THE MISTRESS OF BHATIA HOUSE

Books by the Author
———

THE PERVEEN MISTRY SERIES
The Widows of Malabar Hill
The Satapur Moonstone
The Bombay Prince

INDIA BOOKS
India Gray: Historical Fiction
The Sleeping Dictionary

JAPAN BOOKS
The Kizuna Coast
Shimura Trouble
Girl in a Box
The Typhoon Lover
The Pearl Diver
The Samurai's Daughter
The Bride's Kimono
The Floating Girl
The Flower Master
Zen Attitude
The Salaryman's Wife

THE MISTRESS OF BHATIA HOUSE

SUJATA MASSEY

Published by
Soho Press, Inc.
227 W 17th Street
New York, NY 10011

Library of Congress Cataloging-in-Publication Data

Names: Massey, Sujata, author.
Title: The mistress of Bhatia House / Sujata Massey.
Description: New York, NY : Soho Crime, [2023]
Series: A Perveen Mistry novel ; 4 | Identifiers: LCCN 2022060492

ISBN 978-1-64129-596-3
eISBN 978-1-64129-330-3

Subjects: LCGFT: Detective and mystery fiction. | Novels.
Classification: LCC PS3563.A79965 M57 2023
DDC 813'.54—dc23/eng/20230106
LC record available at https://lccn.loc.gov/2022060492

Map illustration © Philip Schwartzberg
Interior design by Janine Agro, Soho Press, Inc.

Printed in the United States of America

10 9 8 7 6 5 4 3 2 1

To Manju Parikh
And all the visionary women who continue to work for social justice

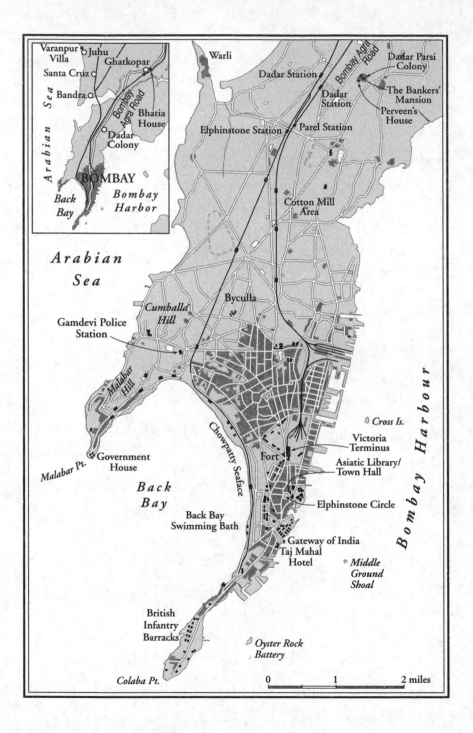

Varanpur
Villa
Juhu
Ghatkopar
Santa Cruz
Bandra
Bombay
Agra Road
Bhatia
House
Dadar
Colony

*Arabian
Sea*

BOMBAY

*Back
Bay*

*Bombay
Harbor*

Warli

Dadar Station

Dadar
Station

Bombay Agra Road

Dadar Parsi
Colony

The Bankers'
Mansion

Perveen's
House

Elphinstone Station

Parel Station

Cotton Mill
Area

*Arabian
Sea*

Gamdevi Police
Station

*Cumballa
Hill*

Byculla

*Malabar
Hill*

Cross Is.

Victoria
Terminus

Asiatic Library/
Town Hall

Elphinstone Circle

Malabar Pt.

Government
House

*Back
Bay*

Chowpatty Seaface

Fort

Back Bay
Swimming Bath

Gateway of India
Taj Mahal
Hotel

*Middle
Ground
Shoal*

British
Infantry
Barracks

*Oyster Rock
Battery*

Colaba Pt.

Bombay Harbour

0   1   2 miles

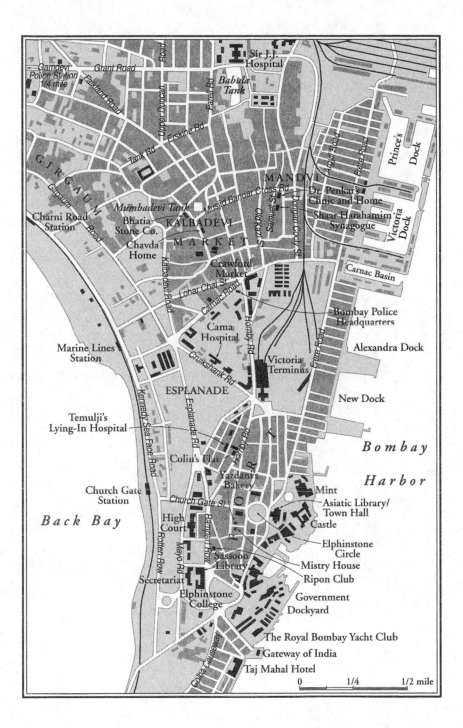

Gamdevi
Police Station
1/4 mile

Grant Road

Falkland Road

Upper Duncan Rd

Parell Rd

Erskine Rd

Sir J.J.
Hospital

*Babula
Tank*

G I R G A U M

Gilgaum

Girgaum Road

Tank Rd

Tank Rd

Mumbadevi Tank

Musjid Bandar Cross Rd

M A N D V I

Argyle Road

Frere Road

Prince's
Dock

Charni Road
Station

Bhatia
Stone Co.

Chavda
Home

KALBADEVI
M A R K E T

Kamaden Road

Olckazi St

Samuel St

Dongari-Gully St

Dr. Penkar's
Clinic and Home

Shaar Harahamim
Synagogue

Victoria
Dock

Crawford
Market

Lohar Chal St

Carnac Road

Hornby Rd

Carnac Basin

Bombay Police
Headquarters

Cama
Hospital

Marine Lines
Station

Cruikshank Rd

Victoria
Terminus

Frere Rd

Alexandra Dock

ESPLANADE

Esplanade Rd

New Dock

Bombay

Temulji's
Lying-In Hospital

Kennedy Sea Face Road

Colin's Flat

Yazdani's
Bakery

Fanby Rd

F   O   R   T

Harbor

Church Gate
Station

Church Gate St

Mint

Asiatic Library/
Town Hall

Back Bay

High
Court

Rotten Row

Bampart Row

Mayo Rd

Sassoon
Library

Castle

Elphinstone
Circle

Mistry House

Ripon Club

Secretariat

Elphinstone
College

Government
Dockyard

Colaba Causeway

The Royal Bombay Yacht Club

Gateway of India

Taj Mahal Hotel

0   1/4   1/2 mile

The Mistress of Bhatia House

PROLOGUE
THURSDAY, JUNE 1, 1922

*S*isters will fight.

It's true whether they are raised together or meet as sisters-in-law in a joint family household. Sisters fight for the better sari, for the chance to do the shopping, for the spot as the parents' favorite. Such rivalry, followed by reconciliation, is as natural as the way summer's punishing heat is chased off by monsoon.

For Oshadi, it was easier to think about the weather. Even in pastoral Ghatkopar, ten miles north of Bombay, the air felt blisteringly humid. The rain was only a few weeks away—it was a shame the party couldn't have waited for the first few days of monsoon, when drops danced lightly. Such a change in weather could have brought forward some harmony between Uma and Mangala Bhatia.

As Oshadi slowly proceeded toward Bhatia House, she waved her walking stick at the wild dogs that congregated on the property across the street, waiting for the daily feeding that the rich Jain family provided. Oshadi wouldn't let the dogs wander near Bhatia House; she had worked there longer than anyone and knew what it meant to protect.

When Sir Dwarkanath's wife had died ten years earlier, Uma, the senior daughter-in-law, had promoted Oshadi to house-mistress over all six female servants at Bhatia House. For this, Oshadi was grateful; but it meant that Uma-bhabhu asked her to do many things that had nothing to do with ordinary service. Today she'd been sent out to walk to the shops in search of extra candles for the many lanterns set out around the courtyard. She'd gone to three shops before finding what was needed.

As Oshadi limped up the gravel driveway, one of the skinny brown dogs edged close, a female with long teats and a whining voice. Again, she brandished her walking stick until the dog shied off, returning to the pack.

Oshadi knew the durwan guarding Bhatia House was afraid of dogs; he ignored their occasional incursions onto the property. And tonight, he was busy polishing the booth and decorating it with hibiscus from the garden. All for Uma's tea party; the guests were already streaming past him in horse-drawn taxis and a few private cars. She could hear the pleased gasps of some women at the sight of the wide, ochre-colored limestone bungalow edged with long verandas on both the upper and ground floors. A series of tiled gables and long-shuttered windows made the house appear even more impressive.

Some of the early arrivals, Gujarati women from nearby, were chattering as they walked behind her.

"My husband wants to donate to the temple only," one lady murmured to her companion. "Therefore, I'm giving a gold-bangle set."

"An excellent donation," her friend opined. "I brought ten rupees."

"Your husband let you give that much?" The first woman's voice lowered to a whisper.

"Don't be silly! I asked my mother."

As if impatient with Oshadi's slow pace, the two women bustled past, giggling as they headed for the courtyard in their crackling tissue silk saris.

On the ground floor veranda, Sir Dwarkanath Bhatia and Parvesh, his elder son, stood watching the arrivals.

Oshadi paused at the servants' door to catch some of the men's conversation. Uma-bhabhu might need to hear about her father-in-law's mood.

"And what is all the furniture in the courtyard? So many mattresses, it looks like the guests have come to sleep!" Sir Dwarkanath thundered.

"But over fifty ladies will be here. They must be made comfortable." Parvesh's voice was anxious.

"You are saying the ladies need something soft for their bony kullas?" Lord Dwarkanath used the vulgar plural for hindquarters.

Parvesh laughed nervously. "Bapuji, remember so many ladies are close by. They might hear you."

"All this tamasha for ladies' work," Sir Dwarkanath grumbled. "Only for your mother's sake, I'm doing this."

"Yes. That is why Uma wants the hospital so much." Parvesh was playing up to his father—just like everyone else.

Oshadi quickly went inside, wanting to steal a few moments' rest in the servants' hall just outside the kitchen. The family had four cooks, all Brahmins. Due to Oshadi's lower caste, she couldn't enter the kitchen, but she made a sound so Aaker, one of the junior cooks, came out to see her.

"The small candles for the cake. Pratip must use the others in the lanterns at dusk," Oshadi said, remembering Uma's instructions.

Aaker winced. "Mangala-bhabhi says to light everything now. Too many people will be sitting at dusk; it will be more difficult."

Oshadi did not like the idea of lighting the flames earlier than necessary. They would add to the heat, and the longer they burned, the more chances for something to catch fire. "Did Uma-bhabhu agree?"

"Don't know."

Oshadi would soon find out. She asked Aaker to bring her a glass of water. Sinking down on the stool that everyone knew was hers, she drank her fill. Revived, she put the glass near the kitchen door and went out again.

Enough women had arrived that she could not proceed straight into the courtyard but had to line up behind others. The woman ahead of her was an interesting sort: wearing an airy chiffon sari in pale yellow, yet carrying a bulky brown case that looked better suited to a man.

"Good afternoon. Are you Mrs. Bhatia?" the strange lady asked Mangala-bhabhi, who was sitting behind a small table at the courtyard entrance.

"I am. If your donation is cash, please count it in front of me." Mangala-bhabhi's voice was as stern as if she'd been talking to any of the family's children.

The visiting lady lifted the fold covering the opening of the briefcase—a man's briefcase, Oshadi noted with fascination. Withdrawing an envelope, she laid it in front of Mangala-bhabhi.

The woman rustled the bills. "Fifty-one rupees. It's from Gulnaz. She wishes you her very best and was thankful for your recent visit to see her in hospital—"

"I never went. You must be talking about my sister-in-law, Uma." Mangala's sallow face showed her displeasure at the confusion. "Please, go ahead inside the courtyard."

"I beg pardon for the mistake. May I ask your name? I'm Perveen. Perveen Mistry."

"I'm Mangala Bhatia. The hospital committee's treasurer."

"Could you kindly point out Uma to me?" the guest persisted. "I don't wish to keep making such a fool of myself! As long as it isn't too much trouble."

Mangala shook her head. "I must stay taking donations. Go in, and you'll see that Uma is the one wearing a pink sari."

As Perveen Mistry moved on, Mangala frowned at Oshadi. "And what are you doing in the middle of these fine people? Trying to make friends—or perhaps pick money from someone's purse?"

"Uma-bhabhu needs me." Oshadi spoke simply, knowing no amount of bowing or scraping would please Mangala. The comment about stealing hurt—Mangala knew that Oshadi had served the family forty years and never taken as much as a match for her own use.

"Very well. What Bhabhu says she needs, she must get."

But not always, Oshadi thought.

1
TEA AND GENEROSITY

*P*erveen felt that getting past Mangala Bhatia had been like running the proverbial gauntlet. No matter what she'd said, it seemed to peeve the woman. But she'd made it into a beautiful stone courtyard half-filled with ladies dressed in pastel-colored summer saris. Many were in shades of pink—quite pretty, but confusing as she started her search for Uma Bhatia.

And soon it would be too late to catch the hostess, as everyone would be sitting down for the presentation. Thin mattresses had been spread across the ground for seating, and in front of them stood short-footed wooden trays. Each tray held a banana-leaf platter, a copper tumbler for water, and a shockingly simple clay teacup. Western-style porcelain, silver, and furniture were in high use amongst Bombay society, so Perveen found this departure an unexpected and very charming setup.

Perveen scanned the courtyard. She'd never been in Ghatkopar before, and she guessed that many of the guests were local. The charitable hospital Uma Bhatia was founding would be built inside Bombay, so Perveen had expected to see some familiar faces. Yet the only woman she recognized was Lady Gwendolyn Hobson-Jones, the prickly mother of Perveen's best friend, Alice.

Lady Hobson-Jones turned from chatting with one friend to the next, and her cool blue gaze swept the crowd. Perveen smiled and began walking toward her, but Lady Hobson-Jones did not return the greeting. Instead, the doyenne of British Bombay took the arm of the full-figured brunette next to her and motioned for a third woman—this one a slender blonde in her thirties—to step closer. Now all three ladies' backs were toward Perveen.

Perveen stood still, wondering if Lady Hobson-Jones had snubbed her. Was this what the British called "cutting someone dead"?

Perveen could never admit to being fond of Alice's mother, but they had always chatted and smiled their way through encounters. Irritation rising, Perveen walked in the opposite direction, resolved that she would complete the mission of locating Uma Bhatia.

Amid the numerous women wearing pinks that ranged from the palest blush to brilliant fuchsia, Perveen finally settled on someone who seemed likely to be the chair of the women's hospital committee. She appeared to be in her midtwenties and wore an expensive-looking rose silk crepe floral sari. Hanging from her neck was a black-and-gold beaded wedding necklace with a floral pendant made up of many small diamonds.

Striving to appear casual, Perveen approached the woman and her social group, who were gathered around a tall woman in a blue-and-white flowered silk sari. This lady, who had a striking, strong-boned face, wore her hair tightly coiled in a bun. Instead of carrying a cloth purse, she'd nestled a large leather bag under her left arm.

"We must make our hospital welcoming to all," the tall woman was saying in fluent Marathi, the language spoken by most people born and raised in Bombay and the surrounding countryside. "Even the hospital sentries could be women. Of course, we will have female nurses, but we need more women physicians. I'll do my best to recruit, but I hope that you'll encourage your daughters to enroll in medical college."

The woman in pink glanced at the others, then spoke in a decorous tone. "Dr. Penkar, we admire you for receiving your advanced and useful education. But medical college is too expensive for most of us."

Hearing the surname, Perveen realized the tall woman had to be Dr. Miriam Penkar, the city's only Indian female obstetrician-gynecologist. It seemed quite a coup for the fledgling hospital to have her on board.

"The girls can study in India!" The doctor gave her a wide smile. "We are fortunate that the Lady Hardinge Medical College has opened in Delhi. One of our committee members at this gathering, Mrs. Serena Prescott, was even involved in their fundraising. She can help your daughters."

Skeptical glances flickered between a few women, as if they didn't believe that an Englishwoman would assist them—or that they could send a daughter as far away as Delhi.

"It's a grand idea. But first, let's get the hospital built. By the time the roof goes on, lady doctors may be plentiful." Uma spoke pleasantly, turning from the crowd to take notice of Perveen. Switching to English, she said, "Good afternoon! Are you a new supporter?" She looked Perveen over, clearly noting the legal briefcase, a cousin to Dr. Penkar's medical kit.

It was a relief to be invited into a group. Smiling warmly, Perveen answered, "My sister-in-law, Gulnaz Mistry, asked me to bring her best wishes. My name is Perveen Mistry."

"The solicitor?" blurted Dr. Penkar. "I've heard tales of you."

Perveen was pleased by the recognition. "Really? I believe we both were in Oxford—unfortunately, not at the same time."

"I had to sit my medical boards in Madras because Oxford wouldn't give me a medical degree." Dr. Penkar raised her eyebrows heavenward. "Therefore, the question sometimes comes to me, was my overseas education worthwhile? But I believe it's served you—Gulnaz is always boasting about your brains and accomplishments. You must join the core committee and handle the legal contracts for us."

"Thank you very much, but I don't know if I can join the

committee at present," Perveen said hastily. "Truly I am here to bring Gulnaz's donation."

"Of course, we understand that your career makes you very busy," Uma cut in. "But sit next to Dr. Penkar during the tea."

Perveen guessed the suggestion was meant to encourage her to reconsider. Normally, she would have ignored such a power play. But Miriam Penkar was intriguing, and she wanted to get to know her.

A tall, thin servant lady had appeared at the outskirts of the group, standing with a slightly bent posture. Uma exited the circle and lowered her ear to the woman, who murmured to her in a stream of low, fast Gujarati.

"It's all right," Uma said soothingly, and then turned to the ladies. "Oshadi reminded me that everyone should be settling in their places. Do spread the word to the other ladies, please. I will fetch the pandit to offer the blessing before we begin."

The women began moving toward the two rows of cushions facing the decorated platform in the center of the courtyard. The three British women in their knee-length frocks had considerable difficulty setting themselves on the cushions while not exposing their legs.

"I don't think they feel pleased about not having chairs," Miriam said in a low voice to Perveen.

"Are they core committee members?" Perveen asked as a waiter came with a silver tray containing a stack of dhokla squares topped with grated coconut, coriander, and roasted mustard seeds. Perveen was fond of the steamed savory made from fermented chickpea batter, so she asked for two.

"Actually, I've only met Serena Prescott: she's the tall blonde," Miriam said. "This tea was planned to recruit new donors. We thought there might be eighty women today, but it doesn't look so. The Bhatias set a rule that the party was for donors bringing at least ten rupees or donated items of higher value."

Perveen thought ten rupees was a very high amount, and

even more difficult to donate because most women couldn't take money from their own household for anything other than groceries. Mohandas Gandhi, the freedom-activist lawyer, was frank about inviting women to donate their personal ornaments to support the freedom movement. And so it was here.

"This dhokla is excellent," Dr. Penkar said. "And I see waiters carrying trays full of aloo tikki and gulab jamun. But where is the tea?"

High-pitched shouting distracted Perveen from answering. A herd of well-dressed but rambunctious children had streamed into the courtyard with three ayahs chasing behind them, herding them like goats. A boy of about four veered away, as if drawn to the sight of Uma lighting incense at the central platform. As he tugged on her sari, she swatted at him. He shouted something that must have been impertinent, because she raised a hand, and he dashed back to the group of children.

In the next moment, Mangala arrived at the platform, holding a tray of flowers and fruit. Just behind her, Oshadi was placing small candles atop a splendid multilayer cake.

Did these ostensibly devout Hindus eat eggs?

"Have you met Sir Dwarkanath and Parvesh Bhatia?" Miriam interrupted Perveen's musing as she gestured toward a pair of men wearing formal Indian suits who had come into the courtyard. Both had strong chins and deep-set eyes. However, the older man's eyes seemed narrow with suspicion, while the younger man's gaze was open and friendly.

"Sir Dwarkanath might be overwhelmed by so many ladies, but his son looks as if he's excited. He must like parties," she guessed.

After studying the two, Miriam said, "I think that Parvesh is also feeling proud of his wife. He supports the project fully."

Perveen wondered whether Miriam felt the same about Sir Dwarkanath, one of the most admired Gujarati businessmen in the city. The gentleman's eyes seemed to soften as he turned his attention toward the little boy who'd been pestering Uma. Now the boy was back with the other children, tugging at their clothes and running back and forth. "What a lively little boy. Who is he?"

"Ishan is Uma and Parvesh's only son," Miriam said, beckoning to a waiter carrying a teapot. "And due to Parvesh's status as Sir Dwarkanath's elder son, Ishan will inherit Bhatia House and the stone business."

"A crown prince of sorts?" Perveen wondered if the other children in the joint family already understood.

"Yes. Uma and Parvesh have two daughters who are older than him, and one about six months old."

"I still think it's a lot to manage, as well as a household like this, and a big charity project!"

"Four children from his eldest son is paltry, as far as Sir Dwarkanath is concerned," Miriam said with a grimace. "Mangala has six children, three of them sons, as she likes to remind everyone on the committee."

"She sounds competitive." Perveen had been close with Gulnaz since primary school. Since they'd become sisters-in-law, their friendship wasn't as silly and full of confidences, probably because Gulnaz's most important relationship was now with Rustom Mistry. "What do you consider the ideal number of children for a family?"

Miriam took a sip of tea before answering. "There's no perfect number. My larger worry is that when girls begin childbearing during puberty, they damage their bodies irreparably. Lady Bhatia—Uma's deceased mother-in-law—suffered pain and infection over the course of many childbirths and ultimately succumbed to her internal injuries," she added. "And there is far too much death for infants in this city—more than half of them die within the first year of life. The outcomes are not good at all."

"What are the causes of death?"

"Tuberculosis, dysentery, cholera, and malnutrition. And they arrive into our world with a physical weakness that stems from growing inside the belly of a child-mother."

"What about death from infanticide? Do you believe that's also part of high infant mortality?" Perveen asked, thinking about some cases in the police court.

"Oh, yes. A female baby is born, and a relative or midwife carries her off. Hours later, the mother is told that her daughter didn't survive. But the truth is, she's a baby nobody can afford."

Miriam's words made Perveen feel ashamed of how much better-off her family was than most people in Bombay. But she reminded herself that the forthcoming hospital would save women's lives. "I suppose you advise female patients about all of the risks of having pregnancies starting at an early age?"

"Advise them?" Dr. Penkar echoed her words with amazement. "I can relay facts to my patients about how pregnancy occurs, but a physician has no authority over a husband. And the fortunate wives who enjoy being with their husbands might not wish to change anything."

Perveen caught her breath quickly. Dr. Penkar had spoken as if it were all right for women to want to touch, and to be touched.

"Miss Mistry? I hope I didn't shock you," Miriam said.

"No!" Perveen blurted. "I was just surprised. Please tell me more."

"The Kalbadevi Ladies' Hospital will provide pre- and post-natal care, and safe, modern methods of delivery," Miriam Penkar answered, dashing Perveen's hopes of another provocative comment. "And that will lead to much better outcomes for both mother and child. You Parsis have a maternity hospital like this. Isn't your sister-in-law there now?"

"Yes. Gulnaz gave birth at Dr. Temulji's Lying-In Hospital. She'll be staying there for forty days following birth. It's actually mandatory because of religious traditions."

"As it happens, that's the proper amount of time to protect

a woman's uterus—" Miriam paused. "I'm sorry, I didn't ask if you know the meaning of uterus?"

"It's where the baby grows?"

"Correct." Miriam sounded like a teacher satisfied with a precocious pupil. "The uterus and vagina, too, should be protected for some time after the trauma of birth. So maternity hospitals are a safeguard during a crucial time."

"Do you find Hindu and Muslim mothers typically stay with their parents after delivery?" Perveen asked. "That would achieve the same purpose."

"If there is room in the parents' home, and if it's clean. We Jews have the same tradition."

"You are Jewish, then!" Perveen exclaimed. She had been wondering about the background of this unusual woman.

Miriam smiled. "Surprised, aren't you? I don't resemble the Sassoons."

Perveen guessed that Miriam was insinuating that Bene Israel Jews were more Indian-looking than the Baghdadi Jews, a later-emigrating group that included the highly elite family she'd mentioned. Perveen was attempting a muddled reply when they were interrupted by Mangala Bhatia.

"Sssh! The speeches are beginning!" Mangala settled herself next to Perveen, as if determined to monitor her behavior.

Uma mounted the stage. She folded her hands in a graceful namaste, inclining her head. In a ringing voice, she said in Gujarati, "Welcome. We are all being blessed by Panditji before the ceremonies begin."

The pandit swirled the aromatic, smoky incense holder and began a slow chant in Sanskrit. Then he held the silver tray of fruit and flowers for Uma and three other women to take. Belatedly, Mangala arose from her place next to them and hurried around the cushions to take the blessed offerings herself.

Perveen was glad that Mangala was gone, seemingly because

she couldn't bear to miss the spotlight. She whispered to Miriam, "Why aren't you also going up?"

"It's a religious observance," Miriam said. "Hindus only. The English ladies on the committee aren't going up either."

As the pandit stepped down, Uma seated herself in a chair near a small table holding the brass box of donations in front of her. Mangala stood nearby; as if to protect the money, Perveen thought with amusement.

"So many donations from this assembled party. The hospital committee wishes to recognize the goodness of each one of you." Uma continued her pattern of speaking confidently in Gujarati, followed by painstaking English. "Sixty rupees from Lady Gwendolyn Hobson-Jones. Please rise, Lady Hobson-Jones." Polite applause rippled through the room. "We also received with appreciation fifteen rupees from Mrs. Serena Prescott, who is very new to Bombay. Sitting beside her is Mrs. Madeline Stowe, who's donated one hundred rupees on behalf of Stowe Ironworks." Perveen watched Gwendolyn Hobson-Jones's companions rise together, holding hands and smiling at the group. "And we are also receiving a magnificent treasure from a royal vault: a pearl and diamond necklace, gift of the Begum of Varanpur. My gratitude, Begum Cora. I should like to note that the begum has also donated the Black Forest cake for this party. It is an authentic European cake."

Perveen guessed the last was said as a warning to those who avoided eggs. She turned her head, looking for a veiled Muslim royal, and nearly gasped to see a young white woman with flowing red hair left uncovered by her silver-on-blue brocaded blue sari.

"It's my pleasure to help a good cause!" the begum declared in cheerful, rough-sounding English, all the while fluttering her hand and smiling like a queen with an adoring public.

A great murmuring in Gujarati followed; Perveen had to strain to hear the words. But the general questions women were asking each other were, *What is she? Muslim or Christian? British—no, Australian!*

"Fifty-one rupees from Mrs. Gulnaz Mistry!" Uma called out, and the begum finally reseated herself. "Because of her new baby, Gulnaz-behen could not attend. Yet the donation was brought in good spirits by Miss Perveen Mistry. Please rise!"

It took two tries for Perveen to stand up, because she had witnessed the begum's easy grace and was desperate not to use her hands to get up from the ground. She managed, though, and became instantly aware she'd set the crowd gossiping.

Gulnaz's sister-in-law. A lawyeress—yes, a solicitor. She is divorced. No, she is not. How much money does she earn? Can she keep it, or does she give it to her father?

As if to quiet the audience, Uma proceeded rapidly with another name. "Next donation is a fine set of six gold bangles from Srimati Radha Shah!" After a brief round of applause, Uma continued. "From Dr. Miriam Penkar . . ." Uma looked up from the envelope and spoke with a trembling voice. "Dear Dr. Penkar, by agreeing to become our hospital's medical director, you have given so much already. And this . . . ten rupees. It is wonderful. Please, will you give us a few words?"

"This is a surprise," Miriam Penkar murmured to Perveen.

"You'll do well," Perveen said, patting her arm.

The doctor rose, and as she walked toward the stage, two other women left their places: Lady Hobson-Jones and Serena Prescott. Perveen expected that they planned to join the doctor on stage, but instead they furtively hurried to the courtyard exit.

Once on stage, Miriam faced the audience with a genial smile. "It is my honor to be the chief of staff for this hospital meant to serve all women, regardless of religion and income. I am grateful because every donation is another brick in the building, another bed in a ward. I know that many of you have given to maximum capacity of your personal finances. And we need more than cash. We need hands."

The doctor opened her palms, and as she stretched her arms forward, Perveen noticed she wasn't wearing bangles. "Sisters, we speak so many languages. Let's use them to ask our neighbors and relatives and the city's wealthiest to lend a hand. And after the hospital is built, how about using your voice to welcome patients to the building? Or your hands to roll bandages, or type medical information? Do you have furniture you no longer need, especially beds, tables, and chairs? All will be greatly needed. And that is all I have to say."

"I shall summarize your words in Gujarati," Uma began, but halfway through the translation, she halted, her gaze fixed on the side of the courtyard.

Lord Dwarkanath was frowning at her, and Parvesh was waving his hands.

Taking the doctor's arm, Uma quickly said, "Thank you, Dr. Penkar. Now, I have the honor of presenting Lord Dwarkanath Bhatia, my father-in-law."

"Dear daughters, are you inviting me to my own home?" Sir Dwarkanath joked as he allowed Mangala to help him ascend the stage.

Dr. Penkar retreated through the courtyard to resume her place next to Perveen, while Uma and Mangala now both stood behind the patriarch. Perveen glanced at Miriam, trying to get a reaction to Uma's interrupted translation, but the doctor stared ahead, her expression studiously neutral.

"Fifty years ago, I came with my father to Bombay. It was a long journey—ten days' walk from Bharuch, where our native village lies." Looking down from his elevated position, Sir Dwarkanath addressed the seated crowd, speaking in a voice that was as relaxed as a storyteller's. "My father found a free school for me and took every job he could find, carrying and selling goods for the merchants who paid him just two paise a day. I helped when I wasn't in school, and it's only through God's grace that we were able to set up our first shop and then save enough to start our stone business. Now I am grateful for all that has come from our work, including the chance to build many fine structures for the use of Bombay's government. Many of you know that my wife, Premlata, died ten years ago." He paused, the light in his eyes seeming to dim. "She was sacrificing, modest, and community-minded. She would have liked this hospital project very much. Perhaps the doctors and nurses of a proper women's hospital could have saved her life. I believe—"

His subsequent words were masked by a child's shriek.

Perveen's eyes shot to the area where the children were congregated. Two of the ayahs were already standing, looking in every direction. Who had cried out?

Then Perveen saw.

At the far edge of the courtyard, Ishan Bhatia was hopping up and down. The sleeve of his kurta was aflame, and as he shook his arm, the fire expanded.

"Hai Ram!" bellowed Sir Dwarkanath, and Uma held a hand over her mouth, as if stifling her own cry. All along the rows, women screamed, some clutching at each other, and others tumbling against each other as they tried to rise—as if their presence around the jumping, screaming child might put out the fire.

Dr. Penkar was already on the move, but she'd forgotten her kit. Perveen grabbed it and hurried after her as best she could in the confusion. As she got close, she saw one of the ayahs throw herself atop the burning, screaming boy. In the next moment, Parvesh was there, dousing the two of them with a pitcher of water.

"Sunanda. Ishan!" the Bhatias' housekeeper called, moving quickly with a twisted gait. She also had a pitcher of water which she streamed over the two of them.

Dr. Penkar's voice was calm as she spoke to Parvesh and Oshadi in Marathi. "The flames are out, but we still need more water. Get more water, please."

"I've brought your bag," Perveen said, dropping it at her side.

"Open it for me, will you? I need scissors first."

As Miriam Penkar bent to touch Sunanda's shoulders, the ayah moaned in pain.

"Sunanda, the fire is finished. Now let me get you apart from Ishan," Dr. Penkar beseeched.

The ayah quieted and, although her shoulders moved, her body didn't follow.

"Get off me, Sunanda!" wailed Ishan.

"How is my son?" asked Parvesh anxiously.

"It's good that you brought more water. Please pour it gently here," Dr. Penkar said, motioning toward the ayah's side. As Parvesh doused the area she indicated, the doctor's strong arms reached forward and swiftly turned Sunanda's body.

"Is the boy alive?" demanded Begum Cora, who was looking wide-eyed at the bodies collapsed on the stone courtyard.

"If he was dead, he wouldn't be crying," Dr. Penkar snapped in English. "Please let me do my work!" She spoke in soft Marathi as she put her hand on the ayah's shoulder. "Sunanda, you were very brave."

Along with charred white cotton pieces of Sunanda's sari, Perveen saw raw pink flesh and blood on her stomach. All that remained of Ishan's silk kurta sleeve was completely black, giving the impression that terrible damage lay underneath. Perveen didn't want to see; yet she could not tear herself away.

"This is your fault, Sunanda! Why weren't you watching him?" Mangala Bhatia was standing over the ayah with her arms crossed.

"Everyone here must be quiet. This is no time for blaming!" Dr. Penkar said, taking a second to glare into Mangala's furious face before returning her attention to Sunanda and Ishan. Taking scissors from Perveen, she cut away the cloth from Ishan's arm. "We need many cloths soaked with cold water."

Sunanda whimpered something, and Dr. Penkar took the

stethoscope out of her medical bag and pressed it to the ayah's chest.

"Why weren't you sitting at the table with the children?" Mangala scolded Sunanda. "You should have stopped him from wandering."

Perveen felt her temper rise. The ayah had behaved heroically and was badly injured. "Mangala-behen," Perveen said, then waited until she had the angry woman's attention. She whispered, "Dr. Penkar gave us orders to be quiet."

Mangala's gaze moved past Perveen. Loudly, she said, "Oh, here you are at last, Uma. Don't worry, he's able to cry to the heavens!"

"I had to help Bapuji from the platform. And then it was hard to get through the crowds!" Uma knelt and put a hand on her son's head. Softly, he moaned, turning his small, ash-smudged face toward her.

"Oh, Ishan! Please don't die," Uma whispered. "You can't!"

"He will most certainly live," Miriam said gently. "Sunanda will be fine as well. Tell me, can ice be found anywhere? We will need to use it for several hours' time."

Parvesh wiped his hand across his brow. "A shop in town sells it. I'll send two bearers to get as many as can be bought."

"Also—we need an ointment from the pharmacy. A thin layer of American petroleum jelly will protect their burns from germs."

"For Ishan?" Uma's voice was shaky.

"*Both* need this treatment." Dr. Penkar's voice was firm.

As if chastised, Uma nodded. Then she touched the sleeve of her husband's jacket and spoke to him in low Gujarati. Perveen caught the word "father."

Perveen had forgotten about Sir Dwarkanath. He was coming slowly through the crowd, the priest at his side.

Seeing them, Uma began to cry. "I've ruined everything. I am so very sorry—"

"It was just an accident," Parvesh said, but his voice was shaky, and he went to meet his father and the priest.

Now that there was more space, Begum Cora moved in closer and stared at Sunanda.

"You poor girl!" she said in her strange English. She pulled a note from her handbag and tried to press it into Sunanda's hand. "I will reward you, even if nobody else will! Remember that Begum Cora herself commends your bravery. This is ten rupees, do you hear? It's for you."

Sunanda's eyes were closed, as if she didn't know that the begum was addressing her.

"Please, no," Uma said in English. "She's not understanding your words. Very kind, but not needed."

The begum acted as if she hadn't heard. She rose, the money still in her hand, and proffered it to Oshadi. "Give it to her later, my dear."

"No, no, I must not take it," Oshadi said in English.

Mangala put her hand on the begum's arm. "Please, Begum. We already take care of their pay."

"Of course. But this is a token of gratitude. A royal recognition from the princely state of Varanpur."

Still, Oshadi would not open her hand.

Perveen tapped Uma on her shoulder. Speaking in Gujarati, she said, "The begum dearly wishes to offer gratitude for your ayah's heroism toward your son. Don't you think Sunanda deserves it?"

Uma's eyes flickered from her toward Sunanda. "Very well. Oshadi, keep the money for Sunanda until she can take it from you."

"I have saved lives, too," Oshadi mumbled in Marathi.

Perveen shot a look at Oshadi, wishing she would say more, but the woman simply tucked the bill into her sari's waist.

"Doctor, what happened to my grandson?" Sir Dwarkanath's English was both precise and angry.

"Ishan has second-degree burns on his right arm, serious but quite treatable. Right now, cooling the burn stops damage from increasing. We will do this for several hours this evening. After that, the burns will slowly heal if the raw flesh is kept quite clean and protected with the petroleum jelly I've requested."

"I thank you for being here." Lord Dwarkanath regarded Miriam Penkar with a favorable gaze. "You saved the life of my grandson."

Perveen thought, *No mention of Sunanda.*

Uma looked up at her father-in-law with a weak smile. "I'm terribly sorry, Bapuji, for all that has happened tonight. It was to be a happy party."

"Yes, there are many ladies here who must be worried," Mangala said. "I'll tell them everything's fine."

"And the cake must be served!" the begum interjected. "Soon, or the cream will become puddles!"

"Nobody will serve that egg-filled cake!" Sir Dwarkanath pronounced angrily. "Ishan must be washed and settled inside the house, and the servant must be cared for as well. Oshadi will tell the staff to take everything down. When I rise tomorrow, this courtyard should be washed clean. Any food left can be given to the poor. But the party has ended."

2

WHEN SISTERS HAVE WORDS

"*B*e glad you weren't at the party. Seeing the behavior of Mangala Bhatia, I was tempted to give her one tight slap! And then her father-in-law closed everything down—although truthfully, I don't see how things could have proceeded. Two people were very badly injured."

Four days after the party, Perveen was recounting the story from a rocking chair next to Gulnaz's bed inside Temulji's Lying-In Hospital. The exterior was a typical imposing stone Gothic building; however, the interior wards had a fresh feeling, with dainty blue-and-yellow tiled floors and crisp white walls. The room had two beds and two modern iron cots for infants, although Gulnaz's roommate had been discharged with her baby son a week earlier.

It was seven-thirty in the morning, and Khushy had just fallen asleep in her cot. Perveen thought the baby looked like a beautiful doll: the kind she kept on a shelf to admire but was afraid to touch. In fact, Perveen had tried to hold Khushy during her last visit, and the infant had screamed so loudly that a nurse had grabbed her from Perveen's shaking arms.

Khushy had Gulnaz's fair complexion and rosebud mouth, as well as the curly black hair that came from the Mistry family. Her exquisiteness was accompanied with what Perveen thought was a chronic fussy nature. Gulnaz's obstetrician, Dr. Mody, had declared that Khushy's agitation was a temporary condition called colic. Nothing to worry about.

Mindful of the baby, Perveen continued in a low voice.

"Thank goodness Dr. Penkar was there. But Mangala Bhatia was absolutely no help, yelling at the ayah as if the accident was her fault."

"Mangala claims to understand the household's customs better than Uma does. And she has more children than Uma."

"Yes, including more sons. But shouldn't Uma have more authority, as the wife of the eldest son?" Perveen winked at Gulnaz, who was just a year older.

"Ha ha," Gulnaz said. "Mangala hates that her husband was dispatched to oversee the family's quarry. She chose to stay with the children in Ghatkopar."

Perveen remembered what Dr. Penkar had said about women being unable to control their pregnancies due to the demands of conjugal life. "I suppose that if the two live apart most of the year, the chance of pregnancy is lessened."

"Though Mangala's managed to drop six already!" Gulnaz sounded awed.

"And how many are you thinking of?" Perveen teased.

Glancing at the cot, Gulnaz said, "As many as it takes until we have a boy."

Perveen inhaled deeply, resisting her urge to swear. "I hope Rustom hasn't made you feel that way. Khushy is a treasure. I know you both waited so long for her!"

"Five years." Gulnaz pressed her tiny lips together. "If this baby were a boy, Rustom would be visiting every day."

Perveen thought of mentioning her brother's exhausting construction project north of the city, but perhaps Gulnaz had sensed something true. So she changed the subject back to the party. "Sunanda, the ayah who saved Ishan, was remarkable. Had you ever seen her before?"

"No. I must hire that sort of ayah to care for my Khushy, one who would lay her own life down for a child." Gulnaz stretched back against her pillows, sighing comfortably.

"That's quite a lot to expect," Perveen said.

"What are you implying?"

Perveen replayed the scene in her mind. "I didn't like the way the Bhatias thought Sunanda was responsible for the accident. They should have been more thankful. Uma arrived to him quite late, but somehow, Sunanda got through the crowd to save him."

"Maybe Uma was in shock. It's awfully hard with babies. When Khushy starts crying, I never know why. Does she need milk, or is it a wet nappy?" Gulnaz glanced down at the crib, her eyes tender. "I'm so grateful for the nurses. Khushy likes them better than me, I'm sure."

"That can't be true!" Perveen protested. "A baby and mother have an irreplaceable bond."

"Tell me more about the tea party," Gulnaz said, as if intent on ignoring Perveen's statement. "Was Lady Hobson-Jones there?"

"Oh, yes. She behaved as if she didn't see me," Perveen said, knowing she sounded bitter. "And when Dr. Penkar was speaking, Lady Hobson-Jones walked out of the party with Serena Prescott. The only whites who stayed on were Madeline Stowe and a very beautiful red-head. A begum, but not from India."

Gulnaz's eyes brightened. "Begum Cora is most notorious!"

"Yes, that's her name—but what makes her notorious?" Perveen asked. "She's married to the ruler of Varanpur State, so doesn't that ensure her social standing?"

"But before that, she was a showgirl in Australia." Gulnaz's eyes flashed with the mischief Perveen remembered from their school days. "The nawab brought her on the ship out of Perth along with two thoroughbreds. When our committee was having lunch at the Ripon Club, she spoke about it being a fairytale romance. Cinderella and her prince. What did she give for the hospital?"

Perveen paused, trying to remember. "A pearl and diamond necklace."

"How many carats diamond?" Gulnaz asked.

Perveen was surprised by the crassness. "Uma didn't announce that. And why should she?"

Gulnaz rolled her eyes. "It sounds like a very grand donation. However, resale of jewelry is inevitably a losing proposition. Unless, of course, one takes one's Indian jewels to a jeweler in Europe." Gulnaz glanced at Khushy, adding, "I wish I'd been able to visit France and England before she came. Tell me, how did Uma like my donation?"

Perveen sensed that Gulnaz was hunting for reassurance. "She expressed her gratitude quite warmly."

"And what was the highest cash gift?"

"Because everyone was sent home after the fire, not all of the donation amounts were announced. But I recall Madeline Stowe gave a hundred rupees."

"Madeline Stowe has unusual status for a boxwallah wife." Gulnaz's mouth twisted as she used the slightly pejorative nickname given to Europeans who were in trade rather than government. "Her husband's company is very successful and old, and she's said to have family money, although she came to Bombay as a fishing fleet girl."

"You mean, hoping to make a match," Perveen corrected, because she didn't like the derogatory word used for single women.

"It's a shame that Madeline didn't add one more rupee to her donation of one hundred! Perhaps that brought the bad luck that caused the accident."

"She doesn't know Indian customs," Perveen said. An extra rupee, to make an odd number, meant the money couldn't be split evenly. It was a signal the gift was meant to be spent in whole, not shared with someone else.

Gulnaz leaned closer to Perveen, as if to share a confidence. "Madeline Stowe probably gave the most because Stowe Ironworks hopes to be tapped for the hospital project."

"The hospital committee should entertain multiple bids," Perveen said. "Even if it ruffles some feathers, it's the right thing to do."

"At least I have my own money. I didn't have to bother Rustom for it." Gulnaz gave Perveen a knowing look. "Please give me my purse—it's in the dresser drawer."

Perveen opened the drawer and found a pink silk purse, which she handed to her sister-in-law.

Gulnaz sorted through the bills and coins. "Here's fifty-one rupees that I'm adding to my previous hospital donation."

"You must adore Uma to double the contribution," Perveen said, although she privately sensed it was a matter of competition with Mrs. Stowe. She put the money in an envelope and slid it into her briefcase, then looked up to see her sister-in-law's petulant frown.

Gulnaz said, "It seems you don't feel the same. Why?"

Perveen struggled to put her feelings into words. "I wish Uma had thanked Sunanda and defended her against Mangala's criticism."

Gulnaz snorted. "People don't need to thank servants. Just because you saw it done when you were overseas doesn't mean everyone has to change to fit your ideals!"

Perveen tensed. "You don't know what I experienced in England. I daresay you're making an excuse for modern mothers who hand off their children to servants so they can spend their time becoming known as goddesses of charity."

"Modern mothers," Gulnaz repeated with a sneer. "How silly that sounds coming from a professional woman. You were so busy you didn't even come to my wedding!"

Perveen caught her breath, realizing that this was something Gulnaz must have been holding on to for years. "But I couldn't leave England. I was in the midst of my legal studies, and it was wartime."

"Now you're the one making excuses," Gulnaz said sharply.

"And you just waltz in after a good night's sleep, expecting me to be all smiles and laughs. You don't know how much I'm awakened at night. Khushy feeds every two hours—can you imagine that?"

Perveen took a deep breath and reconsidered things. Gulnaz's exhaustion was surely driving her nastiness. It was up to Perveen to protect their relationship as loving sisters-in-law. Slowly, she said, "Forgive me. I wasn't thinking about how your days and nights have changed."

"Waaaah! Waaah!"

Both of them turned to see Khushy moving restlessly. She still had her eyes closed but was roaring.

"A bad dream?" Perveen glanced at Gulnaz.

"No. You've woken her. Your terrible words made my baby cry!" Gulnaz retorted.

Perveen gulped, feeling a mix of mortification and anger. Of course the little brat would chime in to prove Gulnaz's point about how much harder her life was than Perveen's.

Brat? How could that word have slipped into her mind?

Khushy kept on crying until a nurse entered, looking at neither of them, just taking the baby from the cot and softly murmuring as she carried her from the room.

"It's going to be all right," Perveen said. "What I meant was—"

"Don't try to tell me anything more," Gulnaz blurted, looking straight at her with venom. "You speak cruelly and then claim that you meant differently. I'm sick of that—of you. Just get out!"

3
A GARDEN BREAKFAST

*S*tanding outside the hospital, Perveen took deep breaths, trying to slow her pounding heart. She imagined that the disharmony would blow off like sugar on a pastry. However, she felt too unsettled to rush off to the contracts lying on her desk at Mistry House.

You speak cruelly and then claim that you meant differently.

Gulnaz's accusation haunted her. Perveen had spoken her frank thoughts to Gulnaz. Was that no longer possible, now that there was a baby and this huge gulf of different experience between them?

Perveen almost stumbled as she passed through a crowd of uniformed boys lingering outside the Cathedral Boys' School. She was so unsteady, inside and out, that she almost missed the turn to Harriman Road.

She knew the street but hadn't come this way before. Hestia House, Harriman Road, was the new address for Colin Sandringham, an unlikely friend of hers, an Englishman with whom she'd worked briefly. Colin had left the Indian Civil Service to serve as a voluntary administrator at the Royal Bombay Asiatic Society, a private library and scholarly group in the city. A week earlier, he'd sent her a short letter giving details of his new residential address. He had also hinted about having some good news he wished to relate in person.

Good news was exactly what her morning needed.

Five minutes later, she was standing in front of a three-story apartment house in need of new paint. A molding of a Greek laurel wreath was missing an edge. Colin's note indicated he would live in Flat 2. There was still a blank space on Flat 2's mailbox, while the other boxes had names filled in.

Turning the doorknob, she entered a small vestibule with two unmarked doors with a bell next to each. What if she rang and a stranger answered? Colin's reputation could be destroyed if word got around about a woman seeking him out.

She decided against ringing.

It was just a few minutes after eight o'clock. Possibly Colin was outside, either taking a stroll in the cool air or spending time in the garden.

Perveen walked along the stone wall until she came to a black wrought iron gate that was padlocked on the inside. It offered a view of the tangled, overgrown garden. An elevated veranda was set out with chairs.

She saw the top of a man's head over one. The hair was dark brown and tousled, making her spirits surge—although she hadn't seen quite enough to be sure. Did she dare ruin the unknown man's morning reverie? She hesitated until she recognized Colin's voice as he thanked someone. Perveen realized that Gulnaz had met Colin and overheard how he spoke to servants. This must have rankled her enough to feel she could accuse Perveen of taking on British ways. The truth was that many Britishers weren't like Colin; however, Gulnaz wasn't someone to whom she'd ever confess such feelings.

Perveen waited until she thought Colin was alone again, and then called out, "Mr. Sandringham? Good morning."

"Per—Miss Mistry?" He stood up, revealing that he was dressed in a white kurta and loose-fitting trousers. Donning his wire-rimmed spectacles, he squinted into the garden. "Where are you?"

"The garden gate. It's locked."

Colin called back, "Please come around to the front."

Feeling a surge of excitement, Perveen walked back swiftly

to the Hestia House door. She stepped into a vestibule and saw Colin was already waiting. Their eyes met, and his slight smile revealed even white teeth that had somehow escaped the curse of English awfulness. The wild-looking hair that she'd spotted in the garden had been combed so it lay neatly, with just a touch of pomade.

He waved her in through the door on the right side of the vestibule. Since he had no cane with him, she guessed he was wearing his wooden leg, though one couldn't see it through the leather brogues on his feet. "You picked the perfect day to visit. Rama just arrived yesterday, and he'll be chuffed to see you."

Looking into his warm hazel eyes, she felt a desire to step into his arms, but restrained herself. "Your man from Satapur?"

"I'm calling him the household manager now," Colin said. "He decided after a few months with the new ICS officer, he'd rather join me. This place is quite a lot for him to learn about—come inside and I'll show you."

Perveen stepped into a wide room with long windows, and above them, a line of jalousie windows that could be kept open to let in breezes at night. The bones of the room were good, but furniture was scant: a long sofa, a single chair, and a low, scratched and worn-looking wooden table. The dining room beyond held a card table and two wicker chairs that looked like they'd come from the garden.

"Do sit down." Colin gestured toward the chair, which had been draped with a cloth that she imagined hid stained uphol-stery.

As Perveen seated herself, the chair's springs rebelled, and she adjusted her posture to avoid tipping backward.

"Sorry!" Colin exclaimed, while settling himself on the edge of the old sage-colored velvet sofa. "This is original furniture included with the place. If it's any consolation, that chair's softer than my mattress."

Perveen's skin flushed at his mention of the place where he

slept. Colin didn't parse his language as carefully as she did. Quickly, she said, "It's a lovely flat, and I think you can find some pieces that will suit you."

"Well, I haven't really got the money for furniture shopping right now. Although I just was offered some part-time work. I'd like to tell you about it, but Rama's making my breakfast. Will you please stay and eat with me?"

Perveen readily agreed, having only had biscuits and tea that morning. And a brief interlude with Colin would mean she arrived slightly late to work. This wouldn't cause her father alarm; he'd believe that she'd spent extra time with Gulnaz, and all was well between the two sisters-in-law.

Colin moved off the sofa and went into the kitchen. Alone, she could hear the low rumble of two voices. When he came back, Rama was at his side. Perveen made a namaste greeting toward the small, silver-haired man dressed in a homespun kurta and faded Madras-patterned lungi. Although most regarded him as a household servant, Rama had the knowledge of an ayurvedic doctor. He'd used herbs to treat Colin after a snake bit him, and while the leg wasn't saved, Colin had lived. Rama had also taught Colin yoga, making it possible for Colin to recover his strength.

"Welcome to Bombay, Rama-ji!" Perveen said. "I'm so pleased you're here. What do you think of my city?"

"Namaste, Mistry-memsahib," Rama answered with a slight bow. "The nighttime was very loud. But I will learn to sleep with it. I would rather work for Sandringham-sahib than stay in Satapur with Mr. Awful."

"Do you mean the new ICS agent who was billeted at Circuit House?" Perveen asked.

"Yes. He was demanding food that cannot be made in the mountains. Shrimp tharr-mee-door." Rama pronounced each syllable with distaste. "He said I must clean the old carpets to be like new or he'd cut my wage."

"He does sound awful," said Perveen.

"The name is O-P-H-A-L-L," Colin said with a chuckle. "Orville Ophall's former post was Bangalore. He expected the same kind of weather, social life, and luxuries. I was very glad that Rama joined me; it will make staying here much more pleasant."

"The landlord said I can plant some of the garden if I do the other work, too."

"What work?" Perveen asked.

"Everything a mali would do. Grass cutting with scissors. Tree trimming. Flower watering."

"But why should you do a groundsman's work? Your wages come from Mr. Sandringham, not anyone else!"

Looking sidelong at Perveen, Colin said, "I convinced the landlord to pay him the old gardener's fee. And I trust Rama will cut a swath through the jungle and make it much nicer for everyone's eyes. Let's eat outside and I'll show you."

"Very well," Perveen said, hoping Rama hadn't noticed her friend's slip in formality.

Outside, Colin showed her mango, pomelo, and papaya trees, all overburdened with vines. When they returned to the weedy veranda, he pulled out a wrought iron chair for her. Perveen paused to appreciate the chair's iron back, a complicated design of flowers, monkeys, and birds.

"What a charming furniture set," Perveen said. "My guess is that it's vintage Stowe Ironworks."

"Oh, that's interesting. Why do you think so?" asked Colin.

As Rama flung a fresh cotton tablecloth over the aged iron table, Perveen continued examining the chair. "The animal faces are the hallmark of a particular artisan named Nadim. Nadim once did metalwork for Mistry Construction, but he was lured to Stowe Ironworks by the Englishman who founded it in the early 1800s. Because of this, my family's company always carried a small grudge. I saw a lady named Madeline Stowe at a tea party for a charity."

"If she's married to Malcolm Stowe, it would be . . . *ironic*." Colin snickered at his pun, and after Perveen rolled her eyes, he continued. "Mr. Stowe's the company owner and also sits the Legislative Council. He's connected to the news I've wanted to share."

"Carry on, then." Perveen settled comfortably in her chair as Rama next presented a tea tray holding a plain white china teapot and cups. Rama poured for her, and she took the cup with pleasure.

"Whilst I was staying at the Yacht Club, I met a fellow called Nigel Prescott," Colin said, accepting a fresh cup of tea from Rama. "Mr. Prescott was interested that I'd made some addenda to maps at the Asiatic Society. Apparently Stowe, in his role at the Legislative Council, was seeking analysis of old maps of the mountainous borders between some princely states and Bombay Presidency. Prescott set things up nicely for me with Mr. Stowe before he moved out of the club."

"So, you've got a job! Is it a full-time position?" she asked, thinking about how Colin would balance this with his time-consuming voluntary vice-presidentship at the Asiatic Society.

"No, I'm being paid by the hour. Stowe and Prescott asked me to examine the borders of several princely states that are close to Bombay Presidency. I've done twenty hours' work so far."

"Really!" Perveen knew she should be pleased for him, but something about the project made her uneasy. "And if this goes well, you might consider setting up a small company for map-making. I'm sure there is a market within the city of Bombay because of all the property disputes."

Colin shrugged. "Such work doesn't hold a strong attraction. This assignment, on the other hand, involves unspoiled forests and mountains, large and small bodies of water, and plenty of political history."

"Thalipeeth!" Rama announced happily when he came out to the veranda again with two plates.

"It's the most delicious pancake, with chilies and greens!" Colin told Perveen.

Perveen hid a smile at Colin's effort to explain a local Indian dish. "I know thalipeeth, but not Rama's version. It smells divine."

Rama nodded, looking even more pleased. "I'll go inside, then. Toast is coming."

"You have such a talented cook!" Perveen said, then hesitated, as she thought more about Colin's situation. "Would you be offended if I ask you a few more things about your work?"

Raising an eyebrow, he said, "I'm always open to unsolicited solicitor's advice."

Perveen smiled, thinking that he seemed on a mission to amuse her. "Did the Legislative Council give you an employment contract to sign?"

He shook his head. "I only dealt with Mr. Stowe. A gentleman's handshake agreement."

Perveen paused, determined to carefully restate what was bothering her. "I think you said that your assignment might involve revisions of borders between princely Indian states and British India?"

"That's what I said." Colin looked expectantly at her.

"You also said that much, if not all, of the territory in question is rural?" After he nodded, she elaborated, "These could be areas where dams can be built for hydroelectric power; trees harvested for lumber, and mountains blasted open for stone. Quite valuable areas for Bombay Presidency to acquire."

"What you say could be true." Colin's voice was steady.

Perveen decided to speak frankly. "These maps you're drawing could literally pave the way for the Empire to grab more of the Indian subcontinent."

"I think you would be surprised by my findings," Colin said, his expression serious.

"Oh?"

"Boundaries change. Not only because of the advancement in surveying techniques, but because of the natural elements. When monsoons pound the earth, rivers swell and new waterways form. This makes it problematic for a landowner to understand the extent of his holdings."

"That makes sense," she acknowledged.

"I'm not sure that I explained it so well to the others," Colin said ruefully. "Or perhaps it's a matter of you having a more open mind!"

"Exactly what did you learn about the borders?"

Colin pressed his lips together for a moment. "I wish I could say, but they asked me to keep the maps confidential for the time being."

Perveen had already suffered one painful argument that morning. She didn't want to have another. "Very well. I understand because I also keep confidentiality for my clients."

Colin's mouth relaxed back into a smile. "Now, might I change the subject to what truly interests me? What's keeping you busy these days?"

"I don't have any cases in front of me that are exciting—just the usual contract work," she said with a shrug. "The biggest news for our family is Gulnaz and her baby, who's named Khushy, will be coming home later this week from the lying-in hospital."

"And how old is Khushy now?" His voice was eager. "Old enough for visitors bearing gifts?"

"She's almost six weeks—and I'm sorry, but I would rather you didn't visit," Perveen admitted, feeling a flash of nervousness. "Gulnaz has been very moody lately, and I can't imagine how she'd behave if you visited. We had a row this morning."

"What about?"

"It turns out she's resented some things about me. And if I'm being honest, I'll admit I'm a little frightened about Gulnaz coming home with the baby and also bringing an ayah into our household." She struggled to put words to her feelings. "Things will never be the same."

"But your brother and his wife are in another house, isn't it true?"

"It's a duplex. The baby's room will be against the same wall as my own bedroom. I'm sure I'll hear her, and if this ayah likes to sing—" Perveen shuddered. "What if she's loud and tone deaf? I've always been a fitful sleeper."

"I didn't know that about you!" Colin's eyes lingered on her as Rama emerged with a silver rack filled with golden-brown toast and a small tray holding saucers of butter and jam.

Of course he didn't know—they'd never passed a night together in the same room. Blushing a little, Perveen concentrated on coating her toast with butter, then the jam.

"I've missed your homemade pomelo jam," Colin said to Rama. "I only hope the pomelo tree in this garden will bear decent fruit."

"We shall see. Bombay is not its native place," Rama said. "Sandringham-sahib, may I ask your permission for something?"

"Of course." Colin laid down his silver. "What do you need?"

"The vegetable man's stand is open. I don't want to miss the best of it."

Colin pressed a hand to his brow. "I'm glad you remembered. Have you the necessary money?"

"Yes, saved from yesterday. Goodbye, Miss Mistry. Please come again."

"I will, and thank you for breakfast," Perveen said as Rama left quietly.

"I'm so glad you visited." Colin's voice had become more intimate, and Perveen felt the tension rise within her. "The days you stayed at Circuit House were the best I ever spent there."

Before Perveen could respond, a scraping sound came from above. Tilting her head, she saw that a European woman in a dressing gown had come onto her balcony. The woman's head hung down, watching them as if a theater performance was unfolding. Colin also glanced up, then grimaced. Underneath the table, he gripped her hand.

"Mr. Sandringham, we shouldn't leave these dishes outside," Perveen said, squeezing back before she released her hand. "Otherwise, the monkeys will make a mess."

It took two trips to carry the dishes inside through the door between the kitchen and veranda. Perveen imagined the neighbor-lady's curiosity rising about what reason a young Indian woman would have to breakfast with a British bachelor. And the two of them, carrying dishes together! That was certainly out of order.

Stacking their breakfast plates on a worn wooden kitchen table, Perveen said, "Have you met any of your flat neighbors?"

"A few have said hello. I've been invited for tea by a couple living upstairs. Why?"

He was so close behind her that she felt his breath on her neck. Turning to face him, she said, "The lady who just saw us. Is she the one who asked you to tea?" When he nodded, she added, "You should mention that a professional acquaintance stopped over with some papers on Monday morning. And that you served breakfast as a courtesy."

"You mean— to lie?" His face was disapproving.

Perveen shook her head. "It's not a lie if I leave a paper from my legal case, is it? And I do represent the Asiatic Society."

"Ah, yes. That fortunate coincidence. Although you know that I came to Bombay for you."

"Without my asking!" Perveen shot back.

At last Colin stepped away, giving her room to exit the tiny kitchen. Perveen made her way to the living room and approached the tall front windows, where the shutters were closed, allowing sufficient privacy.

"Please let's finish this conversation," said Colin, coming up beside her. "Although I know that I've upset you."

Perveen kept her attention on a small reptile basking on the windowsill. Its golden body and legs were covered in square black spots. Softly, she said, "What an incredible creature. Gecko family, I think, from the eyes without lids."

"The Latin name is Hemidactylus gracilis." Colin's voice had a hint of reverence. "I've seen them in Satapur. I especially like its toes—do you notice how they fan?"

As if hearing the praise, the gecko turned its head to regard them with its large, white-streaked black eyes.

"Look at those glorious eyes!" Perveen added. "We both need to keep our eyes open. I'm aware that by coming here unannounced, I'm clearly making myself the instigator."

"Instigating what? My happiness?" Colin took her hand in his, and their fingers twined. She thought of the vines twisting on the trees outside, and how they also were knitted together in an alliance that many would consider detrimental.

"Goodbye, gecko," he said as the reptile slithered out of sight. Looking sideways at Perveen, he said, "Your marital separation was granted by a jury in Calcutta."

"Yes." Why was he stating something she'd told him the year before?

His hazel eyes narrowed as he spoke quietly. "Would you ever consider filing a divorce suit before the Parsi matrimonial court in Bombay? It's been almost four years that you've been apart from your husband. People are more liberal here. Perhaps you'd win."

"The Parsi Marriage and Divorce Act holds across all of India," Perveen said in her most measured, legalistic voice. "I didn't qualify for divorce because I couldn't prove that both adultery and cruelty were committed by my husband. Truly, the only way that Cyrus Sodawalla and I could ever be divorced is if he decides to charge me with adultery—which would ruin my family's name."

"I see," Colin said soberly. "I hope that the law might change as years pass."

"My father suggested that a motivated woman lawyer must convince the establishment to revise the law. But I can't be that lawyer if I'm intending to use the law for my own interests."

"You'd be like Henry the Eighth changing England's religion in order to take another wife." Colin offered a half-hearted smile.

"Yes. I can only play at being the monstrous Henry here!" Perveen stretched out her hands to touch his arms, warm beneath the soft cotton of his kurta. "I must say I'm happy that you've taken this flat."

"Yes," he agreed, drawing her against him. "We can pretend, even for a few hours, that we are a couple. That we can live with the ease of your brother and his wife."

Perveen didn't want to be reminded of them. She tilted her face upward.

The first kiss was tentative, the second more vigorous. It was reckless, and the knowledge of this made kissing him even more exciting. How matched they were in passion, as well as everything else.

Perveen led him by the hand back to the misshapen chair, and the two of them crashed down in it together. More kisses, and hands on silk, and then on skin.

"I love you," Colin whispered.

It was the first time he'd said it. She wasn't brave enough yet to explain what she felt.

She kissed him again.

4

REGRETS AND RESPONSIBILITIES

The liaison in the chair with Colin had gone a bit further than kissing. If it hadn't been for the creaking of the kitchen door, Perveen believed they both would have lost their heads. A man's declaration of love should not have freed her into giving so much of herself.

She'd jumped up and over to the sofa, hiding the dishevelment of her sari blouse under the sari's pallu. Colin gave her a wry smile and spoke about getting off to the library before the heat rose any further.

"A good idea," she'd answered. "I'll leave straightaway. What a marvelous breakfast. My work will surely go well."

Perveen swiftly left through the kitchen door, bidding goodbye to Rama, who was washing the melon he'd brought home. Rama might have guessed something had happened between them; she hoped not, because she didn't want him to lose respect for Colin.

And what might he think of her? An unaccompanied woman should not fraternize with men. She'd behaved impetuously because she was shaken by her argument with Gulnaz. That was the real trouble she should think about.

Ten hours after the argument, Perveen had handwritten a short apology to Gulnaz and had the sealed note delivered by the office messenger, Jayanth. As of Wednesday morning, no response had come. Logic told Perveen that she should return to the hospital, but she imagined Gulnaz had been stewing with indignation and had even angrier words stored up.

Perveen knew her hesitation was ridiculous. She'd survived the sharp inquisitions of the tutors at Oxford, but she was afraid of facing her sister-in-law.

In the end, she decided not to visit because Gulnaz and Khushy's forty days of postpartum confinement were almost complete. They'd be home soon enough for their ritual baths and a celebratory lunch to which Gulnaz's parents were invited.

Another issue was Gulnaz's request for her to carry a second donation to Uma Bhatia. Perveen had spent an undue amount of time thinking that adding this donation to the previous one would create an inauspicious 102 rupees. But Gulnaz had wanted it this way; if she arrived home on Thursday morning and learned it hadn't been done, that could be fuel for another argument.

Perveen asked Arman, the family's amiable chauffeur, to transport her back to the site of the fundraising tea. Traveling to Ghatkopar during midmorning, when the weather wasn't yet as punishingly hot, Perveen was able to better appreciate the scenery. The Agra Road was bordered by farm fields and salt flats, as well as small settlements of people, many cooking alongside the road or quietly lounging in any patch of shade. The ground looked parched, as did the trees. Everyone needed rain.

Perveen guessed that many of the roadside crowd awaited carts transporting them to their jobs at affluent households. It was typical for servants to commute daily to work, and the train was unaffordable for most.

At Bhatia House, she'd seen a bevy of male bearers serving food and a group of female ayahs caring for the children. She also recalled the strong presence of a servant named Oshadi, whose behavior had become emotional when she'd been directed to hold Sunanda's money. Perveen wondered how Sunanda would spend her windfall. Ten to fifteen rupees was a typical month's salary for an ayah; Perveen knew this from hearing her parents discuss finding an ayah for Khushy.

Arman dropped his speed as he left the large metaled road and drove along the smaller main avenue into Ghatkopar. At this time of day, the traffic was largely bullock carts and bicycles. Fruit and vegetable sellers sat behind baskets overflowing with produce, and a number of shops had Gujarati signs advertising that they sold medicines, dry goods, and the like. They passed Vireshwar Mahadev temple, where Hindus were stepping out of sandals and going up the stairs for worship.

The religious landmark and commercial buildings made it apparent the place was outgrowing its village roots. Geographically, Ghatkopar lay outside Bombay's limits and was taxed by a collector for the suburban area. Yet because Sir Dwarkanath had donated generously to Bombay institutions, he had been honored with knighthood and was arguably the most influential Indian member of the city's Legislative Council. This was a formidable achievement for someone who'd described himself as arriving in Bombay as an impoverished immigrant from Bharuch.

At the tea party, Sir Dwarkanath's facial expressions had conflicted with his cheerful words. Perveen had disliked how sharp he'd been with Uma, although it was natural for parents to think the younger generation didn't know how to do things correctly. In the office, Jamshedji kept a tight rein on Perveen's activities, although he'd recently made her partner, which must have meant she was doing some things right.

When they reached the Bhatia House guard booth, Perveen leaned out of her window to explain herself to the durwan, who listened carefully and recorded her name in writing before sending her through. Today, she noticed one side of the field had cricket balls and bats lying about, as if a game had been interrupted.

The house's porte cochere held both a dark blue Rolls-Royce Silver Ghost and a green Buick. A driver lay across the Rolls's wide front seat, a newspaper spread out over his face.

"I didn't know the Bhatias had two cars!" Perveen had to raise her voice over the clamor of dogs barking.

"I think Sir Dwarkanath just owns the Buick; his chauffeur showed it off to me during the party," Arman answered as he opened the car door. As Perveen exited, taking her legal case, she went to ogle the car and saw that it bore a coat of arms with a tiger on either side of a bodhi tree. The Gujarati script below read "Varanpur."

Maybe the nawab himself was visiting Sir Dwarkanath. Perveen felt a surge of nerves as she realized she might be coming at an inconvenient time. Then she heard an odd wailing from a short distance.

"I hope the dogs haven't caught a cat," she muttered to Arman.

"What?" Arman shook his head and followed her around to the house's other side.

Her stomach clenched as she saw a pack of more than a dozen street dogs surrounding a red-headed woman wearing a lavender sari and clutching a purse to her chest.

"Challo, challo!" Arman shouted at the dogs, to no avail.

Catching sight of Perveen, the woman screamed in English, "For God's sake, help me!"

The sharp accent was the last clue that made Perveen certain the young lady was Cora, the Begum of Varanpur.

"I'll fetch the guard!" Arman shouted in English. "Perveen-bai, won't you come back to the car for your own safety?"

"If I do that, she'll feel abandoned." Perveen waved him off, playing braver than she felt. She wasn't afraid of dogs, but this pack was atypically aggressive.

The largest dog sprang up, pushing his mangy paws against the begum's stomach as he gnawed at her large purse trimmed in shining jet beads. The begum screamed even harder. "He'll kill me!"

"What do you have inside your purse?" Perveen called out.

"What? Can't you see they're going to tear me apart?"

"Have you got food or something that smells strongly in there?"

"Blimey! I've got some sausages—"

"Throw it as far as you can. Right now!"

Cora flung away the purse in a wide arc, its jet beads sparkling in the sun. A paper-wrapped package dropped out and the dogs were upon it, battling to see who got the goods.

"The Bhatias should never have dogs running about like this," Begum Cora said tearfully. "At our palace, the guard dogs are caged during the day."

"I don't think those dogs are pets. And it's all right now," Perveen soothed; she was close enough to smell sherry mixed with the rank odor of sweat. "Were you bitten? Let me see your arms."

The woman examined her own lightly freckled arms, which were loaded with jeweled gold bangles that caught sunlight. Some scratches, but nothing that looked like a bite.

"Do you want to go to a doctor?"

"I was on my way home, but I may well do that on the way." She shot a glance over her shoulder at the house. "The bungalow windows are open! Uma probably heard all of it. No worry to her!"

Perveen couldn't possibly know whether Uma was listening, but she had to satisfy her curiosity about something else. "Why ever did you put sausages in your pretty bag?"

Cora looked abashed. "There's a very good Portuguese sausage maker in Santa Cruz. I buy from them so I can have a proper breakfast. It was too hot to leave them in the car and because the Bhatias are vegetarians, I hid them in my bag."

"Probably those dogs never tasted sausages before. It might cause a stomach upset," Perveen said with exaggerated concern.

Begum Cora snorted and then looked toward the bushes with a despairing expression. "Oh, they've ruined that bag. It's—it was—my favorite Vionnet."

Arman and the guard came running around the corner, the two men shouting at the feasting dogs. When the guard brandished his lathi, the dogs loped away from the path toward the open fields.

Perveen followed Cora to the bushes where her beaded purse had landed. The begum crouched, one hand keeping hold of her gold-bordered sari, while the other searched through the grass. Cora hastily picked up a lipstick, some rupee notes, a calling card case, and a pen while Perveen grabbed a book that had landed facedown, its pages splayed. The title was *The Torn Petticoat*. Perveen was turning it over in her hand, amazed by the cover drawing that showed a blonde woman, wearing only a petticoat, pressed up against a wall with a towering dark figure over her, but Cora snatched it away.

"Just beach reading!"

Perveen tried to sound casual. "Is your book from the Oxford Bookshop?"

"Of course not! My books and magazines are posted from Australia. My friends there know what I like," Cora added. "And thanks—there's no need to get your hands dirty scraping on the ground. I've got everything."

"Wouldn't you like to come inside Bhatia House with me?" Perveen suggested, still worried that Cora had been hurt. "You could wash up and have a cold drink of water."

"No. I saw Uma already and have had enough." Cora wiped a hand across her sweating brow, leaving a streak of dirt. "Why did you come? And I'm afraid I don't know you."

"My name is Perveen Mistry. We briefly saw each other at the fundraising party. My sister-in-law asked me to bring another donation."

Cora's hand flew to her bow-shaped pink lips. "Now I remember. You were Johnny-on-the-spot with Dr. Penkar when the ayah got burned." Shaking her head, she said, "I asked to see Sunanda today, but Uma said she was off with the children on a picnic. It seems a bit incredible for her to be so quickly healed, doesn't it? As well as Ishan."

Perveen said, "Good, you're putting my mind at ease. I was fearful about asking Uma and hearing one or the other of them was faring poorly."

"Never mind about them. But good luck to you for trying to get Uma to accept anything." Cora reached into her torn bag and extracted a gold case. After flicking it open she handed over a pale pink calling card engraved in a flowing gold script.

Perveen thought Cora's desire to wish her luck in giving another donation seemed odd; but perhaps it was a matter of not understanding Australian English. Perveen examined Cora's. It had English information on one side, while the other side was typeset in both Gujarati and Marathi. She opened up her legal briefcase to give Cora one of her own personal cards, simply done with black type on white stock. "The Fort address is for my law firm, and the one in Dadar is where I reside with my parents."

The begum pondered the English-language side of Perveen's card. "So what do people call you—memsahib or miss?"

"That depends on the situation. My friends use Perveen-bai, Perveen-behen, or simply Perveen. How may I address you?"

"As you saw on my card, my new full name is Begum Koh-i-noor of Varanpur. He named me after the world's most precious diamond."

Technically, koh-i-noor meant "mountain of light," but Perveen was not going to quibble. "Do you prefer to be called Begum Koh-i-noor?"

"God, no! Princess Cora has a better sound; and Cora is my real name. I'll look up if you call either of those out." She drew Perveen close and kissed her lightly on the cheek, delivering the scent of tobacco and expensive-smelling perfume. "I owe you my life. I'd like to meet you again. Do ring me if you'd like to spend the day at our beach place in Juhu."

"I'd like that," Perveen answered. The weather was so hot, and she fancied the idea of wading into the coolness of the sea. "Is the nawab in town with you?"

"Yes, but sadly for just a few more days. He's truly the prince of my dreams; I like to make the most of each moment. It's as good as in books." Princess Cora pressed her palm to her lips and then fluttered her fingers at Perveen.

She's kissing me twice! Perveen thought with amusement as Princess Cora strolled off, hips swaying, to her parked car. She was relieved that the incident had ended without injury. Perhaps her new friendship could lead to something more than a walk on the beach. In any case, the misadventure with dogs would be a great tale for Gulnaz, once the two of them were speaking again.

5

A CHANGE OF PLANS

"*B*oth of my mistresses are occupied. I cannot admit you."
Oshadi spoke in a voice as starched as her white cotton
sari. She looked Perveen up and down, a turnabout in the usual
relationship between servants and guests.

"I only need a minute with Uma-bhabhu," Perveen pleaded.
"Do you remember me from the tea party last week? I was
impressed by how quickly you came to help when Ishan and
Sunanda were burned."

Oshadi still looked wary, but she stepped back and
motioned for Perveen to follow her. Perveen slipped out
of her sandals and felt the refreshing coolness of marble
underfoot. Soon they'd passed through a tall, handsomely
carved door into a large drawing room with tall windows,
all shuttered from the sun. Uma was seated cross-legged on
a wooden swing, and she looked up from the book she had
open on her lap. Across from this traditional piece of Indian
furniture were several Regency-style upholstered chairs and
a Victorian mahogany breakfront cabinet with glass doors
revealing an array of liquor bottles. A tiny smudge on the
cabinet's glass and a forgotten wooden train were reminders
of the absent children.

"Bhabhuji, this lady insisted," Oshadi said, regarding Perveen
with an expression as tight as her grip on her cane.

Uma uncrossed her legs, shifting them elegantly to one side
and smoothing the fine plum silk sari, and closed the book,
placing it beside her. "Good morning. I must tell you, my

father-in-law is expecting some businessmen for a meeting quite soon. But do sit down."

Clearly, her interruption was unwelcome. Resolving to get the business over quickly, Perveen seated herself in a stiff chair across from the swing. She re-introduced herself, given that Uma had many guests at her party and might not remember her name. "Mrs. Bhatia, you are very kind to admit me without advance permission. How is your son?"

"Please call me Uma. And Ishan's recovery has been splendid—in fact, the doctor cleared him to play with the other children. But did you fall down? Your sari . . ." She trailed off, gesturing toward Perveen's knees.

Looking down, Perveen saw the red-brown streaks marring her blue-dotted tissue silk sari. No wonder Oshadi had looked so dubiously at her! "I'm quite sorry to come in like this. A pack of dogs just outside were bothering Begum Cora, but we managed to scare them off."

"I did hear some barking, but I had no idea about that!" Uma's eyes widened, and Perveen wondered if her reaction was sincere. "Our Jain neighbors feed stray dogs daily as an act of their faith. The dogs might have wandered because those neighbors are away on pilgrimage. Now I must think about whether the children are safe playing outside."

"Yes. It was quite frightening for Begum Cora." Perveen decided she'd better not mention the sausages that had been in the woman's purse.

Uma glanced toward Oshadi, still standing at the door. "Oshadi, you must get a wet cloth for Perveen-behen, and a cup of tea. Unless you'd like something stronger?"

"No, tea would be lovely," Perveen said, noting that Uma seemed to have forgotten the upcoming business meeting.

Oshadi hobbled to the table between them and leaned down to remove a small crystal glass with some golden liquid that Perveen guessed had been Cora's refreshment. As the housekeeper proceeded to the door, Uma said, "Very well, Perveen-bai. Tell me, how are Gulnaz and her baby? Has the family chosen a name?"

"Yes. She's been named Khushna, and they are calling her Khushy as a nickname."

"Khushy is also a Hindu name," Uma said. "For us, the name means happiness."

"It's the same meaning in Farsi. What links we have!" Perveen said. "Although I have to admit that this particular Khushy is behaving against the expectations of her name. She cries often; supposedly it's colic."

"Time will change that," Uma said. "That and proper household help."

"Khushy and Gulnaz are joining us at home tomorrow. That's the reason I descended on you without sending you a note—" Perveen stopped talking because Oshadi had returned, carrying a cup of lemongrass-ginger tea. "This smells delicious. Thank you very much."

Oshadi nodded and bestowed a small smile that made her wrinkled face look unexpectedly younger.

"What were you saying?" Uma prompted when Oshadi had exited the room.

"I was saying I've brought something for you from Gulnaz." Perveen set down the teacup, opened the briefcase, withdrew the envelope, and stretched it across the distance of the tea table to Uma. "Please open it now."

Uma slid a slender finger under the envelope's edge, and after she'd looked inside, pressed her lips together. "How kind and generous she is to give even more. But we can't take it."

"But it's meant for the hospital. An official donation."

Looking away from Perveen, Uma said, "The hospital plan has ended. We are not going to build it."

Perveen wasn't sure she'd heard right. "But your family are the chief supporters! What happened?"

"Sir Dwarkanath changed his mind." Uma spoke lightly, but her eyes had narrowed. She reached across the table, handing the envelope back to Perveen.

Perveen remembered Cora's wishing her good luck in giving the new donation. Now she understood why. "I'm quite sorry to learn this. The cause is such a good one, and you worked so hard to build support among your friends and neighbors. Did Sir Dwarkanath give a reason?"

"He thinks it is too much work for me." Uma's words were halting. "I should spend more time with the children. The accident with Ishan was all he needed to prove his point."

Perveen knew it would be impossible for Uma to contradict the family's patriarch, yet a way might exist to still participate. "What if you remained on the committee but stepped back from being leader?"

"No. I've lost the biggest benefit we had." Uma saw the confusion in Perveen's eyes and explained, "The hospital was going to be built in a part of Kalbadevi where our family owns property. Without this donation of land, nothing can go forward."

Glancing at the open door, Perveen lowered her voice. "I know how it is when family members insist on something. We can be quiet and pleasant, but we can sometimes get what we want with a little bit of time."

Uma shook her head and looked sadly at Perveen. "What is time? After my mother-in-law passed, I believed I would have a little time outside of the house. But now Mangala and her husband are telling Sir Dwarkanath that I'm wasting my days, and my husband is too soft with me."

"How so?"

Uma leaned forward, causing the swing to rock precariously. The book fell onto the table, and as she straightened it, Perveen was startled by the title.

"They don't like that Parvesh let me start the hospital committee. Mangala only joined to keep watch on me. And I know that my husband is disappointed about the cancellation, but to push for my sake would make him look even worse." Closing her eyes, Uma added, "It's so humiliating. I just told Begum Cora, and she didn't want to accept it."

"Do you mean the news—or the begum's donation?" Perveen remembered the extravagant pearl and diamond necklace.

"I tried to give back the necklace!" Uma sounded forlorn. "I told her that it was in my safe, and I went upstairs to fetch it. But when I returned, she'd already gone away."

Perveen recalled how she'd begged off when Uma and Miriam invited her to help. Now she felt ashamed of her reticence. If she'd been involved, she might have averted this crisis. "I'm very sorry, and I suppose it's a good thing you are putting your mind on something else. What's the book about? It's got quite a title."

Uma's cheeks pinkened. *"Woman and the New Race* is a serious book written by an American nurse called Margaret Sanger. She describes her professional knowledge of the hardships cast on women who have more children than they can manage. Dr. Penkar lent it to me so I could understand Mrs. Sanger's ideas. But now that the hospital is cancelled, I don't know why I'm trying to finish it. I should put away any of my outside interests and return to being the head daughter-in-law."

Perveen's initial wariness about Uma was being replaced by compassion. Abandoning the chair, she came over. Uma shifted, allowing Perveen to sit, and then she asked, "How long have you been in this household?"

"I had my wedding when I was eleven—but the ceremony only." Uma sounded defensive. "In the early years, I stayed with Parvesh's sisters in their rooms and learned everything from his mother and Oshadi, who was our ayah. My mother-in-law was often ill, so much of my time was tending to her; I think that's where I became interested in health care."

"And when did you become a mother yourself?"

"My husband and I began living as husband and wife when I was sixteen and he was nineteen. Our children started coming when I was seventeen. Three girls. Just one boy." She smiled wanly.

"When did you have to leave school?"

"I only was in school when I lived with my parents. When I arrived at Bhatia House, an English governess sometimes visited, because my father-in-law had joined the Legislative Council and knew that the family's women would sometimes have to meet with the British. Therefore, we learned some English—even Oshadi learned some English, because she was close by. However, most of my studies—and Mangala's, after she came—were with a Hindu priest. Carrying out religious observances for the family's sake is as important as preparing food."

"There's surely a cook here? I saw staff serving at the tea party."

"It's a large staff for cooking, cleaning, and caring for the children. But a daughter-in-law cannot give orders to cook a dish or mend a shirt if she doesn't know how to do it properly herself. Mangala joined the house a few years after me, and she took more interest in this work."

"Was that why it was so appealing to have a charity project, something meaningful to do outside—" Perveen cut herself off because she heard loud footsteps in the hall.

Parvesh Bhatia stepped in, followed by his father. Parvesh's eyes were anxiously fixed on the two of them. Sir Dwarkanath appeared just as disagreeable as he had at the tea party. What was different today was that both men wore well-tailored European clothing.

"My friend Perveen Mistry just came," Uma said, sliding off the swing so quickly that Perveen had to grab one of its silk ropes for balance. "She is just going home."

"Good morning," Perveen said, getting to her feet. She didn't expect acknowledgment, but Sir Dwarkanath inclined his chin.

"You were a donor at the tea." His voice held a tension that was also different from the jocularity at the party.

"I donated on behalf of my sister-in-law," Perveen clarified, and then dared to add, "but I share everyone's wish for the Kalbadevi Ladies' Hospital to succeed."

Sir Dwarkanath frowned, looking directly at Uma. "Didn't you understand that all of the financial returns should be done next week through the post?"

"I came without an invitation," Perveen said protectively. "And I'm sorry for any confusion."

"And is the red-head begum still here?" Sir Dwarkanath said, feigning hospitality. "What a commotion she caused!"

"She's gone away," Uma said.

"The begum gave us jewelry, didn't she?" Parvesh asked. "What about that?"

"She wouldn't accept the necklace today. Giving back donations is quite complicated," Uma said sullenly.

"If your sister-in-law gave money, it will be returned by courier," Parvesh said, looking at Perveen. "I hope you don't mind the slight delay. As my wife is saying, the situation is complicated."

Oshadi limped into the room, ducking her head as she spoke to Sir Dwarkanath. "Nana-seth, Mr. Stowe has come."

Parvesh looked anxiously toward the tea table. "Take away that cup."

"And that book also." Sir Dwarkanath stepped forward and picked up the book that had been abandoned on the coffee table. As he looked at it, color rose in his face. In a voice shaking with anger, he glared at Uma. "*Woman and . . .* what is this nonsense?"

"It's my book," Perveen blurted. "I'll put it back in my briefcase."

"Please let me show you out," Uma said, taking Perveen by the arm.

"Good day, gentlemen," Perveen said, passing a shocked-looking Parvesh and his fuming father.

As Perveen stepped into the hall, she saw the ironworks magnate seated about twenty feet away on a petite velvet bench. She wondered how much Mr. Stowe had overheard. As she drew closer, she got a better look at Madeline's husband. He was a broad-shouldered, large man of about fifty in a well-tailored white lounge suit that set off his deeply tanned skin. But what did it matter? She must have been trying to distract herself from the recent volatile encounter with Sir Dwarkanath.

Ahead of her, she heard the rapid breathing of Uma, who pulled her sari a bit closer around her head, as if protecting her modesty from Stowe. Perveen's hair was also draped with her pallu, but she didn't make any extra effort to shield herself. She was not connected to the house in any way. It felt like a gift not to have to live with the rigid rules that Uma had endured since adolescence.

Outside, Perveen saw Arman spring out of his reclining spot in the car to open the door for her. Before she moved off, Perveen wanted to make sure Uma was all right. She said, "I'm sorry I didn't get out of the drawing room earlier. That would have given you a chance to get out with your book. I'll give it back to you whenever you want it."

Uma shook her head. "It was very kind of you to say what you did. And I never want to see that book again!"

"Very well. I'll return it to Dr. Penkar, although I may read it first!" she added.

Uma sighed, a soft gust of breath that disappeared in the humid air. "I hope Mr. Stowe didn't hear any of this. It was rude of me to pass by without asking him to give Madeline my best wishes. I probably won't be able to meet her again."

"Please keep some hope," Perveen said. "You have so many women wishing just as you do for the hospital. And perhaps you should not take it so hard about being responsible for every servant. By the way, how is Sunanda's recovery?"

As if startled, Uma paused before answering. "I believe quite normal. Oshadi has been taking care of her."

Perveen thought of inquiring whether Uma had ensured Oshadi gave Sunanda the ten rupees, but she didn't want to put Uma on the spot when she was still shaken from her father-in-law's discovery of the salaciously titled book. "Thank you so much for seeing me, Uma-behen."

Uma touched her elbow. "Would you please explain to Gulnaz-behen what happened? I have so many letters to write."

Seeing the anxiety and fatigue on Uma's face, Perveen murmured that she would.

6

HOMECOMING

On Thursday morning, Gulnaz and Khushy's pending arrival took precedence over everything that was customary. The Mistrys' cook, John, was preparing a dozen dishes, assisted by young Nain whose eyes were red from chopping onions. Gita was dusting and polishing with the help of another maid who'd come in for the last several days. Perveen's mother, Camellia, was in the garden, cutting roses to place into arrangements.

Neither Perveen, Jamshedji, or Rustom had gone off to work. Rustom had dressed in his best suit, and was supervising John's washing of the Daimler, because he would ride in it to pick up Gulnaz and Khushy from the hospital. While they were gone, Gulnaz's parents were expected to arrive, as well as a priest who would offer blessings to mother and baby.

It was a complicated set of arrangements, and nobody noticed that Perveen quietly removed herself after breakfast. She was at peace in her bedroom reading the book by Margaret Sanger. She was startled to learn that excessive childbearing was also a problem in America, and that for the last forty years in Holland, women had the choice to take prescribed remedies that Sanger called birth control. Quickly she became lost in the volume, and only realized how much time had passed when the grandfather clock downstairs chimed twelve.

Returning the book to her bedside table, she went into the hallway outside her room and looked down toward the street. Parked squarely in front of the duplex was their own black

Daimler and the Banker family's large Peugeot limousine, custom-painted a bright green.

Perveen straightened the ceremonial gara sari she wore—a pale blue silk-satin hand-embroidered with pink flowers, twisting green vines, and turquoise parakeets—and proceeded downstairs.

"When did everything start?" she asked, poking her head into the kitchen.

John, bent over the table rolling out rotlis, looked up. "Half an hour ago. Your family and Gulnaz's parents and the priest are taking tea. Gulnaz-memsahib and the new baby are on the other side taking the special bath."

Perveen hastened out the front door and into Rustom and Gulnaz's side of the house. The smell of fresh-cut roses wafted from a silver bowl on an ornately carved table in the hall. She heard the polite chatter coming from what Gulnaz liked to call the "sitting room." The modern term suited the grand room painted lime green and filled with fashionable Edwardian pieces.

Perveen gave a quick smile to her family members before greeting the elderly priest and Gulnaz's parents, Homi and Tajbanu Banker. She then seated herself in a chair near the sofa taken by her parents.

"Gulnaz is still taking her sacred bath," whispered Tajbanu, who shared Gulnaz's fine facial features and pale complexion, although time's passage had thickened her frame and given her an extra chin. "She wished to be alone. Strange, isn't it?"

Perveen wouldn't want people watching her bathe, either, but she didn't say it. Instead, she whispered, "Will she also bathe Khushy?"

"No. She let your mamma and me give Khushy her bath." Tajbanu turned her face to smile at Camellia. "Gulnaz was anxious, so why not?"

Perveen scanned the pristine parlor. "And where is Khushy?"

"Sleeping soundly on the veranda!" said Homi Banker, an affable fellow who was as lean as his wife was rounded.

Perveen wondered why nobody seemed to think twice about the baby being alone, but she felt shy about asking. After a moment, she quietly excused herself to go out.

Khushy lay in the cradle, wearing an exquisitely smocked white dress. There had been many debates between Gulnaz and Camellia about selections for jori-pori, the special trousseau of baby clothes. Finally, they'd decided on ordering the jori-pori from Pestonjee House, a shop in Fort that employed Parsi widows as seamstresses. It was the perfect marriage of good works and tradition.

Perveen bent over the baby so she could better see her tiny nostrils flare as she breathed. Khushy's eyes were shut fast, so Perveen could see her tiny eyelashes, which were as thick and black as her own. Cautiously, she reached down to wave away a fly that was crawling on Khushy's head.

"Memsahib?"

Hearing the soft, uncertain voice, Perveen turned to see a girl dressed in a dull beige cotton sari with a stack of nappies in her arms.

"I'm Perveen, the baby's aunt." As Perveen spoke the last word, she felt a rush of strangeness. She didn't see herself being old enough to be called Aunty, as young people addressed women of a certain maturity. Yet here she was, with a bona fide niece.

"I was away just one minute!"

"Of course," Perveen said, realizing the ayah was afraid of getting in trouble for leaving the baby alone. Looking back at Khushy, she knelt close to the cradle and reached in. Maybe this time, her niece would allow herself to be held; but when Perveen slid her fingers behind the infant's tiny shoulders, she whimpered. Yet she carried on and lifted Khushy up.

Perveen glanced at the ayah. "What's your name?"

"Lakshmi," the girl answered, looking nervously from the baby to her. "That is my job, Perveen-memsahib. Please."

"Do you work for an ayah agency?" Perveen thought Lakshmi looked barely fifteen.

Shaking her head, Lakshmi said, "I worked for the Cowasjee family before this. This baby's grandmother knows them."

"Oh, God! What are you doing to her!"

Perveen turned to see Gulnaz had come out to the veranda. She was fresh from her bath, with tendrils of wet hair escaping from the white mathabana tied around her head. Her sari was new and exquisite—a pale pink silk chiffon with a petit point embroidery border of pomegranates and flowers.

"Welcome home," Perveen said, wondering whether Gulnaz would finally acknowledge the apology note she'd sent to the hospital. "I was practicing with Khushy. I think she'll be happier here than in the hospital—"

"Stop! You'll bruise her head!" Gulnaz interrupted as she rushed up, reaching out to take Khushy. It took Perveen a moment to understand that Gulnaz wasn't trying to adjust her hold but to take away Khushy entirely. Hurt flared within her, but as Gulnaz yanked, Perveen let the baby go.

And in that brief moment, the baby slipped sideways and started to fall toward the veranda's stone floor.

Lakshmi screeched and Gulnaz threw herself forward so that Khushy landed, upside down, on her mother's knees.

Perveen's heart thudded as she watched Gulnaz check the crying baby's head, neck, and limbs for signs of damage. After placing Khushy back in the cradle, Gulnaz said, "You idiot! You dropped my child. Do you really hate her so much?"

Tears had started, and Perveen strained to keep from outright weeping. In a choked voice, she said, "I don't hate her at all. I was holding her because I want to—I want to do better with her."

As Perveen's words trailed off, Gulnaz gave her a disparaging look. "Why are you even here?"

"I stayed home from work to greet you both." Trying to prove her loyalty, she added, "And yesterday, I went to Bhatia House. I tried to give your money to Uma, but she wouldn't take it."

"Why not?" Gulnaz wrinkled her nose at Perveen. "What stories did you tell her about me?"

"I didn't speak of you at all! Lord Dwarkanath decided to reverse his donation of land. I can tell you more later, because it's a bit complicated—" Perveen stopped because she saw Tajbanu Banker barreling through the French doors toward them.

"Darling! It's time to go inside to thank the priest for coming."

Gulnaz gingerly lifted up Khushy, who made a grunting sound. Nestled in her mother's arms, Khushy turned so her shining eyes focused on Perveen. Her tiny rosebud mouth wiggled, and then opened to let forth a scream.

"Waaah!"

"Oh, dear," Perveen said, her face flushing red as the baby kept looking at her and crying.

"Khushy's still angry at Perveen for dropping her," Gulnaz said, sounding plaintive. "Thank God I caught her."

"She fell? Meri Mai!" Tajbanu exclaimed, crouching low to peer at Khushy. "Baby, sweet baby!"

"I am sorry about it," Perveen said, realizing that if she didn't accept blame, it could lead to a nasty argument.

"You should know better." Frowning again, Tajbanu rummaged in the bag hanging at the waist of her sari. She took out a kohl pencil and gently drew a big round spot on Khushy's cheek.

"Mummy, she hasn't been blessed yet!" Gulnaz reprimanded.

"The evil eye is everywhere," said Tajbanu.

Perveen's cheeks flushed even hotter, because she sensed the reprimand was meant for her. Lakshmi also seemed frightened and stepped back so she bumped into Gulnaz, who fell against a chair.

"Ow! Watch it!" Gulnaz snapped.

"Sorry, Memsahib, sorry!" Lakshmi's gaze flashed from Gulnaz to Tajbanu Banker.

"Time to go back inside." Tajbanu put her hand on Gulnaz's back.

Because Tajbanu hadn't said anything more to her, Perveen walked over to her family's side of the duplex. Still shaken from what had happened on the veranda, she seated herself in her usual chair at the long table already set for lunch. As she glanced over the family's Minton porcelain, crystal glassware, and heavy silver cutlery, she wondered what Tajbanu Banker would make of it. She might think what they owned was too old, or too hodgepodge. Homi Banker had founded Majestic Bank, and he and Tajbanu were known for spending lavishly on the latest styles of clothing, cars, and furniture.

Ten minutes later, the priest had departed, and she heard the clatter of footsteps in the hall as the celebratory party arrived, minus Gulnaz and Khushy.

"They're nursing," Camellia told Perveen, taking the chair next to her—as if to offer protection. Perveen imagined that she'd already heard the story of how badly she'd botched things with Khushy.

Lakshmi carried in the cradle from the veranda and set it by the chair that Rustom said Gulnaz would take. The Mistry servants began carrying out dishes. Twenty minutes later, Gulnaz and Khushy joined the rest of the dining family.

After laying Khushy in the cradle, Gulnaz took an appreciative look at the table. "Oh, how I have longed for this, after forty days of plain hospital food!"

"And how I have longed for you!" Rustom said, picking up his wife's right hand and kissing it. Gulnaz smiled back at him, and Perveen felt a surge of annoyance.

John had outdone himself with a luncheon that included lamb chops, pomfret steamed in banana leaves, chicken pulao, spicy preserved prawns, ground beef with matchstick potatoes, a roasted eggplant stew, egg curry, puris and rotlis, and baked custard, as well as raita, dal, and various pickles. There was laughter and chatter about the dull but healthful foods Gulnaz had eaten in hospital compared with the menu when Tajbanu and Camellia had stayed there in 1897 and 1898, the years that Gulnaz and Perveen had been born.

"You surely have the best cook in the neighborhood. Watch out, because Tajbanu might snatch him!" Homi Banker joked, pinching the fingers of his left hand in a snapping gesture.

Tajbanu Banker looked dourly at her Rustom. "I hope that the food is always to this standard. During her first months at home, Gulnaz should not be expected to do cooking herself."

"I'll help, too. Gulnaz is a true talent in the kitchen, but don't worry for a moment about her being tasked with too much," Camellia assured her.

"Don't worry, dear!" Rustom whispered, patting Gulnaz's arm.

"And please remember: the ayah must apply turmeric paste to the baby's face daily. We don't want her turning brown." Mrs. Banker glanced casually at Rustom, who was significantly browner than Gulnaz.

This felt like the last straw.

As her brother tried to laugh off the comment, Perveen stood up. "I'm very sorry, but I must leave."

"To where?" Mr. Banker asked, his tone cheerful. "What could send you off before dessert is served?"

"Gamdevi Police Station."

"A police station?" Gulnaz scowled at Perveen. "Of all the places to go!"

Perveen shrugged. "I must retrieve a bail refund for a client."

"Oh, yes! It's fortuitous that you remembered. Go ahead." Jamshedji's voice was reassuring.

Perveen said a quiet goodbye and made her escape from the dining room. After taking her legal case from her room, she headed out to the Daimler, where Arman was dozing in the front seat.

"Sorry to wake you," she said, tapping Arman's shoulder. "I'd like to go into town, please."

"Of course, Perveen-bai." He struggled from a reclined position to upright. "I thought the luncheon was still on."

"It's still on, but I'm not needed! To Gamdevi, please."

7

THE PRISONERS' LINE

$\mathcal{C}$ollecting a bail refund was the perfect errand for a law clerk—which Mistry Law lacked.

When Perveen had started working with her father, his clerk of twenty years had resigned because he disliked taking orders from a woman. The two gentlemen who'd followed had been sacked due to what Jamshedji called ineptitude, and what Perveen judged to be variations of the same prejudice against female bosses.

Thus, the bail errand fell to Perveen, but at least she was headed to a new police station that was an improvement over most in the city. Gamdevi was built of handsome gray stone bricks in the Adam style. Inside, a sweeping staircase led to various administrative rooms. She felt uplifted treading these stairs alongside others in the field: barristers, solicitors, clerks, police. She was usually the only female doing business at Gamdevi, but a level of professional decorum existed that made her feel comfortable.

Up in the bail office, Perveen produced the papers proving that their client, a rice merchant accused of profiteering, had presented himself to the Police Court a week earlier. The judge had dismissed the case as having insufficient evidence, something Perveen credited both to her research at the rice market and the efforts of Vivek Sharma.

Mr. Vivek Sharma was a barrister and independence activist she'd first met within a small circle of lawyers supporting Mohandas Karamchand Gandhi. Mr. Sharma's education had been completed ten years earlier at the Government Law School in Bombay, giving him old-boy connections crisscrossing all aspects of law. She thought well of him for his memory, reliability, and his open-mindedness about taking direction from a woman solicitor.

The bail refund was returned to Perveen. After she'd placed the cash in an envelope inside her legal briefcase, she proceeded downstairs, thinking about other errands that could fill her afternoon.

Arman and the Daimler were gone. Their space in front of the station was occupied by several horse-drawn police carts. No doubt the police had forced him to move, and she resolved to look for him nearby. But before she could walk along the pavement, she paused to allow space for the prisoners emerging from one of the police carts. Most of the chained men wore the rough clothes of manual laborers, while others were half-naked, wearing rags that marked destitution. Then, she noticed the unexpected: a young woman chained to the end of the group.

The female prisoner appeared to be in her early twenties, with a fuzzy long braid that looked slept on. She had a slender figure covered by a beige sari overlaid with a coat of dust and dirt. As she studied the woman's profile, Perveen thought she looked strangely familiar. She'd seen those high cheekbones and luminous, wide-set eyes before. Who was this young woman?

The prisoners had all been unloaded and were standing in place. While a group of constables conferred with a senior police official, Perveen sidled next to the young female prisoner. Softly, she asked, "Are you Sunanda?"

The woman's head jerked at the sound of her name, but after seeing Perveen, she looked away. Either she didn't remember Perveen; or she didn't want to be recognized.

"I'm Perveen Mistry. I was present when you saved Ishan. Does Uma-bhabhu know what's happened—that you are at this station?" Her words tumbled out fast because she knew the time was limited.

"Nobody knows! The police came to my home last night." Sunanda shuddered, drawing her one unshackled hand toward her stomach, where rusty blood tinged the dirty sari.

Seeing the bloodstain, Perveen flinched. "What happened to you there?"

"It's still the burn. It wasn't ever healing." Sunanda sounded plaintive. "Are you a doctor?"

"No, but I was right next to Dr. Penkar when she treated you. I'm a solicitor." Perveen ignored the inmates right in front of Sunanda who'd turned their heads to watch. "May I ask why you were arrested?"

"They are accusing me of . . ." Sunanda took a long breath. "I cannot say."

Perveen looked at her sympathetically. "Please tell me. I have heard everything."

"They said—child murder. And it's not true!"

The brusque words sent a chill through Perveen, who'd been anticipating an ordinary kind of charge like theft. "Do you have a lawyer?"

"No."

"This is a bail court. There's a chance you could be freed while awaiting trial." Perveen chose her words carefully, because they were in a public space. "Did the police tell you the name of the child who died?"

"Nobody died!" Sunanda's voice cracked with emotion. "The constables say I killed my own child." Again, she pressed her hands against her stomach. "That I made a crime by getting rid of an unborn baby. But it is impossible!"

Several of the prisoners had turned their heads to watch Sunanda. Some faces were contemptuous, others pitying. A guard walked close, shaking a lathi, urging the group to move forward.

Perveen continued alongside Sunanda as the prisoners' line mounted the steps to the station. "Did the constable specify the charge is abortion?"

Sunanda looked at her in puzzlement. "What?"

"Garbhapaat." The word Perveen used was the same in Gujarati and Marathi.

"When the constable spoke to me, he said, killing a child." Sunanda's voice strengthened. "The police had a paper with my name on it, but it's all a mistake! I've not done anything wrong. I only wish to return to work at the Bhatias', and they must be concerned I didn't come today. Will you please tell them? And—"

Sunanda stopped speaking after Perveen laid a finger on her own lips.

"You don't need to tell me everything right now," Perveen assured her. "I'll come to the bail courtroom and examine the documents related to your arrest. But first I must be sure of something. Would you like me to represent you?"

"What does that mean?" Sunanda whispered.

"I'll argue for you to get bail, and I'll help you with everything that comes next."

"Yes, I do. But—"

"Inside, no delays!" a constable shouted at Sunanda, brandishing his lathi dangerously close.

Sunanda stepped back, her face terrified, causing the man ahead of her on the chain to step backward as well. He cursed her, and as the line moved forward, Sunanda was pulled more quickly.

Perveen wanted to shout at the constable, but she feared he could use her intervention as an excuse to have police remove her from the scene. She allowed distance between herself and the prisoners, who proceeded into the building's lobby and upstairs into the bail court, where they were shepherded into an area with a waist-high railing running around it.

The bail courtroom in Gamdevi Station was far smaller and less awe-inspiring than the lofty rooms of the high court, but Perveen still felt intimidated as she approached the bailiff. According to the Empire's law, female solicitors were allowed to work with clients and draft papers for review by a judge; however, because they weren't admitted to any bar associations, they were forbidden from speaking in court. This wasn't a trial, but a bail hearing; she thought the judge might permit her to speak for Sunanda. She wasn't certain, because in the past, all Mistry Law clients looking for representation at a bail hearing had been represented by barristers hired by her father.

But there was no time to stand about worrying; she needed to review the warrant for Sunanda's arrest. Abortion was a non-cognizable offense, meaning it was considered a relatively minor crime. Arrests in such cases were extremely unusual; in fact, prosecution would be impossible without a signed warrant issued by a magistrate.

Perveen gave a reassuring smile to Sunanda, who was watching anxiously from the back of the holding area. Then, swiftly, she approached the bailiff, who stood before a lectern with a stack of papers.

"May I please see the charging document regarding the case of . . ." Perveen realized she had never learned her client's surname. "The lady prisoner on today's docket? First name is Sunanda."

The bailiff, a middle-aged man, regarded her dubiously. "And who are you to be asking for these papers?"

"Perveen Mistry, solicitor." Perveen handed him her business card.

Holding the card at the edge, the bailiff scanned it, then passed it back. He made no movement toward the stack of papers on his lectern.

"Hurry up!" a man barked from behind her.

The civil servant's shoulders tensed, and he found the papers and handed them to Perveen. Sternly, he said, "You must return these before the proceedings begin."

"Of course." Perveen stepped away and began reading. There was enough legalese to warrant several hours of scrutiny, but she had no such time. The gist of the matter was included in the prosecutor's charging document:

> On Tuesday, June 6, Mr. Arvind Vikas Tomar, a Hindu gentleman, presented a complaint to the Bombay Police Department. Mr. Tomar related in an oral affidavit that on Saturday, May 27, he had overheard Sunanda Chavda talking about taking poison in the form of a tea. Knowing that Sunanda was a young ayah serving in a well-regarded Hindu family in Ghatkopar, he wished not to believe that she would have fallen pregnant out of wedlock. However, he heard details of Miss Chavda's admission of obtaining an oral abortifacient by a notorious dai, Oshadi, who also worked in the same home. Therefore, he reported his suspicion of an abortion plot to the police.
>
> Prosecutor Walter Rippington delivered a petition regarding this matter to Magistrate Patrick Symonds, who issued a signed warrant Wednesday, June 7.

A secondary report, issued by the Kalbadevi Police, reported the arrest of Sunanda Chavda shortly after 9 P.M. in the home of her brother, Govind Chavda, residing in a leased property, Lane 3, Settlement 7, Kalbadevi. During time of arrest, the house was inspected and evidence of a bucket of soiled clothing removed for forensic analysis. Sunanda Chavda admitted to drinking herb tea on Saturday, May 27, corroborating the account of Mr. Tomar.

Perveen read through the papers again, transcribing them as best she could on the legal pad she took from her case. She did this leaning against a back wall, because if she ventured to seat herself on one of the courtroom's benches, she might have difficulty getting out to return the papers to the bailiff before the judge appeared.

Perveen sped through her note writing and hurried back to the bailiff with the paperwork just as a knock came at the court's inner door, behind the magisterial bench.

The bailiff grabbed the papers from her and spoke in a booming voice.

"All rise for the honorable James Peale O'Brien, Magistrate of the Bombay Police Bail Court!"

As the people around her rose, Perveen approached the two rows where the barristers had staked their territory. Unfortunately, the spaces close to the aisle were all taken.

The only blessing was that she'd spotted her friend, the barrister Vivek Sharma. He sat directly next to one of the aisle-guarding lawyers, an elderly man whose eyes were shut and who was breathing as if in slumber. Perveen caught Vivek's eye, and he gave her a curious look. She stepped close to the slumbering lawyer and whispered, "Sir, will you please allow me by?"

"Madam, the public sits behind!" The man's tone was irate.

"I am a lawyer!" she whispered with force, but he didn't shift.

Now a new voice thundered from the front of the room. "This is not a bazaar—no talking or I'll have you sent out of the court!"

Perveen flinched. This was not how she had hoped to be noticed by the judge.

The lawyer who wouldn't budge gestured at her with a shooing motion. Quickly, Vivek Sharma turned his face away, acting as if he didn't see or know Perveen.

Perveen gave up, walking back toward an empty spot in the area for the public. Civilians were seated here—family members and friends with eyes on the prisoners' holding area. Their anxieties slipped around her like a heavy, wet blanket. She could feel her blouse dampening under the sleeves. How much she'd wanted a proper seat amongst the lawyers! For her to approach the bench from this position would be controversial. It was also bad that she hadn't got a white wig or black robe, the required clothing worn by lawyers who intended to approach the bench.

What a predicament! If she'd had ten more minutes before the court was called to order, she could have hired Vivek Sharma to handle the argument for Sunanda's bail. But there had been no time: she'd barely had time to read the warrant.

Magistrate O'Brien called a roll for the advocates scheduled to appear. One by one, the vakeels and barristers rose so he could see them. Next, he called for the prosecutors, who were seated in a section together, and they, too, stood to confirm their presence.

Then the cases began. As the magistrate called the names of the various prisoners, they were individually unchained by a guard and brought forward. Each time, a prosecutor came before the judge and presented the charge and his recommendation for bail, if any.

Then the bailiff announced, "Bombay Presidency versus Sunanda Chavda."

Just her luck—the fourth case on the docket.

Two constables brought Sunanda forward from the holding area. In the dim light of the room, Sunanda's sari looked even dirtier, and her eyes appeared sunken in her face. Her mouth trembled, as if she were trying not to cry.

The magistrate announced that Mr. Shah, a court interpreter, would be available to offer translation to Marathi, Hindustani, or Gujarati.

The magistrate turned toward the prosecutor, a pink-faced young man with trouser legs just a bit too short showing underneath his black robe. Speaking quickly in a Northern English accent, the young man introduced himself as Walter Rippington, an assistant prosecutor.

As Perveen rose from her own seat in the public area and came closer, she noticed that Rippington's shoes were unpolished.

Either he was too young to know better, or he was very tight on funds.

Rippington's accent was strong, but she could understand him. He put forward his argument that Sunanda had been charged with abortion, and while the crime was non-cognizable, the likelihood of her running from the city was high, especially since she was homeless.

Perveen's back went up because she'd read the papers and seen mention of a home. The judge rustled the papers and looked at the prosecutor. Sharply, he said, "The warrant gives an address in Kalbadevi."

"The truth is that this home is a shack; a place that can be knocked over in monsoon, which is just weeks away. A stay inside a concrete jail while she awaits trial is a mercy for her." Rippington spoke boldly, and Perveen yearned to call out an objection on the grounds of his supposition. But she hadn't been recognized yet as Sunanda's lawyer.

"Is that all?" Magistrate O'Brien asked Mr. Rippington.

Rippington squared his shoulders. "I'd like to state for the record that Miss Chavda was informed that abortion is a crime under section 312 of the Indian penal code, punishable by imprisonment. The anticipation of potential jailing makes this unmarried, childless shanty-dwelling woman a flight risk before her trial."

Perveen couldn't wait any longer. She had to remind the judge of the fact that Sunanda wasn't homeless, nor was she unemployed. Taking a deep breath, she said a silent prayer, and then spoke into the silence. "If it pleases Your Honor, I request permission to approach the bench."

The judge's eyes narrowed, as if seeking to see her. "Permission granted. Madam, may I ask you to state your name and concern?"

Perveen squared her shoulders and walked the final steps to the lawyers' table. She laid her Swaine Adeney briefcase on the table between her position and that of Rippington, whose blue eyes were wide with confusion as he regarded her.

"I am Perveen Mistry, a solicitor employed at Mistry Law, number ten Bruce Street. I am counsel for Miss Chavda, a hard-working children's ayah in the household of Lord Dwarkanath Bhatia in Ghatkopar. I wish to explain why my client should not be required to pay bail."

Whispers and some chuckling came from the lawyers seated close behind, and her ears picked up Marathi rumblings from the back of the courtroom: "What is she saying?" and "Is she a lawyer?"

"Order in the court!" the magistrate thundered. "Anyone disrupting proceedings will be removed. Now, Miss Mistry, can you state for me the reasons you consider yourself to be a solicitor?"

From this close position, Perveen saw the magistrate's eyes were bloodshot. He was either tired or unwell. She was also close enough to feel Sunanda's hope.

Everything she was doing was for her client's benefit. Perveen tamped down the defensiveness she'd felt at the judge's patronizing question. "I completed the bachelor of civil law education at Oxford University. Following this, I clerked at Freshfields, which granted me the rank of solicitor. I have my business card with me, should it please Your Honor to review it."

He wrinkled his nose. "And what was your mark, when you sat the law exams?"

An innocent-sounding question, but Perveen knew where it was leading. She felt more wetness under her arms. "I couldn't take the test. Female law students were not permitted to sit the examinations."

He harrumphed lightly. "And have you been granted membership to the London Bar, or perhaps the Bombay Bar?"

"No." After she spoke, she glanced at Sunanda and saw the confusion on her face.

"And the reason?"

"I cannot apply because both bar associations deny membership to female lawyers." Perveen spoke without affect, but her heart was heavy. She had told Sunanda she'd help; and now she was doing just the reverse.

"Ah, there we are." Looking toward the assembled lawyers, the magistrate said, "This solicitor's bold approach goes against the rules of our profession. May the record show I only granted her the privilege of speaking to confirm her identity." Clearing his throat, he continued, "All of us—judges, law practitioners, court employees, and civilians—enter this hallowed room with an understanding that rules were set in Britain that are observed throughout the Empire to ensure uniformity and justice." He looked sternly at Perveen. "As Miss Mistry herself admitted, she holds no degree from Oxford nor a recognition from any bar association. She may serve clients as a solicitor, but she has no authority to be an advocate."

Perveen knew it already: this magistrate would not allow her to speak on Sunanda's behalf, and he'd probably enjoyed shooting her down so he could appear to be teaching law to a misguided female.

"Miss Mistry, you attempted to represent your client in court, which is against the Patent of Law set down by the British High Court, which in turn is accepted by the High Court of British India. So we are faced with a situation where you have without cause interrupted a court proceeding. The punishment for such . . ."

Punishment? Perveen gripped the edge of the table. How humiliating it would be to collapse; but the terrible words had given her a shock, and she felt light-headed.

". . . Consists of penalties ranging from simple banishment from the court to a citation and fine," the magistrate continued. "Miss Mistry, I have taken your inexperience into account. Therefore, I shall grant you the mildest penalty, banishment from this room. It should go without my saying that you should never again attempt to work as an advocate."

As O'Brien lectured Perveen in an officious tone, she saw Sunanda's eyes filling with tears. She couldn't have understood all the words the judge had said, but it was obvious to anyone in the room that Perveen was getting a lashing.

Mr. O'Brien rose to his feet and pointed toward the courtroom door. "With the authority invested in me by the Police Court, I order you to leave this courtroom."

"Yes, Your Honor." Perveen wanted to scream, but she held to the mannerly tone she'd used in her approach. She gave a last look toward Sunanda, wondering if the interpreter would explain all that had transpired. If Sunanda were denied bail, she would surely have reason to believe it was Perveen's fault.

Perveen sank onto a long, unoccupied mahogany bench in the hallway. The sweat that had started under her arms had now soaked the back of her blouse. Had her sari been draped well enough to mask this, or was yet another weakness exposed? She wanted to weep, but the hall was full of lawyers and court officers and police, many of them casting curious glances at her. This made her think of the gossip mill; surely the lawyers watching her ordeal wouldn't keep it to themselves.

She could only imagine what was going on in the courtroom. The judge might ask Rippington a few more things and then pronounce his bail decision. Or he might have made up his mind already.

An hour later, she heard scraping sounds in the courtroom. The lawyers and public spectators streamed out, talking. Several pointed at her, although Vivek Sharma, walking by, stopped.

"That was a good try. It's likely the laws will change. I heard that the American Bar Association accepts women. They are more progressive."

Perveen had been annoyed by Sharma earlier when he'd

looked away, but he was proving himself a bit kinder. "Tell me, what did the magistrate decide for Sunanda?"

"Ten rupees bail," Vivek announced with a small smile. "He didn't say this was because you spilled that she worked for Sir Dwarkanath, but I imagine his ears weren't closed."

"Thank you," Perveen said.

"Vivek, come! Your client is looking for you," another lawyer shouted.

Giving Perveen an apologetic look, Vivek hastened off.

Perveen stayed on the bench in the hall, hoping that she'd be able to speak to Sunanda. At last the prisoners emerged, still chained wrist by wrist, with her client at the end. Sunanda was looking at the back of the man in front of her.

Perveen knew Sunanda couldn't see her, so she stood and walked back toward the end of the prisoners' line. Touching the woman's arm, she whispered, "I'm sorry I wasn't able to speak for you. But you are getting bail. Did the court interpreter explain?"

"Yes. I don't have ten rupees. Oshadi gave me ten rupees from the begum, but it's at Bhatia House." Sunanda sounded forlorn as she carefully proceeded down the stairs at the end of the chained line. "Please tell Uma-bhabhu they'll be holding me in the jail here. The trial will not come until the month of Ashadha, the interpreter told me."

Hearing the misery in her client's voice, Perveen stayed close as they headed downstairs. "You won't stay there," Perveen assured her. "Once the bail order is delivered, I'll pay the cost. You won't have to sit in jail until your trial, and that could be quite a while."

Sunanda's eyes were wide with shock. "But how can you do anything? The judge sent you out."

Perveen felt a rush of humiliation. "I'm sorry that I couldn't speak for you in court. The bail office is different. It's operated by clerks, not judges, and any citizen can go in to begin the process of bail release for another person."

Sunanda shook her head. "But you don't know me."

"We'll have time to talk after your release." Perveen spoke hastily because of an approaching constable wielding a lathi. "I'll hire a very good barrister for your defense."

"Don't tarry!" the constable interjected, giving Perveen a fierce stare and tapping Sunanda lightly with his lathi so she'd move along faster. She cringed and tripped, falling against the man in front of her.

"Dirty woman!" the man jeered, and others, including the constables, joined in with variations of the slur.

Perveen longed to snatch the polished wood baton out from the policeman's hand. But that could send her to the lockup, too. And that would be the worst embarrassment of all.

8

NOWHERE TO STAY

Standing in the bail office, alongside peons and a few barristers, Perveen waited for the order to arrive from Magistrate O'Brien's chambers. It was forty minutes before a clerk arrived, laying a stack of papers on the counter. The bail clerk shuffled through them, then spoke to the typist seated at a desk behind him. "Judge O'Brien's papers are here. Sunanda Chavda's bail paper should be done first."

Perveen ignored the scowling of the men waiting around her. Her frequent visits to the office and courteous manner toward its employees had served her well. Within ten minutes, she'd paid Sunanda's bail and had the necessary papers in hand. Reading through it on her way downstairs, she saw the judge had set a condition that Sunanda refrain from returning to Bhatia House in the pretrial period. Perveen shook her head, thinking how unreasonable it was that her client was being denied the ability to work for her employer.

Perveen presented the receipt showing bail had been paid to the officer at the jail's main desk. Shortly afterward, Sunanda emerged from a doorway, unchained, but accompanied by a guard. Seeming fearful, she stepped forward, and Perveen took her arm.

The two women made their way out of the police station. Arman waved from the car, which was back in front of the station.

"I have a new client," Perveen announced to him, as she helped Sunanda into the car. "Sunanda, this is our family's driver, Arman."

Arman nodded toward Sunanda, who gave him a very quick glance before looking down.

"Actually, let's go around the corner. The first matter is Sunanda's lunch." Perveen wasn't hungry, but she didn't think Sunanda could have had much to eat that day.

"Will they let me in?" Sunanda asked nervously. "I feel so dirty."

In the street behind the police station, a well-known vegetarian hotel seemed a likely spot. Perveen knew they looked like an odd couple, and she wasn't surprised when their waiter shunted them to the most invisible spot possible, the back of the veranda. At least the veranda had fans whirring on the ceiling, and a sink with taps.

Sunanda asked permission to wash her hands at the small washstand on the veranda, and Perveen followed suit. Standing behind Sunanda, she watched brown water stream from the young woman's arms and hands. It took a minute before the water ran clear, and still Sunanda washed her hands, scrubbing and scrubbing. Mindful of the dangers of infection, Perveen handed Sunanda her own clean handkerchief. She let her own hands dry in the air.

After returning to the table, Perveen said, "Please choose what you'd like. I'm paying for both of us."

The restaurant was too simple to have a menu, and after the waiter recited the day's offerings, Perveen asked Sunanda if she would allow her to order a full thali for the two of them to share. Soon, the potato and fenugreek curry was steaming in front of them, along with a thick yellow dal, stewed green beans, puris, tomato chutney, pickled turmeric, yogurt, and carrot halwa.

They ate with their right hands, dipping them between bites into the little bowls of clean, warm water that were provided on the side. Half-full from her lunch at home, Perveen ate small amounts, urging Sunanda to take the rest.

Sunanda ate heartily, and after she'd finished the last bit of puri and dal, she spoke. "Thank you. This was the best food I have ever tasted. I worry it is costing too much."

"This lunch is inexpensive," Perveen assured her. "Don't worry."

Sunanda's voice was tense. "I'm grateful to you for freeing me from the jail. But my bail is high: almost a month's wages. My brother hauls stone for the Bhatia Company. Govind earns no more than I do, and there are also his wife, Amla, and three children. My money is necessary for the household."

"What did your brother say about your being arrested?"

Sunanda's eyes were filled with pain. "He didn't believe them at all—he said the story must be made up. Then he begged the constable to let me stay—he even offered baksheesh, two rupees, if the constable would go back to the office and say that I couldn't be found. But the constable wouldn't take it. Amla started shouting at Govind that he was crazy, that I couldn't live with them anymore. When all of that was happening, there was a man walking around looking at everything in our home, and another officer was writing in a notebook. I wonder what he wrote down."

"Did you notice if they took anything with them?"

"They were demanding we show them everything that looked like a stick. Because a stick is sometimes used"—she lowered her face, ashamed—"for that act. Govind showed them he had a lathi—for protection, not fighting."

"Many men keep a lathi. Was that taken?"

"No. All that they took was my sister-in-law's clothing."

Perveen didn't think she'd heard right. "That's very strange!"

"It was her monthly." Sunanda whispered the word, which was not typically uttered in public. "She had left one sari and the cloth wrappings she wore underneath in a bucket of water near the hut. They asked whose they were, and Amla pointed to me. Probably she feared that they would also arrest her. I denied those clothes were mine, but they took them."

"And did you . . ." Perveen wanted to approach the topic of abortion, but it would be complicated when Sunanda hadn't even been familiar with the word. "Do you remember the last time your courses came down?"

"Yes. In Jyeshta." She mentioned the third month in the Hindu calendar.

Perveen searched her memory. "That begins in the middle of May, doesn't it? Do you remember the day of the week?"

"It was a Saturday."

"Do you mean"—Perveen counted backward—"five days ago?"

A closed look came over her face. "No. The Saturday before."

Perveen set the date in her mind. Saturday, May 27. "Do you think your sister-in-law noticed?"

"We didn't speak about it, but she must have known, because of the extra clothes washing I did."

"The prosecutor's charging document said that Oshadi tried to help you," Perveen said.

Sunanda nodded rapidly. "How did the police know that she made tea for me? Just an herb tea, very good for women, but the constable called it poison."

"Just a moment." Perveen opened her briefcase and took out a calendar and her legal pad. She saw that the fundraising tea was five days after Sunanda had drunk the tea. "Were you still menstruating on the evening you were burned?"

Narrowing her eyes in concentration, Sunanda said, "Yes. It finished in the next day or so. I don't remember exactly, because of the burn pains."

"And how are your burns? Did the petroleum jelly help?"

"After two days, the area began to look and feel bad," Sunanda said, shifting the drape of her dirty sari to obscure the dreadful stain. "Just one jar of the jelly was for sale at the chemist. Of course, it went to Ishan. Uma-bhabhu asked Oshadi to make a poultice for me instead."

Perveen caught her breath, feeling shocked that Uma had been so careless about Sunanda's needs. She asked a few more questions, and then she flipped back to inspect the notes she'd taken in court. Arvind Tomar had reported to the police on Tuesday. The warrant from the magistrate had been signed on Wednesday and that very evening, she'd been arrested. Very quick work, and so much effort, for a non-cognizable offense.

"Do you know a man called Arvind Tomar?"

"I don't know of anyone named that. I don't speak to men, except if they are working in the household for the Bhatias."

"What about men in your neighborhood?"

Sunanda fell silent for a moment. "I have reason to speak with the man who allows me to ride in the cart—along with other women and men—between Kalbadevi and Ghatkopar. But his name is Mohan. I've heard some other men calling each other by name in the cart, but not the name you said."

"Well, did you tell any women about drinking the tea? Amla, Uma-bhabhu, the other ayahs?"

She shook her head. "I only talked with Oshadi, and we were inside her storeroom. She gives everyone at Bhatia House tea that suits their health."

Maybe Oshadi had told someone, not guessing the trouble it would bring—or a visitor to the household had somehow overheard. But Perveen would ask one more question, because it had to be asked, since the charge was abortion. "Do you have a friend or sweetheart?"

"No!" Sunanda's face flushed with embarrassment. "I would like to marry someday. Govind said when both of us have saved enough for dowry, he can find someone for a Gujarati of our caste. But now I've spoiled my name."

"Others have attacked your name," Perveen said. "We will clear it, so you will live the rest of your life in the manner you like. But first, I need to know everything. Did Oshadi explain the type of tea she was giving you?"

"No. But she said this one was just dried flowers and bark from plants in the Bhatia House garden. Many women take it every month for regularity. It causes a small stomachache and that brings down the courses."

The police are such fools, Perveen thought. Why did they wish to investigate the business of abortion and menstruation? If the police truly wanted to protect women, they would arrest the family members who murdered newborn girls—a persistent problem all over British India and the princely states.

Sunanda looked toward the street again. "I missed work today. I must go there as soon as I can."

"I'm sorry, but you cannot work at Bhatia House until after your trial," Perveen said, feeling bitter she couldn't have advocated for Sunanda. "It's part of the instructions for your bail."

"But why? I did nothing to harm anyone there!" Her voice rose, causing patrons at a nearby table to turn and look. "I must work. How will I eat? I cannot stay in my brother's house without contributing my wages!"

Perveen put her hand over Sunanda's. "I'm angry about the bail requirement as well. I'm guessing that the magistrate wishes you to avoid contact with Oshadi, knowing the prosecutor might call her as a witness."

"What is a witness?"

"A person who is called to describe for the judge what they saw and heard." Perveen sighed. "Let me be the one to explain to Uma-bhabhu that you've had some unnecessary trouble with the police. I cannot say most of what you've told me, though, to protect information before the trial."

Sunanda looked at her intently. "May I tell my brother what happened?"

"Yes. Let me help you do that, so he knows what is necessary to know, but nothing more. I could tell him about the ban on your working at Bhatia House. Surely you can find other work for a short time in Kalbadevi." Perveen took out her purse to pay the bill. "We'll go to your house together in my car. You mustn't exert yourself on such a hot day."

The drive was short, but it seemed long because the traffic in Kalbadevi was so thick that Arman had to proceed at a snail's pace to avoid hitting the many pedestrians who wouldn't give way, the cows and goats, and the many men pulling long wooden handcarts filled with bags of rice, stones, and all manner of goods.

"And where do we go?" Arman asked after they'd passed Shri Dwarkadhish Temple, a famous site of Hindu worship dating from the 1870s.

"We live in the lanes behind the Bhatia Stone factory." Sunanda answered Arman only after Perveen looked expectantly at her. She whispered, "Tell him to let me walk from here. It's very close."

"Remember, I must speak to your brother." Perveen also wanted to understand exactly where Sunanda lived because they'd meet several more times before the trial.

As they wound deeper into the business neighborhood, the lanes grew narrower and the crowds of people thicker. The conversations floating through the car's open windows were all in Gujarati, a reflection of the area's status as the first place in Bombay where most Gujarati immigrants landed. And wealthy merchants like Sir Dwarkanath had no reason to leave this place, even after success, because of the steady flow of peasants desperate for their first city job.

Because of the regional separation in many neighborhoods, Bombay was a continent in and of itself. Perveen knew that having professional work had widened her landscape and also felt fortunate to speak Gujarati to Sunanda's brother.

And she had to admit—as upset and worried as she felt about Sunanda—she felt grateful for the chance to oversee this case. It wasn't that she had strong feelings about abortion. What she knew was that abortion was considered immoral in the Hindu and Parsi theologies, whereas the Muslim faith acknowledged it was acceptable to save a mother who might die during childbirth.

Sunanda's crime wasn't going to be heard in the Hindu court, though; it was going before the Police Court, which did not recognize religious traditions when meting out justice. It was a critical matter that Sunanda be acquitted. If Sunanda lost, the case could be used as an example to sway judges to quickly convict other women who might face such charges.

"Sir, please stop here. There is no more space for a car to go," Sunanda said as they turned into a lane barely five feet wide, with people hanging out on either side.

Arman switched off the motor.

Sunanda mumbled, "I don't want you to come inside my home."

"Why?" Perveen asked gently. She couldn't work against her client's wishes.

"I don't know what my brother will think. And I believe Amla—my sister-in-law—won't want me back. Especially now I can't work—"

Perveen patted Sunanda's hand. "My job is to defend you. I will do it in a very polite manner. Don't worry."

Arman opened the door for them to step out, and curious eyes passed over them.

"The police freed you, then?" a woman shouted from a window. "What did you do, beti?"

"Stole a car!" a man from the street called back to her and came closer to inspect the Daimler. Arman drew himself up protectively, and the man edged off.

"Arre, Sunanda!" a girl of about six called out in greeting, and Sunanda cast a swift smile at her. To Perveen, she said, "She's my niece."

Perveen followed Sunanda down a rough dirt path of shanties set closely together. Her family dwelling was slightly better than the prosecutor's definition of shack; it had an oilskin roof and walls made from thin boards nailed together. Stepping through the low door, Perveen entered a main room with little furniture. A worn canvas curtain bisected the space, as if to create a second room. A boy of about four and a younger child peeped out from the curtain. They broke into smiles and ran to Sunanda, who hugged them carefully, as if trying to shield her burned belly and arms from them. The girl who'd been outside came into the shanty, followed by a petite, fair-skinned woman of about eighteen wearing a heavy gold nose ring and a red-and-green cotton sari.

"My sister-in-law," Sunanda whispered to Perveen.

"You are free?" Amla Chavda spoke in rapid Gujarati, making the statement sound like an accusatory question. "How is that? And who is this lady with you?"

"Amla, she got me out of the jail! Mistry-memsahib is my solicitor." Sunanda said the last word in English, and Perveen wondered if Amla could understand. She seemed younger than Sunanda and also a bit coarser.

But before she could explain, Amla turned on her, scowling. "So you are an important lady, nah? Get the police to return my sari."

"That probably can't happen until after the trial," Perveen said, taking an immediate dislike to her. "You see, because of what you told them, they believe it's Sunanda's. Of course, you could go to the police and explain the truth."

Amla sucked in her breath. "So there will be a trial? Hai Ram, this is bad. Sunanda is ruining our good name."

Sunanda looked anxiously from Perveen to Amla. "Where is Govind?"

"My worthless husband is drinking toddy in the next gulli. All because of you!"

Perveen needed to speak to Sunanda's brother, but she did not like the idea of being the one to interrupt a drinking man. "Please, Amla-bai, can you ask your husband to come here? We need to explain Sunanda's situation."

"I'll get him, but he will say the same as me. She must go! Tarun and Nila, come with me." Amla's voice was poisonous as she stormed out of the shack, the older children following her. *How old was Amla when she'd had the first child?* Perveen wondered. Probably no more than thirteen.

Sunanda sat on a mat in the corner and the youngest child, a girl wearing just a nappy and tiny earrings, toddled into her lap. Her cheek had a black dot drawn onto it.

"Someone's worried about the evil eye?" Perveen guessed.

"Amla is worried Tapsee might die young. She had tuberculosis a few months ago," Sunanda said to Perveen.

"Hello, Tapsee," Perveen said, smiling at her. The child smiled back and stretched out a hand toward Perveen's wrist.

"She likes your bangle. She's never seen anything so fine," Sunanda said.

Perveen was slipping off her bangle, which was decorated with twinkling blue and green glass crystals, when Amla reentered, followed by Govind. He had Sunanda's expressive eyes, but they were set in a face that seemed hardened beyond his years. His body was wiry, evidence of his punishing work as a laborer in the stone industry.

"Govind!" Sunanda said warmly, but he turned away from her to look at Perveen.

In a slightly slurred voice, he said, "Please take her. Because of the arrest, everyone thinks she fell pregnant. They will cast us out if she comes back."

"But I never did such a thing—" Sunanda protested.

"You shamed us," Amla interrupted. "After all we did for you."

Perveen sensed there would be no way to argue for Sunanda's staying. It was true that a family could be ostracized because of one member's perceived immoral behavior. And where would Sunanda wind up, if she were made homeless in Kalbadevi? Perveen would have to take her somewhere else. But before they went, she needed to make use of the time. "We cannot go until I get information about something. Sunanda was defamed to the police by a man called Arvind Tomar. Do either of you know that name?"

Govind slumped down into a half-reclined position against the shanty's wall. Perveen repeated her question, and he shook his head. "I don't know the name. Is this—is this my sister's, ah—"

Amla cut in with a vulgar word that meant lover.

"No!" Sunanda wailed, and the two older children ran to her.

"Don't cry, don't cry!" said Nila, and the sweetness with which she spoke made Perveen feel like weeping herself.

Resolving to remain strong, Perveen stepped a bit closer to Amla. "Amla, just answer yes or no, do you know the name Arvind Tomar? He is the person whose name is on the warrant. He has falsely accused Sunanda of committing abortion."

"No." Amla pointed to the door. "Go now."

Perveen wasn't ready. Considering the possibility this man had access to Bhatia House, she asked, "Could Tomar be someone you don't know, who works for Bhatia Stone? Perhaps a manager?"

"No. Everyone there is Gujarati," Govind muttered. "Tomar is not a Gujarati name."

"You are right, Govind-bhai. It's probably a Northern name," Perveen agreed. She didn't know how much Govind would recall of their meeting, because of the drinking, but she hoped to make a better impression on him than she had on Amla. "We will go now. If you wish to be in touch, here is my information." She took out her card, avoiding Amla, and dropped it into Govind's lap. He couldn't read it, she guessed, but he could show it to someone, although she suspected he was unlikely to do anything to help his sister.

It was wrenching to bring Sunanda out of the shanty. She held her sari's pallu over her face, but her shaking shoulders gave away what she was trying to conceal—she was weeping. Perveen had thought Sunanda might be angry with her brother, but she seemed resigned to her fate.

Back in the car, Perveen directed Arman to return the way he'd come. When the car had threaded its way out of the gawking throng, she finally felt free to speak with Sunanda. "The hotel where we ate might have a vacancy for tonight. I'll pay for it."

"I've never stayed in a hotel. Where would I wash?"

Perveen hadn't thought it through until Sunanda asked the question. Hotels had communal bathrooms, and most likely some of the guests were men. The more she thought about it, a low-priced hotel probably wouldn't be safe for a woman alone. "Where else can you stay? Who are your close friends from working at Bhatia House?"

Sunanda looked at Perveen with an incredulous expression. "Everyone except Oshadi lives outside with their families—most in places like my brother's, and a few on the pavement. And I've been charged with a crime."

"Well, then." The obvious had been sitting quietly in Perveen's subconscious all this time. "For the night, at least, you will come to my house. It's a quiet place, and it will be very nice for you to wash up there. Yes, it's just the right place to go."

9

A PLACE CALLED HOME

*D*adar Parsi Colony was built for the prosperous; Perveen didn't know any neighbors without at least one servant. The Mistrys had five to handle the work on both sides of the duplex, and Rustom and Gulnaz had always planned to hire more to care for the children they expected.

Housing for female staff was the reason behind the two-room dwelling in a corner of the Mistrys' garden. The cottage was a simple, square limestone building with a sloped clay-tiled roof that had a wide overhang and gutters, so the rain would flow off without drenching the veranda. At the moment, the Mistrys' chief housemaid, Gita, was staying alone in the place, because Taru, her mother, was back in Bengal visiting family.

Perveen directed Sunanda to wait on a chair in the garden while she went to explain the situation to Gita, who'd been standing at the ironing board, hefting the iron that was heated on a stand over the outdoor hearth. Perhaps because Gita was so small—just four feet nine inches tall, a legacy of her near-starved childhood—she always took special care with her appearance. She was still wearing the sari she'd had on during the luncheon, a cotton voile of a vibrant yellow that was further accented by the strand of marigolds she'd woven through her braided bun. This was a dramatic contrast to Sunanda's bloodstained, dirt-encrusted, bedraggled presence.

"Good afternoon. I didn't know you'd be caring for Khushy's clothing." Perveen had immediately noticed the stack of

nappies on the ironing board, and the dampness on Gita's forehead. The day was so hot that the task must have been especially
miserable.

"Lakshmi should be doing washing and this ironing, but
Gulnaz has kept her busy in the house." Eyeing Sunanda, Gita
whispered, "Who's that dirty woman? Is she from the slums?"

"Her name is Sunanda Chavda. She was living in Kalbadevi,
not a slum." Perveen tried to keep her voice low, yet she needed
to be heard over the raucous crying that had started to spill out
of an upstairs window. Was Khushy raising a protest because
she'd recognized Perveen's voice? "At the moment, Sunanda has
nowhere to sleep. I'd like her to stay with us a few weeks. I hope
you'll treat her kindly, because I can vouch for her character."

There was silence, and the smell of scorched cotton in the air.
Gita hastily raised the iron and muttered, "To sleep in the
garden cottage, you mean?" When Perveen nodded, Gita's voice
sharpened. "Is she replacing my mother, then?"

Quickly, Perveen said, "Not at all! Sunanda's already
employed as an ayah in Ghatkopar. She's had a few hard days,
and I want her to have full rest. She will probably be gone by the
time Taru returns from Bengal."

"Probably?" Gita tossed aside the singed nappy and started
vigorously ironing another, making her distress clear.

Perveen could tell from Gita's behavior that she hadn't made
a good enough case, so she thought of what else she could reveal.
"Like you, Sunanda's native place is not Bombay. She was living
in Kalbadevi with her brother's family. The brother and his wife
have sent her off, even though she has burn injuries and needs to
rest so that she can heal."

"If she's healed enough to walk into the garden, why should
she rest? She's taking advantage!"

"When I introduce you, you will be close enough to see burns
on her arms, and markings of dried blood on her sari." Noticing
Gita wince, she went on. "That's because of a stomach burn. If

you really want to know more, I'll tell you the rest. But put the iron aside."

After Gita had rested the iron on its stand, Perveen stepped closer to her and spoke in a whisper. "Do you remember that I attended the fundraising tea party at Bhatia House last week? Sunanda was working there and threw herself atop a little boy who caught fire. She saved his life. She wasn't given the proper medical treatment afterward and now her burns have gotten worse. I feel that I must help her. Just as you and I have helped each other."

Gita's stern expression had softened. Not only was the story dramatic, but Perveen's last words were a reminder of how the two of them had met in Calcutta, where Gita had labored under miserable conditions for Perveen's in-laws, the Sodawalla family. Perveen had paid for Gita and her mother to come across the country to work for double the salary, with reasonable hours, in her family home. Sighing, Gita said, "I hope she can draw the bath herself. I have my hands full here."

"Thank you, Gita." Feeling relieved, Perveen went back to Sunanda and communicated that she would be welcome to wash up and then rest in the garden house—and that Gita might be shy at first, but she would be her companion. She then oversaw introductions of the two women and brought Sunanda into the garden house and showed her the bathroom. Having worked in a wealthy home, Sunanda was familiar with the use of piped water and the in-ground commode.

"I will make everything clean here after I'm done," Sunanda promised Perveen. "And I thank you."

What a day! Perveen thought as she said goodbye to Sunanda, reminding her not to say anything about the police charges to Gita—because the more people she told, the greater the chance they might be tapped by the prosecution and be pulled into court. When Sunanda nodded, Perveen hoped her advice would stick. She knew that the shock of an arrest could be so overwhelming a client might not remember many things from the same day.

Entering the house through the rear veranda, Perveen inhaled the sweet cardamom aroma of the dessert she'd missed. She headed upstairs to her room. Through the wall that split the duplex, she heard short bursts of crying. Perveen also heard a muffled off-tune crooning that surely came from Lakshmi, because Gulnaz's singing voice was high and sweet.

Unable to concentrate, Perveen fled downstairs and entered Jamshedji's empty study. Sitting at his desk, she retrieved a piece of stationery and thought about what she'd say to Uma Bhatia. She struggled for the right words, and in the end, simply wrote a note explaining that Sunanda was staying at her home due to unforeseen events, and she begged permission to visit on Friday to explain the circumstances.

Next, she examined Dr. Miriam Penkar's card, which listed her clinic address on Samuel Street in the Mandvi district. The card also had a telephone number, but when she rang there was no answer. Perveen took a second piece of paper and wrote a note informing the doctor that Sunanda's burns were not healing well, and that she'd taken her in to convalesce. Perveen ended by asking for the soonest available office appointment for Sunanda and provided both the Mistry House and home telephone numbers.

The last letter she wrote was to Vivek Sharma, inviting him to meet with her to discuss a possible barrister role for her new client. He didn't need a phone number or address; he'd been to Mistry House many times.

Once her three letters were in addressed envelopes sealed with a dab of red wax and the Mistry Law stamp, she went outside to see Arman, who was using a bucket of water from the pump in the garden to clean the Daimler. From the dampness of his face, arms, and neck, it was evident the chauffeur had taken advantage of a chance to cool himself.

"I'll take your letters now," he said. "First to Ghatkopar, and then to Mr. Sharma's office and lastly the doctor in Samuel Street."

As Arman dropped the rag he'd been using to wash the car into the bucket, Perveen thought about the hours he'd spent waiting for her earlier in the day. "I hope it's not too much to do after this long hot day."

"Best driving is after the sun's down," Arman said with a shrug. "And I may as well use the time before your father needs his pickup."

"Where did he go?"

"After the luncheon, he took the train to Thane. He had a client meeting and expects to return around nine-thirty."

"Get some dinner for yourself before then," Perveen advised, fishing in her purse for a coin. "Did you hear anyone else needs the car?"

Arman pocketed the coin with a smile. "Ten minutes ago I dropped your brother at the Parsi Gymkhana. He said his friends will give him a lift home. Your mother is attending a kitty party just around the corner. It's so close she said she'll walk home."

Kitty parties were an enjoyable way that women pooled money to help each other. Camellia probably felt she couldn't miss it. But this meant Gulnaz was alone on her first day home with only Lakshmi to help her with Khushy.

Perveen wondered if she should check on Gulnaz. She couldn't hear the crying anymore, though; probably all three of them were sleeping. Feeling satisfied, Perveen walked quickly to the garden cottage.

Sunanda was sitting on the floor, her back against the wall. Her eyes were closed but flew open when Perveen came in.

"Good, you've washed," Perveen said, noting Sunanda's wet hair and the fresh sari she wore—one of Gita's old ones, worn but clean.

"May I ask you something?" Sunanda looked shyly at her. "I

don't know how to pay for this. This room. The food. Your service for me at the court."

"Don't worry. I am taking care of you because I saw how you cared for Ishan," Perveen soothed. Inwardly, she hoped her father would agree to make this a pro bono case.

"I should do something, nah? I heard crying. Gita told me your sister-in-law's got a baby." Sunanda spoke rapidly. "The name is Khushy. She should be happy, but she's not!"

"Your Gujarati is too good," Perveen said with a smile.

"Of course. It's my mother tongue. And there are so many ways I could calm Khushy—I could teach your sister-in-law. What's her name?" Sunanda asked eagerly.

"It's Gulnaz. But she already has an ayah helping her."

Sunanda shook her head. "Many mothers use more than one ayah. May I please be allowed to help? Could you tell her about me?"

"No. You must rest and be quiet." Perveen didn't want to say that she feared Gulnaz would fly into a panic if she ever came to learn Sunanda's state as a criminal defendant charged with abortion.

"Baby work *is* quiet work. Easier than when they are walking," Sunanda offered.

"But . . . I don't know what Gulnaz would think if she heard about your legal situation. It might make it even worse."

As she spoke, she saw the sparkle in Sunanda's eyes fade. "I understand. I am not worthy to hold your sister-in-law's baby."

"Please don't think that!" Perveen said, horrified. "I respect you very much for your bravery and sacrifice. I saw you save Ishan."

As if in memory, Sunanda touched her belly. "The bandage only came off a little bit in the bath. It just hurt too much."

"Let me help with changing it," Perveen offered. "I am not an expert, but I think it would be wise to use boiled water, don't you?"

Gesturing toward the urn in the corner, Sunanda said, "Gita said that water is boiled."

"Good. You must not lift the urn until you've healed," Perveen said, ladling out water into a clean bowl she saw on the room's small wooden table. Reluctantly, Sunanda undraped the front of her sari and loosened the waist string of her petticoat. She dipped a cloth in the bowl of water Perveen had brought and touched it for just an instant to her stomach.

Sunanda squirmed away. "No! I can't bear it."

"We must try." Perveen tried to sound more confident than she felt. The bandage remnants were so grimy, and the burn was a black-and-red oozing mass.

There was a clattering at the door, and Sunanda quickly drew the sari to cover her exposed middle.

Gita stood at the door, hands on her hips. "Perveen-bai, why are you here?"

"I'm helping Sunanda clean her burn."

"It's not proper work for you," Gita said, frowning. "She said she can do it herself."

"Perhaps, but why shouldn't we help each other?" Perveen glanced challengingly at Gita, who she suspected was thinking about Hindu caste law, even though Parsis didn't have a caste system.

"Just leave me," Sunanda moaned, her face flushed with either embarrassment or agony.

"Perhaps she needs a small cup of toddy," Gita said in a low voice. "It is supposed to help with pain."

"What do you think, Sunanda?"

Sunanda exhaled heavily. "If you think it's best."

"I'll get something from inside," Perveen said, rising from her position next to Sunanda.

The parlor was empty as Perveen proceeded toward the tall rosewood cabinet from Hong Kong, fashioned in the Chippendale style. Everything appeared to be in its usual place, although she was hardly an expert. Rustom and Jamshedji were the household's primary drinkers, taking from an assortment of gins, whiskeys, brandies, rums, and some unknown substances in crystal decanters.

She wasn't sure if Rustom and Jamshedji would have something as rough as palm liquor among the expensive spirits, but she eventually came across a small brown bottle with a Marathi label reading FINE TODDY.

The cork was difficult to pull out, and she wound up breaking it. Now she felt hesitant to give it to Sunanda, because she'd begun to wonder if the water used to make it was safe.

A sound at the door made her turn. It was Camellia, staring at her. "Perveen?"

She felt a rush of heat come to her face. "It's not for me."

"I heard from Gita there's a young woman staying in the cottage. Is she demanding alcohol?" Camellia's tone showed disapproval.

Perveen thought quickly about what she could say. In the end, she said she was housing the Bhatia family's former ayah, Sunanda, who'd suffered a burn saving one of her charges. Her family quarters in Kalbadevi were too squalid, and the burn had become infected.

At the end of the recital, Camellia asked, "And so, for treating pain, you are giving her *toddy*?"

"It's what Gita suggested."

Camellia took the toddy bottle from Perveen's hand and put it in the room's small wastebasket. "Let's not give her a new illness! I think you should give her something that has been purified, like the imported brandy."

"Very well." Perveen took a small crystal glass and filled it two-thirds with Raynal et Cie eaux-de-vie. A French luxury, courtesy of Gulnaz's parents.

"I'll come with you. But first, let's get bandages from the cupboard."

Perveen followed her mother to the storeroom, feeling grateful that Camellia hadn't asked more. "This is very kind of you to help. I should have told you about her the moment I arrived."

"Never mind. Better that I do the bandage change. I sometimes assisted nurses at Parsi General Hospital with veterans during the war years. When you were in England," Camellia added.

"That's right, you and Gulnaz used to go together as volunteers."

As Camellia picked up three rolls of bandages and some scissors, she asked, "Perveen, are you angry with Gulnaz?"

Perveen took a deep breath. "I can't believe you're asking that! I love Gulnaz like a sister."

"I know that you love her, but she was saying that you are angry that the baby is home."

"No. I'm only tired," Perveen said with vehemence.

"Remember; your fatigue is different from a new mother's fatigue. Be gentle with Gulnaz."

How could her mother rub in the fact Perveen would never know what it was like to have a baby? Perveen stewed in silence as they walked out of the house and across the lawn to the cottage.

"Here we are!" Camellia said, stepping into the hut. "Sunanda, I am Mrs. Mistry, Perveen's mother. I came to help with the bandaging. But Perveen has something for you to drink first."

Gita got up from the stool where she'd been sitting next to the charpoy. Perveen took the stool and offered the little glass to Sunanda. Eyeing the fine crystal, Sunanda didn't reach for it.

Perveen instinctively knew she was afraid of contaminating the vessel of a higher-class person. "Gita, can you give me an ordinary tumbler?"

Gita went to the rack standing on a table and returned with a copper cup. Perveen poured the brandy inside it and offered it to Sunanda. Sunanda brought the cup to her mouth, then suddenly took it away.

"What is it?" Sunanda whispered.

"It's brandy. Very similar to toddy, but smooth. Better for digestion." Camellia spoke to Sunanda the way she used to when Perveen was home sick from school.

Sunanda scrunched her eyes closed and shook her head.

How childish. Feeling impatient, Perveen brought the tumbler toward Sunanda's mouth.

"No!" Sunanda shouted, turning her head.

Brandy splashed from Sunanda's face onto the exposed skin above her blouse, and she threw her hands over her breasts, frantically rubbing off the brandy.

"You shouldn't have forced it!" Camellia reprimanded Perveen. "Give me a glass of boiled water, Gita."

Sunanda was wailing as hard as a child who'd been slapped. Perveen stepped back, recalling how Khushy had cried whenever she was near. Shame engulfed her again as she realized that she was just as clumsy with an adult woman as a baby. Was it because of the years she'd spent developing her head, rather than her heart and hands?

Perveen went out to the cottage's veranda, gulping in fresh air, trying to exorcise her humiliation. She could overhear Camellia soothing Sunanda, and Sunanda eventually saying that she was feeling better.

If Perveen went back inside the cottage to say goodnight, she imagined her mother might scold her for running off at the sight of tears; for being a sorry example of womanhood.

It would be better for her to go into the study and make sense of the things that had happened that day.

Because when Jamshedji arrived, she had plenty to explain.

10

A LEGAL DISCUSSION

"Hello, hello! Where is everyone?" her father's voice called out some hours later.

"Welcome back," Perveen said, emerging from the study to greet him. "Did you get supper on the train?"

"No, and I'm famished." Jamshedji placed his fetah on the rack and gave her a weary smile. "But first tell me, how is our dear little Khushy?"

"Crying on and off." Perveen spoke offhandedly, determined not to say how annoyed she'd felt about the wailing that had driven her from the comfort of her bedroom.

"Babies must cry," Jamshedji said sagely. "It's a sign of vitality. Only after causing all kinds of noise will they settle down to rest."

"Oh! So you are also the Juris Doctor of children," she joked as her father dropped into the comfortable chair she'd recently vacated. "Shall I ask John to bring your supper to the dining room? Or maybe you'd prefer to sit with Gulnaz and Khushy on the other side?"

"No. I shall take dinner on a tray here so that you can keep taking notes."

Perveen went into the kitchen to tell John, whose apprentice, Nain, was drying a steel cooking pot to a bright shine. John moved toward the stove, which held an array of covered pots. "A full meal for both of you? You missed supper with your mother and Gulnaz-bai."

"I'm not very hungry, but I could do with a spoonful of lagan nu—if anything's left over."

The cook smiled approvingly. "Favorite of you both! I've kept some."

Perveen carried the tray with her father's full supper and her dessert to the study, and as she put it down on a side table, she saw the damp fingerprints that had bloomed on the tray's handles. The humidity, and her nerves.

Jamshedji would likely be horrified that she'd been censured in the bail court, but it would be even worse for him if this news came from someone else. Tonight, she could play up the fact that she hadn't received a formal punishment or fine. And she wouldn't let him dwell on it. The important thing was to obtain her father's permission for Sunanda to stay on the premises, and to obtain his support for the forthcoming case.

Nain carried in the teapot and silverware and finished setting the places for the two of them on a coffee table. Jamshedji looked with pleasure at the savory chicken with potatoes, saffron pulao, and masoor dal with fenugreek. Even the rice flour rotli was freshly made. In between bites, Jamshedji told Perveen about the meeting with a new client in Thane. As Perveen was pouring his cup of tea, the conversation turned.

"You went to Gamdevi this afternoon, but you weren't back with the car before I had to go out," Jamshedji said, taking the cup she handed him. "Fortunately, the Bankers could take me to the train."

"I'm sorry about that. I only returned about six o'clock."

"Was there a delay in the bail office?" Jamshedji rolled his eyes upward. "Those people!"

She paused, gathering strength. *Now is the time.* "I've no complaint about the bail office. What happened is I met a new client and attended her bail hearing this afternoon. Because she had no money with her, I advanced her the necessary bail. Of course, I will settle everything properly by the books."

"What?" Jamshedji put down his cup. "This new client's family didn't pay her bail? What does your contract with her say?"

Swallowing her tea down the wrong channel, Perveen had a brief coughing fit. Her father's eyes widened with alarm, and she waved a hand to reassure him she wasn't dying. When she'd recovered, she wheezed, "I haven't drawn up a contract yet because I met her while she was in police custody. She's suffering from burn injuries that I believe would make incarceration until trial dangerous to her health."

Jamshedji looked keenly at her. "Tell me more."

"Her name is Sunanda Chavda. She emigrated here from a village near Bharuch a few years ago. She's just twenty years old and works as an ayah to Parvesh and Uma Bhatia. Parvesh is the son of Sir Dwarkanath Bhatia, who owns a stone company."

Jamshedji's expression relaxed. "Oh, you should have said that right away. Might the Bhatias pay Sunanda's legal fees?"

Taking a deep breath, Perveen said, "I think they *should*. She saved the life of Sir Dwarkanath's grandson. Remember, I told you and Mamma the other day. She was burned because of her heroism—"

"I recall the story," Jamshedji interrupted. "Just tell me the charge against Sunanda."

"Abortion." As her father's eyebrows went up, Perveen hurried on. "A man named Arvind Vikas Tomar filed a complaint that he overheard Sunanda tell someone that she had committed abortion. Based on this alleged overheard confession, the Kalbadevi police obtained a warrant for her arrest."

When Jamshedji spoke, his voice was calmer than she'd expected. "Is the accusation that Sunanda performed an abortion on someone?"

She shook her head. "The charge is levied against her for actions she supposedly took to end her own suspected pregnancy. When I spoke privately with her, she said she drank a tea made from plants in the Bhatias' garden. The tea was prepared and served by Oshadi, the head woman of the Bhatias' staff. Sunanda believed the tea would regulate her menses. She also told me she has no sweetheart—she was offended at the very question."

"And the prosecutor claims the tea is the abortifacient?" Jamshedji inquired as he dug a spoon into the lagan nu.

"That's the word I read." Perveen had guessed its meaning. "He said the tea was dispensed by a notorious dai named Oshadi. But Uma Bhatia introduced Oshadi as the family's chief housekeeper. That is quite different from a midwife."

"Did the petition also contain a confirming statement from Oshadi about this business?" Jamshedji asked after another bite of lagan nu.

Perveen picked up the legal pad where she'd made notes. "Nothing was mentioned about that."

"Under section 328 of the Indian Penal Code, Oshadi could also be implicated. You do know why?"

"Oh, dear. Let me think . . ." Perveen tried to recall the wording of the section. "A person is liable for up to ten years in prison if they cause another person to take poison or any stupefying, intoxicating, or unwholesome drug with the intention of causing hurt or a crime."

"Well-remembered. Abortion may be a non-cognizable offense, but it's still a crime punishable up to three years. That's why it's crucial for us to prove Sunanda sipped a tea meant to unblock the menses, which does not fall under the law. And we must hope that the prosecutor can't find a man who claims to be Sunanda's partner, because that would point more to abortion than to regulating the cycle." After wiping his mouth with his napkin, he added, "Did the petition set out the date that Sunanda drank the tea?"

"No. But Sunanda told me it was May twenty-seventh— twelve days ago." Perveen circled the number with her pen.

"Just as it is odd for me to be speaking of feminine matters with my daughter," Jamshedji said, smiling briefly at her before turning to the dinner tray. "Who is this second serving of lagan nu intended for: You or me?"

"For me!" Perveen placed the bowl in front of her and stared at the pudding's golden crust. "As I said, Sunanda's an immigrant. She was living with her brother and sister-in-law, but they've cast her out. I don't think her sister-in-law would be willing to testify." Perveen went on to retell the story of Amla's lie about the sari in the bucket.

"Have the police also charged the lady who made the tea—Oshadi?" Jamshedji had pushed away his plate and was writing notes. The fact of this—her father taking the case seriously—lifted Perveen's spirits, and she took a first bite of lagan nu. Its comforting sweetness filled her mouth, and after swallowing, she answered.

"Sunanda hasn't been to Bhatia House since her arrest, so she doesn't know." Putting down her spoon, she added, "Isn't it true that prosecution for abortion is more commonly wielded against dais than pregnant women?"

"Correct," Jamshedji said, scribbling away. "In fact, arrests are also made of family members who administered toxins or used physical means to cause miscarriage. Prosecutors are most often driven to investigate for abortion if the woman has died."

Perveen finished the dessert quickly and laid down her spoon. "I plan to do research on past outcomes of cases brought to court. But based on what I've said about Sunanda, do you think we have a good chance?"

Jamshedji ran a hand through his wiry salt-and-pepper hair. "In my opinion, it boils down to convincing the judge that Sunanda was only taking a health remedy. And what does our barrister think?"

Summoning up every bit of courage, Perveen said, "I didn't have enough time at the bail court to enlist a barrister. I tried to speak up for her, but the magistrate declined to recognize me."

"You . . . approached the bench?" Jamshedji spoke slowly, as if he could not fathom her words.

"I thought I might be allowed to speak because it wasn't the actual criminal trial!" Perveen said in a rush. "I made clear to him I was her solicitor. I showed my card."

"But you were still in a court of law—a bail court—and you yourself broke a law speaking to the magistrate. You know full well that you aren't a member of the Bombay Bar." Jamshedji's voice was anguished. "You say that he threw you out?"

She had used a different word for what had happened, but he'd got it right. "There was no fine, at least. And Sunanda got bail. I believe it occurred because he'd heard me mention Sir Dwarkanath's name."

Jamshedji stared into the circle of light cast by the green-shaded lamp on the desk. "What's done is done. Let's hope you don't become the Bombay legal community's favorite joke. And in the meantime, it is your responsibility to sign on a barrister who can speak before a judge. You also need to find someone who'll pay for Sunanda's barrister."

Perveen gulped. "Perhaps a barrister would agree to work pro bono?"

"You are ginning cotton on the stool!" Jamshedji huffed.

"I'm not talking rubbish at all," she protested. "What do you think about Vivek Sharma? He happened to be present at the hearing. He's done well for us before."

Jamshedji shrugged. "He's a solo practitioner, so I imagine he counts every rupee. But yes, he might."

"I also hope for a formal written statement about Sunanda's fine character from her employers." Perveen thought again. "Or should I depose Uma or Parvesh Bhatia as a character witness for the trial?"

"Actually, I think your chief request of the Bhatias should be asking them to pay for Sunanda's defense. However, they may not be willing. If Uma's husband or father-in-law were involved with Sunanda, things become difficult."

Perveen was horrified by his thinking. "I think Sunanda would have told me if one of them was her lover."

"Or her assailant?" Her father raised his thick eyebrows. "Don't be so sure she'd speak up. She's a servant. They rarely make complaints for fear of being sacked, or worse."

"We can't assume this is the case," Perveen said firmly. "And if I go to Bhatia House, I'll also be able to speak with Oshadi. She might know something very crucial about the tea or who else drinks it."

"So be it." Jamshedji rose from his chair, as if declaring the conversation over. "Where is our client staying, if not with the Bhatia family or her brother?"

Perveen took a deep breath. "I did the only thing I could think of: I brought her to stay in the garden cottage with Gita."

"Oh Khodai!" Jamshedji exclaimed. "What in God's name?"

"You've never said we couldn't bring home someone in need," Perveen countered.

"What I haven't disallowed doesn't mean it's allowed!"

"I understand, Pappa." Perveen knew her father's bark was worse than his bite. She'd play on his natural compassion. "But there was nowhere else she could go. How could I let her fend for herself on the streets?"

"When will you explain her presence to the rest of the family? You have a defendant staying just beyond Gulnaz's hibiscus hedge!"

It struck Perveen as odd that her father hadn't any trouble with her taking on Sunanda's controversial charge but was exploding now at the prospect of her staying in the garden.

"Are you ashamed that we have someone on our grounds who's been arrested? That isn't like you, Pappa." She affected a lightness to her voice.

"It's a matter of professionalism! Lawyers simply do not bring their clients to live with them. It brings up the whole issue of too many people in the household knowing the client's particulars." Jamshedji rose from his chair and paced the small room. "What if Mamma and Gulnaz are called to testify about Sunanda's behavior? Things are complicated enough with a new baby in the house."

"Mamma knows already and is helping with her care," Perveen said, jumping up to stride alongside him. "All I said was that Sunanda used to work for the Bhatias and needs a clean place to stay while she recovers from the burns. Mamma knows how to change a bandage—in fact, she sent me off to take care of things properly. Gulnaz doesn't need to know; I already told Sunanda not to try to help with Khushy."

As if he hadn't heard any of it, Jamshedji continued with his arguments. "The other trouble with a lawyer who decides to house a client out on bail is the outcome if the accused disappears before the trial."

"If Sunanda were homeless, a disappearance would be more likely. That's the argument the prosecutor was using to try to keep her in jail," Perveen pointed out.

Jamshedji's steps slowed, and he halted, looking past Perveen through the open window and the darkness of the night. "I suppose that if she didn't stay here, her health would worsen."

"Yes. Infections can become toxic very quickly," Perveen added, feeling relieved that her father had calmed enough to understand her logic.

"A wound is obvious," Jamshedji said soberly. "If only recognizing the truth was as clear."

"What do you mean by that?" Perveen demanded.

But this time, her father didn't answer her.

11

A RUDE AWAKENING

"*Wah! Ahhh! Ah ah!*"

A forty-six-day-old human couldn't speak—or so Perveen had thought. Yet Khushy already had a veritable glossary of different sounds. Perveen's sleep had been shredded all night long by the infant. Adding to the injustice was knowing that the coming day promised to be full of hard work and uncertainty.

It was six-thirty, because the cries now were punctuated by avian squawking. Her parrot, Lillian, who resided in a large brass cage on Perveen's bedroom veranda, kept regular hours. She knew when it was time to rise.

A thump came on the wall, followed by Rustom's voice. "For God's sake, shut up the damn bird!"

And what about your child? Perveen suppressed the retort that would be too unseemly for an aunt. Instead, she dragged herself out of bed and unlatched the French doors to the veranda. The air was beautifully cool at this hour. But her pet bird was mischievous and flew into the bedroom to perch on Perveen's headboard. As Khushy cried on the other side, Lillian squawked again.

"Come, come!" Perveen shooed the bird, who hopped away, but then fluttered after her into her black-and-white tiled bathroom. Watching Perveen take her morning bath wasn't a normal behavior for Lillian, but now that Khushy was part of the household, nothing would ever be the same again.

After her bath, Perveen noticed the baby was no longer

crying, but it was too late to do anything but go on with the day. She dressed rapidly, wondering if Gulnaz had gone back to sleep. As she was twisting her damp hair into a bun, Gita came into the room.

"Sorry to be late with your tea. I had to help them on the other side. They are going to the temple." Gita put down the tray with tea and biscuits and carried a saucer with vegetable scraps onto the balcony. Catching sight of her breakfast, Lillian rushed back to her cage.

"It doesn't matter. I'm late, too. How was last night for Sunanda?" Perveen asked when Gita returned to strip the wrinkled sheets off her bed.

"She was crying in her sleep. I had to wake her, and then she was all right."

Perveen was surprised to hear the sympathy in Gita's words and tone. "That was good of you. Her burn might be agonizing. She may also have other worries."

Gita moved swiftly around the room, making a bundle with the sheet around Perveen's discarded nightdress and towels. "Sunanda asked me what else she could do today, and I said she could finish the ironing. In my home village, babies this age only wear a nappy in hot weather. Probably all the tiny fancy clothes and blankets are what upset Khushy!"

"You might be right," Perveen said. "I hope the iron isn't too heavy for Sunanda. She should be resting, remember?"

"She feels useless if she's not working. I would be the same!" Gita dusted Perveen's bureau in vigorous sweeps. "I'll set her to washing the basket I collected from Gulnaz's room. It's the least she could do. Lakshmi is coming soon."

After Gita had remade the bed, Perveen sent her off, determined to take care of her own hair, which only needed to be brushed before disappearing under the shelter of her sari's pallu. Since the previous winter, her hair had been shoulder-length, a bobbed style she'd adopted not because of the modern fashion, but only after her long hair had proved dangerous in her work.

Perveen went downstairs and out to the garden veranda, where her mother was setting the table. Unseen by her mother, Perveen took a moment to admire her. Camellia was a beautiful woman of forty-nine with thick straight hair that was just beginning to silver at the temples. Camellia's hair was pulled up in a proper bun, but she wore a casual cotton-silk sari today. This, and the fact that she was setting the table herself, seemed more evidence that the house had been turned upside down. Camellia's expression as she fussed with the tablecloth seemed troubled.

"You're here quite early, Mamma," Perveen greeted her.

"Yes. Your pappa left early for the office by train. He left the car for you—he thought you'd need it. I've already been out to see Sunanda. I don't like the look of that burn."

"I plan to take her to Dr. Penkar's office today for treatment." Camellia frowned. "Isn't Dr. Penkar an obstetrician?"

"An obstetrician-gynecologist," clarified Perveen. "Dr. Penkar has a full medical-school training from Oxford, so she will certainly know the proper course of treatment. And she knows Sunanda."

"The doctor might treat her gratis." Camellia sounded thoughtful. "But if not, I can petition for the medical cost to be covered by my women's association. We do this sort of thing all the time, as long as you can prove she's needy. What are her home living conditions like?"

Perveen put down the fork she'd been examining and imagined that selling it on a backstreet could have paid Sunanda's expenses for a month. "She lives in a shanty in Kalbadevi with her brother and his wife and their young children. But right now, they can't keep her, and I suppose it's just as well because the hygiene is not suitable for someone recovering from infection."

"Things can be so hard in that neighborhood," Camellia said in a somber tone.

"You're absolutely right." Perveen was relieved that her mother didn't sound as if she wanted to throw Sunanda out.

Camellia pushed back a damp strand of hair that had escaped her bun. "Do you mind finishing the table? And let's not tell Gulnaz about Sunanda. She's highly anxious and doesn't need another sad story crowding her mind."

"Very well, Mamma." Perveen thought Camellia's wish lined up very well with her own and that of Jamshedji. "I'll go around to the cottage right now to explain to Sunanda."

Camellia cast a glance toward the kitchen. "John's baking dal ni pori. If it's ready, why don't you take her some?"

The baked cake, wheat studded with dal, nuts, and raisins, sat resting on the kitchen table. John cut two pieces for her and she put them on a metal plate.

When she walked through the garden, the scents of just-opened flowers were overtaken by the pleasant smell of laundry starch, made from rice-cooking water. Sunanda was ironing on a board set out near a small brazier burning with a few pieces of wood. Upon seeing Perveen, she finished her ironing stroke and used two hands to slowly place the iron atop the brazier.

"Good morning," Perveen said brightly. "It's very kind of you to help with the ironing."

"I want to help. Not just with this—but the baby. She cried so much last night."

"Yes." Perveen saw the eagerness in Sunanda's face, so she spoke carefully. "But truly, it's not your work. You aren't an ayah here, but our guest."

"Your father came out a while ago and introduced himself to me. He also said I shouldn't come near the baby. I don't understand," Sunanda said, her eyes downcast as she moved the heavy iron across cotton. "Is it because he thinks I'm too low or too dirty?"

"No, not at all!" Perveen said hastily. "It's just that the baby's mother—my sister-in-law, Gulnaz—would ask so many questions about you. I don't want trouble to arise. Look, I've brought you something nice."

"I ate already. There is no need." Still, Sunanda's eyes lingered on the squares of cake.

"I'll put it inside, then. And don't let it go too long, or the ants will come." Perveen stepped into the cottage, looking around more closely than she had the previous evening. The space was dark, with the only air and light coming from high windows close to the ceiling of the low structure.

As her eyes adjusted, Perveen saw a few pieces of plain wooden furniture. One charpoy stood against the wall with a sheet folded on it, and the other rope bed, slightly wider and longer, was bare. Unlike the Mistry house, this cottage was not electrified, although it did have piped water in bath and sink. There was also an enclosed open-air privy, a ceramic platform with a hole in the earth that was cleared with buckets of water. This style of arrangement was common for most Indians. But now, Perveen thought about her family's home, with its grand square rooms, wide windows, and ensuite bathrooms. Did Gita ever think, *why do the Mistrys live this way, instead of me?* And did Sunanda harbor such thoughts about the Bhatias?

Soberly, Perveen left the cottage and went over to speak again with Sunanda. "I've left dal ni pori on the table. Tell me, where did you sleep yesterday evening?"

"I slept inside. Gita was outside. Why?" As Sunanda spoke, she ironed steadily.

"I mean, did you lie on a charpoy?"

"No. I always sleep on the floor." Sunanda looked at Perveen as if she was speaking another language. "Gita kindly gave me a mat and a sheet. I was fine."

Although you cried at night, Perveen thought. Aloud, she said,

"Because of your burns, we must ask Dr. Penkar whether it's all right to lie on the floor—and if you can handle heavy objects."

Sunanda looked warily at her. "I will try to remember that. Is my stomach all that I must show her?"

Perveen realized Sunanda might never have had a medical examination. "I'm sure that she will only examine what is necessary for your welfare."

Sunanda nodded at her and resumed ironing. Feeling awkward, Perveen said goodbye and went around the side of the house intending to gather some flowers to make a bouquet for the interior of the garden cottage. Because she wasn't carrying scissors, she had to use her hands to snap off the dahlias and marigolds. Although the flowers bloomed brightly, the stems were dry. She found it a marvel that flowers could survive, holding their beauty, in conditions that made her wilt.

She caught sight of the family Daimler pulling up in front of the house and walked closer to see Rustom and Gulnaz were emerging from the car. Khushy was bundled in Gulnaz's arms, and Perveen remembered her mother saying they'd gone to the fire temple. Lakshmi, whose sari was damp in front from doing laundry, ran out of the duplex to take the baby from Gulnaz.

"Khushy's not crying anymore." Perveen tried to share a smile with Gulnaz, but her sister-in-law looked away.

"Have you brought that posy for Khushy?" Rustom smiled at Perveen and then turned back to look at the baby in Lakshmi's arms. "What a good baby she's been. She fell asleep before we went to the temple for her appointment to be blessed. Thank goodness for that!"

The flowers hadn't been intended for Khushy, but Perveen could hardly say that. She put the flowers in Rustom's hand and was glad for the interruption of a horse-drawn taxi, which appeared on the street and stopped near the house.

A tall young woman stepped down from the platform,

refusing the driver's assistance. When she reached back into the carriage to lift out a heavy doctor's bag, Perveen recognized her as Dr. Miriam Penkar.

"Dr. Penkar?" Gulnaz looked anxiously at Rustom. "Did you call her without telling me?"

"No! I've no idea who this doctor lady is," Rustom hissed as the doctor caught sight of their group and nodded in greeting.

"Good morning, all!" called out Miriam Penkar, stepping briskly toward them, the medical bag swinging heavily in her left hand.

"You must have received my request. How kind of you to come and visit me." Perveen spoke quickly because she didn't want the doctor to inadvertently mention Sunanda.

Dr. Penkar turned toward Rustom and Gulnaz. "I presume you are Mr. Mistry, the proud father of that sweet baby? And dear Gulnaz, it's been too long since I've seen you!"

Gulnaz's smile was a brief spasm. "Yes. And did you say that you came to see Perveen?"

"We have little time, Dr. Penkar. Please come." Perveen looped her left arm through the doctor's right and marched her through the house. This way, Gulnaz and Rustom wouldn't see them going through the back and swiftly through the garden.

"Remember, I said you may call me Miriam," Dr. Penkar said in a low voice. "You are behaving somewhat strangely. I hope your sister-in-law wasn't offended that we walked off from her."

Perveen glanced over her shoulder to make certain that Gulnaz and Rustom hadn't followed. Then she whispered, "They don't know about Sunanda staying here. She's in the garden cottage with our maidservant Gita."

"But why wouldn't you tell them?" Miriam objected.

"Sunanda had some trouble with her family," Perveen improvised. "I'm not sure how much she will tell you."

"The poor girl. Problem on top of problem!" Miriam exclaimed. "Don't they know what a heroine she is?"

"I think not." Perveen wanted to say more, but it wasn't the right time.

Sunanda looked up from her ironing as they approached. Softly, she said in Gujarati, "Doctor-ji. Hello. Thank you for what you did."

"Hello, Sunanda. I am glad to see you again." Miriam spoke back in courteous Marathi. "I hear that you are still in pain from the burn. Are you still using the jelly that I recommended?"

Sunanda hesitated, then shook her head.

"The Bhatias only gave it to Ishan," Perveen explained. "Sunanda had a homemade poultice from Oshadi, and for the last several days, she hasn't had any treatment."

Miriam pressed her lips together. "That's a shame. Where can I privately examine her?"

"We can go inside there," Sunanda said, gesturing to the garden cottage.

"Perveen, why don't you wait for me on your veranda," Miriam said, looking at the area where the breakfast table was set.

As she watched Miriam going into the hut, Perveen was ashamed. Could the doctor undertake a proper examination in such a dark space? As Perveen sat on a chair, she checked her watch. It was already eight-thirty; at nine, everyone would be assembled for breakfast. What would she say to Rustom and Gulnaz if they saw the doctor emerge from the cottage?

Twenty minutes later, Miriam emerged and crossed the garden to Perveen. Her easy smile was gone.

"What is it?" Perveen asked apprehensively.

"First, may I properly wash my hands?"

"Certainly." Perveen walked the doctor to the washbasin in the dining room. "And have you eaten breakfast?"

"Yes, my mother made sure I ate properly before I left home." Turning off the taps, Miriam glanced at the watch on her left wrist. The behavior was a reminder of how Perveen kept track of time doing legal work for a client. She hadn't done that yet for Sunanda.

"It was extremely kind of you to take time to pay a house call. I truly expected to bring her to the clinic," Perveen said, handing her a fresh towel.

"I work a shorter day on Friday, because of our Sabbath. I wouldn't have been able to fit her into the office schedule." Miriam dried her hands vigorously and hung the towel on the rack next to the sink. "Sunanda's allowed me to speak about her condition with you. Where can we speak with complete privacy?"

"The family is about to eat breakfast," Perveen said over the clattering sound in the kitchen. "I'll ask John to pour out two cups of tea for us, and we can talk upstairs in my room."

12

THE MEDICAL FACTS

"How pleasant—and large!" Miriam made a slow inspection around Perveen's bedroom suite, with its freshly made bed and opened windows letting in the morning breeze. Perveen set down the tea tray in the bedroom's visiting area, which had two golden velvet slipper chairs and a low table painted with flowers and birds. Many tiny round mirrors were inset on the table's top and sides. When she was very young, Perveen had caught glimpses of color and movement in the tiny mirrors and believed they were fairies. Now she wondered if there could be any truth to the idea that mirrors held spirits—and if so, how they'd react to hearing a privileged conversation.

"Where I live in the Mandvi district, the buildings are older than this," Dr. Penkar said as she settled down in the chair facing the windows. "We are blessed that my father paid the entire mortgage before his death. But our medical clinic takes up the entire downstairs, so our living quarters upstairs are rather cramped."

"Town living is more convenient, but it's true that there is more space in new suburbs." Perveen didn't want to say that Rustom was one of the contractors building out Dadar Parsi Colony, a prime reason they could afford having such a large property.

The doctor lifted her cup of tea and took a brief sip. "Very nice. Assam?"

"You're right." Perveen imagined the doctor was wrong

about very few things. She went to the wall to switch on the electric fan and then came back to seat herself in the other chair.

"Let's begin," Miriam said, placing her cup precisely on the saucer. "There's much to discuss, but I'll explain the medical aspects first."

"May I take notes?" Perveen motioned toward the pen and notebook she had near her.

"Certainly. It's important that you can recall the exact directions. As you suspected, her stomach burn is infected. I'm shocked that Uma didn't understand that the petroleum jelly was as necessary to treat Sunanda as her own son." Miriam grimaced at Perveen. "So we must try something stronger. I've left Sunanda a partially used jar of a special silver cream I had with me. I'll also write you a prescription that you can take to the European Hospital's pharmacy. Most pharmacies don't carry it, I'm afraid."

"The European Hospital is close to my office. I'll fill the prescription today." Although Indians couldn't receive medical treatment inside the hospital, the pharmacy would take anyone's money.

"Now, about Sunanda's daily schedule. She can do light housework, with regular rest periods. The kind of work I'm talking about would be done sitting down. Not squatting or standing or holding anything heavy. No ironing!" Dr. Penkar looked sternly at Perveen, as if holding her responsible. "Sunanda can do something like hold Khushy in her lap, but she could not walk around carrying the baby in her arms."

"I hope she didn't ask you about caring for Khushy?" When the doctor nodded, Perveen groaned. "We don't need that kind of help. Gulnaz already has an ayah."

"Now the next bit is very important!" Miriam looked intently at Perveen. "Sunanda said she's accustomed to sleeping on the floor. I explained that sleeping on a charpoy is essential for healing because it's more likely to prevent her from turning over and putting pressure on her burn. Please make sure she does this."

"I'll remind her, and also tell Gita about it." Perveen turned back to her notebook. "How many days must she apply the cream?"

"Until her wound is completely healed, a light coat of cream should be applied every morning after washing the wound. Use boiled water only. Do you have bandages on hand?"

"Certainly. Gulnaz cut up so many sheets for bandages during the war years—I know there are lots that never made it out of our house." Perveen noted a change in the doctor's expression. "What is it?"

"Nothing important." The doctor gave her a quick smile. "About the bandages—they must be changed every morning and night. She should be able to do it, but she will need help if it's too painful. If the skin around the burn becomes red and hot, you must ring me." Miriam took another sip of tea. "There is something else, but it's not a good idea to put it in writing."

Perveen put both sweating hands in her lap. "Of course."

"Sunanda had widespread abdominal tenderness, so I told her that I thought a pelvic examination was necessary. Never having had such, she was quite hesitant. Eventually, she allowed me, and then—she started to weep."

"So she has another injury, then?" Perveen tried to sound detached, but her thoughts were racing.

"No. She told me she'd had a very heavy menstrual cycle after drinking a medicinal tea that gave her stomach pain. And that the police believe that she drank the tea intending to abort a child. Given all of this, you were very kind to help her, Perveen."

Perveen's face was warm. "It's not much that I've done. And I'm grateful that you are compassionate to her. Plenty of people would regard what she's told us as a sign of immorality," Perveen said. "I'm trying to prove differently. In fact, anything you can tell me about the ingredients of the tea could be very helpful."

"There are probably more plants used as a so-called wife's help than there are flowers on your pretty tea table," Miriam said with a sigh. "These teas contain an irritant—something the body reacts to that makes the intestines or uterus contract. I've treated a few women who don't feel well after these teas, but they all improved. Far more dangerous are the situations where sticks or other materials are forced up inside the birth canal."

Perveen grimaced. "Who would do such a thing?"

"Situations are sometimes desperate, and medical doctors are prohibited by law from giving women anything that might prohibit conception." Dr. Penkar's voice was sober. "It is unusual for a woman to be able to disregard a husband's demand. And what if they are impregnated by someone other than a husband? To bear a child out of wedlock means a life on the streets."

"It's an impossible situation, isn't it?" Perveen recalled Amla and Govind's expulsion of Sunanda.

"Yes. Another point: when I made Sunanda's pelvic examination, I did not see a hymen," Dr. Penkar said briskly. "Such breaks can occur for a number of reasons. But it might mean that something happened."

Perveen stared into the tiny mirrors of her table, wondering how much Sunanda had held back from her. Sunanda might be romantically entwined with someone she couldn't marry—just as Perveen was with Colin Sandringham.

"How else can I help you, Perveen?" the doctor asked, glancing again at her watch.

"I've been reading a book that you lent to Uma. Do you need it back now?"

"*Woman and the New Race,*" Miriam said, smiling slightly. "Mrs. Sanger is a brave thinker, and she writes from the experience of having tried to help women who are desperate to be done with childbearing. Take as long as you need to read it."

"I was intrigued that Holland, which has birth control available to women, also has the lowest infant mortality rate in

Europe. It made me want to know more about the contraceptive devices and remedies. Do you think any of these are available in India?"

"Contraception isn't yet available in India." Miriam shook her head. "Doctors are afraid it might be harmful to women, or they worry that the government could arrest them for distributing obscene materials. It's a shame, because so many women ask me what they can do to prevent more children—and I have no answer that could satisfy both them and their husbands."

And it was also a shame, Perveen thought, that she could never avail herself of some method that might allow her to explore her utmost longings with Colin without fear of pregnancy. Worried that her face would give her away, she arose from her chair and went to the French doors that were open to the veranda. Watching Lillian napping in her cage, she produced a response that was impersonal, yet honest. "This situation sounds harmful, not only for the unplanned children who might die early or live with less food—but for the women who cannot control what happens to their bodies."

"Yes." Miriam stood up and put a handkerchief to her damp brow. "Who can blame Sunanda for taking the same tea as many women?"

Perveen waited for Miriam to come alongside her. Then she asked, "Would you consider being an expert witness in Sunanda's case, if there is a trial?"

Miriam took a deep breath. After a moment, she said, "I truly wish I could, but it's not a good idea. Firstly, because she's been my patient. They might try to push me to give the results of her physical examination. That wouldn't bode well for her. And there's another problem as well."

"And what is that?" Perveen asked.

"God save the Queen!" croaked Lillian, who had come awake.

Miriam laughed, and Perveen briefly explained to her that the bird was of unknown age but had been acquired by her late grandfather during the Victorian era. Then, Perveen opened the cage for Lillian, who flew out, her green feathers flashing.

Watching the bird at play, the doctor spoke again. "The other thing that concerns me is that if the papers report that Dr. Miriam Penkar gave expert testimony on abortion, it might give Sir Dwarkanath a false impression I'm knowledgeable about the topic and might administer abortions in our future hospital. You've seen how his anger can flare. I'm very sorry I can't help."

Miriam gave Perveen an apologetic smile before turning to go back inside.

"Never mind, then." Perveen followed her into the bedroom, slowly realizing from the doctor's words that Uma hadn't yet told her about the change in plans. "I'm sorry to bring it up this way, but . . . have you heard about the cancellation of the women's hospital?"

"What nonsense are you talking?" Miriam picked up her doctor's bag as if readying to leave. "Our hospital is well on its way."

"Last Wednesday, Uma told me that her father-in-law has decided the effort is too much of a distraction for her from family duties. He's rescinded his offer of land."

Miriam went stock still and stared at Perveen.

"I'm very sorry," Perveen said. "I just learned myself. You should have known before I did."

"No!" Miriam whispered as she collapsed onto the gold chair she'd sat in earlier. "How can it be? Sir Dwarkanath spoke in favor at the fundraising party."

Perveen summarized her conversation with Uma, watching Miriam's strong-boned face become even more rigid.

"Sir Dwarkanath should know better than to call this off!" Miriam's voice wavered. "He knows there are too many women dying. His own wife perished from gynecological trouble!" Miriam covered her face with her hands, as if to hide her tears.

Perveen left her chair to comfort Miriam, but the doctor shook off her touch.

"I'm all right!" Miriam said, taking a handkerchief from her bag to wipe her face.

A soft flurry of knocks on the closed bedroom door startled both of them.

Perveen sprang up and went to the door, finding Camellia on the other side.

"Sorry!" Camellia's voice was hesitant. "I don't suppose I could ask Dr. Penkar for a small favor?"

Perveen shifted her body, trying to block her mother's view of the doctor, who was putting away her handkerchief. "Perhaps another time?"

"Perveen, it's very important! Don't tell the doctor what to do."

Miriam closed her eyes for a moment and breathed deeply. Then she arose and came to the door herself. "Mrs. Mistry, what is it?"

"How kind you are." Camellia delivered the imploring smile that had brought so much to her various charity efforts. "I wonder if you could come next door to check on my new grand-daughter, Khushy? Gulnaz and I worry that she's sleeping too hard."

"Mamma, why in heaven's name would you want to wake her? The crying has been unbearable," Perveen protested. "Dr. Penkar has to get on her way, after giving us so much time—"

"It won't be long," Camellia said, giving Perveen an exasperated look.

"I'm pleased to check." Miriam picked up her doctor's bag and started for the door.

Perveen marveled at the doctor's ability to switch into professional mode after such a shock. Softly, she said, "Thank you very much."

"It's my pleasure." Looking over her shoulder at Perveen, Miriam said, "I'll let your mother bring me. After that, I'm headed out to the clinic. I think we've covered everything, haven't we?"

"Yes, thank you." Trying to duplicate Miriam's cheerful professionalism, Perveen turned to address her mother. "I'm off to the office. Ring me if I should bring anything from the shops or the chemist for Khushy. You are in good hands with Dr. Penkar."

13

A LADY'S DECISION

In the late-morning traffic, the ride into South Bombay was easy, even with a stop at the European Hospital to buy the cream.

"Aadab, Perveen-bai. Here is the morning's post." Mustafa handed her a sheaf of letters when she entered Mistry House.

Upstairs, she settled down in her spot at the partners desk. Usually her father, seated on his side, would comment on every letter she passed to him or inquire about the ones addressed to her. Today, her pulse raced as she opened an envelope with the return address of the Bombay High Court. Inside was a letter reminding her of the trial date of July 7, with a pretrial hearing with Magistrate O'Brien on June 29.

So much had to be organized: hiring and instructing a barrister, reviewing the evidence, preparing Sunanda, and deposing witnesses. The defense team also had the right to examine all the exhibits of evidence. The only exhibit she knew about was the soaking bucket with Amla's sari. She'd initially focused on how she'd need to convince the judge that the sari hadn't been worn by Sunanda. But as she thought about it, the prosecutor's timeline established that the tea was taken on May 27, which meant it was unlikely that any sari collected June 7 could fit the narrative. She wouldn't even need Amla's cooperation to win this point.

Feeling righteous, she decided to proceed further with research.

In the nearby storage room, she opened a steel almirah

holding many reference books. She selected Woodman's *Digest of Indian Law Cases* and brought it back to the main office. After she'd found mention of cases that involved abortion, she requested Mustafa to bring the corresponding volumes of *Indian Law Report.*

As she slowly read through the abortion prosecution cases, she noticed they tended to fall into three categories. Most often the women involved were widows or wives, although there was one case with a British woman living apart from her husband. In all the cases, though, the named defendant was somebody else: a husband, or a mother-in-law, a physician, or a dai. And in almost all these cases, the women involved had died from gynecological infections caused by abortion sticks, uncontrolled bleeding, or poisoning by substances like arsenic and gunpowder. So the defendants weren't the women; they were people who had either allegedly made the woman abort or performed a fatal procedure.

A baby's wailing caught her ear, and she flinched.

Not Khushy—someone else.

Through the open window, Perveen saw the source. A girl of about sixteen was walking along with a baby swaddled in the folds of her worn cotton sari. Behind her walked an extremely thin boy who appeared no older than four. When two men approached, the woman beseeched them, her free hand waving an array of pencils for sale.

One of the men laughed and the other made a shooing gesture with his hand.

The ragged family continued slowly down Bruce Street. Perveen stared until they were out of view. They seemed emblematic of the problems she'd been reading about: early marriage and uncontrolled fertility.

On impulse, Perveen hurried downstairs and into the kitchen to open the petty cash box.

"What's this?" Mustafa said, looking up from the silver teapot he was polishing.

"I need to buy a pencil." She grabbed a handful of coins, not looking at the denominations.

"Won't you record it?" Mustafa called after her, but she was already out the door.

The young woman, baby, and boy were at the end of Bruce Street when Perveen caught up. The boy turned at the sound of Perveen's fast footsteps. This close, she could see his ribs sticking out. She pressed a rupee into his hand.

As she did so, the woman turned and swept an arm protectively around the child. "Get away from my son!"

"I'm only paying him," Perveen said, realizing that the child's mother looked younger than sixteen, although there was a gauntness to her face that would soon age her beyond her years.

"Show me!" the mother demanded of her son, and when she saw the coin, she looked with confusion at Perveen.

"I want to buy some pencils." Perveen smiled at her. Female street sellers in Fort were uncommon. Had the young woman taken over for her husband or father—or had she convinced a pencil-shop owner that she could sell for him?

"I can't give change for that, Memsahib. One pencil for two paisa." She plucked the coin from her son's hand and gave it back to Perveen.

"It doesn't matter. Give me two pencils, then. Keep the rest."

Thanking Perveen profusely, the pencil seller pressed the rupee to her forehead before tucking it away in a purse tied under her sari. Then she instructed her son to choose the very best pencils from her hand.

As Perveen took the pencils, she had a second thought. If the pencil seller didn't have a lot of change, she'd probably have to give up the entire rupee to whoever had provided her the pencils. She reviewed the coins she'd taken from the petty cash box and found an anna, a coin equivalent to four paise. In a low voice, she said, "This is what you give back to the man who sent you. Promise me you'll keep the rest to take care of your family."

"May Lakshmi bless you," the woman said.

The pencil seller might have thought Perveen was Hindu. And Perveen could be mistaken about her being someone's employee. What did it matter? She would accept any blessing that came her way.

Across the street, she saw that Jayanth, their occasional errand-runner, had been watching her exchange. The sight of him was welcome, for more than one reason.

"Arre, Perveen-memsahib!" The thin, wiry young man rose. "I saw you hurrying to that young woman and thought, why are you tiring yourself in the heat when I can run errands for you? How much did you pay for those pencils?"

"Oh, that doesn't matter. I have a request for you." Perveen explained that she was looking for a man named Arvind Vikas Tomar who might live or work in Kalbadevi. Could Jayanth discover whether he was a known person in the area?

"It's a very crowded place." Jayanth, who'd come from a fishing community, looked aggrieved. "Finding him would be like a needle in the haystack."

"Ask at any tea and food stands and amongst the cart drivers. And the local police may know him."

"I don't like police, and they don't like me," Jayanth grumbled.

"They may have records of tenants in rental houses. And don't worry about the police! You are past all those troubles," Perveen reminded him.

"Because of you." Jayanth squared his shoulders and sighed. "Very well. What shall I do if I learn his address? Shall I go to him?"

"I'm curious about what his dwelling looks like," Perveen said after some consideration. "And if you see that he is a man with a family, that sort of thing. You could linger in the area and give me details. But there's no need to make direct contact. Go whenever you have time."

Jayanth finished his tea quickly. "I'll leave now."

Perveen took two rupees from her purse. "For expenses. And note how much time you spend, if I don't see you again today."

"I will go," he said, pocketing the money. "And look, here's the sahib coming!"

Perveen followed Jayanth's gaze. Jamshedji Mistry was walking slowly with his briefcase in hand, his eyes on her.

"Already back from court. Thank you, Jayanth," Perveen said and quickly crossed the street. Either her father had an unsatisfactory outcome, or he was suffering from the heat.

"And what are you doing away from your desk?" he asked, taking a handkerchief to his gleaming forehead.

"I'm sending Jayanth on reconnaissance to Kalbadevi," she said as they turned back onto Bruce Street. "How was court?"

"I won my motion," he said, his voice casual, but his eyes shining. "They said it could not be done. So our exhibits in favor of the client's character will be allowed."

"Congratulations!"

"Too soon for that—do not jinx the case." Jamshedji motioned for her to precede him up the steps into Mistry House. "Let's have our lunch. As you know, I left before you this morning, but I did see Sunanda in the garden."

Perveen had entered the hall first, and now she spun around to look at his expression. "What happened, then?"

"She was ironing—trying to make herself useful," Jamshedji said. "At least the setup was not visible to the other side of the duplex. It's a shame about her looks, isn't it?"

"She should not have been ironing!" Perveen said, frustrated. "And why are you talking about her appearance? What does that matter?"

"Thank you, sahib!" Jamshedji said to Mustafa, who appeared with a silver tray holding two tumblers of water. Jamshedji drank before speaking. "She's very pretty. That could make the judge suspect she has a lover. He might ask, why isn't she already married?"

"Because her brother can't afford dowry," Perveen shot back. "Sunanda dresses modestly and is clean and respectable. The man you are defending has a pocked face and shabby clothes. Does that make him successful?"

"I will instruct him on what to wear before the day of trial." Jamshedji glanced at himself in the mirror by the hat rack as he handed his fetah to Mustafa to put away. "Sunanda told me that she was worried about the Bhatias thinking she'd left them without giving notice. I said that you would be going to Bhatia House to explain what you could of the situation."

"Yes. I'm glad you agree with my plan," Perveen said, remembering the caution he'd expressed the night before.

"I'm not terribly optimistic, but we shall see what unfolds."

As they entered the high-ceilinged, sunny office, Perveen went straight to the letters she'd neglected to finish sorting that morning. Quickly, she passed Jamshedji letters from his clients, keeping her own and throwing away unsolicited advertisements. At the bottom was an envelope addressed to her from Vivek Sharma's office.

Swiftly, her eyes scanned the letter.

Dear Miss Mistry,

I am in receipt of your invitation to a meeting with the purpose of discussing my assistance with the trial of Sunanda Chavda, who you attempted to represent in bail court a few days ago. Let me congratulate you on your bravery and idealism.

I appreciate your invitation to participate in Sunanda Chavda's representation, however I am heavily committed. Therefore, I offer my regrets. Please give your father my very best wishes and let him know that I hope he keeps me in mind for future cases.

Yours sincerely,
Vivek Sharma

Perveen read it again, feeling a rush of disappointment. Heavily committed, yet still looking for future cases? It was also offensive that he'd written of wanting invitations from Jamshedji. Perhaps Vivek was not the progressive man she'd believed. She recalled how Vivek had seemed not to notice her when she wanted to get into the lawyers' seating area; perhaps that was intentional. He'd quickly turned away when the magistrate was railing at her.

"The bastard!" she muttered.

Jamshedji looked up from his work. "What is it?"

Holding out the letter, she said, "Vivek Sharma won't take Sunanda's case. He gave no reason other than being heavily committed."

"Typically, he's eager for whatever business we bring." Jamshedji scowled as he reviewed the letter. "Now who will be the next possible barrister?"

Perveen took a deep breath. "You could?"

"No!" Jamshedji spoke in an admonitory tone. "I prefer to do solicitor work. Besides which, the Lahiri murder trial starts July fifth. And I choose my clients; they aren't assigned to me by my junior partner."

"Touché." Perveen tried to play off his reprimand. "Do you mind if I use the car for a few hours?"

Her father shrugged. "As long as it helps your case."

"I'll do my best to ensure that."

After her troubling visit with Miriam and the bad news about Vivek Sharma, Perveen needed something to go right today. If Uma came through, it would feel like a triumph.

14

THE ANSWER IS NO

"At least no dogs to fight!" Arman joked when they arrived at Bhatia House. Perveen had kept her eyes on the fields as well, not seeing dogs, only children playing cricket.

One car was parked in the round driveway at Bhatia House—the dark green Buick she'd seen before and understood now was the Bhatias' vehicle.

"This visit might take some time," Perveen told Arman as he opened the car door for her.

At the Bhatias' door, Perveen took a deep breath, but before she could knock, the door swung open. Oshadi stood there, glowering at Perveen as if she'd already seen her through the window and wasn't pleased about it.

"You are Mistry Memsahib. I remember from before," Oshadi said in Gujarati. "I gave Uma-bhabhu your letter."

"Thank you. I've come to call on her," Perveen answered in the same language.

"No." Oshadi's hand gripped her walking stick. "She's with Nana-seth and cannot come to you."

Perveen recognized that Oshadi was using the term for lord of the house. "I can wait until she is finished speaking with him. I must speak with Uma-bhabhu about Sunanda."

"Sunanda doesn't work here anymore." Oshadi's mouth trembled as she said the name.

"Why?" Perveen asked, curious about how much she knew.

"She committed a crime, Nana-seth told everyone." Oshadi's hard face seemed to crumple with grief.

"Sunanda was arrested, but she has not harmed anyone at all," Perveen said, fearing the woman was about to burst into tears. "I've been keeping her safe with me. In fact, because I'm helping her as her lawyer, I would like to know whether you prepared any tea for her recently?"

Oshadi's hand clenched tighter on her walking stick. "I brew homemade tea from nature's gifts for anyone who is feeling poorly."

Perveen lowered her voice. "You must remember how much I liked your tea when I visited before. I'd like to see the tea to try to clear Sunanda's reputation."

Oshadi looked over her shoulder and then motioned for Perveen to come inside. They walked along the main hall, into a secondary hall and then a small, musty room.

"Sunanda might have been overheard talking with you here," Perveen said, looking at the open window. "I wouldn't want that to happen for us, either."

After Oshadi latched the window, she turned to a shelf that was filled with jars of various sizes. Some had contents that bore the unmistakable yellow color of turmeric, while others were gray, brown, and black.

Oshadi held up a large jar that had about an inch's worth of brown twiggy matter. "Just flowers and bark. Very mild stomachache follows drinking. This keeps the menses regular. This is a bit I have left. The police took the other one."

"One question I have—did Sunanda ask you for the tea, or did you tell her she should take it?"

"The police asked this also." Oshadi frowned. "Sunanda was feeling very upset," she said after a pause. "I thought it might be an irregular cycle. So I told her, drink this tea."

Perveen wanted to write down the statement, but that act might frighten Oshadi into being less forthcoming. "How many women in the household have taken this tea?" Perveen asked.

"I have been making it for many years now." Oshadi touched

her gnarled right forefinger to the jar's lid. "Since the hardships of the nana-sethani."

Perveen recalled what Dr. Penkar had said about Lady Bhatia's death due to gynecological ailments. "Did Lady Bhatia drink the tea?"

"No. But after her mother-in-law became bedridden, Uma-bhabhu asked me if I could make a remedy for regulating menstruation. Lady Bhatia had too many children. Damage to her body from those births caused her great trouble in later years."

"I know about Parvesh Bhatia and his younger brother," Perveen said. "How many children were there?"

"They are the only males who lived, as well as two daughters. Lady Bhatia had three stillbirths, and many miscarriages. Not even Lady Bhatia could guess the number."

Speaking Marathi with Oshadi, it struck Perveen again that the word "garbhapaat" was used to describe both unexpected miscarriage and abortion.

"Have you ever assisted anyone with childbirth or an abortion?"

"I was here when all the children in this household were born. Of course, a dai was always in charge. I brought water, clean sheets. And my prayers." Her rheumy eyes drifted past Perveen, as if lost in memory.

Perveen thought that Oshadi's assistance sounded like that of a typical female helper, which contrasted with the nefarious role described by the prosecutor. However, Oshadi had stated that she'd suggested the tea to Sunanda. If the prosecutor argued that Oshadi made the suggestion because she'd believed Sunanda was pregnant, both women were at legal risk. Perveen would have to tread carefully, stressing the case that the tea was commonly used by many for unblocking the menses. "You have been a great help. Now I need just a moment with Uma-bhabhu. As I said, I can wait as long as needed."

Oshadi's face tightened again. "It is better that you wait upstairs. But she may not be able to come."

"Thank you very much for telling her I'm here." Perveen followed Oshadi, who slowly climbed the steep stairs, her gait off-kilter, one hand on the wall. The hall was an open gallery with a roof overhead to protect from rain and sun. Oshadi opened the door to a small sitting room and directed Perveen to a low teak chair. Her attention was caught by a portrait of an unsmiling woman in her forties wearing a sari draped over her head and heavy jewelry. The photograph sat in an ebony frame draped in a fragrant jasmine garland. It was very likely the deceased Lady Bhatia. Perveen gazed at her, thinking about how her life's work had been bearing children—and how it had ultimately killed her.

The door to the sitting room was half-open, and a few servants passed by, darting glances toward Perveen, who looked back, wondering if any of these young men or women might have been involved in reporting Sunanda to Arvind Tomar. Then she heard the soft sliding of sandals and saw Uma Bhatia had arrived. Instead of silk, she was in a simple cotton sari, which was crumpled.

Perveen rose to greet her, but Uma held up a hand. "Stay in that chair, and I'll sit far away, to avoid the possibility of infection. My father-in-law is ill."

"Oh, I'm very sorry!" Perveen said, noting Uma's use of the English word for *infection*. "Does he have a fever?"

Uma settled down on a narrow bench near the open door. "No, he is thankfully cogent. However, his mood is bad. The Legislative Council meets today for voting, and he thinks if he's not there, the outcome may not be good. But he is not strong enough to walk or even stand."

Perveen felt a trickle of misgiving. "Have you called a doctor?"

"Someone examined him yesterday morning. The doctor

said it would be all right—just to give him lots of fluids and simple foods, assuming this is either a virus or food poisoning. But surely, you've not come about this."

"No." Perveen arose and went to close the door for privacy. "There was more to tell you than I could write in the letter."

"Yes," Uma said, leaning away from Perveen as she passed close to her on the way back from the door. "The children have been wild since Sunanda didn't come to work yesterday morning. A policeman came later in the day and said to my husband something about her being arrested. Is it true the crime is garbhapaat?"

"The arrest is on suspicion of induced miscarriage," Perveen acknowledged. "However, it was a groundless arrest for a number of reasons."

Pursing her lips, Uma said, "We thought we hired a virgin, but we were misled. She is a different sort."

"That's incorrect," Perveen said, feeling her back go up. "Sunanda is the same brave and selfless woman who saved Ishan's life!" Uma looked away, as if embarrassed to be reminded, and Perveen soldiered on. "The person who reported Sunanda to the police is a man named Arvind Vikas Tomar. Have you ever heard of him?"

Uma appeared to be thinking, and after a long moment shook her head. "Tomar is not a Gujarati name."

"It may be a name more common to North India," Perveen said. "There are many immigrants to Bombay."

"Almost all the people we know are Gujarati," Uma said. "We don't have friends who are men or have personal acquaintance with men who sell food and whatnot. Our cook or Oshadi takes care of that."

Perveen thought Uma seemed to be striving to portray herself as being part of a clan, as opposed to an individual—typical for an Indian communal household. "Could there be a Tomar among the many employees at Bhatia Stone?"

"It's unlikely. Sir Dwarkanath and my husband only hire Gujjus or Marathas."

"Might you inquire whether Arvind Vikas Tomar is an employee or business associate, or known in any way? His bad-mouthing of Sunanda led to her arrest, after all."

Uma's face didn't reveal the displeasure with Tomar that Perveen had hoped for. Instead, she spoke in an even tone. "Do you mean I should ask my father-in-law?"

Perveen understood the need for caution around Sir Dwarkanath. "Since your father-in-law is ill, why not ask your husband?"

Uma smiled tightly. "It's not a good idea to involve him in the controversy. I'm sorry, but you can learn about this another way."

Perveen felt nervous about her next request, but she couldn't return to Jamshedji without asking. "There sometimes are discreet ways to help. I know that you liked having Sunanda care for your children."

"That's very true," Uma said, her eyes soft. "We all miss her."

Perveen held her gaze. "I'm working to help Sunanda pro bono, but a barrister will expect to be paid to speak up for her in court. I wonder if you could find it in your heart to cover that expense?"

Uma was shaking her head before Perveen had spoken the last words in her request. "You are asking, would he give a rupee toward the defense of a woman accused of abortion? No."

"Sunanda saved Ishan's life—"

"I would have been there myself, but Mangala was in my way," Uma interrupted. "I would have done the same as Sunanda, but how lucky that she was so fast. In fact, we wanted to give her a financial gift as thanks, but Sir Dwarkanath didn't agree."

Perveen noted that Uma had slipped back into formality. "I won't ask you again about money. But could you write a letter in praise of Sunanda's character? You could include the story of how she saved Ishan's life. Sunanda's barrister could present that to the judge."

"A written statement with my name attached?"

"Yes."

"I'm very sorry, but I told you what they expect of me. I got in trouble for trying to do something outside of the house. So my answer must be no."

Uma rose, and as she straightened her sari, Perveen saw that it was flecked with a brown substance. Following her gaze, Uma said, "Please excuse me—my father-in-law is ailing, and I haven't had time to clean up. Do you know the way downstairs?"

"Yes, I'll go on my own. Please give Sir Dwarkanath my best wishes for his recovery—"

Vehemently, Uma shook her head. "He would be most perturbed to know you were back."

"He doesn't approve of me because I'm defending Sunanda?" Perveen could not hide her sarcasm.

"He doesn't know about that part." Uma's expression was serious. "He doesn't believe it's proper for women to work alongside men. In this house, even the servant work is separated. Oshadi is in charge of the female servants. We have a bearer supervising the men."

After that, Perveen saw no point in talking further. She'd gotten what she could from Uma, which wasn't much.

Riding back to the office, Perveen felt herself flummoxed by what she did and didn't know about Uma Bhatia. The lady's swift decision not to help seemed hypocritical in the face of her praises of Sunanda. But as Ghatkopar vanished from her window, replaced by fields, Perveen wondered if Uma had been harsh out of self-preservation. What if she thought her husband or Sir Dwarkanath had impregnated Sunanda?

Perveen couldn't subpoena Uma to the witness stand, because the law was written to allow women the decision whether or not to appear in a public court of law. It was an accommodation made out of respect for families who thought it immodest for women to have strangers' eyes on them.

Perveen thanked Arman and dragged herself back into Mistry House, so deep in thought she forgot to greet Mustafa.

"Aadab," he said to her retreating back. "Didn't you see Jayanth outside? He has returned and wants to give his report."

"Didn't you let him come inside?"

"I offered. He was not comfortable." Mustafa's voice was stiff, as if he was angry that Perveen had thought him inhospitable.

"That sounds like him. I'd better go out." Perveen rummaged in her legal case to make sure her notebook was there and felt a sharp prick. The wound came from one of the pencils she'd recently sharpened.

A warning that for every impulsive act, there'd be a consequence.

Jayanth was at the same place on the curb near Yazdani's. He was utterly drenched in sweat and accepted the tumbler of cool water she procured from the bakery.

"Shall I bring you another glass?" she asked, after he'd gulped the cup down.

Smacking his lips, he said, "That's enough. Now, I'll tell you about it. First, I went through the neighborhood asking casually after him. I found several men near the Bhatia Stone buildings. They didn't know the name. Neither did any of the men in the bazaar, nor the chaiwallah."

"Did you try the police?"

"Only because I promised you." Jayanth's voice held the resentment of his past mistreatment by the law. "They asked why I wanted to find him, and I said I had news from his village. The duty sergeant said that to check if his name was in the registrar could take weeks. To get it right away, payment was needed."

A bribe. "How much?"

"Four annas," Jayanth muttered, showing his annoyance.

"They looked, but they said there was no record of such a man living in the area. They didn't ask for more money, so I don't think they were hiding anything."

"Hmm." Perveen didn't like spending money for nothing.

"I've got more," Jayanth continued. "The sergeant said he'd read an order from Bombay Police Headquarters that included that name. Tomar was a complainant to the police with no address listed."

It was the same information Perveen had before—but now she thought about it differently. Tomar wasn't a denizen of Kalbadevi; furthermore, he was someone confident enough to go straight to police headquarters or to have called the police for a meeting elsewhere.

"Jayanth, you've worked so hard. Thank you." Perveen put the four annas that Jayanth said he'd paid in baksheesh into his palm. She was feeling fatigued in the heat and could only imagine how much more he'd been through.

He thought he hadn't found out anything. But what he was doing for her was eliminating possibilities. A. V. Tomar was not anyone hanging at the edges of Sunanda's community. He was distant, and that might very well work in her favor.

15

WHERE IS SHE?

"Let's go. We must see Khushy before she's asleep."

Jamshedji's cheerful declaration put a stop to Perveen's work. Packing up her legal case, she realized that she'd hardly thought about Khushy all day, even though she'd left the house knowing the baby might be ill. *I am a pitiful excuse for an aunt*, she thought, staring out the open window on the car ride home.

"Where is my beautiful granddaughter?" Jamshedji called as they entered the quiet hall.

John stepped out of the kitchen to take the tiffin containers and answered Jamshedji with a nod. "On the veranda, Mistry-seth."

Perveen followed her father through the house and out the French doors to the garden, where Gulnaz was slumped in a rattan chair, Camellia seated nearby with Khushy in her lap. Perveen's eyes strayed toward the garden cottage, feeling a flutter of satisfaction that Sunanda wasn't visible. She was abiding by the rules Perveen had set.

"Here you are at last!" Camellia looked up and gave Perveen a significant glance. "What a day we've had."

Jamshedji knelt at her side so he could look straight into Khushy's half-open eyes. In Gujarati, he crooned, "There you are, my little dear! A very good afternoon to you!"

"Surely Lakshmi could help," Perveen suggested, noticing they'd set up on the veranda without her.

Camellia stared at Gulnaz, who grimaced before speaking. "I had to sack her."

"What happened?" Perveen tensed. Surely one day wasn't long enough time for an employee to prove herself useless.

"Dr. Penkar said that Khushy's breathing revealed that she'd been *drugged*!" Gulnaz announced.

"What on earth?" Perveen thought she hadn't heard right, but when she glanced at Camellia her mother gave a quick nod.

Jamshedji knelt in front of Khushy and looked closely at the baby, who began making odd little grunts. "Is she all right now? What was the drug?"

"The exact drug is unknown, but it must have been brought in," Gulnaz said. "Lakshmi gave Khushy something dangerous enough that she could have never awoken! It could have *killed* her."

Jamshedji's eyes widened. "Did you witness Lakshmi doing this? What did she say?"

Camellia pressed her lips together, and then said, "Nobody saw her. Lakshmi told us she didn't understand why we were accusing her. She cried very hard; it was difficult to understand."

"Dr. Penkar said Khushy was dangerously over-sedated." Gulnaz's words poured out rapidly. "We had to wipe her face with cold water. Finally, she came awake when I pinched her. I was so frightened!"

Perveen recalled how annoyed she'd been that Khushy had cried all night, only to quiet in the morning. Now she felt sick about it.

Jamshedji pulled out a handkerchief and wiped his eyes. He whispered a few words of an Avestan prayer, then he motioned for Camellia to pass the baby to him. Perveen watched as her father gently took the baby into his arms. After smiling and cooing for a moment, he looked over at Camellia. "When Perveen was a baby, she never wanted to settle to sleep. Always battling, she was. I remember that in those days, her ayah would put something on her finger for Perveen to suck."

"Rum," said Camellia. "My mother and the ayah didn't think

a touch was harmful, but Grandfather Mistry put an end to it, saying it could lead to trouble."

"There's always rum in your parlor cabinet. Was it locked?" Gulnaz asked, her voice accusing.

"I should hope so! But I admit that I carelessly threw away a half-filled toddy bottle yesterday."

"Ah!" Jamshedji raised a finger. "Servants commonly take discarded materials. Lakshmi could have come across it."

For Perveen, the scenario had too many unproven and unseen elements to make sense. She asked, "When did Lakshmi arrive this morning?"

"I am a new mother, and I should be looking always at the clock?" Gulnaz grumbled. "I don't know."

"Eight-thirty," Camellia said. "She arrived when you and Rustom were at the temple, so I instructed her to wash nappies and freshen—"

She stopped talking, because Khushy had burped, and a milky stream shot out onto Jamshedji's suit jacket.

"Oh Khodai!" Jamshedji cried out in shock. Perveen laughed, unable to restrain herself.

Jamshedji continued to look alarmed, and Camellia quickly took the baby, slipping a tea cloth over her shoulder to expertly burp the infant.

"What will we do?" Gulnaz's eyes were wet as she looked at her mother-in-law.

"I'll call a domestic service agency," Camellia said, her voice firm. "I shall help you as best I can when I'm home, but I do have my charity meetings. What about your mother?"

"Mummy's terrible with children." Gulnaz used her fist to wipe her reddened eyes. "And if I can't trust our neighbors to send me a good ayah, how could I possibly trust an agency?"

"We could give the ayah a one-day trial, fully supervised," Camellia said. "You and I will interview her rigorously."

Camellia had not included Perveen in the proposed interviews. Logically, Perveen knew it was because she worked outside the house; but part of her also sensed it was because they thought she had scant knowledge of a baby's needs.

When Perveen left the veranda, nobody noticed. She passed the high hibiscus hedge to the other side of the garden to face the servants' cottage. Gita was nowhere to be seen. When Perveen stepped through the door, a patch of light coming from the high window revealed the neatly made-up charpoy, but no Sunanda.

Hearing the sound of splashing, Perveen guessed that Sunanda was in the bathing house just behind the cottage. Perveen laid the jar of silver cream on the charpoy so Sunanda wouldn't miss it and went back around the house, avoiding the veranda entirely. She'd refresh herself with her own bath and then lie down a few minutes. The scene with her family had been exhausting.

She slept for a while, although she briefly awoke to Khushy's plaintive cries. It was dark, and she could hear the clinking of cutlery and conversation from the windows. Dinner had begun without anyone calling her, but was that such a bad thing? She was wary of any more conversation with Gulnaz. She might as well do as her faith told her and work against her bad thoughts by replacing them with good ones. *Good thoughts, good words, good deeds* were the foundation of Zoroastrianism.

She switched on her bedside lamp, which shone down on the legal briefcase she'd brought upstairs. A potential good deed lay amongst the jumbled papers.

Perveen opened the case and pulled out the history of a case in Bengal leading to an acquittal on the charge of abortion. It was possible to win; how could she do the same for Sunanda?

When a knock came on the door, she ignored it. She had no interest in a tray of dinner or anything else. Khushy's crying waxed and waned as the hours went on. After midnight, the cries were accompanied by Gulnaz and Rustom's high-volume quarreling.

Perveen had been genuinely excited for Gulnaz and Rustom to have a child. She had never expected to feel such resentment, and it went far beyond her awkwardness at holding the fretful infant. Gulnaz and Rustom had achieved something she couldn't ever have for herself—and Perveen's parents were part of this new family unit. They had a grandchild; something Perveen could never give them.

All she could offer them was her professional accomplishments—and now, that idea was precarious. She imagined how the events of yesterday could be relayed by a reporter. *Miss Perveen Mistry, the city's sole woman lawyer, works with clients in a most unorthodox manner. The Parsi woman lawyer insisted that a young female client live on her property in a meager dwelling meant for servants. The lawyer subjected the client to an unrequested medical examination and tried to force the client to drink alcohol under the guise of assisting with her medical treatment.*

By the time she was done imagining the news story, Perveen could envision herself facing charges for unethical behavior.

She put away the law journals and turned out the light. The baby was quiet—temporarily, surely. But some sleep was better than none.

At six o'clock on Saturday morning, the sky was lightening from black to a deep indigo. Perveen could hear the rough sound of wheels going over roads. She used to find the noise irritating, but it was nothing compared to what she'd heard the last two nights.

She took a quick bucket bath with cool water and dressed in a yellow tissue silk sari with a black-and-white embroidered border. Her hair was already rebellious, so she brushed it behind her ears and decided to tie a mathabana over it—at least, until it was dry.

She went downstairs and found John was already in the kitchen, humming as he chopped vegetables. "Good morning. Do you see the teapot? I can serve you in a minute."

"I don't mind doing it." Perveen chose a plain cup from the cabinet and poured for herself.

"Your father is also awake early. He's in the parlor with the newspapers. I'm just getting his tea tray ready."

Spotting the saucers of spices and a bowl holding bread dough, Perveen shook her head. "You're busy enough. I'll pour him a cup and bring it to him."

"Tea must steep three more minutes," John admonished. "And don't forget the sugar and milk!"

A few minutes later, Perveen carried the tray into the living room. "Good morning, Pappa. You are up even before me."

"As you know, there is no point in wasting time lying awake." He was dressed in his light white undershirt and pajama trousers, the typical clothing worn at home by Parsi men.

"Did you also hear that raucous crying last night?" Perveen asked, feeling that the two of them were coming back into alignment.

Jamshedji snorted. "Raucous is a term for men in taverns. Our Khushy's a sweet baby doing what babies must do."

Your Khushy, Perveen thought as she sat down heavily across from him. She smarted from his rebuttal, but she had to accept that it was true: infants didn't have any way to voice their feelings except through crying.

Jamshedji sipped his tea, not seeming to notice that Perveen had made it rather than John. She supposed that this was a good thing. He drank while slowly reading through the *Bombay Chronicle*, while she read an article in the *Times of India* reporting that, from his prison cell in Poona, Mohandas K. Gandhi was spinning thread on a small wheel. Reading about the freedom activist's six-year prison sentence made her ashamed of feeling sorry for herself. She couldn't do everything that she wanted;

but at least she had physical freedom. After her father refolded the *Chronicle*, he offered it to her.

"I'll read it later," she demurred. "Would you like to take a walk with me?"

Sunlight glinted through the branchlets of casuarina trees as they walked side by side, nodding hello to the other neighbors walking and servants arriving for a day's work. Going through the ordinary motions calmed Perveen enough to voice something she'd been thinking about since the previous evening. "After what happened in the police court, I won't be rash enough to approach the bench again. But could I run the deposition for A. V. Tomar? That would be done privately ahead of time. No judge is present, so I don't see how it would break any laws."

Jamshedji walked another half block before delivering his answer. "Perhaps. It would also be necessary for our barrister to be present so he understands every nuance of the situation. We need to identify our barrister as soon as possible. I spoke with Sunanda briefly yesterday morning. She's very shy. Let's hope she will become comfortable enough to speak in court."

"Yes. It's a shame that a female lawyer can't be the one who questions her in court," Perveen said pointedly. "Anyway, last night I drafted the letters to the barristers you recommended and will have them delivered by courier to their offices."

"To their homes," Jamshedji corrected. "Remember, not every lawyer works on Saturday. I expect interviews with these gentlemen to commence on Monday."

"Very well. But I want to depose A. V. Tomar very soon, especially since getting to him might take time. I don't know where he resides." Perveen had been bothered by the lack of detail in the charge sheet she'd reviewed at the bail court.

"That must be among the papers filed for court. The

prosecutor's office is close enough to the High Court that I can get that information on Monday."

Jamshedji's commitment to participating in the case heartened her, and when she returned to the house, her nose wrinkled with pleasure at the smell of sausages frying. A clatter came from the dining room, and she looked in to see Gita arranging plates.

"Eating inside this morning?" she inquired. Most of their meals were taken outdoors in the high heat.

"Gulnaz's wish is to avoid insects." Gita looked sideways at her and said in a low voice, "You didn't answer last night when I knocked."

"Sorry—I didn't hear. Must have been asleep." As she spoke, Perveen wasn't sure if she even remembered the sound of a knock. She knew she'd wanted to avoid going downstairs, even if it meant missing dinner.

"Yes, you must be tired. And now—"

Perveen turned to see whom Gita was anxiously regarding: Gulnaz, who was wearing a rumpled nightgown, with Khushy nestled in her arms.

"Oh, good morning!" Perveen spoke brightly.

"Perhaps good for you, but not for me!" Gulnaz grumbled. "I was awake all night holding Khushy. She could not make up her mind to feed. It's as if she forgot everything she learned in the hospital!"

"John is making akoori for you today. Eggs are especially important for new mothers!" Jamshedji said to Gulnaz, coming in and stopping to tickle Khushy under the chin. The baby looked up at him and he cooed.

Gulnaz turned her attention toward Gita. "And where is Khushy's cradle? I can't eat with her on my lap."

Perveen gave Gita a sympathetic look as she stopped table-setting and went off to fetch the cradle.

"Why don't we have two cradles? One to keep upstairs in your quarters, and one that stays on our side?" Jamshedji said.

"If one could be found. But it's too hot for me to take Khushy shopping."

"For goodness' sake!" cut in Rustom, who'd just stepped in, fully dressed for work, his hair damp from bathing. "You are looking for reasons to be unhappy."

"Gulnaz, one of us will get to the furniture shop today," Camellia promised.

Perveen had supposed she might improve her image by offering to help, but she hadn't liked Gulnaz's tone with Gita, so she stayed silent.

Eventually, Gita came, breathing heavily as she lugged the cradle. Once Gulnaz laid down Khushy, breakfast was served. The scrambled egg dish known as akoori had been cooked with double the amount of ghee, and the sausages were crackling hot, but Perveen found herself less hungry than usual. She watched Gita silently walk around the table, pouring tea, which was then followed by rotlis. Usually, she and Gita spoke in the early-morning hours when she dropped a cup of tea and biscuits to every bedroom. Now Perveen realized how early Gita's days began—and how late they ended.

Camellia chatted about going to the ayah agency at eleven, and Jamshedji delivered a lecture on the life-giving benefits of eggs. Rustom didn't speak much, but he kept his eyes on Gulnaz. Khushy cried several times; the first two, Gulnaz picked her up, and the third time, she left her lying, saying it was important for her "to cry it out." This was a term she had heard the British mothers using, and it started a debate between her and Rustom on whose advice was correct: Indians, who believed in mothers' duty, or the nonchalant British.

The crying and arguing were too much. Perveen stood up, put her napkin on the table, and walked out. She'd thought of checking on Sunanda that morning, but the walk with Jamshedji had derailed the plan. Now seemed the perfect moment to visit.

It was a few steps across the lawn to the garden cottage, and she knocked at the closed door. No answer. It was hard to believe Sunanda was sleeping so late, so she cracked open the door to peek.

The silver cream jar was set on the charpoy, which still had the sheet folded in the same manner as the night before. Hadn't Sunanda slept there?

"Sunanda?" Perveen asked, approaching the door that led to the bathing quarters, but nobody answered.

Hearing a flurry of footsteps, she turned and saw Gita had followed her from the house.

"She's not here. That's what I wanted to tell you last night!" Gita said breathlessly.

Perveen stared at Gita. "When did she leave?"

"Yesterday, right after the doctor finished the examination. Sunanda told me she needed to meet you to go somewhere together. I said, but where? Perveen-memsahib might be in the office, maybe not. She seemed to think about it and then she said that she'd meet you and your father."

"I didn't have a plan with her." Perveen felt as if the rich eggs she'd just eaten were about to reverse course.

"So she lied," Gita said, her eyes narrowing. "After all we did. To think she would accept your mother's tender hospitality, John's meals, and the doctor's care—and then tell a story to me and run out the door."

"I'm sure we don't understand all of it." Perveen leaned against the cottage's rough lime wall, thinking about what all this meant. Sunanda was not only suffering from an infection, but grave mental stress. But why would she run off, when the Mistry house was so safe? Perveen picked up the expensive unused silver cream to put back into her legal case, just in case she were to find Sunanda in the city.

"I didn't want to let her stay here. But then you told me those things, and I felt sorry," Gita said, her voice heavy.

Something could have happened to Sunanda when she went out. The expedition was so tiring that she collapsed, or someone might have seized her.

The only thing Perveen didn't want to consider was that Sunanda had skipped bail and headed out of Bombay.

16

MISS ARBISON

*P*erveen didn't want to jump to the worst conclusion. Should she tell Jamshedji what Gita had told her? *Yes—but not right away.* She would rather check with Mustafa first about whether Sunanda had stopped in.

Saturday, the traffic into town was lighter, so the drive was swift. Her father was reading through papers for his corruption case; he handed her the newspaper. But looking at the print in the fast-moving car made her feel sickly. This was even more reason not to bring up the complicated problem of Sunanda's unknown whereabouts.

Upon reaching Mistry House, Jamshedji paused to chat with Mustafa, inquiring after his well-being. Perveen wished her father would go straight upstairs as usual so she could speak with Mustafa privately. Her heart skipped when Mustafa turned to her and said, "I have news for you. A lady caller."

"Oh, good!" Perveen felt her misgivings slip away. "Did you let her in?"

"No. She telephoned," Mustafa said. "I wasn't sure of your arrival time, so I told her two o'clock."

"A potential client who is a female?" Jamshedji gave Perveen an approving look. "Our advertising efforts in the Gujarati and Marathi ladies' magazines are paying off."

"But she's a foreigner!" Mustafa declared dramatically. "I know from the accent and her name. Miss Arbison."

Jamshedji scrutinized Perveen, who was no longer smiling.

"Aren't you pleased to have a female client? Your stated mission is to fight for the rights of women."

"I'm simply surprised," she bluffed. "I don't know who referred Miss Arbison."

As Jamshedji stepped briskly upstairs, Perveen lingered to speak with Mustafa. In a low voice, she asked whether a young woman had stopped by the day before.

"No. I am certain of it. Are you expecting someone else?" His voice was soft with concern.

"I was hoping to hear that Sunanda came by," Perveen whispered.

"Your new pro bono client, isn't she?" When Perveen nodded, he said, "If she does come, I'll let you know."

"And if I'm not here—please take her in. She's not very well and will need food, water, and rest until I can take her back with me."

Mustafa's brow furrowed at the words, and she realized she might be going too far with her directions. The man's job was to ensure the safety of Mistry House and the smooth scheduling of appointments and necessary errands. Opening up her legal case, Perveen handed him the letters she'd written to the barristers. "I appreciate all you're doing. Will you have time today to hail a courier to deliver these?"

"Without fail," he said, and the steadiness in his gaze was reassuring.

Routine was everything. Climbing the stairs, she told herself that it would be unwise to halt trial preparation out of fear the defendant was gone.

Jamshedji was reading and writing on his side of the partners desk, not even looking up as she sat down. Perveen pulled out her notebook and the legal journals she'd read the night before. She still needed to keep looking for a prior case in which tea was the alleged abortifacient. If no such case could be found, it was another reason for acquittal.

Therefore, tedious work with no answer was ultimately what she needed.

"Miss Arbison is here early," Mustafa said, interrupting her shortly before two. "And she's brought a cake."

Perveen guessed the woman had been drawn to the offerings in the window at Yazdani's Bakery across the street. It was a common experience for anyone who came to Bruce Street. "Did you offer to put her cake in the icebox?"

"She put it in my hands and told me to serve it during your meeting!" Mustafa said with a chuckle. "When I opened it, I saw it is very fancy, with whipped cream and some red fruits on top. You must see it, Perveen-bai."

"Perhaps her father owns a bakery," Perveen said, deciding that Miss Arbison might be using the cake to negotiate a better rate with Perveen.

"I believe I smelled chocolate." His eyes sparkled with excitement. "For this reason, I suggest coffee rather than tea."

"Enough talk of cakes!" Jamshedji grumbled. "This is a working office."

Perveen walked quietly downstairs and paused outside the half-opened door to get a look at the potential client. The lady was dressed in a fashionable sleeveless azure silk dress. Her calves were slim and not properly covered in stockings, but bare and tanned golden brown.

Miss Arbison was standing in profile; her face was shadowed by a blue cloche hat decorated with an oversized spray of white feathers. She was wiping her nose delicately with a handkerchief, and it wasn't until she tucked that away that Perveen could get a full look at the pretty young woman.

Perveen stepped into the room and spoke pleasantly. "Good afternoon. I would introduce myself, but I think you may already know me. Miss Arbison, has anyone ever said you could be the twin of the Begum of Varanpur?"

"I'm not a twin. I just use my maiden name when I'm being discreet!" Princess Cora answered with a sniff. "It's all right for you to call me Cora, now that the door's closed."

She might be thinking about divorce. Perveen held out a hand. "How are you healing after last Wednesday's mishap?"

Cora inspected her tanned right arm, turning it to show Perveen a red scratch. "Not much damage done, thanks to your help. I've had nastier gashes from shikar with my husband."

"Really!" Perveen said, motioning to her guest to take a seat. She had only heard of such hunting trips, which were mostly the business of royalty who owned miles of undeveloped land, where elephants, tigers, leopards, and other game freely roamed. "Don't tell me you suffered a tiger bite?"

Settling into the large tapestry armchair most foreigners preferred, Cora laughed. "No, from crouching inside the brush. You've got to hide in order to catch them."

"Your husband must think you a jolly good sport to go along for that kind of thing?" Perveen asked exploratively.

"No chance of that! I've hunted all manner of wildlife since I was a young girl. Out in the bush. No servants, no tents, nothing but a rifle and a sharp eye."

Perveen smiled at Cora's use of the phrase "young girl." Even with the fancy clothing, she didn't look a day over nineteen. "Then he's very fortunate to have found you."

Cora shrugged, her wide collar slipping to reveal a delicate lingerie strap. Pushing her collar back in place, she said, "Yes. He wants to teach me to sail, and he has the loveliest yacht. It's bigger than anything in the docks at the Royal Bombay Yacht Club, which is probably why they won't grant him membership!"

"They don't let any Indians in," Perveen said, seeing a look of disbelief cross over Cora's face.

"Not even the royal ones? What about women? White women, I mean?" She looked intently at Perveen.

"No. That club is closed to female membership, as far as I've heard."

"Did you know I brought a cake for you?"

The abrupt change startled Perveen. "Yes, Mustafa told me. How generous! Did you bake it?"

"I can barely boil an egg," Cora said with a giggle. "On the way in, I had the driver stop at the German bakery in Bandra for a Black Forest torte. So we'll have a taste of what I brought for Uma Bhatia's tea party. Another donation she can't give back."

Mustafa carried in a silver tray that held two perfectly upright triangles of cake set dead center on small Minton plates, with matching coffee cups and an elegantly chased silver coffeepot with matching cream pitcher and sugar bowl. Cora picked up a saucer and turned it over for examination. "Quite posh, aren't we?"

Perveen flushed, not used to such sarcasm about the household's possessions.

"Coffee, Miss Arbison?" Mustafa asked in his starchiest tone. He took great pride in the china.

"That's a nice change from the usual," Cora said approvingly, after Mustafa had served both of them and slipped out. "This isn't what I expected a law firm to be."

"What did you expect, then?"

"Lots of serious men hunched over desks," she said, rolling her shoulders forward and grimacing. "I didn't expect it to be so much like a home."

Perveen laughed in appreciation and slid her fork into the cake. First, she tasted a tangy, soft fruit—then a cloud of cream—and a light chocolate flavor, far less sweet than the desserts John prepared at her home. "It's delicious! You must tell me about the little red fruits atop the cream. Are they berries of some sort?"

"Cherries," she said, shaking her head. "They grow on trees, but these are the tinned sort. The German baker has found a way to import them—and Dutch cocoa as well. That's what is flavoring the cake. The baker said his recipe comes from people who live in the Black Forest."

"It seems remarkable to taste this German cake in India, brought to Mistry House through the kindness of an Australian." Perveen was laying the flattery on thickly, but she was pleased by the possibility of Cora as a client.

Cora brought the cup to her lips. After a long sip, she said, "The Bhatias never thanked me for the cake I brought to the party."

The cake again. Was the visit just a social call? Perveen reminded her, "We didn't get to it because of Ishan's accident."

"Right." Cora ran a finger under her nose, and then said, "But I don't believe that's half of it!"

Perveen felt herself being drawn in. "What do you mean?"

"Sir Dwarkanath's stone business has been losing ground." She grinned at the pun. "My husband says that Bhatia Stone wants assistance and had not yet found a bank loan. So the party was a kind of fundraiser for their own purposes. Once the money went into the box, there was no more need for us."

"What makes you think this?" Perveen asked, suspecting that Cora might be repeating a rumor.

Cora brushed the cloche's feathers from where they dipped over her face. Looking intently at Perveen, she murmured, "Everyone who didn't bring cash or jewelry was writing checks addressed to Lord Dwarkanath Bhatia. The nawab says a proper bank balance is important to show to lenders. Sir Dwarkanath would have had a full bank account after putting in all the checks. Uma had written to everyone about the cancellations and got the bank to issue them checks."

Perveen recalled how the letters and refunds were supposed to be sent to the women this week. So perhaps there was truth in what Cora said.

"What are you thinking?" The begum's eyes were shrewd as she studied Perveen.

"The kind of maneuver you are talking about—placing money for a charity in one's own account for different purposes—is illegal. The lawyer who established the charity would surely have warned against it."

"The ladies didn't have their own lawyer. Though they could have got one because we once had a meeting at a social club that was full of lawyers."

"It must have been the Ripon Club," Perveen said, recalling what Gulnaz had mentioned.

"Right. There's going to be a ball next weekend. I'm discussing with the nawab about whether he should stay in town longer so we can go. And did you know that he was willing to donate stone for the project?"

"No, I didn't know that. This is the first I'm hearing of it."

"Yes, the ladies would rather not be upstaged by me." Cora's green eyes narrowed. "Varanpur rock is the most gorgeous green. Imagine a stunning green stone hospital, something as handsome as the college and court buildings in the city. But in that crowded, shabby neighborhood."

"That's quite generous." Perveen's estimation of the Nawab of Varanpur was rising.

"I asked my husband, and he said that if he gives it, I'll officially become the most expensive wife. Even though at nineteen, I am the youngest."

"How many wives are there?" Perveen asked.

"Three preceded me—and I won't let him get a fifth! He promised not to," she added, sounding defensive. "He said he had to have all the earlier marriages because of family demands."

"Did you know about his wives when you met him in Australia?" Perveen asked.

Cora turned her face away, her cloche's feather falling so her expression was masked. When she spoke, her voice was controlled. "I only found out about them when he brought me to Varanpur. I was angry but what could I do? I'd never dreamed

I'd be able to get out of Australia, let alone married to a prince. And he told me I was so young that I needed them to help guide me to be a proper begum."

Perveen thought the nawab clearly had misjudged his young wife's spirit. Gently, she offered, "It must be very difficult to enter into a household where a man already has spouses."

"Hard is not the word for it. I would say—it's hell!" Cora took off her hat to push back her damp auburn hair. "The wives and some others at the place think I'm selfish to live apart, but it's a matter of saving my own life."

Perveen swallowed, trying to suppress an instinctive rebuttal. "What makes you think this?"

"I was miserable on the sea voyage. At first, I thought it was just seasickness. It turned out I was carrying a baby." Cora looked seriously at her. "But I lost the pregnancy—miscarried—within the first three weeks at the palace. I recovered, but I kept getting stomach sickness. Everyone said it was because I couldn't eat Indian food."

"Do you think you have the capability to be pregnant again?" Perveen smiled encouragingly, but she wondered whether Cora would find happiness as a mother. Gulnaz's reaction had made her rethink everything.

"At the European Hospital, Dr. Flynn tested my blood. He said I was poisoned by lead, which can cause illness, miscarriage, and death. I come to him every month to check the level. If you don't believe me, speak to him!" Her voice had risen, as if she expected dismissal.

Perveen thought the details she'd given were complex enough to be authentic. "Have you told your husband?"

"Oh, yes! But he says the tests must be wrong." Cora slumped back in her chair and regarded Perveen sadly. "I think he doesn't trust the European Hospital because he can't be treated there."

"That's rotten," Perveen said with feeling. "Does this make you feel upset with your husband?"

"Not really. He did buy the villa for us to be away from his other wives. That should keep me safe. Really, it's a storybook romance. If it only wasn't for the wives, and the damned government."

"Bombay Presidency government?" Perveen asked.

"That's right. A councilor told my husband that he created an unstable future for Varanpur by marrying me! But how could that be, when he already has four sons in line to inherit the throne? It's ridiculous."

Perveen remembered something she'd learned whilst working with Colin on a special investigation in Satapur. "The trouble is that each princely state has a relationship with a government official. It's expected that the government knows about a royal's intentions and either approves or disapproves."

"What rot!" Cora said passionately. "Nobody can control Manny."

"Manny?" Perveen raised her eyebrows.

"His first name is Mansoor, so that's what I call him. So do his very best friends," Cora said with a soft smile. "When we are alone, we are informal."

Perveen thought the government's reticence surrounding Cora and Mansoor's union was a strong example of its desire to prohibit interracial marriage. "The two of you undertook a daring adventure in the name of love. And what a long way you've come from Australia—and at a young age."

"Yes. Like I was saying, I've never hidden where I come from. And I'll tell you that I wanted to be away from my father and brothers—they've been in and out of the boot for as long as I can remember. I had to care for myself. My uncle's friend said I was too pretty to waste in the outback and gave me a job singing and dancing at his club in Perth."

"I admire all working women," Perveen said, realizing that Cora was desperate for someone to understand her. "And how old were you when you started at the club?"

"Seventeen. I'd just turned eighteen when the nawab came in one night. Because of my particular costume and hairstyle that night, he mistook me for a film star. It was hilarious because the newspapers were always calling him the Sheikh."

Perveen ventured, "Oh! Do you mean he resembles the Italian actor in that film . . . Rudolph Valentino?"

"Righto!" Cora chuckled. "And he's every bit as dashing as the Sheikh, I tell him that all the time. Though he really doesn't need so many wives." Cora ate a bite of cake with relish and then said, "I heard Sunanda's not staying at the Bhatias' place anymore. Do you know where she's gone?"

"Sunanda?" Perveen repeated, feeling surprised to hear Cora using her client's name. It seemed out of context.

"Yes, the nanny who saved Ishan Bhatia. To think she did such a great thing and then lost her job. Right? Is that what happened?"

"I agree that she was brave. I can't say—I mean, I don't know—much more."

"Oh, you must be her lawyer, then." Cora's eyes seemed to brighten. "Are you suing the Bhatias?"

Perveen bit her lip, wishing that she'd responded to Cora in a way that would have halted the conversation. Yet the turn in topic showed that the princess had compassion for Sunanda and might be willing to pay the barrister's fee.

"I think that's a brilliant idea!" Cora declared, as if Perveen had answered in the affirmative. "I actually came to you because I want to sue the Bhatias for mismanagement of the hospital project."

Perveen felt knocked sideways. "But—on what grounds?"

"You said yourself they were breaking the law with that financial funny business." As if noting Perveen's disapproving expression, Cora added, "Don't worry about the cost. Manny wants me to be happy doing something I enjoy. And I want to set up the Princess Cora Hospital for Women."

Perveen struggled for the right words. "How wonderful that you wish to save the hospital project. But you have no case to bring to court against the Bhatias. If you want to build the hospital, invite the other ladies into conversation. And you have the advantage of royal connections—you can reach out to other princesses, Muslim and Hindu, for contributions."

"I don't have royal Indian friends," Cora shot back. "All the princesses I've met live in purdah. But if I founded a hospital, the Europeans in Bombay would have to receive me. They'd respect me just like they respected Uma. And who is she now? Just the mistress of Bhatia House; nothing more."

Perveen understood Cora's hardscrabble background and the pain she felt at social exclusion. But using the hospital for social advancement was a folly. Quietly, she said, "Doing voluntary work can bring about friendships and other social benefits—but we must keep our eyes on the cause itself."

"If your eyes are on the cause, why won't you take this as a lawsuit? Join me in suing them!" Cora settled more deeply into her chair.

"You've already explained that Uma tried to return your donation. The Bhatia family has not wronged you in any way." Perveen stood, hoping Cora would follow her lead.

"But you said"—Cora jabbed her emerald-heavy index finger in the air—"you said the money wasn't properly collected for a charity. That could be exposed in a lawsuit. Then the judge would let me take everything over."

"You don't need a judge's permission to work on fundraising for a hospital." Perveen moved closer to the door. "Princess Cora, quite honestly, my plate is full. I've got a complicated pro bono case with discovery in just a few weeks."

"Ha! You sound like you're the Bhatias' lawyer trying to protect them—or are you representing Sunanda for another reason?"

Perveen suppressed her desire to push the irritating young

woman out of the room. She spoke calmly. "To return to your original query about seeking representation, I can certainly refer you to another solicitor. I would suggest Bradbury and Kulkarni, who have an office in Elphinstone Circle—"

"Don't you bother telling me what to do." Cora jumped up so quickly that her clutch bag toppled off her lap. "Now I understand that I'm truly alone in this country."

Perveen leaned down to retrieve the silken bag, which was smaller than the other bag the dogs had torn. This one also had the feeling of a book inside it; Perveen wondered if it was the same romance. "I'm sorry I can't help more."

"I don't believe you." Cora laid a hand atop her shapely bosom and looked angrily at Perveen. "My heart is beating too fast again. It must be the mercury."

Perveen struggled not to roll her eyes. "Shall I have my driver take you to the European Hospital?"

"No! I've got my own car." Cora gave her a withering glare and flounced out.

17

BREAKING NEWS

*P*erveen felt shaken by the dramatic ending to the meeting, although she was proud of herself for resisting Cora's entreaties for representation.

She sat down, penning a few more notes on the conversation in case Cora had revealed something that might be useful later. It seemed strange that she'd asked so many questions about the Bhatias and Sunanda. Perveen thought the alleged poisoning by her sisters-in-law and her unfair legal treatment by the government would have been her chief concerns. But Cora was immature.

Because of the large slice of cake, Perveen had no appetite for the usual 2:30 P.M. lunch. When she went into the dining room to tell Mustafa, she saw he was already clearing away the dishes from her unoccupied place, while Jamshedji was finishing a cup of tea.

"I'm sorry I didn't let you know I couldn't eat lunch," she apologized to both of them.

"Not to worry. Arman has taken the letters to the barristers' homes," Mustafa said.

"Let's make it an early day and go home as soon as he returns," Jamshedji said. "The heat could not be any worse."

Hot as it was, Perveen had wanted to get to Kalbadevi to look for Sunanda. But Saturday was traditionally a shorter workday—not only for her and her father, but for Arman.

Perveen used the next ten minutes to give a summary to her father about Begum Cora, and why Perveen hadn't wanted to take her on as a client. At the end, Jamshedji shook his head. "I wish you hadn't closed the door so hard on things. One never knows what legal bounty a controversial bride could bring."

Perveen considered his words. "If you're thinking about divorce, it's unlikely. She's besotted with him."

"A known philanderer," Jamshedji said dismissively. "I would not take a bet on that marriage surviving."

When Arman returned from his errand a half hour later, he was soaked with sweat. He gulped the large tumbler of water Mustafa gave him and nodded with relief when Jamshedji said the workday was done.

Arman drove as fast as he could out of the city, and as they passed men pulling handcarts stacked with bolts of cloth, Perveen thought of Sunanda's brother, Govind Chavda, who hauled stones. Very likely he was working today. Had Sunanda gone to him, and perhaps not been turned away? She hoped the Chavda family relationship could be restored, just as she wished things would improve between Gulnaz and herself.

As they pulled up to the Mistrys' wide bungalow, the sound of sobbing cut the air.

Jamshedji turned to Perveen, his face alarmed. "Someone must be hurt!"

"Again?" Perveen said, rolling her eyes.

Arman jumped out of the car and tilted his head toward the house, waiting a few seconds before opening the passenger door. "The trouble is on Rustom-sahib's side. Mother or baby; I can't tell."

"Go to them," Jamshedji said, nudging Perveen out of the car. "I'll take your legal case inside."

Perveen didn't answer; she was fully annoyed that her father thought it her job to manage the situation. All because she and Gulnaz had once been friends—

Perveen swallowed hard, regretting her thought. Was she now as terrible a sister-in-law as she was an aunty?

The front door was locked, so she went around the side of the house, past the thick hedges of hibiscus, to the veranda.

"Hello!" she called out cautiously as she opened the French doors to Gulnaz and Rustom's dining room.

Gita rushed into the room holding the nappy bucket. "Good thing you've come. Gulnaz is very upset."

"Why? Is Khushy ailing again?" Perveen stepped back, trying not to breathe in the foul scent.

Gita whispered, "Gulnaz knows about Sunanda!"

"What?" Perveen said loudly, because it made no sense to hide conversation if the discovery was made. "How did she learn about her?"

"It happened like this." Gita looked behind her, as if fearful of an observer. "John was preparing a tiffin for Sunanda's lunch, and I had to tell him it wasn't needed. Gulnaz was just outside the door with Khushy. So she asked us whether the Sunanda we spoke of was the Bhatia family's ayah."

At least Gita didn't know all the facts about Sunanda—namely, that she had been charged with a crime. Slowly, Perveen said, "But why would Gulnaz be crying so hard about Sunanda? They didn't meet, did they?"

"I don't think so. But Gulnaz thinks everyone was keeping secrets from her." Gita winced as she spoke.

"I suppose I'd feel the same way. I'll apologize to her." Perveen forced herself to smile reassuringly at Gita, who had rushed outside with the bucket of nappies.

Perveen counted to three, calming herself, and then climbed the stairs.

Through the half-open door to the master bedroom, she spotted Gulnaz in a rocking chair, her face in her hands as she wept. The bedroom had a nauseating odor of roses and urine that caused Perveen to stop inhaling. She turned on the ceiling fan, and as a breeze started, the odor faded slightly. It hit her then that Gulnaz wasn't holding Khushy; the baby was nowhere in sight. Nervously, Perveen asked, "Does Mamma have Khushy?"

Gulnaz raised her tear-stained face. "No, she's gone out to a charity meeting. And why do you care? You want me to fail!"

"Where's Khushy?" Perveen repeated, because she didn't understand Gulnaz's point, and her anxiety was rising. Shouldn't the baby be crying like she usually did?

"In the nursery. She wouldn't feed, and I was hurting, so I laid her down to sleep."

Gulnaz didn't follow Perveen to the nursery, where the smells were even worse. Feeling a surge of fear, Perveen stepped close to the crib. She was relieved to see Khushy's nose flaring as she breathed evenly—but she smelled of excrement.

"She's still asleep," Perveen said, returning to the bedroom and opening the curtains so air could flow more freely. "But when she wakes, she needs her nappy changed."

"Are you ordering me?" Gulnaz tilted her head, as if to better examine her. "That's quite outrageous."

"I'm not ordering you to do anything," Perveen said evenly. "I'm just informing you, in case she awakens crying."

Gulnaz rocked sharply in the chair. "And why didn't you inform me that you had the best ayah in Bombay sitting in the garden cottage? Sitting idle, instead of helping me when I needed it? And now she's gone!"

Perveen struggled for a satisfactory response. "I didn't tell you because I didn't want to cause trouble for your relationship with Lakshmi, and—"

Gulnaz interrupted, "No. You didn't tell me because you don't believe mothers should even have ayahs to help them."

Weakly, Perveen said, "I used the wrong words. Now that Khushy's here, I think differently—"

"You're lying!" Gulnaz shook a finger in the manner of a

school prefect admonishing her junior. "Gita admitted that Sunanda had offered several times to help with Khushy. Yet you said Sunanda had to stay away."

"She couldn't work!" Perveen exclaimed, feeling righteous. "She's got an infected wound—that's the reason Dr. Penkar came. To diagnose her and prescribe a medication!"

"And I'm not sick?" Gulnaz muttered, curling her legs up into the rocking chair. "I cannot sleep, and I can hardly remember my thoughts. Yet you didn't send me an ayah to help."

"Well, she's gone now!" Perveen said, turning away from Gulnaz. "There's no more point in arguing."

"She left because she needed work!" Gulnaz's voice rose. "Gita said that Sunanda was desperate to be earning. She had no home anymore with her brother. This was the perfect place for her!"

Perveen cursed herself for the details she'd given Gita. "I am truly sorry you are in a state about this, Gulnaz. But it's illogical for you to be upset about someone whom you never met."

"Sunanda saved Ishan Bhatia's life. She is the rare person who puts another life before her own." Gulnaz wiped a tear from her eye. "She would have been perfect for me."

"I will try to find her," Perveen protested.

"As you should! Things won't be right until you bring her back."

Khushy started crying, and Gulnaz's head jerked toward the nursery. Rising to her feet, she muttered, "I'm going to her. But will you tell Gita to come back? At least she tries to help!"

Perveen knew she should have volunteered to assist, but she was afraid of Gulnaz's reaction after the last time she'd touched Khushy. So, she watched her sister-in-law plod mechanically to the nursery, and then she slipped downstairs, relieved to flee the noxious smells and emotions.

As she emerged into the late-afternoon heat, the sound of the Victrola playing in the parlor told her she'd be unable to go inside without passing her father. He played Brahms if he felt a need for extra calm, a sign that he would be anxious to hear what she had to say. And this time, she couldn't reassure him.

Perveen reminded herself that her priority was to find Sunanda before giving premature news. And as she saw the neighborhood's newspaper boy skipping from house to house with a stack of papers under his arm, she decided to question him.

"Arre, Arjun!" she called, and he stopped.

Perveen started by asking if he'd noticed an unfamiliar young woman walking by herself in the neighborhood the previous day. She described Sunanda's stature and face, adding that she wore her hair in a braid and had been last seen dressed in a blue-and-red checked sari.

Arjun shook his head before she'd finished speaking. "I never look at ladies! Why are you asking?"

"Sunanda is an ayah who was staying with Gita in the garden cottage," Perveen explained. "We all are wondering if she got lost yesterday. Or—if something bad happened."

"If I see someone like that, I'll tell you." Handing her a newspaper, he said, "The *Samachar* came late today."

"Thank you," Perveen said.

Arjun hurried off, as if making up for the lost time the minute of conversation had caused him. Perveen was unfolding the paper when she was interrupted by the roar of a familiar motor. As Arman parked the Daimler, she waved one hand at Camellia and Rustom in the car's back seat.

Arman opened the door, and Camellia emerged first. But Rustom came quickly behind her, calling out, "Do you have today's paper?"

"Yes, but . . ." Perveen was surprised that her brother wanted to read the newspaper. He only seemed to care if his picture was in it. "It's better for you to first speak with Gulnaz. She's feeling upset."

"Why?" Camellia's voice had the slightest hint of exasperation.

"Is Gulnaz still fretting about caring for Khushy by herself? She made it clear she didn't think I should go to my meeting, but I really had to do it."

"Actually, it's more than fretting. She's—" Perveen stopped speaking because Rustom had grabbed the paper out of her hands. "Why so rude, Rustom?"

"There! It's not a rumor!" Rustom shouted, turning his head toward Jamshedji, who had just emerged from the house.

"What rumor?" Jamshedji said, coming up to him. "And why are all of you clustered outside? Do you think it will bring the monsoon?"

"It's true about Lord Dwarkanath Bhatia!" Rustom said, facing his father. "He's gone. Now I wish I talked to him last week."

Camellia looked inquiringly at her son. "Why do his activities matter?"

But the name had sent a shiver through Perveen, and she ripped the newspaper out of Rustom's hand, ignoring his curses. On the front page, she saw a small photograph of an unsmiling Sir Dwarkanath wearing an elaborately wrapped pugree twice the size of his head. The banner headline in Gujarati proclaimed: "Gujarat's Own Emperor of Stone Is Dead."

Without pausing, Perveen read the rest of the article.

At sixty years, Lord Dwarkanath Bhatia, one of Bombay's foremost citizens, has passed. The noted business leader was afflicted with stomach pains for several days. He was admitted to Sir J. J. Hospital early today and was pronounced dead at 11 A.M. of cause yet to be determined. What is certain is that the city's business community has lost a man who had gone from rags to riches, beginning as a small merchant in Kalbadevi and growing into one of India's largest stone contractors. His predominant accomplishment was receiving an OBE knighthood awarded by

King George in 1916. Lord Bhatia has been a past president of the Bombay Merchants Association, and the Gujarati Club. His highest civic achievement was being amongst the first Indians appointed to the Legislative Society. He was also the chief donor for a forthcoming maternity hospital in Kalbadevi."

As Perveen pondered the last line, she recalled Uma Bhatia saying her father-in-law had directed her not to write about the cancelled hospital plan until Monday. This was still two days hence. This might mean that no one outside of Bhatia House knew about the cancellation, excepting the Nawab and Begum of Varanpur, Dr. Miriam Penkar, and Jamshedji and herself.

"Perhaps we should talk about this," Jamshedji said, looking meaningfully at Perveen. "In my study."

She would tell him her thoughts about the Bhatias. And along with that, she'd explain about Sunanda.

18

A MISSING PERSON

"As I said yesterday, it was a risk to take personal responsi-bility for a client's bail and housing."

Jamshedji's words were as heavy as the heat in the study. The two of them were occupying the same positions, in the same room, as they had the night before. The difference was that Perveen had once been filled with confidence she was doing the right thing. Now her father was pointing out her error, and she couldn't stand it. "Maybe she's run; but it could be that some-thing else happened. Perhaps there was an urgent reason she had to come to the office rather than wait for my return."

"Such as?"

Perveen leaned forward from her place on the settee. "Dr. Penkar said Sunanda became emotional during the medical examination yesterday. Perhaps she was going to admit to me having a lover. Or—an oppressor," she added, thinking of the late Sir Dwarkanath. "With Sir Dwarkanath deceased, how might this affect Sunanda's case?"

"There is no case for you without your client!" Jamshedji exploded. "Perveen, you have a habit of falling into the hands of unscrupulous people. Sunanda is doubtless a victim of injus-tice, but she has acted in a manner that imperils your status as a solicitor!"

"Nothing's happened in the courts yet," Perveen said, speaking in a deliberately calm manner. "We have a few weeks yet before the trial."

Her father glowered at her. "It was outrageous for you to

spend today writing to barristers with the knowledge that she'd absconded."

"I didn't know that she was missing until this morning," Perveen protested. "It made complete sense to proceed as usual. Now, I understand you might not wish me to use billable hours during the workweek for her case. But I would be grateful if you'd allow me to use Sundays and any evenings to look for her." She looked imploringly at Jamshedji. "I have an obligation to represent her best interests."

Jamshedji stared at her, and then shrugged. "I won't tell you how to use your free time. But eventually, you'll have to deliver the news to the prosecutor about your missing client. And you know what that means."

"The police will go after her," Perveen said, feeling ill.

That night, Perveen tossed in bed, distracted by Khushy's crying and her worries about Sunanda. This was her second night away. Was she still alive? Why hadn't her father thought of the same dreadful possibilities that Perveen had?

Perveen finally slept, and awoke late, with sun streaming through the muslin curtains.

It was nine o'clock on a Sunday morning. The traditional day for family time. Perveen washed and dressed in a lightweight blue cotton sari. The tea that Gita had left on her bedside table had gone cold, so she went downstairs into the kitchen, where John made her a fresh cup while he stirred a pot of keema.

"Breakfast in half an hour," he told her. "Let's see if Gulnaz-bai is well enough to come."

"I heard that Gulnaz was eavesdropping yesterday when Gita told you about Sunanda leaving," Perveen said, spooning sugar into her tea.

John dropped his cooking spoon, swore under his breath, and put it in the basin. "Yes. I'm very sorry about how it affected Gulnaz-memsahib."

"It's all right. I was wondering, did you ever speak to Sunanda yourself?" Perveen hoped he might know something that could lead to finding her.

"No. Gita took all the meals to her. She said that Sunanda was especially fearful of men—and so I stayed here." John's voice was grave.

"Thank you," Perveen said and then carried a cup of tea outside for Gita. Sunday was supposed to be the maid's free day, but she stood ironing at the board set up in the garden, a tight expression on her face. When Perveen offered her the tea, she accepted it with a grunt of thanks.

"Working hard today as well? I'm sorry," Perveen said, glancing at a line of wet diapers drying on the clothesline.

Gita shrugged. "If I don't wash the nappies today it will be all the worse on Monday."

"I hear from John that Sunanda told you about some troubles with men," Perveen said. "Did she mention anyone?"

Gita shook her head. "I tried to talk to her about how she got into her situation, but she wouldn't answer. Though she was very upset the night she stayed here. She had a bad dream."

"Did she tell you what it was about?"

"No. But it sounded like she called a man's name."

Perveen was eager to know more. "That could be very important. Do you remember it?"

"She said 'brother.'"

"Brother?" A chill ran through Perveen, despite the heat. "Did she say the name Govind?"

"No."

What if Govind had violated his sister? If something terrible was going on, Amla might blame Sunanda, rather than her husband. But would Sunanda feel drawn to return to Kalbadevi? Perveen realized there might be signs that Sunanda intended to leave. "Gita, are any of Sunanda's personal items gone?"

"She went out with a shopping bag I gave to her, but not anything she owned," Gita answered readily. "She didn't take anything of mine. What does your mother say? Is everything in place in the house?"

Perveen was momentarily struck dumb. She hadn't even thought Sunanda would steal from the house, but she understood Gita's suspicion. "I haven't heard about anything."

"Your mother should look closely. And Gulnaz, too."

Perveen had no intention of creating new hysteria, but she knew some sort of conversation was needed with Gulnaz. She'd already caught sight of her sister-in-law and Khushy on the veranda, nestled together in a rattan chair.

Gulnaz's eyes had been closed but fluttered open as Perveen arrived.

"Good morning," Perveen said. "I thought you didn't like being outside."

"I don't." Gulnaz yawned. "I only came because the cool air settles Khushy better. Have you found Sunanda?"

"Not yet." Perveen should have expected her sister-in-law would linger on the topic that had consumed her the previous afternoon. "Gulnaz, can we talk about what's happening between us? I feel like it isn't the same."

"It can't be the same." Shifting the baby slightly, Gulnaz said, "Do you think Sunanda was kidnapped or killed?"

Perveen had had the same thought—but looking at the dark circles under Gulnaz's eyes, she didn't want to burden her further. "Anything could happen, but as Pappa says, if worries carry us away, we can't be present in life."

"Your family and its sayings!" Gulnaz grumbled. "Don't give me another excuse. You hid the woman—and now you're hiding the truth."

Taking a deep breath, Perveen said, "It's because she is—or was—my client."

"But your legal work is contracts." Gulnaz's eyes bored into hers. "What kind of contract did she need? Just tell me that."

Perveen thought about the facts as they were laid out in the prosecutor's charging document. To share this would not be a violation.

"Sunanda was accused of garbhapaat."

Gulnaz gaped at her. "But that happened to me. It's nobody's fault!"

Perveen realized her sister-in-law was referring to her own experience with miscarriages. "The trouble is that if the court believes a woman tried to end a pregnancy, that is a criminal charge."

Gulnaz whispered, "Men can do as they wish. What if someone jailed me?"

"I don't think it would happen to you. Women in families like ours are above suspicion."

"It makes sense for Sunanda to run away. She was afraid about the trial. I would also be."

"So, you really think she fled?" Perveen hoped Gulnaz wasn't right—but this was what her father believed, too.

Gulnaz's eyes were shining with tears. "I longed for children. It's not until you face the child that you understand whether you are mother material or not."

"Oh, darling!" Perveen reached out impulsively to touch her hand. "You are a good mother. You are simply tired out and needing help."

"Why should all women be forced to bear children? So many of the babies will die. The world is not safe from cradle to grave," Gulnaz said, carefully pulling Khushy out from under the sari, where she'd been nursing.

Perveen shivered hearing the bleakness in her sister-in-law's tone. She also feared she had said too much. "You are very safe here, Gulnaz. And so is Khushy."

Shaking her head, Gulnaz laid Khushy down into the

cradle. "Shhh. We must talk very quietly now that she's fallen asleep."

Perveen sat quietly, watching Gulnaz move the cradle slowly with her bare foot. Gulnaz whispered, "If only Khushy could stay here."

"In the cradle? Why is that?" Perveen whispered, feeling a portent of some unknown calamity.

"She's away from my heart beating too fast, and my sweating." Smoothing back a damp strand of hair, Gulnaz croaked, "It's miserable! When will the rains come?"

"A week or so, the same as ever. Shall I bring you some water?" Glancing at the full cup on the cast-iron table, Perveen said, "You didn't drink any of your morning tea."

"Rustom brought it to me."

"Did he go back to bed?" Perveen asked, thinking that her brother had also had a restless night.

"No. He went around eight o'clock this morning to visit Bhatia House."

"Oh." Perveen remembered her brother's extreme reaction to the news of the death. "Is it because Rustom is friends with Parvesh?"

"No. I think it's because of business. That's the only thing Rustom loves." Gulnaz continued the slow rocking of the cradle. "I wonder if any family members were with Sir Dwarkanath, or if he died alone in hospital."

Perveen was surprised by Gulnaz's particular interest. "I imagine that Parvesh would have been there with him—otherwise, how would he get to hospital?"

"There's a younger son, too. Somnath Bhatia stays in Lonavala, near the quarry, but Mangala says she won't live so far from society," Gulnaz said. "Now that Sir Dwarkanath is gone, perhaps Parvesh and Uma will be able to get rid of Mangala and her children."

"Oh?" Perveen glanced at Gulnaz, whose expression had changed from tearful to malicious.

"Mangala let everyone know she was the favorite daughter-in-law. You see, she has three sons, while Uma only has one. In fact," Gulnaz said, running a tongue over her dry lips, "if Ishan had burned to death at the tea party, Mangala's eldest boy would inherit Bhatia Stone."

"What a gruesome thing to say." Perveen wondered if Gulnaz was hinting that the fire was a setup. Gulnaz's expression was tight, as if she resented Perveen's reprimand. It was an uncomfortable moment that only ended when Gita appeared.

"Breakfast's ready. Are you all coming?" Gita asked, looking at the cradle with obvious misgiving.

"I can help carry the cradle," Perveen offered, aware of how many hours the maid had been working. So she took one end, and Gita the other, and Khushy was transferred without waking up.

Gulnaz didn't thank them, but Perveen still felt a sense of accomplishment as she sat down to the table on her father's right side. John had made a fine Sunday breakfast—not just the savory keema curry and rotli, but eggs poached on drumstick flowers, prawn ghee roast, and sweet ravo pudding with raisins. Camellia took pains to make sure Gulnaz had proper servings of everything, saying that she'd lost too much weight.

Jamshedji said that the morning edition included another article about Sir Dwarkanath's death, although the cause was still unknown pending autopsy results.

"That's unusual," Perveen commented. "Because he's in hospital, a doctor should be able to easily state cause of death. There shouldn't be a need for forensic examination."

"And no reason to spread rumors," Jamshedji said, annoying Perveen, because he'd been the one to bring up the gentleman's death.

"Tests are often done looking for poisons." Gulnaz leaned forward, her elbows on the table. "When Rustom comes back, he'll tell us if that's it."

"The tests look for everything," Jamshedji said. "In any case, it's grievous for the family to have extra waiting time before the funeral and cremation."

Gulnaz's eyes moved in Perveen's direction. "Once the mourning period is finished, I think the hospital project will go forward again."

"Are you saying that the hospital project was stalled?" Camellia looked curiously at Gulnaz. "That is your favorite charity, isn't it?"

Gulnaz nodded, but didn't explain, so Perveen summarized the situation. At the end, Camellia said, "Well, it seems to me that the family's in a difficult position. If Parvesh and Uma reverse the father's pronouncement, that could be seen as disrespect."

Gulnaz scowled. "But Hindus often make a charitable contribution on their deathbed. Maybe Lord Dwarkanath changed his mind."

"If he was well enough to speak," Perveen said. "There's a lot to—"

"Oh, you've started breakfast without me! Terrible state of affairs, isn't it?"

Rustom's sharp voice interrupted her midsentence. She hadn't heard him entering the dining room, but now she watched him slide into the empty seat next to Gulnaz.

"Sorry, we didn't know when you would return from Ghatkopar," Camellia apologized.

"No matter, there are plenty of eggs left for you. And look, little Khushy is here, sleeping nicely in her cradle. Her dreams will be fragranced with ginger and cardamom," Jamshedji joked.

As Rustom reached down from his chair to stroke his daughter's head, her eyelids fluttered and she let out an unhappy cry.

"Welcome home indeed." Rustom took his hand away and picked up his fork. "From one home of misery to another."

"Are the Bhatia family very distressed?" Perveen asked, ignoring the insult to their own family, although it annoyed her.

"They were putting on a very calm front, remembering good things about Sir Dwarkanath. So many people were chatting about this and that. Dozens of people had come to pay their condolences."

"Who?" Jamshedji asked, his eyebrows raised.

"Many Legislative Council members, other construction magnates, and, of course, so many of their neighbors in Ghatkopar. Everyone speaking Gujarati. I even saw some Britishers coming into the house as I was leaving, Malcolm Stowe amongst them."

"Did you speak with Uma?" Gulnaz asked.

"Of course not!" Rustom answered crossly. "My business relationship is with your friend's husband. It was important to give condolence to Parvesh and get a sense of his plans for Bhatia Stone."

Gulnaz's expression tightened. "That's a shame. She would know about the dying wish!"

"What do you mean by that, dear?" Camellia was speaking in the soft voice that had now become customary for her with Gulnaz.

"Uma would be aware of what Sir Dwarkanath wished as a last gesture of charity. As I was saying, he probably reversed his decision about the hospital."

"We have no idea of what is happening in that family," Jamshedji said curtly. "Gulnaz, will you pass the salt?"

Gulnaz thrust the salt cellar across the table so rapidly that salt flew through the air. "So you're silencing me from speaking my opinions. It is like my mummy said—watch out after the baby comes home."

Perveen shot a warning look at her parents and asked, "Please tell us what you mean."

"You don't like me anymore. Everyone's watching me and

scolding." Gulnaz turned her head to glare directly at Rustom. "Even you—such a sorry excuse for a father!"

"I won't stand for this," Rustom said, shoving his chair away from the table. "You are as witchy by day as you are at night."

"So you think I'm not doing my duty? Go ahead, say it to everyone. Tell them what you were shouting about last night."

Camellia began, "Please, children. Let's not fight at the table—"

Rustom slapped a hand on the table. "No, I've had enough. I said to my wife that some women are better at being motherly than others. Forty days they spent at the lying-in hospital! I thought it was because she was learning from the nurses. It seems our Gulnaz is as terrible at learning this as everything else when she was at school with Perveen!"

"Out of line!" Jamshedji thundered. "I will not have such words at the table. You will apologize to your wife."

Rustom muttered something unintelligible, but he did not sit down. Instead, he stood with arms crossed, looking challengingly at Gulnaz. She seemed to have shriveled into her seat, her head dropped, as if ashamed to look at any of them. Perveen went to the chair next to her, but Gulnaz edged away. Rustom's words must have delivered the false impression that Perveen had mocked her.

"Gulnaz, Rustom doesn't mean any of what he said. You are both so tired," Camellia said. "We must get the help you need. I will ring the agency on Monday morning."

Gulnaz's voice was barely audible. "You mustn't put words in his mouth he doesn't believe. And I don't want a stranger taking care of Khushy. It's not safe."

"Then let Gita help as she can," Rustom shot back. "Why are you even downstairs? The baby will be brought to you when you are needed."

Perveen couldn't restrain her fury any longer. "Does this mean you're volunteering to carry Khushy up when she wakens? That would be a very fatherly act," Perveen said sarcastically.

"Don't meddle in our marriage!" Rustom snapped. "We all know Gulnaz is a failing mother. She needs to see a doctor."

"What?" Gulnaz's fork clattered to the table. Her voice was no longer quiet, but now shook with rage. "Is that the real reason that Miriam Penkar came, Perveen? Because you wanted her to treat me?"

Khushy started to cry, small noises that quickly escalated, causing Rustom to clap his hands over his ears.

Camellia reached into the cradle and lifted the baby into her lap. Over the crying, she said, "I was the one who asked the doctor to examine Khushy. And she was helpful, wasn't she? Please forgive Rustom. He is tired, and that's why he's spouting such foolishness."

"Not as tired as I am," Gulnaz said pointedly. "It sickens me to hear you make excuses for your son. Because he is your *true* family."

"You are a daughter to me, Gulnaz. Don't say such things," Jamshedji implored.

"Very well, Mr. Mistry! I won't say anything to you anymore, ever again." Gulnaz's furious glance swept the table. She stood up, her napkin falling to the floor. She looked at Khushy, now at full throttle crying in the cradle. Shaking her head, she walked out.

19

A PERSON OF INTEREST

And just like that, Gulnaz was gone.

After the front door slammed, Perveen felt as if shame had physically locked her in place. She glanced at Rustom, whose face was still red with anger.

"It's a tempest in a teapot!" Camellia's voice, though, sounded uncertain. She bent to pick up Khushy, and after a few minutes, the baby quieted.

"Give Gulnaz time to restore herself," Jamshedji told Rustom. "And then, you must apologize."

Perveen could understand Gulnaz's needing distance from Rustom. He'd been utterly loathsome to his wife in the manner Perveen remembered from their youth. And the worst part was he'd tried to make Perveen seem allied in his despicable behavior. Perhaps Perveen had boasted once about beating out everyone, including Gulnaz, on a geography test. But Gulnaz was better at French! Didn't Rustom remember that?

Pondering the murky depths of her tea, she was startled by the familiar starting-up sounds of the Daimler. Rustom must also have heard, because he strode out of the room abruptly.

He was back just as quickly. Looking anxiously at all of them, he said, "Arman's taken the car out—and Gulnaz must also have gone."

"For a drive? How could she, when she was wearing her night-clothes?" Camellia said, fussing with Khushy's simple white gown.

"What an embarrassment." Rustom's voice cracked. "Arman shouldn't have taken her out."

"Don't blame Arman," Camellia said soothingly. "His duty is to take any of us where we want without question."

"Perhaps she wants to ride around to the shops to get a box of sweets or some other comfort," Jamshedji suggested.

Gita came in to start clearing the table. Hesitantly, she said, "Maybe Gulnaz-bai asked for a ride to her parents' house; her mother is often calling on the phone."

Camellia gave Gita a grateful look. "Yes. Best thing is to nurse her wounds."

"But she's left Khushy behind." Perveen motioned to the baby in her mother's arms. "Isn't that concerning?"

Camellia murmured, "You visited with Gulnaz this morning, Perveen. When did she last nurse Khushy?"

Perveen had to concentrate to remember. "She was nursing when I saw her, and that was about nine o'clock."

"Khushy will probably be crying for milk by eleven-thirty," Camellia said, looking tenderly at the granddaughter in her arms. "I'm sure Gulnaz will remember."

"And if she doesn't?" Perveen asked. "Then what do we do?"

"Perveen, weren't you going into Fort today?" Jamshedji said, frowning slightly.

Perveen felt he was cutting her off—and perhaps it was because he was afraid to think about the prospect she'd raised. "I have a long-standing lunch planned with Alice at the Taj, and then . . . I was going to look around."

"And how will you do that without a car?" Rustom interjected. "Now do you regret throwing fat on the fire?"

"I'll manage something," Perveen said between gritted teeth. "Every now and then, I'm allowed to take the train. Will you allow me today, Pappa?"

"Wait to see if the car returns. And Rustom, I want you to walk with me to the fire temple." Jamshedji's tone brooked no room for disagreement.

"What?" Rustom said. "I was there yesterday. I've done the rites."

"The men's group is having its monthly meeting. Now that you are a father, it's proper that you participate."

After the dining room was cleared and the men were gone, Camellia laid Khushy to rest in the cradle again, and she spoke softly to Perveen. "I'd like to know your opinion about something."

"Of course, Mamma." Perveen was surprised by her mother's deference.

"The obvious thing is to call the Bankers to see if Gulnaz arrived there. But Tajbanu has a way of twisting one's words." Camellia looked from Perveen toward Khushy, who was making soft, chucking sounds. "I don't want Gulnaz believing I'm ringing her mother to complain about her."

"But if we don't call, we won't know if she's safe," Perveen said, thinking about Sunanda. "Tell you what? I'll call. Let me take the brunt, as usual."

"Oh, Perveen!" Camellia sounded anguished.

Perveen's reply was cut off by the faint sound of a telephone ringing in Jamshedji's study.

"Can you believe it? Not five minutes, and Gulnaz is calling to apologize!" Camellia's eyes shone.

But the woman who answered Perveen's greeting was Miriam Penkar, asking whether she'd heard about Sir Dwarkanath's death.

"Yes, Dr. Penkar," Perveen said, so Camellia, who had followed her, would understand that it wasn't Gulnaz calling. "Lord Bhatia's passing was mentioned in yesterday afternoon's newspaper. It's a big shock, isn't it?"

"Actually—the police came to ask me about it."

"Really? Did they give any reason?" Perveen tried to sound dispassionate, but she was already on alert.

"Apparently Parvesh Bhatia told them that I was the last doctor who saw his father before he became incoherent." There was a catch in Miriam's voice.

"I don't understand." Perveen tried to put together a possible scenario. "Were you visiting the hospital before he expired?"

"No. On Friday I was so distressed to learn from you rather than Uma about the hospital being cancelled. After I'd gone back to work, I realized I couldn't concentrate. When my final afternoon patient didn't appear, I closed up the clinic and went to Ghatkopar." Taking a deep breath, Miriam said, "Mangala denied me entry, saying that Uma was busy tending to Sir Dwarkanath due to illness. When I told her that I didn't believe her words, she finally relented.

"When did you arrive?" Perveen asked, thinking about her own timing when she visited that day.

"About four o'clock. I wasn't there for more than a half hour, but it was difficult getting back, and I walked through my door just after sundown. I was late for Shabbat and my mother was very upset. Another reason I shouldn't have gone!" The doctor sounded close to tears.

"You didn't know that you'd be late," Perveen soothed. "Just tell me what happened at the Bhatias'."

"Mangala told Oshadi to take me to a small upstairs room to wait—a prayer room of some sort. I felt very restless, and then I heard Uma's voice nearby. I realized she must be with Sir Dwarkanath, because I heard a man groaning. It struck me that it was true that he was ill—and if I helped him in his time of need, he might be grateful enough to reconsider cancelling the hospital."

Picking up a legal pad on her father's desk with one hand, Perveen said, "Before you continue speaking, I want to make sure that our conversation is protected as confidential. That would mean that you are engaging Mistry Law for your protection—whether or not anything does happen with the police."

"Yes, I want that." Miriam cleared her throat. "All right, then, I went inside the room, which reeked of vomitus. Uma looked surprised to see me, but she didn't tell me to leave. You see, Mangala had told her a guest was waiting, but she hadn't said it was me."

"Did you bring up your concern about the hospital cancellation when you went in the room?"

"No. I knew it wouldn't have served either of us to have an argument in front of her father. I told her that Sir Dwarkanath appeared ill, and I would be willing to check his vital signs. After all, I had my medical kit with me."

"What did Sir Dwarkanath say about it?"

"He moaned something or other in Gujarati." Shakily, Miriam added, "Physicians often proceed when patients are too ill to speak clearly. Uma didn't forbid my actions!"

"Of course," Perveen said reassuringly. "Uma knows what a good doctor you are. We all do!"

"As I was starting to take the man's pulse, Mangala came in. She started shouting that he was being morally compromised if a woman looked at his body. That it was against what he would want, as an orthodox Hindu."

Perveen could imagine the scene, the tension, and the smells. A doctor's experience treating a patient could be as tense as a barrister's standing in court. In both cases, a life could be at stake. She asked, "What happened, then?"

"I told Mangala that I had examined male patients before and would be as professional now as in the past. Uma then chimed in that Mangala hadn't complained about a difference in gender when I'd treated Ishan after his burn. That sent the two of them off! Uma went into the hall, and Mangala followed to scream in her face. I saw my chance, then; I shut the door and locked it."

"And then what?"

"I finished taking his pulse. It was slightly elevated—and I found his heart beating quickly, too. I spent most of my time on the abdominal examination. He was able to speak to me, after all. I asked about foods he had recently eaten. He insisted he'd only eaten at home or from the tiffin Uma packed for him to go to work the previous day. He'd also taken tea made by Oshadi, and a milk pudding specially made by Uma as part of the evening supper on Wednesday. In this heat, dairy dishes can spoil faster than usual."

"What was your diagnosis?" Perveen asked.

"I could rule out appendicitis, but I didn't feel comfortable saying anything else without laboratory testing. I told Uma two strong possibilities were food poisoning or a viral illness. I gave some directions on food and diet and said that he would very likely improve, but that they should call his regular doctor if he developed a fever."

"It all sounds like a reasonable account of your behavior," Perveen said. "And it was generous of you to take the initiative to help someone in need."

"But the police pointed out that I didn't say to take him to the hospital!" Miriam interrupted. "Sir Dwarkanath only was admitted to Sir J. J. Hospital because Parvesh became so worried that he drove him there during the night."

"Did Uma ring you about it?" Perveen asked.

"No. I haven't heard anything from her. The police told me about it. And I think the police might believe . . ."

"Might believe what?" Perveen prompted.

Silence crackled on the line. Then she spoke. "The police might believe I didn't recommend hospitalization because I wanted him to die."

Perveen was outraged by the idea. "If anyone hinted that, it would be the worst kind of speculation. English common law states persons who attempt to help someone who's ill or injured cannot be punished if the outcome is poor."

"But there's more." Miriam took a shuddering breath. "I locked the door for part of the time I was with him. And a lot of people in that household know that I was very angry about the hospital cancellation—and he was the obstacle. They'd think it would be in my interest for him to die."

Miriam was essentially saying the same thing that Gulnaz had. Perveen realized that the outcome of the autopsy was going to be very important—but she had to limit her questions to immediate concerns. "Did the police involved give their names?"

"The only one with a badge was called Vaughan. A British man—small and unpleasant."

"I've met DI Vaughan." It had been on a case where he'd bungled things so badly that women might have died if Perveen hadn't intervened. For a homicide detective to visit a person of interest before an inquest occurred meant that the coroner already suspected foul play—and that was not good for Miriam. "Did Mr. Vaughan have questions that you haven't yet mentioned?"

"Yes. He asked me my mood when I went to the house. I told him it was normal, but he shot back that the servants reported I was enraged and shouting. I denied it because I was afraid. So, he already caught me out!"

Perveen swallowed hard. Miriam hadn't exactly lied, but she had omitted information.

This could make her time with a dying patient in a locked room seem more suspicious.

"Did you give him any medication?"

"No, nothing at all."

"That's good. I'm glad you kept things brief," Perveen said.

"What now?" Miriam's voice had risen to an anxious pitch.

"Don't speak to the police again without me present. I'll send you a contract to sign and return to me with a small retainer. I'm sorry to bother you for money, but it serves as proof that I am your designated legal representative and can protect you in future matters." As Perveen finished, Khushy began wailing.

"Thank you," Miriam said in a heavy voice. "Is that Khushy I hear?"

"Yes. In fact—" Perveen paused, feeling torn. Did she have the right to ask Miriam for help, when the doctor was in such a distressed situation? Not to mention, Gulnaz would take offense.

"In fact?" Miriam repeated.

In a rush, Perveen said, "Gulnaz left our house without the baby this morning. I don't know where she is, or if she's coming back."

"Oh, I am very sorry to hear this." Miriam's voice had reclaimed its calm timbre. "On occasion, women have mental disturbance postnatally. So what's your plan?"

"Khushy's being watched over by my mother and one maid-servant, but we feel rather panicked. Especially about feeding."

"If Gulnaz is having a mental problem, her departure may be safer for the baby," Miriam said, and Perveen wondered if the doctor had noticed something ominous when she'd tended to Khushy in Gulnaz's home. "However, as you rightly point out, Khushy requires mother's milk to survive at her young age. An ayah is needed, preferably one who can properly nurse her."

Perveen considered the choice of words. "Do you mean—"

"Yes. A wet nurse is what you need, around the clock. Not like that last girl, Lakshmi. Did you hear that she possibly gave the baby alcohol?"

"Gulnaz spoke of a drug. We don't really know it's true," she added, remembering Gulnaz's depressed views about every-thing.

"The baby was very heavily sedated. If she hadn't come to wakefulness, I would have advised taking her to hospital."

So it was a serious matter. "I am sure that my mother would also welcome the idea of a wet nurse, and we would pay well for it. But I'm worried that Gulnaz might not consent to have her baby drink from another woman's breast."

"If she is gone, she cannot say yes or no," Miriam reminded her. "And her husband will surely approve this lifesaving mea-sure. That's all you need, really."

Perveen felt like she was seeing an example of Miriam's

fast-moving, firm decisions—just like decisions she'd made in the cases of Ishan and Lord Bhatia. Sometimes the decisions turned out in a patient's favor; other times, not. "Mamma did speak at breakfast about the need to find a new nurse."

"And not just any nurse. My group of wet nurses have learned health care from me, which is why they also are paid a bit more—about forty rupees a month. I require the households where they work to permit them the proper amount of sleep and food. Hiba has just finished the weaning process with one of the babies in my practice. She is in Byculla right now, not far at all. I can send her in a taxi to you—hopefully quite soon."

Perveen was reminded of the doctor's own crushing worries. "You have so much to think about at present. I'm grateful to you for doing this."

"What are thanks inside a family?"

As she hung up the telephone set, Perveen thought that her father would be pleased to learn that Miriam Penkar had become a client. But it didn't feel like a victory of any sort. She was as worried for Miriam as she'd been for Sunanda.

Perveen opened the study door and stepped back in surprise to see Gita holding Khushy. "Have you been here all this time?"

"No, I've just come." The maid spoke in a whisper. "I've got the baby for the next two hours because your mother said she needs her hands to be free. She's cleaning up the nursery. I want you to see—look how Khushy is quiet. I cannot believe it!"

Perveen watched Gita's expression become even more pleased as she explained the possible arrival of Hiba, the wet nurse Dr. Penkar had recommended.

"A nurse is what we need. But has Hiba ever run away?"

"I don't think the doctor would recommend someone like that." As Perveen spoke, Khushy came awake in Gita's arms and let out a tiny cry.

"Khushy doesn't want anyone but Gulnaz," Gita fretted, shifting the baby awkwardly. "It's very hard to keep her happy."

"I could try." Perveen was surprised by how quickly Gita handed over the baby, and how easy it was to hold the light, sweet-smelling child. Still whimpering, Khushy rubbed her face against Perveen's bosom, and something inside Perveen melted.

"She's looking for milk," Gita said. "I have been giving her my finger dipped in boiled milk and a little bit of sugar. You can try it, too!"

The memory of Khushy screaming wildly returned, so Perveen decided not to test her luck. Handing the baby back to Gita, she said, "I must tell Mamma what's happened."

She found Camellia in the nursery, where the fan was whirring and piles of clean and dirty laundry sat on the floor. Looking up, Camellia listened to Perveen's account of Hiba and agreed that this was the best possible decision.

"So we can afford this nurse?" Perveen said, having explained that her fee was higher than Lakshmi's.

"What choice do we have?" Camellia said, sliding a stack of dry diapers into a drawer. "And I think I hear a car stopping outside! If not Hiba, maybe it's Arman."

20

THE LADIES' RACE

*G*lancing out the window, Perveen was able to confirm that Arman had returned all by himself. When she rushed down to meet him, he spoke straight away.

"Gulnaz-memsahib is still at her parents' house. I waited for an hour, but then Mrs. Banker came out to say that I should leave."

"Did she say when Gulnaz needed to be picked up?" Perveen asked, wondering if the tempest was still raging. "I've always thought that they are close enough for walking, but Gulnaz went in her nightclothes!"

"I noticed that!" Arman said, shaking his head. "So strange—and she was crying very quietly all the time. She would not say to me what was wrong—probably I should not have asked. Mrs. Banker said she didn't know when Gulnaz would be ready to return."

"Is Mrs. Banker also upset with us?"

"How can I tell? That woman's face is like a dried plum. She is always looking angry."

Perveen couldn't help smiling, because Arman's view was the same as hers. "Very well. I'll ask you to take me into town, then."

Perveen had thought she'd be late to the Taj's outdoor dining pavilion, but it turned out Alice was not even there. Her friend had a sharp memory and wasn't the type to forget an engagement.

"What do you wish, madam? Will you come to the table

now and wait?" The round-faced Anglo-Indian man in his early twenties spoke politely, but Perveen was distracted by the faint sound of women's voices calling out to each other with British inflections. They were not on land but quite distant, moving along in a series of sailboats. Suddenly, Perveen could guess where Alice might be.

"The Yacht Club's races are still on—that must be why my friend isn't here. May I give up the table for the moment and come back with her in, say, forty-five minutes?"

The maître d' consulted the book in front of him. "Very well. I'll make a note of your name, Miss Mistry."

Perveen thanked him and began a swift walk toward the Yacht Club pier. She had never observed a sailing race before, and she was unsurprised to see that the small crowd assembled to watch were all Europeans.

Alice's father was the one who held a Yacht Club membership; wives and daughters were allowed. Civil service officials could join Bombay's exclusive clubs for lower fees, if any. Colin had a mentor in the Indian Civil Service who had granted him a month's stay as a temporary visitor in the Yacht Club's residency building. He'd left as soon as he had another housing option, saying that he didn't want to stay in a club that didn't admit Indians.

Perveen had felt gratified by his conviction, although at the time she'd played devil's advocate and told him that the late Solomon Sassoon had belonged there, proving an exception. Colin had swiftly countered that the Baghdadi Jew was "de facto European" in British eyes. So in the end, they both were in agreement that the club discriminated.

She had reached the timbered clubhouse. The boats were still out on the water, slowly streaming in. Just to be sure her hypothesis about Alice was true, she went to the open-air stand near the clubhouse door.

"Are the ladies' teams practicing today?" she asked the man who was checking people into the club.

"Yes. They're out," he said shortly.

"Do you know whether Miss Hobson-Jones is racing?"

Glancing down at the guestbook before him, he said, "What business is it of yours?"

The Garden Room's maître d' was a paragon of politeness compared to this fellow. Coolly, she said, "We have an appointment. I'm trying to locate her."

"The club is members only. Go on, now." He made a shooing gesture with his hand.

She resisted the impulse to utter a curse word. Lingering just a moment, she said, "And the dock is open-air, which means that by law, it belongs to all of Bombay."

She left him muttering to himself and walked across to the dock to watch the fast-moving yachts. They were too far for her to make out the people on them, but a small group standing at the dock's edge—a few men, but mostly ladies, and some children—were clapping. The only Indians waiting appeared to be ayahs to the children and Yacht Club attendants.

We are in your country, but we can make rules about buildings and associations to keep you out. And even the very rich, like the Nawab of Varanpur, were excluded.

The sailboats were skimming along the water, piloted by women who hadn't such concerns. A trim yacht with a blue flag came up swiftly on the tail of a larger one named *Queen of Bombay*, and the crowd broke out in applause as the second boat sailed past the finish line, a buoy speared with the club's jaunty blue flag.

Perveen could see women scurrying around the winning boat, *Pretty Bird*, pulling at ropes to draw down the sails. A tall blonde standing on the boat's rim flung a rope to a Yacht Club worker standing on the dock so he could tie it to a pole as the boat slowly came in.

"Hi, Perveen! Hold up a minute, I'm coming!" Alice, who'd been the rope-thrower, called out as she easily bridged the two-foot gap to the dock, her wide-legged trousers flapping in the wind. "Sorry to be late. Although we did come in first."

"Alice, what is this? You can't miss the awards ceremony," interjected one of the sailing women walking behind them. She was a tall blonde in her late thirties, with conventionally pretty features. She seemed familiar, although Perveen couldn't place her.

"Oh, that's right." Alice stopped, allowing the lady to catch up. "My friend Perveen Mistry has come to meet me. Perveen, Mrs. Serena Prescott is the skipper of *Pretty Bird.*"

"Congratulations on your victory!" Perveen said. "What a beautiful yacht."

"*Pretty Bird* belongs to the Stowes," Mrs. Prescott said. "Mrs. Stowe doesn't sail, but she said we could use it today because her husband only comes on Saturdays, now and again."

"How kind of her," Perveen said, remembering how Madeline had stayed after Serena and Lady Gwendolyn Hobson-Jones had walked out of the tea party. Casually, she said, "I believe I've seen you before—was it at Uma Bhatia's fundraising party?"

"Oh, yes." She gave Perveen a second, more approving, look. "I adore Uma. We just came from Delhi four months ago, and she's been very helpful to me."

Serena's vague compliment led Perveen to believe that she didn't yet know about the hospital cancellation. Casually, Perveen asked, "How has Mrs. Bhatia been helping you?"

"The biggest problem for any newcomer: finding servants!" Serena chuckled, but Perveen saw that Alice was looking annoyed. "We were placed in such a small flat in the area near the Bombay Gymkhana. There was only a cook and cleaning boy, which was simply impossible for our needs, given that we had ten rooms in Delhi and a household staff of six, plus driver. Uma sent me an ayah whose English is passable. I feel quite fortunate."

"Bully for you!" Alice said at the same time Perveen asked, "Where is your flat?"

"Harriman Road."

"Oh!" With a sinking feeling, Perveen realized that Serena Prescott could be in Colin's apartment building.

"Palm Villas. Do you know it?" Serena asked, looking inquisitively at her.

Not Colin's building. "I do know the name. It's a lovely modern building, isn't it?"

"So they say." She rolled her eyes. "Electric fans and lighting and piped water. That's what modern means here. Whereas in Delhi—"

"Sorry, Serena, but if we natter on, we'll miss the trophy presentation," interrupted Alice. "And then I must run to change before lunch."

"Don't worry—sporting clothes are permitted during the day. They already have a large table prepared for our group," Serena said.

"Perveen and I are having lunch elsewhere," Alice cut in.

"Could she just come along with us? Be my guest!" Serena came to a halt and turned to smile patronizingly at Perveen.

"It's kind of you to offer, but Indians are prohibited from entering the club," Perveen answered, wondering if Serena Prescott really was so new that she had not noticed.

"Oh! I'm sorry." Serena Prescott put a hand to her mouth and looked sideways at Alice. "I didn't know."

"It's fine," Perveen said. "Alice, we still have a table in the Garden Room."

"It's too hot to be in a garden, surely," Serena said. "But I suppose Indians have stronger skin!"

"The Garden Room's at the Taj, and there's an awning," Perveen said, privately happy to again prove Serena's ignorance. "In fact, I'll go ahead to hold our table while you enjoy the trophy ceremony."

When Perveen reached the Garden Room, the maître d' apologized that lunch orders would be ending in twenty-five minutes and only one table for two was left—close to the wall. Did she mind?

"Thank you very much!" Perveen said, glad for the shade and greater privacy this table provided. A young man dressed in a crisp white coat and black trousers dashed over from the next table to take her drinks order: a sweet lime for Alice, and salt-lime for herself, both with plenty of club soda and ice. Within ten minutes, the waiter was back with the drinks, and Alice rushed up, face pink from exertion, with wet hair hanging lank to her shoulders.

"You are her guest?" The waiter looked in confusion at Alice, who answered with a cheery nod.

After he'd left, Alice murmured to Perveen, "Sorry to look like a drowned rat—I came straightaway after my shower."

Perveen laughed. "I rather think his surprise was because of your missing chapeau."

She clapped her hand to her crown. "I must have forgotten it in the changing room."

"Never mind. Just look at the menu—I want to get in the orders before lunch service ends."

The Taj's menu steered toward France and sometimes Italy; there were only a handful of Indian dishes on the menu. Given the heat, both women opted for a chilled shrimp cocktail and Salade Lyonnaise. Perveen selected a dish she'd never heard of called Chicken Americaine. Alice inquired about the ingredients contained in the day's special, a fish called bombil that bore the Anglo-Indian name "Bombay duck."

"Breadcrumbs fried," the waiter answered, as if he'd said it a thousand times.

"That's all?" Perveen asked, disappointed. The small, scaleless fish that belonged to the lamprey family was typically cooked with many spices.

"This is a Continental restaurant, madam." The young man gave her a faintly reproving look.

Alice shrugged. "And a very good restaurant, too. I'll try it. And did I spy a Black Forest cake on the sweets trolley?"

"Yes, Memsahib. I shall set aside a slice of the torte for you. And as for you?" The waiter turned to Perveen.

"No pudding today, thank you." She had the urge to look at her watch. It felt like the day was almost done, and she had so much left to do.

The waiter recited the order and then sped off.

"How interesting that a German cake is appearing on the Taj's menu so quickly after the war," Alice said. "In any case, I'm excited to taste chocolate. It's a rare treat in India."

"Yes, maybe that's why it's so popular," Perveen mused, and as she glanced around the restaurant, she saw several people eating a chocolate cake topped with cream and cherries. "Begum Cora of Varanpur brought a Black Forest torte to Uma Bhatia's tea party. Did your mother mention the party to you? A child caught on fire and barely escaped serious injury."

Alice had been sipping her lime drink, and now put it down. "How terrifying!"

It was fortunate that the two tables of people nearby were finishing up and leaving, because ears would have been burning as Perveen continued the story of how Ishan Bhatia caught fire and Sunanda saved him.

"I might have heard that last bit," Alice commented. "In the locker room, I caught a bit of chatter from Serena Prescott to another lady about an accident happening after they left the party."

"And did Serena talk about why she left early?"

Alice shrugged. "She and Mummy had to avoid someone."

"An Australian woman married to a nawab?"

Alice chuckled. "Did you have a spy in the room? Apparently, Begum Cora cannot be spoken with or socially received by anyone because she's not officially the nawab's wife, in the government's eyes."

The shrimp cocktail and salads arrived. Alice immediately dug her fork into the icy goblet to scoop out the contents. After she'd finished three shrimp, she asked, "And how is Sunanda in the aftermath? Will she make a full recovery?"

"That's what I need to talk to you about," Perveen said, squeezing extra lemon on her own shrimp. "A week after the party, Sunanda was improperly arrested. I happened to notice her in a prisoner's line at the police station and took her on as a client. My father's unhappy about it because, as you know, I'm a solicitor, not an advocate. And she can't pay for my service."

"You haven't told me what she's charged with."

Perveen ran her tongue over her lips as she thought of how much she should say. Because of Alice's prior help with some of her cases, she was considered a part-time employee of the firm, and thus couldn't be compelled to divulge their conversation. "She was arrested on suspicion of abortion—or, as legal language states, causing herself to miscarry."

"Really?" Alice put down her spoon with a clatter. "What a dreadful bit of meddling the police did this time! I suppose Sunanda is a mother who needs to keep working to feed all the mouths at home? Someone who could not cope with another pregnancy?"

"No, she is unmarried and childless." Perveen glanced around again to make truly sure that nobody was within twenty feet of them. Then she told the rest, including how Sunanda had wound up staying with Gita in the garden cottage.

"What does Sunanda tell you about her life? Was there a man who loved her, or"—Alice's brow contracted—"who abused her?"

"Sunanda's gone now. I suspect something, but I'll never know."

"She's gone?" Alice's voice rose. "But what about the case?"

Perveen raised a hand in a patting gesture to remind Alice to keep her voice low. After Alice nodded, she said, "I must find her. Pappa thinks she jumped bail out of fear, but I can't believe that's possible. Her home village is too far away for it to be likely for her to travel, especially since she's got an infected burn."

Alice frowned. "It makes me so angry that the Bombay Court decided to nose into her life. The prosecutor sounds scurrilous. Who is he?"

The waiter took that moment to arrive and set down their filled plates. Perveen thought the Chicken Americaine could have been a double to Alice's Bombay duck: both entrees were heavily breaded and fried to the same golden-brown hue. Alice pronounced her fish scrumptious but Perveen found the chicken disappointingly bland.

Once the food was analyzed, Perveen picked up the conversation where it had paused. "The prosecutor is named Walter Rippington. Have you heard of him? He seems young."

"He hasn't presented himself for a social call, if that's what you're asking," Alice said dryly.

"Your father is friendly with people in the prosecutor's office, isn't he? I wonder if Mr. Rippington has a reputation of any sort."

"What do you mean by reputation?" Alice rested her chin on her hand, studying Perveen.

Perveen struggled to put her feelings into words. "The strategy of prosecuting Sunanda for drinking herbal tea—from which she recovered without illness—is inconsistent with typical abortion cases. I wonder if Rippington is either terribly naïve, or he's tremendously clever or perhaps is behaving at the behest of someone else who has an ulterior motive. It would be helpful to find out before he presents his opening argument."

"Loads of possibilities there—but I can't think of how to ask Pa about the fellow without making him suspicious I'm digging into government business." Alice straightened her posture. "I wonder if your Mr. Rippington might be at the Lawyers' Ball."

The ball was the premier fundraiser for Government Law

School. Because of Perveen's brief, miserable tenure there before enrolling at Oxford, she didn't wish to support the institution, but her father paid for two tickets and always encouraged her to attend as his companion. She said, "It's next Saturday. I might go."

"Oh, good, here's the cake!" Alice clapped as their waiter set down the dessert, a thick slice of chocolate cake with a whipped-cream middle layer and cream and cherries on top. As they oohed at it, the cake toppled to lie flat on the plate.

"Sorry, madam." The waiter looked consternated.

"Never mind," Alice said with a grin. "Everyone knows a fallen slice means one won't get married."

"Where did you hear that nonsense?" Perveen asked, tasting a bite of Alice's cake with her unused teaspoon. It was soft and mildly chocolatey, and the whipped cream a perfect cloud.

"Someone said it when I was in Austria." Alice had spent her sixteenth year in an Austrian sanatorium, her parents' response to her expulsion from Cheltenham Ladies' College.

"Oh, a religious belief!" Perveen joked. "Regarding the Lawyers' Ball; might you attend?"

"No. It was on my father's calendar, but he just said he's got to change plans to attend a dinner at the Bombay Club for an important government visitor." Alice swirled cream on her plate. "He'd bought two tickets earlier, but I don't know that I'd be allowed to go to that ball without an escort. Mummy's been making a lot of noise lately about my decline in what she considers acceptable social activity."

"May I?" Perveen asked, holding up her spoon. When Alice nodded, she reached over and stole another bite of the airy torte. "If you've got a spare ticket, you could offer it to Colin Sandringham. Or should I say, he could escort you there?"

Alice put down her fork. "I hardly know Colin. He's your friend."

"You've had a few dances together at government events,"

Perveen reminded her. "And your mother knows him. Wouldn't a date with Colin throw your mother off-kilter?"

Alice's eyes sparkled as she answered, "Possibly. But we all know I'm not his type."

The thought of a party seemed ridiculous after all the worries she'd had—but it was also irresistible. Seeing Colin always made her feel better. "I suppose you could tell him I'll be going."

"Oh!" Alice lit up. "Then the two of you can have a rendezvous. How mischievous of you to plan this."

"We are not up to mischief, I assure you." Perveen flushed, remembering what had happened in Colin's apartment. As close as she felt to Alice, she couldn't ever confess it.

21

THE STONE YARD

After the last crumbs were gone, Alice walked off to the Yacht Club to retrieve her hat. Perveen found Arman parked in the same spot and told him the next stop was Mistry House.

"Ma'ashallah you are here," Mustafa said, greeting her with a surprised air when she came to the door.

"Sunday is unusual," Perveen agreed. "So much to do, and it's sometimes easier when Pappa isn't around!"

"I'm very glad to see you, because I telephoned to your house and could not find you," Mustafa said, closing the door behind them. "A rough-looking man came earlier asking for you. He said he wanted to tell you about Sunanda. Isn't she the one you mentioned yesterday?"

Perveen's pulse raced at the unexpected news. "She is. Did he give his name?"

"No. He seemed very nervous."

"Please describe what you remember, then."

"He was small-small." Mustafa moved his hands gracefully, shaping a figure just a few inches taller, and thinner, than Perveen. "But his arms looked strong as steel. He wore the kind of shoes poor men wear when they are dragging carts or doing work in the street."

Perveen remembered giving Govind Chavda her card. "That man might be Sunanda's brother!"

"A brother?" Mustafa rubbed his beard, as if considering things. "Yes. That could be why he spoke her first name."

"I am so glad you notice the small details," Perveen told him.

"If it really turns out that it was Govind, I know just where to find him in Kalbadevi. Perhaps he came today because it's his day off."

"Won't you attract too much notice in Kalbadevi? That's why you sent Jayanth." Mustafa's brow creased with concern.

"That was for a wide search for someone else," Perveen said. "Don't worry. I know exactly where to go—Arman and I visited there before."

"You must have him accompany you throughout the neighborhood," he said soberly. "I would not like to explain to your father about a disappeared daughter."

It only took ten minutes to travel from the quiet of Fort to the vibrant chaos of Kalbadevi. Today, wives carried baskets and tugged at their husbands' arms, pointing out wares they wanted from roadside stalls. Children skipped in and out of the streets, the lucky ones holding balloons and paper cones filled with nuts. A small grassy area near the Bhatia Stone business was taken over by young men and boys playing cricket.

"This way?" Arman was stopped at an intersection, looking indecisive.

Perveen was also stymied, so she stepped out of the car, awkwardly lifting the edge of her sari so it didn't trail in the muck. She walked this way and that until someone recognized Govind's name and pointed out the right direction to his home. She got back into the car with Arman, and he drove to the same point as the day before, when the lane was too narrow to go farther.

"Mustafa wants me to follow you all the way."

"Very well." She approached the shanty, Arman following. As she peered in the door, it was neat—but there were no inhabitants.

"Govind must still be working," said the neighbor man in the next shanty when she walked over to inquire.

"Working on Sunday?" She was surprised. "And where are Amla and the children?"

"Gone home."

If they had gone back to Gujarat—did this mean Sunanda was with them? It seemed unbelievable, given Amla's reaction. Maybe that was why Govind had come to see her.

All she could think of was driving to Bhatia Stone. Arman followed her directions to proceed to the warehouse area, where men went back and forth with carts loaded with stone.

Many times, Grandfather Mistry had brought Rustom and her to watch his company's bricklayers at work on the city's emerging grand buildings. But he was a contractor, not a stone purveyor, so this was the first time she'd laid eyes on the brick-making process. She imagined the glorious mountains turned into quarries, and the peasants who broke the dense expanses of rock into boulders that could be transported by other men, down steep slopes and rough landscape to trains and ships. One couldn't see the bruises of the men in the uniform bricks that formed the proud faces of Mistry House, the High Court, and the University of Bombay. But now Perveen had witnessed the pain.

Perveen watched until she spotted Govind, among several others, tortuously pulling a cart loaded with boulders into a stone yard. The cart was unloaded by other men. The four then walked off at varying speeds, leaving Govind to pull the empty cart by himself.

"That's him! Now I've got to let him know we are here." Perveen realized that because Govind was working, the need for discretion was greater so she explained to Arman how he could help.

A minute later, Arman had parked the car and walked over to a spot along the road where Govind would pass him. Then, Arman ducked his head and began speaking to the small man. Govind's cart slowed to a stop. After a moment, Govind spoke back in an aminated fashion, using his hands to gesture something to Arman. Govind's journey resumed and Arman strolled back toward the car.

"He told me there's a chaiwallah around the corner. You can walk and wait behind the closest building to that. He will leave the cart hidden in the stone yard and go directly there."

"I'm leaving my briefcase with you." Perveen drew her sari over her head, so little could be seen but her eyes, and she passed the tea stand and went around the corner. As she waited, a few men eyed her curiously, and she wondered what she would say if they approached her. She knew that her appearance marked her as someone who didn't belong.

Suddenly Govind was passing by, barely glancing at her. She realized she was meant to follow him, so she did, winding up in a narrow space between two shops. It smelled dreadfully, a mixture of rotting vegetables and urine, a good reason nobody else was there.

When he was close enough to hear her, she said, "Are you the man who came to my office this morning?"

"You should know what happened," he muttered. "The police have taken Sunanda back to jail!"

Perveen gasped aloud, for this was entirely unexpected. "Why? And how did you find out?"

He sighed, a long rattling sound. "Sunanda came back to the house on Friday late afternoon. She was crying very hard about something, so I gave her a glass of toddy so she would calm. She didn't use it before, but she does a little bit now."

"So, you are saying that she willingly imbibed?" Perveen's voice sounded sharp to her own ears; but she'd been thinking about what a man might do to a woman who'd had too much to drink.

"Just one glass, but she became very tired." He looked sideways at her, as if embarrassed to have provided the alcohol. "I told her that she better stay the night and return to your house the next day. Amla was upset and took the children to stay with her parents."

"Where exactly did Sunanda sleep?"

"Always with the children. On the other side of the curtain." Govind's voice was sharp, as if he sensed her suspicion.

Perveen didn't want to give the impression she thought badly of him, so she chose her next words with care. "Sunanda must be quite beloved to them. Their special aunt." After he nodded, she said, "Sunanda said you wanted to help find a match for her."

"She wishes to marry. But between all of us, there is very little to give for dowry." Studying the stones in the cart, he added, "My sister shouldn't be made to marry a man who is too old or bad-tempered. Those are the usual types who accept low dowry marriages. I told Amla we won't put Sunanda with such a man."

Perveen had heard similar stories about lack of dowry leading to huge mismatches between young women and old men. He was good to have insisted on Sunanda being matched with someone appropriate. "Did the police come for her on Friday?"

"No. They came Saturday morning. Before she had time to return to your house."

Perveen guessed that the arrest might have occurred because of an error. "Didn't the police know that she was out on bail?"

"The constable said she broke the bail rule by going to the Bhatias'." Govind's eyes were damp. "But why is it a crime to go to your old employer for back pay?"

"So that's where she went on Friday!" Perveen couldn't hide the incredulity she felt.

"Yes. She said a barrister needed to be paid."

So Sunanda had understood Jamshedji's monetary concerns. "What happened when she went there?"

"She only said that her mistress was too busy to see her. I said to her, what do you expect? Plenty of people don't get the pay from the Bhatias." Govind's voice was desolate.

"That's a real shame," Perveen said, thinking the words

weren't strong enough for the distress she felt. "Is there anything else you think I should know?"

Govind's eyes flickered, as if looking for someone who might interrupt them.

"Sunanda had a bad dream at night and woke screaming."

Perveen suspected the bad dreams might be key to understanding what Sunanda wouldn't tell her. "Really! Do you remember any words she screamed?"

"It sounded like she said 'motabhai.'"

The word was startling; it lined up with what Gita had said about Sunanda crying "brother" in her sleep. "Does this mean Sunanda was calling for you?"

"No!" he looked startled. "Motabhai means elder brother. I'm a year younger than her. She calls me by my name."

"I see. And did she say anything about the dream?"

Govind stared into the empty wagon, as if the answer lay in its dusty depths. At last, he said, "She was talking about the sea. Big waves. She said something about children, too."

Perveen had an immediate thought. "The Bhatia children?"

"I didn't ask. And Ghatkopar is not near water!" Govind's voice was low. "Sunanda was very confusing when she spoke. She said she thought she would die."

While in Oxford, Perveen had read some of Sigmund Freud's *Interpretation of Dreams.* Diving into water, or being rescued from it, was described as a theme relating to birth. Now she thought that Sunanda had faced so many accusations about ending a pregnancy that her anxiety was being replayed through her dreams. "She wasn't afraid of the children dying?"

Govind raised his hands helplessly. "I didn't ask much. I only wanted her to be calm. She slept again. And then, a little after sunrise Saturday morning, the constable came. I was so upset I didn't understand where he said she was going. I don't think he even told me."

"Perhaps it's Gamdevi Station, where she was placed before. I'll go there now. Do you plan to visit her?"

"Yes. No matter what Amla says."

"I think that would be a great comfort to her." As Perveen readied herself to leave, she felt bad for even suspecting that Govind had harmed his sister. But she could not get past the feeling that someone else had caused her trauma. "Was your sister afraid of anyone?"

"Of course!" Govind looked back at her earnestly. "She was afraid of both the mothers at the Bhatia House, worrying they would find fault and sack her. She loved the children, but the work was very hard."

"The Bhatias are a demanding family," Perveen said with sympathy.

Govind put his rough hands on the cart. Looking up, he muttered, "I carry stones for the Bhatias. It pains my back, but at the end of the day, I am free. She is also a carrier of stones— those precious Bhatia children. She did not say, but I think they are part of the reason she went to the house on Friday."

A dust-smudged teenager darted into the lane. Looking straight at Govind, he said, "There you are! The boss is coming."

Govind slipped past in the narrow space before she could say goodbye.

22

INCARCERATION

*P*erveen was quiet on the way to Gamdevi Station, her head bent over her legal pad as she wrote down what she remembered Govind telling her. She thought the dream was significant, and maybe it could provide a conversational opening with Sunanda.

Upon reaching Gamdevi Station, Perveen advised Arman to wait around the corner, so he wouldn't be subject to any police order to move. Inside the station, she went to the jail section and introduced herself as Sunanda Chavda's counsel to a rotund clerk sitting at the counter.

"The prisoner told us your name when she came." Dryly, he added, "I remember both of you from before."

"Any chance you have the papers relating to her arrest?"

The clerk itched under his arm before he answered. "It's a great deal of effort to look for them. And I was going for tea."

"A tea break is good for everyone." Subtly, Perveen fished in her purse and pulled out a rupee. It was barely on the counter before it vanished in the clerk's hands.

"Why don't you go out and have tea, too," the clerk advised. "You'll see what you need in an envelope when you return."

Totally improper, Perveen thought as she exited the waiting room. Lawyers should not be paying the police. Especially when the record was public access, not secret information. It was just that she wanted it now, not the next day.

Perveen waited ten minutes and then returned to see a different clerk at the desk: a slender man with neatly oiled hair.

When she reintroduced herself, he handed her an envelope with her name on it. "Return afterward, yes?"

"Of course. And I'd like to pay a lawyer's visit to Miss Chavda." Perveen settled onto a hard bench and opened the papers. As she read, she recorded swiftly in her notebook.

Sunanda had admitted being at Bhatia House from approximately ten to ten-thirty on Friday morning. Although she had been turned away at the door by Oshadi, she had entered the house through other means and was discovered by Mrs. Mangala Bhatia to be lurking upstairs in the bedroom wing. When questioned by Mrs. Bhatia, Sunanda claimed to be collecting money. Mrs. Bhatia reprimanded her and sent her out of the house.

Perveen stared at the long, dreadful account. Sunanda's presence near Sir Dwarkanath's bedroom shortly before his death was surely another reason the police wanted her in custody. If the death were to be ruled a homicide, Sunanda could be even more likely to be charged than Miriam Penkar.

Perveen was in a state of high anxiety by the time she'd finished reading. She returned the paper to the second clerk. He said, "It's a wait to see prisoners in the women's block."

"Very well. May I speak with the jail doctor?"

"What business do you have with him?"

Perveen was glad that the silver cream was still in her bag. Taking it out, she said, "I brought a medical remedy prescribed for my client. She needs to have a wound cleaned and treated twice daily. Otherwise, you might have a dead lady on your hands."

The clerk sucked air through his teeth. "She can't keep the cream with her. Nothing allowed."

"Then she'll need to be seen in sick bay twice daily." A good break for Sunanda, Perveen thought. "What is the jail doctor's name?"

"It's Dr. Gupta. He's in the men's area now making examinations."

Perveen wasn't surprised the doctor would be male, but that could create another frightening situation for her client. As she placed the cream on the counter, she met the clerk's eyes. "Please make sure Dr. Gupta receives this, then. The instructions are on the paper attached to the jar. If she's not treated, she might die."

"We have a messenger who can bring it to the doctor later. But because it is Sunday, there is, well, a difficulty . . ."

Perveen slid two annas toward him. "Thank you for doing this. And I will speak to the doctor later, without fail, about the treatment plan."

Anxiety rising, she waited, watching the clock, thinking about how things had gone wrong. Sunanda had ignored the bail instruction—was that because Perveen hadn't explained it well enough? There was plenty of blame to spread around.

When the guard finally came, he took extra time searching her legal case before bringing her into the humid, odorous cell block.

The guard showed her into Sunanda's cell and locked the door behind her. Late-afternoon sun splashed through the barred window, casting rows of gold on the floor. Sunanda moved from the shadows to stand in the light, revealing reddened eyes and a distraught expression.

"You found me!" Sunanda's voice cracked. "I prayed, and you did come."

Perveen walked over to her and wrapped her arms around Sunanda. She felt the younger woman's thin body shaking, but gradually she calmed.

"My dear, I am glad to have found you—but very sorry you are incarcerated. I've been quite worried. I brought the medical cream to be given to the doctor. How is the condition of your wound?" Perveen released her and stepped back to get a look at her.

"I haven't been thinking much of the wound. Now the pain is in my head."

Perveen walked around her client, inspecting her. "What kind of pain? Is it sadness, or headache, or—"

"A big bruise," Sunanda said, putting her hand gingerly on the back of her head. "The police put me in a different room in the station before I was put in the cell. They made me stand before them and then they asked questions. I said I mustn't talk without you. When I wouldn't talk, they hit me."

"May I?" Perveen asked, and when Sunanda nodded, she touched the inflamed spot on Sunanda's head. She parted her hair, looking for blood, but only saw redness. "Were these men the constables who seized you at your brother's home?"

Sunanda shut her eyes tightly for a moment. "The constable who hit my head today was also at my brother's place. The other man was called Mukesh. I hadn't seen him until that day. He hit me on my arms and back."

Perveen gently took Sunanda's arms for examination, and then lifted the sari's pallu to look at her back. Mukesh knew what he was doing to hit someone without leaving marks. "Did a supervising officer ever appear before or after you were hit?"

"A white man came in afterward. They called him Detective-Inspector." Sunanda said the English words carefully. "They were talking about me to him, but I didn't understand the words. Everyone was angry; I was afraid."

From her briefcase, Perveen removed her legal notebook and the small battery torch that was of good use in dark places. "Did you hear the name Detective-Inspector Vaughan? And what did he look like?"

"The constables were translating his words, but they never said his name. He was short for a Britisher, and I think the hair that I saw was an orange color." Sunanda shook her head. "Maybe he is ill?"

Orange-hued hair was a sign of malnutrition, so Perveen could understand Sunanda's comment. The officer sounded as if he resembled Vaughan—the same officer who had questioned

Miriam Penkar. "Let's start at the beginning. I heard you told Gita that you were going out to meet me. Why?"

"Because of your father," Sunanda murmured. "He spoke to me in the garden on Friday morning. He was asking me if I could think of anyone who would be willing to pay barrister fees. I felt very bad I couldn't think of someone, but I did have saved money and back pay due to me at Bhatia House."

"Did you tell him you were going to try to get that?"

She shook her head. "I didn't want to say, in case it didn't work out. I told Gita I was going into town to see you, because I hoped you could take me there in your car."

Perveen knew her father had no idea how he'd influenced Sunanda's actions. But Perveen might also have had a role in it. "I'm trying to remember if I made clear to you that getting bailed out meant you were restricted from going to Bhatia House."

Sunanda's mouth twisted in misery. "No. I can't remember much from that day."

"What's done is done." Perveen sighed. "Make yourself comfortable and tell me what happened after you left my home."

"The weather was cool when I set out," Sunanda said, moving away and sliding down to rest against the cell wall. "But it became very hot while I was still in Dadar, and my stomach was paining me. I checked my directions with a peddler who said going to Fort might be four hours' walk. But to Ghatkopar, it would be less than two hours." She gave Perveen a rueful glance. "A cart driver recognized me walking along the Agra Road and took me the rest of the way, no cost. Then I walked fifteen minutes to Bhatia House."

Perveen wondered about the police's timeline. "Did you see the watchman when you entered the Bhatia House driveway?"

"No. I didn't go that way—I went through the open field nearby. I saw the children playing with Chandini—the other ayah," she added for Perveen's benefit. "They all saw me. Ishan ran to me, and the others followed."

"And then?" Perveen prompted.

Sunanda had been sitting with her back against the cell's wall, and now she shifted her legs. "Ishan was very upset—he thought I quit. I didn't want to say that the police arrested me. I said I would come back to see them again. The children weren't so upset anymore. It touched my heart so much that I cried a little bit."

"How long were you with them?"

"Not long," Sunanda answered, her eyes tearing up. "Chandini was worried that someone would see me, so I went back to the house."

Sunanda described going to a side door that was unlocked and slipping inside. "Oshadi appeared from around a corner and was very surprised to see me. She said I should not be there, or it could be trouble."

Perveen paused in her note taking. "So did you leave?"

"I told her that I very much needed my back pay. She said that I mustn't bother Uma-bhabhu for anything that day because Sir Dwarkanath had fallen sick. But I thought I would still try because I had come such a long way. I didn't want to go back with nothing." Sunanda went on to describe saying goodbye to Oshadi and walking out of the house, but then quietly returning by an exterior stairway.

"Why did you go back, when she'd refused you?" Perveen tried not to sound judgmental, but she was frustrated to see how many pieces of advice Sunanda had rejected. None of this would play well in court.

"Remember the money the begum gave after I helped Ishan? I had it saved inside the house. Then Mangala-bhabhi saw me before I could get it. She shouted at me that she would report me to the police for coming in the house to steal. I ran out as quickly as I could, and I know that made it look very bad. They will never accept me again." As Sunanda ended her report, her voice dissolved into sobs.

Perveen went to her, crouching down and stroking her hair. "Why did you go to your brother rather than back to us?"

"I was upset about how things went at Bhatia House. Govind is the one who always listens."

"You are his older sister. And this time, he defended you against Amla," Perveen said.

"Yes. And he also said I should sleep the night because it wouldn't look well for me to come to you in such a state."

Perveen waited for Sunanda to say something about drinking toddy. When nothing came forth, she said, "He says you had a terrible dream that night."

Sunanda shut her eyes tightly and gave a slight nod.

Perveen wondered how much she remembered. "Was it the first time for that dream?"

"No. But it's not a good dream to talk about," she said.

Perveen reshaped her next question about the dream. "All right, then. Did you ever take the Bhatia children to the sea?"

Sunanda stiffened. "Just one trip. It was a party at a big house. Right behind the house, there was the sea."

"Did Uma or Mangala also come?"

"No. But Uma-bhabhu's husband drove us." Sunanda's lip trembled as she spoke.

"Did any of the children come close to drowning?"

"No. Please, I would not like to talk about it anymore."

Perveen was getting the impression that something had happened at the beach, but she wouldn't learn about it today. The point was to protect Sunanda from further legal trouble. "Very well. Let's talk about what's happening now. I want to know what the police have said."

Sunanda exhaled heavily before speaking. "They told me that they knew I was alone with the nana-seth the day before he died. This meant that I could be convicted of two crimes: abortion and murder! I was crying very hard then. That's when Mukesh said my sentence could be light if I were to tell the truth about things. He said the white officer wanted to know who the bad man was."

"The bad man? What did you take that to mean?" Perveen asked carefully.

"A man who gave me a baby in my belly!" Sunanda mumbled. "You know that I don't go with any man."

Sunanda was standing by her story, Perveen thought.

"Then Mukesh said, 'If you lie about that, we know you are lying about killing Sir Dwarkanath.'"

Perveen had feared the police would take note of Sunanda's presence in Bhatia House when Sir Dwarkanath was ailing. "How did you reply?"

"I said only your name. That you were my lawyer."

"May I ask you another thing about Sir Dwarkanath?" Perveen paused, trying to find a way to make her question less personal. "In some households, the men take advantage of female servants. Did that happen with him toward any of the other females?"

"No. He would shout if his slippers were not just so, or to hurry with tea if someone was late. He was strict with rules. But he did not bother any ladies that way."

The calm with which Sunanda spoke made it seem clear that Sir Dwarkanath hadn't raped her. "What is Parvesh Bhatia like?"

"A good man. Brave and kind."

Perveen listened to the change in tone. If Sunanda liked him so much, could she have been his willing partner? "How much did you see of him during your time working there?"

Sunanda took a fraction longer to answer the question. "Every now and then. He called for me to do things with the children, like play ball. Sometimes he wanted me to sit in the back of the car with them—if he was taking them to a festival or the theater."

Perveen remembered that Parvesh reached Ishan before Uma had. She would have spoken again about him, but she heard the guard's footsteps. "I know that you will stay strong, Sunanda. I can come at any time to sit with you, if they have questions. They know where my office is, and that we have a telephone. Don't tell them this now, but I'm going to file a complaint about the physical attack on you."

"Will you get me taken out of here today?" Sunanda's eyes were pleading.

Perveen could not give her false hopes. "I wish I could. I will see you many times before the trial. And remember that you must see the doctor twice daily for your medical care. I brought your prescribed cream to this jail." She added the last bit for the benefit of the guard, who was unlocking the cell door and motioning for her to come out.

The guard brought Perveen back out to the waiting area, where she paused to speak with the first clerk she'd dealt with. "Thank you for your help earlier. I only have a few questions. Superintendent Graves runs this station, isn't it true?"

"Yes." He looked uneasy.

"And what about Detective Vaughan?"

"Oh, he is based at Bombay Police Headquarters."

"And lastly, a man I believe is a constable who came through here. His first name is Mukesh?"

Suddenly, the clerk's eyes shifted. "We have no Mukesh."

Either Mukesh was a false name, or the clerk was protecting the violent constable. Perhaps this was a routine process at Gamdevi, which meant the shining new star of the justice system was as dirty as any old police station in Bombay. After all, they'd demanded bribes; and she'd paid them without question.

Leaving the station, Perveen felt so very tired. All she wanted was to go home and wash herself. The sweat and dirt would come off, but not the corruption that she'd heard about and even engaged in herself.

23

CHANGING OF THE GUARD

*P*erveen reached home a half hour later. She stepped into the house and inhaled the scent of potatoes fried in butter, and a long-simmering lamb. These were dishes that Gulnaz particularly enjoyed. Perhaps John was cooking them to welcome her back.

Putting down her legal case, Perveen quickly went through the ground floor rooms to the veranda. Camellia was on the settee, her face buried in *Stree*, the Gujarati women's magazine. Rustom lounged in a nearby chair, a glass of golden whiskey at his side.

Camellia put the magazine down and smiled at her. "Glad you are home, but you look worn out. The heat is unbearable, isn't it?"

"I found Sunanda!" Perveen said. "Unfortunately, she's in jail. I can't tell you any more about it other than the police took her in because she accidentally violated the conditions for her bail."

"Gulnaz was crying about her. But she doesn't sound like a very good character, if she's committed a crime!" interjected Rustom, his voice slurred.

"She's a heroine," Camellia said, frowning at him. "She saved one of Uma Bhatia's children. That surely is why Perveen is taking care of her."

Perveen wanted to change the subject. "Did Gulnaz return?"

Rustom glowered at Perveen. "No Gulnaz."

"But the new ayah came two hours ago," Camellia said brightly. "Hiba seems perfectly suited for the work."

Perveen turned to Rustom. "Wonderful. Have you spoken with Hiba, too?"

"I don't need to. She looks very capable. Loaded with milk." Rotating his palms in front of his chest, Rustom squeezed his fingers emphatically.

Perveen put her hands on her hips and stared down at him. "Shame on you for that vulgarity!"

"Let that be your last drink, Rustom," Camellia said softly, giving Perveen a helpless look. "I very much like that Hiba is twenty-nine. Her age gives her confidence and experience. We are doing our best to make her feel appreciated. Actually, she's staying on our side of the house for . . . convenience."

Perveen could understand that a nurse wouldn't wish to stay in a household with just the baby's father—especially if she'd seen him drinking. "Which of our rooms is Hiba sleeping in?"

"Would you mind terribly if she slept on your balcony? The garden cottage is too far for her to hear a baby's cry. And she said she likes to be in cool night air."

"I hope she doesn't mind Lillian's squawking." Perveen would also have to adjust to not using her balcony as she liked for early morning tea—unless Hiba had already gone off to care for Khushy.

"I'm glad you are agreeable," Camellia said. "And we found that Khushy's crib fits nicely into your bedroom near your little tea table and chairs."

Perveen didn't think she'd heard right. "Why is Khushy's crib inside my room?"

"Because it's near Hiba! Don't worry, dear. Remember that I ordered a full-sized cot to be installed in Khushy's nursery, meant for Gulnaz's benefit? You'll be comfortable there."

Not only did Perveen dislike the idea of giving up her room, the last face she wanted to see in the morning was Rustom's. Settling down next to Camellia, she said, "No, that's not suitable for me. Why don't Hiba and Khushy both stay in the nursery?"

"Absolutely not!" Rustom looked thunderous. "Everyone knows that it's improper for me to be alone in my room with a maid next door. If Gulnaz hears, she's got grounds to divorce me."

Perveen stared him down. "What nonsense are you talking? Gulnaz is just napping at her mother's place."

Camellia glanced at Rustom, and then at Perveen. "Tajbanu rang. She said Gulnaz decided to stay with them for a while."

Perveen remembered what Dr. Penkar had advised about struggling mothers needing time away from babies. Sharply, she answered, "I'm very sorry that Gulnaz isn't well, but I shouldn't be forced to move into Rustom's side. My work at the moment is very challenging. Let me stay in my own room that allows me the rest I need."

"Rest is important," Rustom opined. "I also want my nights without the sounds of crying."

Perveen shot back, "She's your child. You will hear crying for years!"

"Don't start fighting again," Camellia reprimanded. "We don't need more trouble than we already are facing. What if Hiba hears this hubbub and is so put off that she quits? I certainly would, if I were in her shoes."

"Right. We can't lose her." Perveen shifted in her chair, thinking. She would have to adjust somewhat. "Let's keep Khushy's crib in my room. However, I'll remain in my own bed."

Rustom put down his glass and looked closely at her. "Won't you hate being in the same room with Khushy?"

"I don't like being awoken any more than you do. However, Khushy is my niece, and I have every intention of being a proper aunt to her. As long as Hiba's nearby, we shall manage." As she spoke, Perveen realized the idea wasn't as horrifying to her as it would have been a few days ago. So much had changed.

"The relationship of an aunt and niece is one of the most precious," Camellia said approvingly. "And it is always a better idea for a baby to sleep in the same room as a family member. It doesn't need to be the father or mother."

"Speaking of fathers, where is Pappa?" Perveen asked.

"Over at the Bankers'," Rustom said. "Trying to make things better, which I'm sure he cannot."

Perveen went upstairs and paused before stepping into the room that no longer belonged just to her. The fan whirred overhead as usual, but the curtains were drawn, and the air smelled like coconut. She sniffed again, expecting a bad odor, but it wasn't there.

She walked softly over to the cot and saw Khushy resting on her back, tiny eyes closed so her lashes fanned her cheeks. She looked like the most angelic doll.

With a soft rustle, the new ayah stepped in from the balcony. Perveen was impressed by the confident way Hiba greeted her, and liked that instead of drab beige or white, she wore a cheerful yellow-and-blue-printed cotton sari with a matching blouse. Her skin glowed with good health and coconut oil, and her shining black hair peeped out from the edge of a pink hijab.

"I am so grateful to you for coming the very day you heard about our situation," Perveen said, using her right hand to copy the adaab gesture of greeting. "Please call me Perveen-behen."

"Perveen-behen, I'm glad to be here." Hiba smiled warmly at her. "Dr. Penkar said you are a very kind family in need of some help."

"What do you think about Khushy's condition? She is sleeping now—but she can really cry!" Perveen said, glancing back toward the crib.

"The baby is fine. She was only hungry before. Now she will learn to sleep. I will teach her about lifting her head. Has she had her daily massage?"

"Massage? I don't know. I am gone most days." Perveen wondered why Hiba hadn't asked Camellia.

"Daily massage is very important for babies," Hiba said, walking over to Khushy's crib to look approvingly at the sleeping baby. "Often ladies in the family like to do this themselves, but I will gladly do it. I can also show you how."

Hiba was speaking as if Perveen, being the aunt, was the most responsible person for Khushy. It should have rankled, but Perveen felt strangely pleased. "I'd like to learn. And please tell me the truth about whether you want to sleep on our balcony. You must have noticed our parrot, Lillian."

"I like birds. She ate from my hand." Hiba fluttered her fingers. "Birds close by remind me of home—so many birds singing morning, noon, and night."

"Do you come from outside of Bombay?" Perveen asked.

"Yes. From Lonavala. My children are there being brought up by my parents."

"Do tell me about them," Perveen said, sitting down on the edge of her bed.

"Zainab is twelve and Nadim is four. I became a nurse when I was weaning Nadim." She spoke without emotion.

Watching the nurse's face, Perveen said, "You must miss Zainab and Nadim and your husband very much."

"Yes, but my children are no longer needing my milk. My wages pay their school fees," Hiba said.

Feeling awkward, Perveen said, "It is still very generous to give so much of your own body and spirit to Khushy. I'm gone to town most days, but I sleep in this bedroom. Please tell me when you need to rest or anything at all. We want you to be happy."

Hiba smiled. "Dr. Penkar said you are a good lady—as good as having the baby's mother in the house. And little Khushy is happy to be close."

Khushy gurgled and Hiba stepped to the cradle, reaching deftly to pick her up.

"She's not thirsty yet," Hiba said, tilting her head as she examined the baby. "I fed her just half an hour ago."

"But she called out," Perveen objected. "Didn't you hear?"

"She only wants to be close." Looking at Perveen, Hiba said, "You can hold her."

Taking a deep breath, Perveen opened her arms to take Khushy. It wasn't the first time she'd held her niece, but today she felt a tiny bit heavier. There was a pleasant scent about her, Yardley's English Lavender soap and something else. Perhaps it was Hiba's milk.

Khushy's small brown eyes fixed on her, as if watching for a reaction.

"Surely she can't focus," Perveen said.

"By this age, they are seeing very clearly," Hiba said. "She is looking at her aunty. She says, 'Aunty, I love you.'"

"She doesn't know me to love me," Perveen protested.

"I will be on the veranda. I'll come if she cries."

Hiba disappeared through the French doors, and Perveen settled down into the rocking chair. Looking back at Khushy, she said, "Well. We spend our days apart, but tonight we are roommates. Just as I was in college with Alice-aunty."

Nobody was watching to say she wasn't holding Khushy's head correctly. But she remembered where to place her palm, and Khushy did nothing to move away. Nor did she cry. A powerful feeling rushed up inside of Perveen as she held the baby. This was her niece. Not a daughter, but the closest she would have.

24

TO POLICE HEADQUARTERS

On Monday, Perveen woke up at her usual time: six-thirty. She lay still for a moment, marveling at how comfortably the night had passed.

Khushy had awoken during the night. Three times—or was it four? Each time, Hiba arrived quickly from Perveen's balcony and settled in one of the velvet lounging chairs to nurse the baby. Perveen had insisted that she take a chair rather than sit on the floor. As the nursing went on, Perveen drifted in and out of sleep, hearing the occasional pleasant whisper or sucking sound. How intimate it felt: just the three of them together.

Hiba had restored calm to an uprooted household. And what about Gulnaz? As Perveen tiptoed into her bathroom, she found herself hoping for just a few more days of calm without her sister-in-law's presence.

After Perveen's bath was done, Gita appeared with tea for her and cut-up fruit for Lillian. The sound of the tea tray being set down awoke Khushy. As the baby wailed, Gita began apologizing.

"She needs to wake," Perveen reassured Gita and reached confidently into the cradle to pick up her niece. When Hiba hurried in, Perveen said, "Will you show me how to change her?"

Learning was not as complicated as Perveen had feared. After the baby was washed and pinned into a dry nappy, Hiba settled herself cross-legged on her sleeping mat on the veranda to nurse Khushy. Perveen opened the birdcage so Lillian could strut along the railing, and Gita went on to do her other morning chores.

In all, it was an unusual and engaging early morning, and Perveen felt almost reluctant to go downstairs to go off to work.

She packed up her legal case, not only with the material for Sunanda's case, but also with the book about women's health that she intended to return to Miriam Penkar.

Jamshedji was already in the hall, adjusting his necktie before the mirror. Glancing at her, he said, "You must have had a hard night."

"To the contrary. I did some reading before bed, and I slept quite well." Perveen joined him to look at herself in the mirror. "Do you see something wrong?"

"Not on your face. But I know that Khushy has been in your room."

"Hiba comes so quickly when the baby needs a feeding that there's never more than a few seconds of crying. It's quite amazing."

Jamshedji nodded and said, "Well, we don't have time for breakfast at home. I must reach court before ten."

"Very well. We can get something to eat from Yazdani's," Perveen said, thinking that he was the one who'd clearly had a hard night. "Let's both say goodbye to Khushy before we go out."

He looked startled. "I—well, if it doesn't disturb the child and her ayah."

"Hiba recently finished a feeding, and Khushy is resting under Mamma's care on the back veranda."

Perveen followed her speedily walking father to the veranda, where he halted at the cradle to bend and chuck Khushy under the chin. His mouth curved upward for a moment. Then he told Perveen, "Let's go."

What is it about Pappa and Khushy? Perveen mused as they hustled toward the car. She'd wanted to hug Khushy goodbye, but she sensed that if she'd picked her up, it might take too long, in her father's opinion.

She startled, realizing that as she'd been brooding over her desire to go back inside, she'd stopped in front of the open car door, with Arman looking curiously on. She climbed inside, with Jamshedji following.

Clearing his throat, he said, "Mamma told me that you found Sunanda, and that she's in jail. What has the girl done this time?"

"She didn't do anything wrong except for misunderstanding the bail agreement!" Perveen went on to tell him about how Sunanda had been anxious about the barrister fees and gone off to try to obtain her saved funds to pay for it.

"We can't shelter clients from knowing that lawyers work for pay," Jamshedji's voice was tight, as if thinking that what he'd said during his brief encounter with Sunanda had been the catalyst. "We are already doing our side of the work as pro bono. It was my hope someone might support the cause."

"Like . . ." Perveen thought through the various women at the tea party who'd seen Sunanda's valor. "Begum Cora of Varanpur?"

"The so-called Miss Arbison who consulted you two days ago?" When she nodded, he said, "But you rejected her entreaty for representation. A bridge burned," he snapped. "But tell me what Sunanda said when you went to see her."

After Perveen had explained how Sunanda had resisted the questioning and been physically abused, he shook his head. "This is not good for her at all. It sounds like she could possibly be charged other actions. Let's hope they don't include murder."

"But multiple visitors came to Bhatia House that day—" Perveen stopped, realizing she hadn't told her father about Miriam Penkar's phone call. She did so, and he argued with her about how best to protect the doctor's rights all the way to the Bombay

High Court. Here, he disembarked, and Perveen rode the rest of the short distance to Mistry House.

Mustafa handed Perveen the morning's mail. Sorting through it upstairs, she was disappointed to see one of the potential barristers had already sent a rejection. But two other men wrote with the times that they could come for a meeting.

Perveen gave Mustafa the appointment details to write on the schedule he kept downstairs. She got to work on filling out a deposition form for Mr. A. V. Tomar, angry that she was still stymied by not having an address. Would the prosecutor give her the missing information? It might be unlikely, given that the magistrate had censured her. What to do?

She was nowhere close to an answer by afternoon when the first barrister, Mr. P. K. Dastur, arrived.

Dastur, an old friend of Jamshedji's, waited in the parlor with a big smile. After they had both inquired after each family's health, Perveen gave an outline of Sunanda's situation. She noticed the man's smile fading, and she felt convinced that she'd won him over with the importance of the mission.

"It's a very important battle to win," she said, leaning forward to make her final point. "If we succeed with this case, it will be very difficult for the Bombay prosecutor's office to mount similar accusations. We could protect the privacy and free choices of women in the city."

As she finished, the lawyer shook his head. "No, not for me."

"Why not?" Perveen asked, feeling perplexed. "You've got two daughters studying at university. I know you believe in women's progress."

"Abortion is not allowed in our faith." He spoke heavily. "Therefore, I shouldn't be involved in this case."

"We will prove she *didn't* have an abortion. So how could that be a conflict?"

"My reputation."

Perveen counted slowly in her mind, trying not to lose her

temper. What more could she say? "Mr. Dastur, isn't it true that your surname means 'priest'?"

"Yes. As a Parsi, you should know that." His voice held a hint of reproof.

"Yet you decided not to be one."

Clenching his hands, he said, "Law is a very good field. We don't all have to be priests."

"Regardless, I suppose you do recite the Nirang-i-kusti several times each day?"

He shifted in his chair. "There is no set pattern."

"We should make this prayer daily, according to the rules of our faith."

He shook his head. "I don't understand your point, Miss Mistry."

"I'm saying that it's impossible to define what it means to be a faithful Zoroastrian. And Zoroastrian barristers, including you, routinely represent persons accused of many crimes that we find distasteful."

"You speak cleverly, Miss Mistry. But it's still my decision to decline this case. You need someone who is more daring than this old gentleman." He made a self-deprecating smile. "And do say hello to your father."

The interview had lasted twenty minutes. Afterward, Mustafa came in to clear up the cups and tell her two things: the second barrister for that day had called to cancel, and her father had sent a note to her by courier. It read:

I stopped into the prosecutor's office to seek Tomar's address for the deposition. They received a complaint in letter form from the police without an address for the complainant. No deposition can be made until we have an address; and I suggest you trace back to the Bombay Police for the necessary details.

This was an irregular process; Perveen knew the police would not be amiable to any sort of questions from a lawyer outside of a courtroom. Yet because the prosecutor's office hadn't been observant, she'd have to demand the information herself. She packed up the copies of documents that she had—as well as a finished contract for their real estate client, Mr. Hariani, to drop off later.

The Bombay Police Headquarters building in Palton Road was a three-story Victorian Gothic structure designed by John Adams, the public works architect-engineer who'd designed Wilson College and the Yacht Club residency building. Perveen asked Mustafa to park near the lengthy outdoor gallery that spanned the ground floor, and as she passed well-dressed civilians and uniformed British officers, she caught a few curious glances. She was not a regular at this location, so she imagined nobody knew her as a solicitor.

Perveen gave her name and business to the armed constables guarding the building entrance and was allowed through.

This office was much better appointed than a typical neighborhood station waiting room, with comfortable chairs and settees rather than wooden benches. Portraits of Bombay's governor, Sir George Lloyd, and the country's viceroy, Lord Reading, and King-Emperor George V stared soberly from the walls.

Nobody else was waiting, and Perveen went straight to the clerk behind the Burma teak counter. "Good afternoon. My name is Perveen Mistry—"

The Anglo-Indian clerk's voice was brusque as he pointed to a large book on the counter. "Sign in. Then you will be called."

She signed her name and listed her business address. There was no space for telephone numbers, because telephones were still rare in most homes.

Nobody else was in the room, but it took five more minutes for him to call her up. Immediately, he said, "If you wish to file a police report, go to your local precinct."

"I'm not wishing to make a report. I'm a solicitor with a case who needs to trace the background for a complaint filed with the police on Tuesday, June sixth." As she spoke, a British superintendent wearing Bombay Police khakis came into the waiting room and shot her a curious look. Ignoring it, she kept her attention on the clerk.

"That information is with the prosecutor's office, madam." He looked past her to the police officer, as if ready to serve him.

Perveen could not let him end the encounter like this. Pulling the charge sheet from her case, she laid it on the desk. "You'll see here that the complainant's address isn't in their possession. That's why I've come here—to get what's missing."

He smiled patronizingly. "Actually, the complaints are made in individual stations. We would not even have the document you seek."

"But there's no mention of a neighborhood station. Just Bombay Police Headquarters."

"Enough. Out of the way—some of us have real business to do!" the officer behind her said gruffly.

Knowing the officer would not tolerate any more arguments, Perveen stepped aside. But as she walked out of the room, she felt on the edge of a new idea. Wherever Tomar had made his complaint, he should have signed a log. If she could get hold of the book on the counter, she would at least know if he'd come to the main headquarters; that she was right, and the clerk wrong.

As Perveen headed toward the main doors, she noticed a familiar-looking Indian officer in a khaki police uniform walking briskly in her direction. When she caught his eye, he stopped, giving her a nod of recognition.

"Miss Mistry? Good morning to you," he said with a warm smile.

"Inspector Singh! It's very nice to see you again."

"I'm still a sub-inspector," he corrected her. "What brings you here?"

Why not try for what she wanted? Casually, she said, "I

was hoping to see if there are details here of the address of a complainant. It isn't present on the prosecutor's charging document."

"How strange. You could ask at reception," he said. "But if you've got a minute, I want to ask you something . . ."

"Certainly." She looked at him expectantly.

"Detective-Inspector Vaughan heard that you went to Bhatia House recently?"

If the police were interested in her activities at Bhatia House, it could mean she too was a person of interest in the case. And she also would be in a similarly vulnerable spot to Miriam Penkar and Sunanda.

"Yes. I visited with Uma Bhatia several times over the last few weeks," she said. "For a charity project."

"Was it not to talk about Sunanda Chavda?"

Perhaps Uma or Mangala had told him. "I am representing her, so I would hardly gossip about her. Now, I wanted to ask you about something else. A way that I might be able to see the police reception log for June six, to see the address for a complainant."

"Someone who's behind the warrant for Miss Chavda's arrest?" He paused. "The police really can't talk about that kind of thing outside of court. It's an active investigation."

"What's the trouble here?"

Perveen turned to see another police official—not Singh's boss, but a stranger in the white uniform of the Bombay Police.

25

AN IMPERIOUS REQUEST

Serena Prescott's husband was a fitting match for her: a tall, slim gentleman with the bone structure of a film star. Somewhere in his forties, he wore his salt-and-pepper hair fashionably slicked, and he had a narrow mustache that was waxed into a thin line.

"Inspector Prescott, may I introduce Miss Perveen Mistry?" Singh said in a rush. "She is a solicitor who arrived here by mistake. She will be heading on for the prosecutor's office."

Perveen looked at Singh, feeling a mix of irritation and sympathy. Was his anxious reaction because he feared the man, or because he was trying to deflect attention from her direct request for information?

"Miss Mistry, your reputation precedes you." The man put out his tanned hand, and Perveen felt obliged to shake it, her hand gliding over the hard black stone of his signet ring.

"Oh. Did your wife mention me?"

As he released her from his steely grip, he said, "She told me she put her foot in her mouth in your presence yesterday—I apologize on her behalf. But let's start again. I was informed you are Bombay's first female solicitor. This interests me greatly."

"I see." Perhaps he was part of the investigation, which meant her conversation with Singh would be repeated verbatim.

Prescott smiled and asked, "Have you a moment for a cup of tea?"

"Sir, we do have the meeting with Mr. Stowe in a half hour," Sub-Inspector Singh said, while Perveen paused, deliberating what to do. The fact was, Prescott was so high up, he might do her the favor nobody else could.

"Just knock on my door when he arrives. Come along, Miss Mistry." Prescott ushered her down the same corridor she'd traveled and toward a closed door which was quickly opened by a peon who'd been standing nearby, as if opening the doors of seniors was his duty.

Perveen sensed that his office could be as much an interrogation chamber as Sunanda had faced; even though it appeared as a pleasant room with a damask sofa, comfortable rattan chairs, and a handsome desk decorated with silver-framed photographs.

She shifted her gaze from a plaque on the desk reading PRESCOTT, IMPERIAL POLICE ADVISOR TO THE BOMBAY POLICE to an ominous curved spear hanging on the wall behind the desk.

"A gift from the Maharaja of Rajputana," he commented with pride.

"It's quite a splendid work of art." Perveen dropped her gaze to look directly at him. "Did you meet the maharaja when you were stationed in Delhi?"

There was a knock, and when he called for entry, a constable came carrying a tray with a teapot and two cups. The young man began pouring tea for Prescott, but he cut him off sharply. "Ladies first."

The constable flinched, splashing a bit of tea, and then turned to serve Perveen.

"Milk and one sugar, please. No, I'll stir it myself." She held the cup in her hands, watching as the man wiped up the spill he'd made on Prescott's saucer before serving him.

Prescott spoke after the constable had exited. "Actually, I met the maharaja when I was stationed in Rajputana as an advisor to his military command. It was a memorable tour of duty in a paradise of unspoiled nature. Bombay is quite the opposite, in terms of land development. However, Serena does enjoy the sailing and social life that goes with it. She sails with the Honorable Alice Hobson-Jones, who I gather is a dear friend of yours?"

This was an abrupt segue, but the topic seemed innocuous, so she answered. "Our friendship goes back to student days at St. Hilda's College in Oxford. When Miss Hobson-Jones arrived here from Britain in 1921, I was so pleased to rekindle our friendship. But she's quite busy most days teaching at Wood-burn College."

"Apparently a job your family helped her get?" His voice was faintly teasing.

"She's a brilliant lecturer and dean—does it matter who introduced her?" Perveen realized belatedly how defensive she sounded.

"I'm only thinking it's an example of how Parsis are connected all through society. Almost like . . . an intelligence network!" He smiled as if it were a compliment. "Were you at the fundraising party for the women's hospital?"

Perveen was sure he knew the answer. "Of course. Didn't Mrs. Prescott mention it?"

"Yes. My wife helped organize the women's medical school in Delhi, so this is a natural progression for her. But now Sir Dwarkanath has passed away. Such a tragic loss. Did you hear the cause of death?"

Perveen was startled by his expectation. "This morning's newspaper didn't have the autopsy result."

He raised his eyebrows. "Just as the papers haven't reported on Sunanda Chavda's second arrest."

This was the moment she'd feared; she would have to stay strong and reveal as little as possible. Chuckling, she asked, "Do you think my client is important enough in this city to have her story publicized?"

"It's not that she's unimportant." After taking a long sip of tea, he spoke in a casual tone. "But why should a woman's reputation be ruined needlessly? What the police share with the press is part and parcel of the progressive ideology I'm bringing to the department."

Perveen stared at him, thinking that it sounded like he supported the casual censorship that was a matter of course for newspapers in Bombay.

"Miss Mistry?" he prompted. "Did I surprise you?"

"Sorry. I'm a bit overcome." Perveen widened her eyes, as if she were very naïve. "What an unusually frank tea-time conversation! Are the police keeping Sir Dwarkanath's cause of death as confidential information?"

"The autopsy finished two hours ago—not enough time to make tonight's papers, but in my opinion, it's public information. Sir Dwarkanath showed signs of acute lead acetate poisoning. An interesting result." He looked intently at her.

Lead acetate was very different from what Miriam Penkar had thought in her brief examination. Perveen asked, "What is the police response?"

"Obviously, we will search for the source. For the time being, it remains a suspicious death."

"I've heard his stone business is located in Kalbadevi. I wonder if lead acetate is ever used to color stones?" Perveen asked.

"Perhaps. We know that Sir Dwarkanath had a number of visitors from outside the house in the week that he died."

"You already know that I was there," Perveen commented with an easy smile. "My question is whether that coincidence should inspire me to hire my own lawyer."

"Actually, Miss Mistry, I am interested in you, but not for that reason." He looked penetratingly at her, and she felt nauseated. "I wanted this time alone to ask you some things. Specifically, about your interest in women's welfare. Sir David says that you've represented several Indian ladies in Bombay Presidency and the princely states."

"True," she said, wondering at his use of the term "welfare."

"Most of my clients came to me because of cultural taboos that preclude male lawyers' assistance."

"Just the situation I am concerned about!" Leaning forward slightly, he said, "The viceroy dispatched me here with the mission to make the Bombay Police a modern, ethical institution. One of my first questions is why no office exists within the Bombay Police that protects women and offers sincere compassion when they fall victim to crime?"

"I don't know," Perveen answered. "I imagine that the past chiefs of police thought other matters were more pressing."

"Miss Mistry, what's your opinion of the value of the Bombay Police establishing a special unit, perhaps called Women's Safety and Protection?" He ended on an exultant, upward note.

Perveen sensed that he wanted her approval, but she felt reluctant to become his supporter. "I think it would be difficult to get customers."

"I don't understand," he said, putting down his cup of tea.

"How could women rally the courage to tell someone outside of their household—who is not even the same gender—about abuse?" As Perveen spoke, she felt a chill, remembering the miserable months of her short marriage. "These feelings are inculcated in us—just as men are trained not to think of women as being intelligent."

"So, you are saying that gender difference would impair such a police unit."

"I am. Also, there's the matter of the British Indian government permitting different legal codes for the different religions."

"I'm somewhat familiar—but tell me more." He put down his cup and looked toward her with warm eyes.

"From the early 1800s, colonial judges used translations of Hindu and Islamic classical legal texts for guidance. When British rule was formalized, so were different systems of family law for Hindus, and for Shia and Sunni Muslims. Sikhs were placed under Hindu law, and the remaining smaller faiths:

India's Jews, Christians, and Buddhists fall under English common law."

He interjected, "And what about Parsis?"

She couldn't believe she'd omitted her own people. Skin flushing, she said, "In the 1860s, male leaders in my community advocated for exceptions in matrimonial and inheritance law."

Prescott smiled. "I think these differing systems show cultural sensitivity. And there's no reason to think such a framework would inhibit my suggested police unit for women's well-being."

"Actually, it does. The differing codes affect at which age a girl can legally be married." Perveen's voice was tight, because she felt fearful of showing too much emotion. "And there are varying rules against the type of violence the court deems acceptable for a husband or father to mete out on her."

Prescott had been watching her raptly. He kept silent for a minute and then said, "Violent crimes come under the standard Indian Penal Code, which applies to everyone. Rape is a violent crime."

"Section 375," she nodded. "Within the definition of rape, there's an exception to protect the perpetrator if he is the husband of a female aged thirteen or older. And the truth is, most rapes and beatings of women occur within joint family homes. And tell me, what family would want to report a patriarch or son's actions? And what would lead a woman to think she had a right to complain?"

"I agree." He looked away and picked up a pen on his blotter. As he examined it, he said, "So, let's say that such cases are unlikely to come forward. Still, if an unrelated man attacked a woman, the unit would make it faster and easier for us to charge him. And the penalties for rape are severe—up to ten years of prison. Wouldn't female victims wish to report these types?"

"Of course, but . . ." Perveen thought about how Amla Chavda had reacted to gossip about Sunanda's alleged sexual activity. "Even if a stranger raped a woman, her family would probably tell her not to report it. She'd be considered perma-nently defiled."

Prescott shook his head. "Perhaps there could be a way for this department to put shame where it belongs: on the attackers. Surely there are some situations with powerful men abusing women," he continued. "What happens when gentlemen in Bombay are accused?"

Perveen felt a prickling go up her spine. Was he asking because he knew about a crime not yet reported?

"Miss Mistry?"

"I'm not aware of any cases wherein a white man was charged. And isn't it almost time for your meeting with Mr. Stowe?" She checked her watch, desperate for an excuse to leave.

"He must not have arrived yet." Smiling unctuously, Prescott said, "I am very curious about what typically happens to elite men who are accused."

"I wish I could tell you, but I don't have access to the police records of Bombay." She smiled tightly. "Don't you have that?"

Ignoring her jab, he asked, "What about civil suits? This is the type of thing Mistry Law specializes in, isn't it?"

"It's true we do many civil suits. But in our firm's experience, I can't think of a case wherein a client has come forward to sue a European for rape. However, the British have been in Bombay since the 1600s, and I have only worked as a solicitor since 1920."

Quickly, he said, "I meant elites of all nationalities. I wonder if the common law has loopholes that protect elites?"

There were many ways to answer this question, but she didn't want to help Prescott with his inexplicable mission. "I know there's a standing law in British India that prevents the poor from raising a charge of assault against an employer."

"But that's absurd!" he sputtered.

"It seems to me that the law is intended to allow employers to discipline workers as they see fit," Perveen said.

"You have many interesting observations." Prescott steepled

his fingers and said, "For this reason, you are first on my list as a potential officer for an office of women's safety, should it ever come to be."

Perveen swallowed hard as she realized she'd been ridiculously suspicious of him, for all the wrong reasons.

"What do you think—would you like to have such a job?"

"I am tremendously flattered," she said. "However, if I leave my father's firm, it would certainly harm that business. My father is counting on me to succeed him."

"So you are enjoying everything about your work?" Studying her, he added, "You don't occasionally feel a bit limited?"

"The discrimination of the courts against women is frustrating—but that is hardly a reason to abandon what I'm doing." Perveen also imagined that having police as her colleagues would be even worse than facing hostile judges.

"Very well, I have noted your opinion," he said, giving her a look of resignation. "In any case, let's keep this conversation private."

Perveen stiffened as his meaning hit her. If she couldn't divulge the conversation, it might mean he wanted to keep private some of the questions and comments he'd made, especially about rape and whether elite men had avoided persecution in Bombay. *Damn it*, she thought. He was not only imperial; he was imperious. Smiling widely, she spoke in a light manner. "Usually, my clients sign contracts before we enter a situation of privileged conversation."

He didn't smile back. "I am not confessing anything to you. It's only that if I'm to move forward on this new department, it would be better not to have rumors flying about it before I've proposed it."

Perveen's heartbeat returned to normal. Not all Englishmen were enemies. Perhaps Mr. Prescott had been sent out of Delhi because his ideas for the police were considered unsettling. If he sincerely wished to create a police office to help women, and women worked within it—maybe things might change a little bit. "I see your point. And I wish you the best of luck."

A knock came at the door, and she heard Singh's voice. "Mr. Stowe has arrived."

"I'm just coming," Prescott called out. As he stood, he shook out each leg, like an athlete preparing for a race. "Will you be at the Lawyers' Ball this Saturday?"

Again, she had an instinctive feeling of caution. "I haven't yet decided my plans."

As Prescott opened the door, he said, "There will be many highly placed officials in the police attending. That's a benefit for you."

Perveen found it annoying that he was still hinting about how good it would be for her to join forces with him. "If I do go, I'll be with my father."

"You must introduce us," he said.

"As you wish. Goodbye, then." As she walked out, Perveen didn't glance at Malcolm Stowe sitting on a chair in the reception area. In fact, it wasn't until she reached her car that she took her first full breath.

26

A GENTLEMAN'S LUCK

*A*rman was waiting with the car, and when she got in, he asked, "All's finished to your satisfaction, then?"

"No—I still don't have A. V. Tomar's address." Seeing the concern on Arman's face, she forced herself to smile. "Let's go to Elphinstone Circle. At least I can deliver the Hariani contract."

Mr. Hariani's office was on the second floor of a handsome office building decorated with black wrought iron grilles on every window and an especially elaborate grille on the front door. As Perveen entered the building, she found the curved stairway going up had a similar metal banister with railings in which carved monkeys, birds, and even a mongoose played. Very likely it was the work of the long-gone artisan, Nadim, at Stowe Ironworks.

Mr. Hariani was pleased to receive the contract, and she offered him the chance for a personal explanation of a few points.

"This is done just as I'd hoped! But you must take a rest in the heat. Please take a glass of water." He clapped his hands loudly and a peon appeared to take the order.

Perveen was parched, so she was glad for the drink. Sitting down in a soft chair across from the client, she said, "This is a handsome building. And the wrought iron stairway is so beautiful."

"Stowe Ironworks made it," he said. "Did you know they own this building?"

"No. I hadn't seen any sign when I was coming upstairs."

"'Stowe' is carved outside, over the building's doors. Can't miss it."

Perveen chided herself for doing just that. She felt curious about the man who'd inherited the historic company and who'd given work to Colin—and had existing appointments on days she'd visited Bhatia House and the Bombay Police. Perhaps he already thought she was suspicious of him. "What is Mr. Stowe's schedule like?"

"I rarely see him. Sometimes I see him leave the office already dressed for a dinner party." He uttered the last words with obvious distaste for frivolity. "They say that he's different from his father. The company isn't doing as much furniture and fittings, but more industrial uses, including steel."

The word "industrial" reminded Perveen of Sir Dwarkanath's lead acetate poisoning. Probably the police would trace his movements at work and come to an answer about the origin of his poisoning. Then she wouldn't have to worry about a serious charge for Sunanda, or for Miriam Penkar. Shifting her mind away from these worries, she said, "Now, to our business.

"As I've explained, I've worked carefully to preserve your interests in this contract. Now only your signature is needed, and I shall deliver it to the other party's lawyer."

Hariani raised a bony finger in her direction. "Before signing, I'll pass the contract back to you for your father to check."

"Please don't worry. I am the lawyer who drafted this contract, and I've already reviewed it with you." Perveen was frustrated to be treated like a law clerk, rather than the partner in a solicitor's firm.

"He is the reason I hired the firm. I expect his attention," Mr. Hariani said sternly.

"I understand," Perveen said, trying to hide her desire to snatch the contract back. In the end, Hariani would pay more, because Jamshedji would bill for his time. A win for the accounting books, but not for her.

On her way out, she paused on the ground floor. The door to Stowe Ironworks was cast iron over glass, and through it she spotted a young Indian clerk in a European suit sitting at the desk. Perhaps Mr. Stowe had returned from his meeting with Prescott.

Impulsively, she entered the office, causing the clerk to look up, startled.

"Ah . . . the hair salon is two buildings down!" he said after taking measure of her.

"I'm not looking for any salon. Is Mr. Stowe in?"

"Have you business with him?" The clerk's gaze fell on her legal case.

"No. I'm involved with the women's hospital—his wife's pet project." Perveen delivered an ingratiating smile.

"He is out of station until day after tomorrow. What is your name, madam?"

Perveen hesitated, knowing that he might be getting an earful about her from Nigel Prescott. "He won't know me: I'm one of many on his wife's committee. I'll check with her again."

Perveen directed Arman to drive the short distance to the Royal Asiatic Society of Bombay. She told him she'd spend an hour doing some light research in the reading room. If Sir Dwarkanath had been murdered—as she guessed the police were thinking—she wanted to know more about his recent activities and associates.

Perveen felt the heat rising like a blanket around her as she left the car and climbed the society's lengthy flight of white marble steps. She was damp with sweat when she entered the periodicals reading room. As she'd hoped, she saw her elderly friend, Abinash K. Dass, with the *Times of India* in front of him.

"Good morning, Miss Mistry! A nice surprise after so many months."

"Yes, Mr. Dass, I haven't seen you since that lecture last November." Perveen slid into the empty chair next to the retired postal clerk, who prided himself on reading at least six newspapers daily. "Tell me, how many newspapers have you checked today?"

"This is the third." He closed the newspaper. "And what can I tell you about?"

"I was looking for more information on Lord Dwarkanath Bhatia than was in the obituaries. But I suppose that means I must go back many issues."

"Oh, yes." He nodded. "The death of a powerful man often raises suspicions. And frankly, I am thinking it will be ruled foul play."

Perveen thought of telling him what Prescott had told her about the lead acetate, but she could run into trouble if the information got out. "Why do you think this?"

"If Sir Dwarkanath died of age or disease, the doctors should have already declared." Dass tapped the newspaper. "They should have said it on Saturday or Sunday. But many could have wished for his early demise."

"Like who?" Perveen tried to sound dispassionate, although Dass's theory was exactly what she needed to protect her clients.

Dass removed his spectacles to look frankly at Perveen. "The Legislative Council had a bill to vote on last Friday. That day, Sir Dwarkanath was absent, so he was marked as not voting. The bill narrowly passed, and it was something he opposed."

"Please tell me about the bill!" Perveen recalled her own thoughts that Bhatia could have rivals for power within the Legislative Council.

"It would give government the right to enforce fines on any houses of worship who do not report donations to the satisfaction of the Bombay Municipal Corporation. Sir Dwarkanath opposed it strongly."

"I can understand why. A closed temple or mosque could create quite a bit of unrest." Perveen shivered, imagining police beating back protestors, and the fight spreading.

"And more!" Mr. Dass raised his bony index finger. "Sir Dwarkanath wrote an editorial positing that when houses of worship could not afford to pay the fines, they would lose their properties. And that perhaps having more plots of land to sell within the city was the true motive. It was a brave thing to say, as he himself has accepted honors from the government."

"Yes, it would seem so!" Perveen thought Dwarkanath Bhatia was a conflicted man. She'd disliked him because of how roughly he'd spoken to his family members, but she also believed he loved and missed his wife. Now, Sir Dwarkanath seemed to have tried to protect Bombay from over-reaching hands.

Mr. Dass murmured, "Sir Dwarkanath could see ahead to what might happen to Bombay. That's why he was against the bill. Now, who on the Legislative Council can take his place?"

Perhaps someone who wanted power enough that they'd kill him. Perveen was about to ask Mr. Dass if there were any businessmen he suspected, but the librarian suddenly called out to them to be quiet: the library was for research, not conversation.

Mr. Dass blushed and began fiddling with his spectacles, and Perveen knew it was time to go. She whispered goodbye to her dear old friend and headed out of the reading room. The research had been faster than she'd expected. Now she had a spare forty-five minutes, and a good idea of what to do with it.

The map room was empty save for a pair of students whispering together in the back. Right away, she saw Colin Sandringham leaning over one of the wide teak tables with a tracing paper spread out over an old map. Perveen let him finish the section he was tracing before she quietly approached and spoke his name.

"Why, hello!" He straightened and turned to smile at her. "Miss Mistry, what a nice surprise."

Perveen was glad he'd remembered the proprieties.

"And hello to you, Mr. Sandringham. Do tell me about the map you're tracing."

"It's an early nineteenth-century map of the hills outside Varanpur. At that time, all the land was held by Marathas." He indicated a mountain with his finger. "Muslim forces came over this mountain and conquered. That's when the name changed."

"Is this part of the work we spoke about earlier?"

He hesitated. "Not exactly. That job's completed."

"Well done! And do you think you'll do more for the Legislative Council?"

Colin began folding up his tracing paper. "I'm not sure what to think about them. I can leave this map here without worry. Shall we have a cup of tea?"

Colin's office was underground and, thus, windowless. Since she'd last visited, she noticed he'd decorated his walls with framed maps of India's princely states. Perhaps some of the maps showed the areas that Colin had been reluctant to discuss.

A young man in a neatly pressed gray shirt and trousers paused at the open doorway.

"Hullo, Kabir!" Colin waved him in. "We need two cups of tea, please."

Kabir regarded Perveen with open curiosity. "Sugar, milk?"

"Just milk. And if I could have a glass of water, I'd appreciate it," she said, seating herself in the straight-backed mahogany visitor's chair set in front of the cluttered desk, and Colin moved to take the larger chair behind it.

"I mustn't visit your office, but you can come to mine. Clever!" Colin said, leaning back to smile at her after Kabir had gone.

Noting how Colin's manner had relaxed, Perveen resolved to keep from falling victim to her own desires. Smiling, she said, "Please don't distract me from the question I was asking you upstairs. What happened with your project for the Legislative Council? You were so excited about it."

"Well, I'm not quite sure." Colin sounded uneasy.

"You already have presented it, didn't you say?" Perveen asked just as Kabir returned with their tea and the extra water for her.

"Right. The first time I presented was on Friday, June second, at Malcolm Stowe's office, which is very nearby."

Kabir departed, closing the door behind him. Colin gulped his tea, and Perveen slowly sipped her water, thinking that he wanted to tell her something but wasn't sure that he should. She asked, "And someone asked you to present a second time?"

"Informally," he said with emphasis. "Prescott, the Yacht Club member who introduced me to Stowe, invited us both for drinks at his new flat on Sunday evening. That's when he brought out the maps."

Perveen had finished her water, and now she looked into the golden depths of her tea, using her spoon to tamp down an errant tea leaf. It had run away into her cup, just like her anxious thoughts. "I've met Inspector Prescott myself. He was quite friendly. He brought me into his office for a spontaneous chat, and then he told me I could repeat none of it."

Colin rolled his eyes. "Prescott was good natured when I met him, but he became rather challenging once I'd done the maps. He even drew his own lines over the map, showing me where I should correct borders."

"Which zones did he want to revise?"

Colin's face had developed two pink spots close to his cheekbones. "As I said to you last time, I cannot divulge more details. It's not important, anyway."

Impulsively, Perveen reached a hand across the table to touch Colin's wrist. As his pulse beat under her thumb, she said, "Sorry—I don't want to make you uncomfortable. Just be aware that there's no law prohibiting you from sharing previously published material, such as the original maps, with anyone else. Perhaps you could garner a supportive opinion of your work and share that with them. That is—if you feel it's worth fighting for."

"Or maybe that person would agree that I'm wrong," Colin

said, taking another chug of tea. "As you know, I read geography at university, but that isn't the same as a cartographer's training. I overstepped myself."

Geographers ranked higher professionally than cartographers, just as solicitors were in comparison to barristers. It seemed an interesting coincidence that their supposed advantage wasn't serving either of them well. Trying to lighten the mood, she said, "You will create more maps and have better experiences in the future, but I am sorry about how this job ended."

Colin snorted. "Frankly, I want to wash my hands of this whole ordeal."

"The rains are coming!" Perveen said dramatically. "Your hands will be washed and everything else, too."

Colin glanced wistfully at one of the maps on his wall. "It's already been raining in Satapur for three weeks. How divinely cool the air must be."

Noting his melancholy, Perveen decided to press forward with her purpose. "I've got an invitation for you—and I hope you're free this weekend."

Colin's eyes slowly brightened as she told him about her planned attendance at the Lawyers' Ball, as well as Alice's extra ticket and need for an escort.

"I'm chuffed to go, but remember, I'm a dreadful dancer!" Colin gave her a lopsided grin.

"We mustn't dream of dancing together!" Perveen said, shocked he'd raised the prospect. "My father will be there!"

"I thought your father liked me?"

Seeing the hurt in Colin's eyes, Perveen said, "It would be better for him to continue thinking of you as a friend of the law firm only. He expects me to behave respectably everywhere, especially at a ball being held at a club where we belong."

"Love cannot conquer all, you are saying."

"Not in my country, and perhaps not yours, either. " Perveen stretched out a hand across the table toward him. Softly, she said, "What we have together is special—but I hope you understand it can't ever be a happily-ever-after fairy tale."

Colin squeezed her hand gently—the opposite of the unpleasant handshake she'd had with Prescott. And she didn't remove her hand, wanting the touch as long as it lasted.

"When will you come to my flat again?" he murmured.

"I feel like we got awfully close last time," she said, hiding her nervousness with a laugh.

"We should be close! I am in love with you," he said earnestly.

"And I—" Perveen cut herself off, still feeling fearful of declaring herself. "I've been reading about how things work—I mean regarding human conception," she amended, seeing the confusion in Colin's face. "If a woman falls pregnant, there's no escape except abortion, which is hard to find safely and is also labeled a crime."

"Heaven forbid," Colin said, releasing her hand. "And I'm ashamed of myself for making it seem that conjugal relations was chief in my mind. At least we are in the same city and can see each other here and there. Will you promise to keep dropping in at the Asiatic?"

"Yes. And the Lawyers' Ball is exactly the kind of moment we can enjoy, in some small fashion," Perveen said, trying to sound more cheerful than she felt. "Taxis can be expensive. Why don't I tell Alice to come with a car for you at six-thirty? Then you're sure to be on time."

"Why not?" Assuming the boisterous voice of a stage comedian, he said, "A man moves to Bombay and finds that etiquette is upside-down. Ladies are the ones who come to call, who pay for the evenings out, and even supply transportation. Fellows new to town should be advised to dress to the nines every evening, just in case a lovely lady should knock at the door."

Perveen collapsed into giggles. "I think you're a very lucky gentleman."

Colin winked and said, "The luckiest gentleman of all."

27

A CLINIC IN SAMUEL STREET

"We must talk," Jamshedji said the next morning as he was proceeding from the house to the car.

"Of course," Perveen said, sliding into the back of the Daimler. As he followed suit, she had an ominous feeling she was in for another scolding. He hadn't been pleased that she couldn't get past the police's resistance to looking up A. V. Tomar's address. Nor had he liked learning that Mr. Hariani wanted his oversight on the contract that Perveen had prepared. With all the criticism heaped on her, she'd thought it wise not to bring up her meetings with Nigel Prescott and Colin lest he jump on her for wasting time.

"Let me be frank about something," he said, settling himself into the car. "We are leaving later than we should today, and I'm sorry about it. I was forced to attend an early meeting today."

"With a potential barrister?"

As Arman started driving, Jamshedji said, "Homi Banker called for Rustom and me to meet him in Five Angles Park this morning. He informed us that Dr. Pandey has advised them not to move Gulnaz back to us."

Perveen wondered if by meeting in the park, Mr. Banker was trying to keep Rustom from reuniting with Gulnaz. But at the same time, she felt relief that Khushy's other grandfather hadn't asked for the grandchild to be delivered. "Who knows what the truth is? But thank goodness we have Hiba, and I truly don't mind Khushy sleeping in my room."

"Don't forget that you are a lawyer, not a mother!" Jamshedji said, grimacing slightly. "Keeping a baby in your room is not right."

"I'm sure it's only temporary. I can bear it." She used understated words because he seemed fixated on Khushy being a thorn in her side.

"Everyone in this house has tried to see Gulnaz and been turned away. But you have not tried." He looked closely at her. "If you succeeded, you could tell Gulnaz how well everything is going now that Hiba's joined us. And perhaps her mood would change. She seemed perfectly fine until she lost the first ayah."

"I've been far too busy to call on Gulnaz," Perveen began.

"Excuses, excuses," he interrupted. "We shall stop there on the way home from work. You'll go to the door. I shall remain in the car waiting."

A waiting car was a reason to have a very short visit. Still, Perveen felt reluctant to try. "I might only make matters worse. Things haven't been easy between us for quite a while."

"You will do your best. And the other thing I wish for you to do is get her consent to see Dr. Penkar."

Perveen stiffened. "I don't think that's a good idea! Remember how Gulnaz accused me of having the doctor come to look at her? And Dr. Penkar is now my client. To ask her to see Gulnaz complicates the relationship."

Jamshedji raised a finger. "Then do this. When you see Gulnaz tonight, find out how she feels about Dr. Pandey. And if she seems indifferent or unhappy, provide her with Dr. Penkar's telephone number."

"It doesn't sound like I have a choice," Perveen muttered.

At the office, Mustafa seemed to recognize Perveen's glumness, because he stirred an extra lump of sugar into her cup of tea. How many cups had she taken that day? Perveen was too distracted to count. Setting aside the half-finished cup, she decided to slightly subvert her father's orders by calling Dr. Penkar's office. She would find out, ahead of time, if Dr. Penkar thought having an appointment with Gulnaz would be a professional conflict.

It took several calls to get through to Dr. Penkar's clinic. A nurse answered, saying the doctor was very busy and that there were no appointments available for the next two days.

"I'm not seeking a medical appointment for myself. I'm the doctor's friend," Perveen clarified, choosing not to say "lawyer." "Could she please ring me back?"

"Oh, that's different." The nurse paused. "You said your name is Mistry?"

After Perveen affirmed this, the nurse said, "The doctor has mentioned you with respect. Come at four o'clock. She takes a tea break at that time before returning to work."

Perveen agreed and wrote down the appointment in her book. Then she settled herself on her side of the partners desk and began reviewing the document Mustafa had set on the center of her blotter, a real estate contract. It was refreshing to do something completely unrelated to Sunanda's case. But after about five minutes, her concentration was broken by Jamshedji rising.

Gathering up his legal case, he said, "I'm off to the Ripon. Too difficult to concentrate with your sighing and grunting and sour expressions. What is on for you today?"

"A potential client interview—Mr. Thakkar." Trying not to look as morose as she felt, she added, "And I'll interview two more barristers—if they come."

Two of them did appear, each an hour apart. Perveen introduced the basics of the case to Mr. Ravi Malhotra, who cut her short and said that he feared he would have too much difficulty arguing the minutiae of feminine health. After lunch, she saw the second barrister, Mr. Dubey, who opined that he might consider taking the job except that he was booked solidly through July. Would she consider asking the judge for postponement? Thinking of Sunanda's misery in the dark, fetid cell, Perveen declined.

She was in a very dark mood when Mr. Thakkar, the prospective client, finally arrived. She had tea with him in the parlor, learning that he was a pharmacist being sued for allegedly dispersing the wrong prescription to an elderly woman who'd vomited for two days. His argument was that the customer had grabbed a bottle off the counter that wasn't intended for her, so he was not at fault.

"This is just the sort of case I like. Recently, I represented a restaurant owner facing a lawsuit related to food poisoning. The settlement we reached was a fraction of what the plaintiff's solicitor had asked."

"Settling is not winning." Thakkar's thin lips curved downward. "What about your father? I want to hear his opinion."

"Mr. Mistry is meeting a client," she said, not wanting to divulge that he'd decamped to his club. "He assigned me to represent you based on my experience with similar civil suits."

"Mr. Jamshedji Mistry handled the Rajamatha Medicine Shop case," he said with an air of heavy disappointment. "He is the one with real experience. And I have too much trouble to take any risks."

"Mr. Mistry hears about every case I manage," Perveen said tightly.

"Pride is unbecoming in women," Mr. Thakkar said with a reproving look. "If your father is not available to help me, I'll go elsewhere."

He rose and walked out, Perveen trailing behind him with a promise that her father would call. She felt pain in her chest when he left. Was it indigestion—or heartbreak? Why did Mr. Thakkar have to become another failure to report to Jamshedji? She paced the office until three-thirty, when she judged it close enough to four to be on her way to Miriam Penkar's clinic.

The doctor's clinic was in Samuel Street, which had been named after Samuel Ezekiel Divekar, a Bene Israel Jew who'd served as an officer in the East India Company Army in the late eighteenth century. He was captured by the kingdom of Mysore's army, and he vowed to God that if he ever regained freedom, he'd build a synagogue in his home city of Bombay.

It was a colorful story that Rustom had told her during the time that he was new to construction and excited about every street in the city. Now she walked along, her eyes running over unusual names on shops and offices, wondering if these were names of Bene Israel people who had built a community around that first synagogue, Shaar Ha-Rahamim, a squat synagogue with a walled courtyard entrance. This was a house of worship that would be subject to the new bill that had passed the Legislative Council. She thought it likely that the synagogue would survive; although the Jews were a small population in the city, they were growing in number and influence.

Miriam Penkar's clinic had two signs. The older painted one, running across the top of the three-story brick building, said DR. ABRAHAM V. PENKAR, MEDICAL DOCTOR. On the newer glass window, a sign read: MIRIAM ABRAHAM PENKAR, GYNECOLOGY AND OBSTETRICS.

Perveen's attention was caught by a tiny ceramic cylinder exquisitely painted with blue flowers affixed to the right side of the door frame. She had never seen anything like it but had no more time to ponder it because the door was opening toward her, and she stepped back, holding its edge, to permit the exit of a heavily pregnant woman in a burqa followed by two children holding hands.

Entering the clinic, she saw an array of teak chairs and benches, where a few women sat, as well as girls, some not more than twelve, but with bellies swollen from pregnancy. The walls showed the doctor's framed certificates from Oxford and the Medical College of Madras. There was also a hand-colored illustration of a Muslim lady cradling a baby, and another of a Hindu mother and children, and finally, one of a Jewish mother at a table set with an elaborate candelabra and children clustered around.

A short table in the room's corner was surrounded by children drawing with colored pencils on paper; she saw other children holding books, pretending to read to each other.

"Dr. Penkar is finishing up with a patient," said the nurse she approached at the counter. "She wants you to go upstairs to the apartment. Her mother is waiting."

Perveen went back out to the hall and took the narrow stairway up a flight, where she faced another doorway affixed with a small cylinder, this one decorated with tiny sapphires and gilding.

She tapped the knocker. A Muslim maidservant wearing a sari over her salwar kameez welcomed Perveen into a sitting room brightened by light coming through a large bay window across from old upholstered mahogany furniture.

Perveen's eyes were drawn to several framed pictures. She saw a large document with Hebrew lettering, and a hand-tinted photograph of a handsome man who looked somewhere between thirty and forty. The deceased Abraham Penkar, she guessed.

"Good afternoon, Miss Mistry. I'm Bathsheba Penkar. Please come in."

Mrs. Penkar was in her fifties, Perveen guessed. Her black hair was threaded through with silver and there were laugh lines creasing the edges of her eyes. Perveen's eye was drawn to the fact she wore no jewelry, and her finely woven silk sari was a modest gray hue.

"This is the best seat. Take it, please." Mrs. Penkar gestured to the most luxurious piece of furniture, a velvet settee. "Miriam is late because she always takes the extra patient. I am glad you've come to see her. She was disconsolate last week but is now thinking that the hospital might resume."

"Has she received a firm indication?" Perveen asked,

retrieving *Woman and the New Race* from her legal case as well as a notebook and pen.

"Uma Bhatia hasn't spoken with Miriam because she's still in her mourning period. But it's entirely possible that she can convince her husband." Smiling at Perveen, she asked, "Will you take some of my halwa with your tea? Miriam tells me to ask first, because of people's health. It has sugar, you see."

"That sounds delightful," Perveen said, and Mrs. Penkar gave directions to Rehema, the maidservant who'd admitted Perveen.

After Rehema had gone to prepare the tea, Mrs. Penkar told Perveen in a low tone that the maid was a daughter of one of Miriam's poorest patients. Rehema had turned up one day saying to Miriam that she didn't want to be married to the elderly man her stepfather had chosen. It had been a risk for Miriam to take in a girl whose father was trying to arrange a marriage. However, when Miriam agreed to pay the family a small sum equivalent to the mahr they would have received from a groom, all objections were dropped.

"Rehema was just fourteen when she joined our house," Mrs. Penkar said. "Miriam's hope is that the maternity hospital will have a grant fund to make it possible for poor women to study there and stay in a hostel with other girls. Rehema is a gifted artist; she drew and colored all the pictures of women and babies in the downstairs clinic. She works for me part-time, and we pay for her high school."

"A happy ending," Perveen said.

Mrs. Penkar looked wryly at her. "Rehema's life has many chapters left to write. Will she get a scholarship to the Sir J. J. School of Art? That is our hope."

Rehema served the tea and sweets, bringing a third cup and plate for the doctor, which she arranged prettily near the empty chair. Even though it was four-thirty, Miriam still hadn't arrived. Perveen imagined her father would be impatient if she arrived back to Mistry House late.

"Eat, eat," Mrs. Penkar urged, so Perveen bit into the sweet, creamy halwa flavored with rose water and cardamom. Mrs. Penkar asked about Perveen's family, and then she chatted about Miriam's brothers, one who was principal of a boys' boarding school in the mountains, and the other who worked as a dentist and lived in Kemps Corner.

"My son Boaz would have liked to set his dental practice in the space downstairs, but Miriam was older and finished her studies first. So she took the space, and I'm glad she will always be nearby. What is better than having a daughter care for a mother as she ages?"

"Two daughters," Rehema said, as she refilled Mrs. Penkar's cup.

"Yes, yes! You are also my daughter now," Mrs. Penkar said. "Will you sit with us and ask Perveen-aunty about her work?"

"Sorry. I must study for my English exam," Rehema said.

"Go, go! I will make the second pot of tea when Miriam comes." Turning back to Perveen, Mrs. Penkar said, "I wouldn't have thought Miriam would be unmarried and living here still. My good fortune comes out of her misfortune."

"Her father's death?"

"That brought her back to us, yes. But she would very likely have been elsewhere, if her sweetheart had not died."

"A sweetheart? I didn't know!" Perveen was struck by the English-language word used by Mrs. Penkar, who'd been speaking Marathi.

"Miriam met Jacob at the Madras Medical College. When war broke out, he served as an army medical officer in France, and unfortunately, didn't survive." Mrs. Penkar picked at the border of her sari as she continued. "To the neighbors, my daughter is a spinster who is too old to match with the few eligible men in our community."

Perveen thought about the simple military watch Miriam wore, as well as the plain clothing for a woman so young, and she felt a pang for the doctor's hidden loss.

"The situation for finding a groom is difficult. I believe our population is smaller even than you Parsis. There are also Baghdadi Jews in this city—this is the origin of Miriam's sweetheart's family. His family was not pleased when he wished to become engaged to her."

Now Perveen understood Miriam's flippant comment about not looking like the Sassoons, and she felt angry about what had happened. "Those people should have been happy he was marrying another Jewish person, when there are so few in India."

"Many Baghdadis don't see the Bene Israel people as equals." Mrs. Penkar spoke softly, as if she did not hold anger. "Even though we are most certainly descended from the Ten Tribes of the Kingdom of Israel, so many years ago."

"And your tenure in India is almost two thousand years, isn't it?"

"Nobody really knows. One story is that some Jews from Yemen shipwrecked along the coast. They settled in villages and repeated what could be remembered of our faith. What an accomplishment it was to stay Jewish with only stories of heritage passing from parents to children. But in the last century, some religious men from Cochin—where a different group of Jews settled, a bit later than us, but sooner than the Baghdadis—traveled to Bombay to teach my great-grandparents about the Torah and everything else."

Perveen sensed that Bathsheba's devotion meant she could freely ask about the little ornaments near the doorways.

"Each one is called a mezuzah and contains a tiny scroll inscribed with a Hebrew prayer." Bathsheba's eye crinkles deepened as she added, "I touch the mezuzah each time I pass through and kiss my fingers. Yet I have told Miriam not to do it."

"Why?"

"Because of treating so many patients." Bathsheba's smile faded. "My husband, who treated so many patients, died from influenza. She washes her hands downstairs, and she washes them again upstairs."

Perveen looked at the portrait of the man on the wall and then back at Bathsheba. "I am so sorry to hear about your loss. And Miriam's."

Mrs. Penkar nodded. "Thank you. We have our double grief tying us together in a manner that enriches the typical love of a mother and daughter. Now, let's speak of what lies ahead, not behind. I see you've got that odd-looking book of Miriam's."

"Yes." Perveen touched the book, which she'd kept near her, but not put on the tea table, because she remembered Sir Dwarkanath's shocked reaction to its title.

"*Woman and the New Race,*" Bathsheba said with a twinkle in her eye. "Miriam discussed Mrs. Sanger's thesis with me. I told her that birth control is the wrong idea for religious minorities like us. If we want a stake in the country, we need offspring."

The door creaked, and Perveen saw that Miriam had arrived.

"Hello, Perveen. Thank goodness you are still here. I'll just wash my hands." Miriam disappeared and Perveen heard the sound of running water in the apartment's hallway.

"She's very careful," Mrs. Penkar said. "Thank goodness the influenza epidemic has finished, but many patients who come for treatment of female matters also suffer diseases like tuberculosis or dysentery. It is hard not to catch infections when homes are so close. Let me boil some more water to freshen her tea."

Miriam returned at the same time as her mother, who poured hot water into the half-full pot. Miriam held her cup with both hands, as if she received comfort from its warmth.

"And how was it today, dear?" Mrs. Penkar asked.

Miriam's lips drew together in a thin line. "Difficult. One of my patients died of sepsis at home this morning. And then another patient couldn't come because her sister died during childbirth—a ruptured uterus. The girl was only thirteen." Her voice tightened. "You see, many women can't safely convalesce at home. It's not clean enough, and they aren't allowed to rest. If only women were just a bit older when they gave birth . . . that would save so many."

"Yes," Perveen said, thinking about the many sad examples in the Sanger book. "Do these vulnerable women who need more care transfer from you to Cama Hospital?"

"She refers them, but very few of them go," Bathsheba interrupted. "The chief barrier is that almost every doctor there is a man. So many patients are afraid their virtue would be compromised if a male doctor examined them."

"Even if the situation changes and the women's hospital goes forward, will you truly be able to staff it with women doctors?" Perveen asked. "I think of you as one of a kind."

"Throughout India, most female doctors have had medical education, but little work experience due to employment discrimination. Therefore, I'll advertise far and wide, looking not only in India but also Ceylon, Burma, Europe, and America. Just watch—they will come." Miriam's voice held a proud defiance that Perveen had heard in many of their earlier conversations.

"But then there is the matter of paying them!" Mrs. Penkar said, her expression grim. "And of course, Europeans and Americans would want more."

"We'll need to get approval for the city of Bombay to pay them. That's how things work for Cama Hospital; why shouldn't it work for us?"

"Are you thinking that Madeline Stowe's husband, who is in the Legislative Council, could be a leader in that effort, since Sir Dwarkanath is gone?"

"I expect we'll need someone in our committee to lobby the Legislative Council." Miriam sighed. "Malcolm Stowe is wealthy, but I don't know whether he holds enough clout."

"What about Lady Hobson-Jones?" suggested Mrs. Penkar. "I hear that her husband is a fair-minded man."

"Sir David is on the Governor's Council, a different body from the Legislative Council. Although he does work closely with the governor," Miriam reflected. "But why do we have to worry about wives pulling in their husbands? Frankly, we could use Perveen, who is a skilled negotiator with power in her own right."

Mrs. Penkar turned her bright gaze from her daughter toward Perveen. "Miriam told me your family has been in Bombay for centuries. They must have many good friends in both business and government."

Perveen looked away from the women's eager faces. How could she sit at a table hammering out strategy with Alice's haughty mother and Serena Prescott and Madeline Stowe? She wouldn't be able to suppress her disdain for them, and she imagined the feeling was mutual.

She also feared Gulnaz might feel that her own role was usurped. And that made Perveen's thoughts wander to Gulnaz's feelings, and whether she knew that Khushy was spending every night close to Perveen.

"I can't commit yet, although I thank you for your confidence," Perveen demurred, while Mrs. Penkar glanced at her daughter in disappointment. "I will think about it, though. Now, if you don't mind, I've got a few things to ask you—that's why I came."

"As you indicated in your telephone call!" Mrs. Penkar said, rising from her seat and beginning to stack the empty plates and cups. "Let me give you privacy."

When they were alone, Miriam said, "My mother knows you're my lawyer. But she doesn't know much detail about why."

"I didn't say anything revealing," Perveen reassured her. "Have you heard anything from the police?"

"Not yet," Miriam said with a shudder. "But I did send off your retainer—did you receive it?"

"Yes, thank you. Everything arrived yesterday afternoon

and has been filed." Perveen hesitated, wondering how much to reveal about her activities on Monday. "I was told something that isn't yet common knowledge, so please don't repeat it. The autopsy revealed Sir Dwarkanath died from lead acetate poisoning."

Miriam fell silent. At last she said, "How did I miss that?"

Perveen wanted to comfort her. "Perhaps the symptoms overlap with food poisoning?"

"Some things are similar—but it's obvious that I didn't look hard enough." Miriam bit her lip. "The police might conclude that my misdiagnosis was intentional. Would that make me an accessory to murder after the fact?"

"No," Perveen replied emphatically. "You did not help the poisoner—who might not even exist! Sir Dwarkanath might have accidentally ingested the poison at his factory in Kalbadevi."

"What does lead have to do with stone?" Miriam objected. "Lead and its byproducts could be on a construction site. But he was far too senior to go to such places, wasn't he?"

Perveen saw her point. Very likely, the lead was obtained and dispensed to Sir Dwarkanath without his knowledge.

"Now, tell me—any news about Sunanda? How is she healing?"

Perveen realized she'd never told Miriam about Sunanda's troubles. Now she decided to be brief. "Unfortunately, she's back in Gamdevi Station's jail. I brought the silver cream to the jail."

"But I thought the police had given her bail. Is she being accused of something new?" Miriam looked intently at her.

"By mistake, she broke one of the conditions of her bail."

Miriam narrowed her eyes. "And how did that happen?"

Perveen reminded herself of her obligation to Sunanda—and how complicated things would be if either Sunanda or Miriam were implicated. "I can't talk about more than what's public record. Sorry."

"Yes, our professional obligations." Miriam straightened up. "If you don't mind, I'd like to ring the station to speak to the jail doctor. I'll make sure he knows that if he doesn't treat Sunanda's burn, the outcome could be as terrible as death."

"Truly?" Perveen shivered.

"Yes," Miriam said. "Especially since I hear prisons are very unclean."

Perveen wasn't able to bear any more thoughts of Sunanda's plight worsening, so she turned to the topic of Gulnaz. She started off with high praise for Hiba, and then moved to the complicated part. "Gulnaz is still with her family—supposedly at the recommendation of her family's doctor. My father is doubtful of Dr. Pandey's expertise with postnatal women's care and wondered if you might be able to make a judgment."

"My goodness." Miriam shifted in her seat, looking uncomfortable. "I certainly can understand your father's concern, but he is not the patient needing help. This isn't an emergency situation, so I shouldn't go to Gulnaz unless she rings me to make an appointment."

"I see your point," Perveen said, although she remembered that Miriam had come to treat Sunanda without a direct request from the patient. Perhaps Miriam saw Sunanda as incapable of reaching out, while she regarded Gulnaz as part of an elite coterie who were waited on a bit too often.

Miriam checked her watch and looked apologetically at Perveen. "It's time for me to head downstairs again."

"And I should get on, too." As Perveen gathered up her legal case, she gestured toward the Margaret Sanger book. "I read it front to back. Thank you."

"And what do you think?"

Perveen gave her a wry smile. "I think the ideas about conception control are wise—but the censors won't like it."

"That's exactly it! As I've said before, doctors cannot share written information about reproduction without putting ourselves at risk for breaking laws against obscene material." As if disgusted, Miriam shook her head. "Please don't give up on joining the hospital committee, Perveen. If something happens to me—if I'm arrested—another doctor needs to be found. I would trust you to move heaven and earth to find her."

28

A MOTHER'S WISH

*P*erveen's mind was roiling after she returned to Mistry House and climbed into the Daimler to return to Dadar. Had Miriam sounded fatalistic because she knew there was good reason she'd be arrested? There was more than Miriam's misdiagnosis to worry about. The doctor could have been correct about Sir Dwarkanath having a virus or food poisoning—because she poisoned him, while the door was locked.

Perveen didn't want to believe it, so she shifted her attention toward Jamshedji, who was regarding her with an eager expression from his seat beside her. When Perveen explained the doctor wished for Gulnaz to telephone, he threw up his hands in frustration.

"Gulnaz doesn't know what she needs. Still, I suppose you could write down the doctor's phone number on paper before you go in. And keep it in your pocket," Jamshedji instructed her.

Perveen raised her eyebrows. "It sounds like you're suggesting that I slip it to her secretly."

"As girls you both used to pass notes back and forth. I remember being called into the school head about it," Jamshedji said nostalgically. "And her parents were there, too."

"The good old days," Perveen said as the car rolled toward the block where Homi Banker's vast mansion sprawled across five lots, surrounded by a tall wrought iron fence, spiked sharply on top, with two guards and an Alsatian dog always patrolling. Mr. Banker, the owner of Majestic Bank, had a valid fear of kidnapping. Such crimes had happened to other banking families in India.

As the guards recognized Jamshedji and Perveen, one of them trudged to the mansion's door, presumably to notify the household.

"Look up there!" Jamshedji said, pointing to the house. "The upstairs window."

Perveen saw a hand holding a drapery slightly open and thought, *Could it be Gulnaz?*

The guard came out of the house and walked to their car. Speaking through the open window, he said, "Mrs. Banker has requested just one visitor, due to the memsahib's delicate state. Mr. Mistry, tea will be brought while you wait."

"Does this mean I'm being admitted?" Perveen felt confused.

"Yes, Mistry-memsahib."

"It's so rude," Perveen whispered to her father before she got out.

"Never mind. I am relieved you are being allowed in."

When Perveen reached the door, it opened right away. She found herself facing an unsmiling Tajbanu Banker.

"How good of you to come, Perveen." Her sharp eyes looked over Perveen. "You are sweating and disheveled, aren't you? Did you have to work in town today?"

"Yes, I'm just coming home. We've all been worried about Gulnaz, Tajbanu-aunty. I hope you'll allow me to see her."

"Your father and Rustom said a wet nurse is now employed. Is she clean?"

"Her name is Hiba, and she is very clean," Perveen said, trying to keep her voice even. "Also, she's very kind and hard-working. Dr. Penkar trained her."

"Never heard of him," Tajbanu said. "And how is Khushy growing?"

Perveen restrained her urge to correct Tajbanu about the obstetrician's gender. "Hiba says Khushy's neck and head are stronger, and it's my opinion that her hair is coming in very thickly. She is a beautiful baby."

"Yes, our Khushy resembles Gulnaz so strongly." Tajbanu chuckled approvingly. "What's her weight now?"

"I'm not sure, but I don't believe she's lost any weight." Perveen guessed that Tajbanu was probably anxious to see her grandchild again. "And she cries so much less—she feeds as much as she likes."

"Isn't the wet nurse checking her weight?" Tajbanu retorted.

"I'm away most days, so I'm not sure." Perveen had a sense she'd said the wrong thing. "You are right that checking weight is important. I'll ask her."

"Do you have a baby scale?" Tajbanu was watching Perveen closely, as if to catch her in a lie.

"I don't know." Perveen had a sudden inspiration. "Our cook, John, has a large scale in his kitchen—"

Tajbanu put a hand to her head. "Oh, meri mai! To lay my grandchild on the same place as onions and meat!"

"We will be sure to have a proper scale by tomorrow," Perveen said, realizing how much Tajbanu must be missing the transition to grandmother. "Arman will go to the shops."

Shaking her head, Tajbanu said, "I'll check if Baby wishes to come down. Please wait here." She ushered Perveen from the hall into the drawing room. "Sit wherever you like, dear."

Perveen had forgotten that the Bankers often called Gulnaz "Baby." She was the youngest of four, and she'd often complained about the nickname when she was a teenager.

Perveen seated herself on a pink velvet chair that was surprisingly rigid and studied the drawing room, which had changed from a rose-and-green scheme to rose and gold. She also noted new drapes of lustrous gold silk, trimmed in a braided rope of black and pink. The Belgian chandelier with hundreds of crystal drops had been removed for a new fixture that looked like a giant downward-drooping flower. The chandelier was surely the latest style from France, an endless source of inspiration for the Bankers. Mrs. Banker and her husband had spoken of making a grand tour of France, but Gulnaz's pregnancy had postponed their plans.

A few minutes later, Gulnaz trailed into the room wearing a voluminous pink silk dressing gown that matched the rose paint of the walls. Her features were sunken, and her skin looked unwashed.

"Hullo, Gulnaz," Perveen said, rising from her chair.

"Good morning." Gulnaz's voice was rough, as if she'd just awakened. A maidservant in a black dress with a white lace apron and cap followed her all the way to the lounging area where Perveen sat. She held the chair steady as Gulnaz seated herself across from Perveen.

"You may go," Gulnaz said, and the maid obediently turned and left the room. Perveen noticed that although the maid closed the door, she did so slowly, so that it remained slightly ajar.

Perfect for unseen listeners.

"Actually, it's almost evening. How are you feeling today?" Perveen's voice was loud and studiously cheerful.

"Quite fine." Gulnaz's eyes shifted to the door. "Is Rustom also here?"

"No. He's tried to visit a few times, but he heard that you were too tired to see him."

"I'm such a disappointment. I can't bear to see him." Gulnaz dropped her head, as if she was very tired, or ashamed.

"Are you telling people to send him away?" Perveen spoke bluntly, because she had to know the truth about who was controlling the situation.

Gulnaz wrinkled her tiny nose, an act that reminded Perveen of Khushy. "How could I, when I didn't know he was here? But Mamma knows about the things he said to me so she must have sent him away. She doesn't want me to keep crying."

"My dear—I'm so sorry. I didn't like what he said at breakfast on the day you left. But it sounds like you would like a chance to talk again." Perveen waited for a response, but getting none, she said, "You've probably wondered about Khushy's well-being. That's the main reason I've come."

"It took so many years to conceive," Gulnaz said dreamily. "Do you remember all those years that we tried? Then Khushy came."

Perveen noted Gulnaz's lack of response to her mention of Khushy's needs; it seemed her brain had jumped to a different place. "Dr. Penkar referred a wet nurse named Hiba to us. She's experienced and is tremendously kind. Khushy is feeding well and only wakes twice in the night."

"Lovely." Gulnaz drew her hands together to clap, one of her palms hitting lower than the other. "They are both better with me gone."

Perveen knew she should protest the statement, but perhaps Gulnaz was speaking an unfortunate truth. Perveen was slowly but surely building a bond with Khushy; and shouldn't the child be closest to someone who would never leave her?

"Khushy's better with me gone, I say!" Gulnaz was slurring every *S* that she uttered.

Was she intoxicated or heavily medicated? Watching her sister-in-law closely, Perveen said, "Khushy has received plentiful feedings and all kinds of attention—and Hiba can keep working after you return. The question is whether you believe staying here is better for you than coming home. Are you feeling happier?"

"Dr. Pandey said to Mamma I must stay." Gulnaz regarded Perveen with the eyes of a much younger child. It was as if she'd regressed twenty years in her age, back to their days at school.

"Did Dr. Pandey explain why?" Perveen asked, noting that Gulnaz hadn't affirmed or denied her happiness.

"I don't remember. But he left medicine to help me sleep."

"If you would like to get another medical opinion, Dr. Penkar could come. But she'd like you to telephone her to set up a time." As Perveen spoke, she reached one hand into the waistband of her sari, where she'd tucked the paper with the doctor's information.

Gulnaz shook her head slowly, as if it hurt. "No. I mustn't use the telephone."

Perveen felt her rage mounting at the situation. "Gulnaz, you absolutely have the right—"

"Oh, hello, Perveen, I didn't know you were still here! What on earth are you talking about?"

Perveen jerked her gaze away from Gulnaz to see Mrs. Banker standing in the doorway. Now she kept the paper folded in her hand, fearful of what Tajbanu might ask if she caught sight of it.

"Oh, there you are! I was telling Gulnaz it might be the *right* idea to wear a different dressing gown," Perveen said quickly, in the hopes she could bluff Tajbanu. "She's perspiring so heavily."

"That is her favorite wrapper." Mrs. Banker folded her arms across her ample bosom and stared coldly at Perveen. "I'm afraid that your father needs you. He's jumping in and out of the car complaining to the guard about checking for you."

Perveen felt a surge of irritation that was followed by wariness. Certainly, her father would be hot, but she couldn't imagine him short-changing her chance to visit Gulnaz.

"Goodbye, then." In a natural gesture of friendship, Perveen put her hands over her sister-in-law's, which were warm and sweaty. Nobody could see her push the small paper into Gulnaz's hand.

Leaning close to Gulnaz, Perveen whispered, "Have you any message for Rustom?"

"Give him my love. And say that he must kiss Khushy for me." Gulnaz's voice trembled, and she buried her face in her hands.

As Perveen exited the room, Mrs. Banker put a hand on her back. "I could see that Baby was getting upset. I wish you had taken notice and asked for me to help. She might need another dose of medicine."

Perveen jumped on the topic now that it had been introduced. "What is she taking?"

"Veronal. It was prescribed by Dr. Pandey, an elixir good for
sleep and mood." Tajbanu took her hand from Perveen's back to
lightly touch her cheek. "Perhaps you should try something like
that to calm yourself. You don't look well."

As a child, Perveen couldn't have answered back. But now,
she had the strength. "I feel perfectly healthy. Do you hope to
keep Gulnaz here for quite some time?"

"A woman should have as much time as needed with her parents. Look at you—a girl who left and was back within the space
of a year."

Perveen felt blood rush to her face as she understood the reference to her own failed marriage. "I'm home for a very different
reason. And while Rustom can speak thoughtlessly, he wants to
personally apologize to Gulnaz."

"Husbands and wives sometimes are happier living apart,
don't you agree?" Tajbanu spoke as casually as if they were discussing home decoration.

Perveen suspected that Tajbanu was hinting at the possibility of separation. Was Tajbanu feeling bold enough because
she knew Perveen was both a lawyer and a legally separated
woman? "Separation is something for spouses to discuss, and
they will certainly have strong feelings about the best interests
of Khushy."

"What a sweet baby Khushy is—I'll visit when I have a
moment. But let her stay where the ayah's working. It's better
for her to grow up calmly." She spoke without emotion, and Perveen sensed that Tajbanu's chief desire was caring for Gulnaz.

But Perveen didn't think the care was safe; now she put on
her solicitor's hat. "I agree that a calm family life is good, and
that goes for Gulnaz, too. I wonder if you might ask Dr. Pandey
if Gulnaz might be somewhat overmedicated? If she's more
alert, we would understand her true wishes for the situation.

After all, she is showing concern about missing her chance to see Rustom."

"Actually, she requested that you give her love to both Khushy and him," Tajbanu said with a hint of malice. "That's a bit removed, isn't it? But don't let me keep you here a moment longer. Your father's waiting."

As Perveen got into the car, she hardly knew where to begin, but she replayed the conversation as best she could as Arman drove the few blocks home.

"Tajbanu's behavior sounds deplorable," Jamshedji said at the end of her agitated summary. "And let me say it wasn't true that I was jumping out of the car asking for you. I only stepped out to stretch my legs."

"Rustom needs to know that his mother-in-law is perhaps thinking of encouraging Gulnaz to file for a separation," Perveen continued. "And Gulnaz needs to meet him so they can settle that last argument."

"Given what you've said, I doubt Tajbanu will allow it." Jamshedji gazed despondently at her. "I'm unhappy to hear about the medicine. Veronal is a strong hypnotic and can sicken people to the point they are hooked on it. The question is whether Tajbanu seeks to weaken Gulnaz's mental abilities so that she doesn't think about her husband and child or because she wants to disempower her from speaking her wishes."

Perveen's skin prickled because she also had come to feel Tajbanu Banker was an adversary. Quickly, she recounted how Gulnaz thought she couldn't use the telephone. "At least I gave her the paper with Dr. Penkar's information. You had the right idea for me to bring it inside discreetly."

"My only good idea. I hope Gulnaz can rally herself enough to call." Jamshedji leaned his head against the car seat, as if too tired to hold it up anymore.

29

A BROTHER'S SECRET

"Look, Khushy. Lillian's making a dance for you!" Hiba said. Perveen had been snuggling Khushy close, but Khushy raised her head and turned it toward the parrot, who was ruffling her feathers as she strutted on the railing that ran around Perveen's veranda.

"She can't be understanding language already!" Perveen said in amazement.

Hiba laughed softly. "No. But her eyes are sharpening. She will especially love birds, because of this one."

"Khushy thinks Lillian is a family member," said Gita, who was crouched in a corner, mending one of her own blouses.

Khushy cooed and Perveen reached down to adjust the baby's small downy head so she could see into her eyes. "Thanks to you both, she seems to have woken to the beauties of our world."

"And what about you? Her second mother!" Hiba smoothed the last of the diapers that she'd been stacking in a basket.

Perveen subdued the warm feeling that Hiba's words gave her. "I mustn't try to take Gulnaz's place."

"Hiba is right!" Gita kept her eyes on her sewing. "The most special place in a girl's heart is saved for the mother's sister, who always is there to comfort rather than scold."

Gita began singing a Bengali lullaby, a melody that tugged at Perveen even though she understood few of its words. It felt so beautiful, to be holding a baby and to be close to other women who were enjoying the child as well. Why couldn't it always be that way?

"I hope you aren't lonely in the garden cottage, Gita," Perveen said after the song was done. "When does your mother return?"

"She said she'd come before monsoon."

"Any day, then," Hiba said. "I wish she would come now, because of the man."

"What man?" Perveen asked, as Gita shushed Hiba.

"It's nothing." Gita looked at Perveen shamefaced. "I told Hiba earlier that a stranger started talking to me over the garden wall yesterday when I was ironing. Perveen-bai, I tell you, I didn't speak to him first."

"I believe you," Perveen said, seeing the anxiety in her face. "What was he asking about?"

"He asked my name several times." Because of Hiba's presence, Gita was speaking Marathi, which she was still learning, so the words came slowly. "I said 'Not your business.' Then he said, 'Who stays in this nice cottage?' I did not answer at all, wishing him just to go. But he didn't, and asked, 'Do you stay by yourself?' I didn't like that," Gita said, looking at them both. "I shouted that a lot of people stay in that house with me. Then I said I was going inside the big house to get my brother. I locked up and looked through the windows, but he was already gone."

"Shabash!" said Hiba as she clapped her hands.

"Yes, that was splendidly done," Perveen agreed. "Men shouldn't feel free to annoy women like this. Although I suppose the fellow might have truly been inquiring into housing. He might think that place had room for another person."

Gita shook her head. "He was a badmash. I could tell from his voice."

Perveen noted that both Hiba and Gita were regarding her with disappointment. Quickly, she said, "I don't mean to doubt your judgment. I'm sure Pappa and Mamma will agree that you can sleep inside our house until your mother returns. There's plenty of room on the verandas outside the bedrooms and in the upstairs and downstairs halls."

Gita shook her head. "Your house has fans. It is too cold for me. I will stay and keep the door locked."

There was a sound at the French door, and all three of them turned to see Rustom standing awkwardly. He had changed out of his suit and into a sudreh, the fine cotton undershirt worn by Parsi men, and a pair of light cotton trousers. Dressed like this, he did not look like a company president. His eyes were on Khushy, and suddenly Perveen saw him with new eyes. He was a father.

"You are welcome to join us. Sit down." Perveen patted the space beside her on the swing.

Rustom obeyed, looking shyly at Khushy. He said, "Pappa said you saw Gulnaz today. Did she say anything about me?"

"Oh!" Perveen said, playing for time. "Our time together was quite short. I'll tell you what I remember."

"Let's go inside," Gita said to Hiba.

As Hiba walked toward Perveen to take Khushy from her arms, Perveen shook her head. "I'll bring her to you if necessary. Rustom wants to practice holding her."

"What?" Rustom sputtered as the servant women departed.

When they were alone, Perveen shifted Khushy into Rustom's lap. "Here you go."

Rustom's hands shook. "But you don't understand. I didn't learn to hold babies. I might drop her."

"You won't if you pay attention to her," Perveen advised. "Keep her head supported. She likes when you rock back and forth on the swing."

Khushy's warm brown eyes fixed on Rustom as the movement began.

"She's not crying yet. But—but look!" Rustom's voice cracked. Khushy was foaming at the mouth, and, suddenly, white fluid was running down her face.

"Too much milk," Perveen said, lifting Khushy so she lay against Rustom's shoulder. Awkwardly, his hands held her as Perveen tapped lightly on her back.

"I'm sorry about your sudreh," she said with a chuckle. "Next time that you come to her, put a clean towel on your shoulder."

"Very well," Rustom growled. "Now, tell me about how Gulnaz is. You have been delaying. Pappa wouldn't say anything."

"He hardly knows anything because he wasn't permitted inside," Perveen said smoothly. "Gulnaz wanted me to give you her love."

"That's all? She walks out, and she has nothing more to say? Is she coming back?" Rustom's voice cracked with anxiety.

Perveen considered how to word things. "She believes that you're very disappointed in her performance as a mother."

"I am," he said bluntly. "Also, I regret the way I've spoken about it to her. It was unkind." He looked down at Khushy and slowly raised his hand, holding it close to her hair. "If I touch her hair, could her skull be bruised?"

"Not at all," Perveen said, hiding a smile. "After all, she has your curls. There's a lot of protection."

Rustom's fingers stroked tentatively, and he asked, "So when will she come back?"

"She didn't say anything about that." Perveen watched her brother's face; he looked calmer than she expected.

"Was she asking anything about Khushy?" His voice was strained.

Perveen hesitated, not wishing to make him too unhappy. "I tried to explain how well things are going, but she did not show an interest. I don't think the medicine her mother's insisting she take is motivating her to return to us."

"That's good," Rustom muttered.

Perveen looked at him sharply. "Are you even listening?"

Khushy made a cooing sound, and Rustom shot an amazed glance toward Perveen. "Khushy's speaking to me! But what does it mean?"

"I think it means she loves you," Perveen said, determined to build his confidence. "And your daughter understands that you love her. But I'm not going to let you forget the serious matter we are talking about. Gulnaz might be taking too strong a medicine."

"Well, that would be just deserts," he muttered. "Gulnaz was the one who sedated Khushy the day after they came home. She denies it, but I know it must be her."

Perveen absorbed the words slowly, and with shock. "But Gulnaz said that someone else must have done it!"

"I found our sherry bottle amid the baby clothes." Rustom stroked Khushy's hair more rapidly. "How did it get there? The ayah didn't have a key to our drinks cabinet."

"Oh!" Perveen paused, realizing that she'd been thinking about the alcohol coming from her parents' parlor, especially since Camellia had thrown away a half-filled bottle of toddy.

"And how many keys are there to your own cabinet?"

"Just one. When she was away, I had the key, but once she returned she asked me for it. She keeps it with her other keys on a ring tied to her sari. She wants me to drink less." Rustom's expression, as he spoke, was bleak. "She must have fed the alcohol to Khushy before we went to the fire temple. I remember being relieved that Khushy was sleeping at last. Now I feel such shame!"

Perveen watched a tear fall from her brother's face and land on Khushy's downy head. The evidence of his growing sense of responsibility—and love—tugged at her. Softly, she said, "I don't know what the future holds, but I am so grateful you trusted me enough to tell."

Rustom looked warmly at Perveen. "You can be everything to Khushy."

"No, I can't. She needs a parent. You are already proving yourself an excellent father."

Rustom lifted his hand in protest. "But I know nothing about babies!"

"I also knew nothing when Khushy arrived." Perveen spoke firmly. "I'm learning from Hiba and reading as much as I can of these baby books Gulnaz has. You should read them, too."

Rustom adjusted Khushy so she could see his wide, mischievous smile. "Darling, I would rather read nursery rhymes than a guidebook!"

"One last thing!" Perveen felt she owed her brother the full story of what she'd noticed while visiting the Bankers' home. "Gulnaz didn't know you'd tried to visit her. I think it would be wise to keep pushing for contact with her—that is, if you want to keep trying."

Rustom looked searchingly at her. "If the Bankers loathe me so much, why did they ever agree to the marriage?" Rustom said, grumbling.

He knew the answer, just as Perveen did. Gulnaz's parents had welcomed the Mistry family's proposal only after learning that the knighted families weren't interested. Homi Banker also knew that Rustom and Perveen's grandfather had lent money to his own father, who'd arrived penniless from Persia.

Reaching out to touch Rustom's hand, Perveen said, "I doubt that the Bankers considered much about you beyond your job. The important part is that Gulnaz was thrilled by the proposal and truly wanted to marry you. She had a crush since she was twelve."

Rustom's eyes were heavy with sadness. "Tajbanu-aunty has her own love for Gulnaz—and too much time on her hands. She's not like Mamma with her social interests and activities. Gulnaz admired Mamma and said it was her goal to take over a lot of Mamma's charities as time went on." Rustom gazed down at his daughter. "What do you think, little one? Should I write a letter to your mother, at the very least?"

So Rustom was conflicted—he wanted his baby safe, and deep down, he didn't want to lose Gulnaz. She said, "I don't know whether Tajbanu would give Gulnaz anyone's letters. She wants to protect Gulnaz. They even call her Baby."

"I know. Gulnaz told me never to call her that." Rustom's hands were trembling as he kept them on the tiny baby's sides. "May I move her?"

"Yes," Perveen said, and he awkwardly shifted the baby to her lap. Winking at him, she said, "You did fine work cradling her head. It must be your construction background."

Rustom chuckled as he stood up. "I'm going in to change my shirt. Thank you, Perveen."

After Rustom left the balcony, the two maids came back.

"Men come for the smiles, and they leave when it's time to wash the baby's bottom!" Gita said.

"Yes, it is time for a nappy change." Hiba held out her arms.

"Actually," Perveen said, "you taught me how. Remember?"

"You don't have to—"

Perveen laughed. "I can't teach Rustom if I don't do it myself."

It was ten o'clock when Gita left to go to sleep in the cottage, and ten-thirty when Hiba finished nursing and laid a sleeping Khushy in the crib. She carried her own mat from the veranda into Perveen's room, saying that Lillian was just a bit too loud that evening.

"She thinks rain is coming. She is crying out for it. All the animals are!" Hiba said.

"You are very welcome to sleep here." Perveen washed and dressed for bed, climbing into the four-poster, drawing the mosquito nets around. She had with her one of Gulnaz's books on baby development written in Gujarati that offered specific healthy recipes and rituals.

The book was nowhere near as engrossing to her as *Woman and the New Race*, but it did cover things she needed to know about Khushy's upcoming months of growth. After her mind felt over-crowded with details, Perveen put a book-mark in the text and returned it to the shelf. Crossing back to her bed, she looked down in the crib, trying to picture Khushy as a chubby ten-month-old crawling across the floor. But Gulnaz kept coming into the frame. What Rustom had said about finding the sherry bottle was disturbing—especially since Gulnaz had laid the blame for Khushy's sedation on another woman.

She considered whether Tajbanu Banker might also have witnessed strange behaviors that were irrational. After all, she'd visited Gulnaz during her time at the lying-in hospital more often than anyone. And she'd told Perveen that she didn't think Gulnaz needed to have Khushy with her. That Khushy needed calm.

Perveen's throat suddenly felt dry. Tajbanu might not be acting entirely out of selfishness, but partially for her grand-daughter's protection.

But it seemed inevitable that Khushy would someday ask questions about her mother's abandonment. She might suspect that the Mistrys had willfully kept her from her mother. And that would be a tragedy that no number of words could obfuscate.

30
FEARS AFLAME

In Perveen's dream, she was nestling Khushy in her arms. A moment of tranquil peace for the two of them on the veranda, until a bird was flying hard into them. It was Lillian, not playful but angry, butting at her, and squawking to the high heavens.

When Perveen came to consciousness, she heard both Lillian's squawking, and a soft coughing sound that could only have been Khushy.

The sound must have been too soft to awaken Hiba, because when Perveen pulled the chain on her bedside lamp, she didn't see her. Recalling the perils of babies who vomited while lying down, Perveen bolted out of her bed toward the crib. Here, she pushed aside the mosquito net draping the cot and picked up Khushy.

Perveen held the baby against her chest and thumped her with one hand. No milk or bile came out, and her thin cotton nappy was still tightly wound and dry.

Khushy coughed again, and Perveen caught the scent of smoke from outdoors. Clutching Khushy, she walked through the open doors to her veranda, which overlooked a softly moving field of smoke and red light. The birds, normally quiet at night, were squawking and flying through the trees. Lillian was rushing around her cage, cackling with anxiety.

The fire's source wasn't in view, but she guessed it might be the outdoor hearth in front of the garden house. In such dry weather, grass was like tinder—the fire could sweep the garden and take not only the Mistrys' duplex but everything else around it.

"Gita!" Perveen said aloud. The maid typically slept on the cottage's narrow veranda, and if she were there now, she might be dead from smoke inhalation. Khushy coughed more and squirmed, perhaps startled by the movement of Perveen's rapidly beating heart.

Perveen opened Lillian's cage, and the bird flew behind her into the bedroom. The urgent cackling slowed as the bird breathed different air. Ignoring her, Perveen hurried into the hallway to find Hiba, who struggled to her feet, straightening her sleeping sari and reaching out to take Khushy. "Does she need feeding?"

"No! There's a fire in the garden! Khushy and Lillian smelled it and woke me up!"

Hiba switched on the hall light. Urgently, she asked, "Where is Gita?"

"I don't know! I'm going to find her," Perveen said as she transferred the baby. "Will you please take Khushy downstairs to the parlor? You should be near the front door, just in case."

"Yes, and we will go out the door if necessary!" Hiba's voice was reassuring. "What about your parents? And John-sahib?"

"John lives in the same flat building as Arman. Go down with Khushy, and I'll wake my parents."

As Hiba departed downstairs, Perveen rushed down the hall and flung open her parents' bedroom door.

"What?" Jamshedji asked sleepily. "It's too dark to be morning yet. And is that a bird on your shoulder?"

"There's a fire!" Perveen shouted, turning on a second light in the room. "Outside in the back. I haven't seen Gita!" Perveen motioned for Jamshedji to follow his wife's lead in rising out of bed.

"Gita usually sleeps outside on her charpoy," Camellia fretted as she hastened out of bed, tying a wrapper over her nightdress. "If she hasn't come to us—oh, this is dreadful!"

Perveen waved in her father's face until he started to move. "Pappa, come out with me now. And we must rouse Rustom, too!"

"I'll go next door," Camellia said, getting her key ring from the bureau. "For once, he will listen to his mother!"

"And ring the fire brigade!" Jamshedji called as he got out of bed and headed toward the door.

Perveen led the way down the staircase, her father's footfalls fast behind her. They went through the back of the house, throwing open the doors to the veranda. Running across the warm grass toward the smoke, her worst fears came to fruition.

The garden cottage was on fire—chiefly, the roof and one of the walls.

Perveen ran toward the flames, coughing in the smoke, noting that the veranda was clear, but no charpoy was there. However, an iron garden table had been pulled in front of the door, blocking it from being opened from inside.

She turned and saw her father also staring at the obstacle that had been placed to eliminate the possibility of escape.

"Gita, we are here!" Perveen screamed as she began struggling to move the table. Joining her, Jamshedji pulled away the chair. Touching the hot knob, Perveen pulled her hand away so fast she tripped backward.

Behind her, she heard her father's voice. "The door is too hot—it's not safe to open. Gita might be overcome by smoke. I don't think we can do anything before the brigade arrives."

"I won't give up!" Perveen protested. What if a wall of fire lay between them and Gita, and she was desperate for rescue?

"Mr. Mistry! We have water!" someone called out from behind them. Perveen's tortured thoughts were broken by the sight of almost a dozen neighborhood men streaming onto the lawn from the street, while others climbed the garden wall, reaching for buckets handed to them by people on the other side.

"Thank you. The brigade was called, but we don't know how long they will take," Jamshedji shouted back.

Perveen remembered an urn on the back veranda that collected rainwater. She ran to it and found that Rustom was there and had tipped the urn toward her, showing there wasn't any water within.

"Mamma told me Khushy's still inside the house!" His voice was sharp with anxiety.

"Yes. Hiba's got her, and it's a short distance to the front door, if they have to leave." Perveen looked desperately toward him. "Pappa thinks Gita's been overcome by smoke or might be burned up inside the cottage. But we can't know!"

"We must try." Rustom abandoned the empty urn and took off running toward the small inferno ringed by men throwing water that evaporated quickly in the heat. Looking back at Perveen, he called, "We can use the windows!"

Perveen ran after him as he hurried to the building's north side, where a long, narrow series of windows were set close to the ceiling.

"Get me the ironing board!" he shouted to the neighbors, and three men rapidly went for the metal ironing board Jamshedji and Perveen had found near the door. The men and Rustom drew the sturdy board up to the cottage wall under the windows. Swiftly, Rustom clambered up.

"Do you see her?" Perveen called, afraid of what he might answer.

"Yes," he answered shortly, then shouted through the window, "Gita, don't be frightened. Can you come up to the window? No? What about moving your table and standing on it?" Turning back to Perveen, Rustom said, "Gita's raised herself to the window height, but she says the window's too small for her."

"Then make it bigger!"

"I would gladly do so, but I don't have a company toolbox," he snapped.

Perveen suddenly had an inspiration. "What about the iron?"

"I'll try anything!" Rustom said, his eyes hopeful.

"Bring us the laundry iron. It's by the hearth!" Perveen shouted to the neighbors.

In moments, the heavy instrument used for clothes was in Perveen's hands, and then she handed it up to Rustom. With the iron, he hammered hard at the window's edge until the limestone wall around it began to break.

"Gita! Try to come out now!" Rustom shouted through the window.

Gita's face appeared in the window, and then her shoulders. Her face was slicked gray with ash, and her eyes shone with fear.

"We will catch you," Rustom urged. "Just come farther."

Gita wiggled until her upper body was out, all the while keeping hold of the window's edge with her hands. Her face crumpled with despair as she moaned, "My hips are stuck! And the flames—" Her voice dissolved into coughing.

"I can't widen the window more," Rustom said to Perveen. "There are structural supports that can't be broken. And there's no time to get tools."

Perveen stared at the window, noticing that the height was greater than its width. Gita's hips were too wide for the width, but if she could turn her body completely sideways, she might be able to get out. But she'd need something to help her balance.

Perveen's thoughts were faster than words, so she dashed off and got two men to help her carry the heavy table from the Mistrys' veranda to the side of the cottage. Returning to Rustom, gasping from the exertion and smoke, she explained her idea: that he could stand on the table and lift Gita's ironing board to the window so Gita could cling to it and climb out.

Rustom slid the narrow end of the board to the window's edge. "Gita, grab tightly to this. We'll use it to pull you out."

With effort, Gita scrunched up her face and turned so her shoulders and the side of her body were at the same angle.

Rustom slowly pulled on the board, his muscles straining with effort, and Gita's head, shoulders, torso, and hips emerged. Suddenly so much of her was out of the window that she lost balance. The men in the garden who'd been watching surged forward to break her fall.

Perveen knelt by Gita, who was covered in black dust and coughing. The maid's arms were covered with gashes, and her sari was almost the same gray as her skin and hair. Anxiously, Perveen asked, "Are you burned?"

"No," Gita whispered hoarsely. "Just—hard to breathe."

Then came the clanging of many bells. Two horse-drawn wagons had arrived in the lane behind the cottage.

Perveen turned to watch Rustom slip through the gate into the lane. How strong and sharp he'd been in this crisis—much better than she'd expected. He'd not hesitated to try to save Gita, when her father had feared all was lost. He'd also immediately understood her idea about the ironing board as a rescue instrument. It was the first time in many years that the brother and sister had been in league.

Soon, the firemen were dousing the cottage with buckets of water to the cheers of neighbors in the garden and many others who were watching from their balconies and verandas. Quickly, the sound of rushing water coming from hoses drowned out the crackling wood. The brigade extinguished the fire to cheers from all.

Camellia took one of Gita's hands, and Perveen, the other. The three walked slowly indoors, where Hiba was waiting with a tumbler of water. After Gita had swallowed it down, she, Perveen, and Camellia walked slowly upstairs to Perveen's bathroom, where Camellia tenderly undressed the maid while Perveen filled the tub with barely warm water. The girl shuddered and cringed as Camellia discovered patches of skin rubbed raw and cut.

Perveen remembered her disastrous attempt to help clean

Sunanda's burns, so she kept her hands to herself and concentrated on speaking to Gita. "When did you notice the fire, Gita?"

"I was asleep and woke up because of a banging sound. I saw flames in the darkness and ran for the door," she said weakly. "I could not get out the door. I didn't know why."

"Someone jammed the garden table against it," Perveen said. "An intentional act, meant to trap you."

"I don't usually sleep inside," Gita said, as if not understanding the gravity of what Perveen had said. "I only was there because of the man who talked to me yesterday."

"What man?" Camellia asked, and Gita tearfully recounted the conversation that had ended with her fleeing into the main house.

"Most suspicious," Camellia said. "And don't blame yourself for anything!"

The chief fire officer, Deepak Sule, came inside at six-thirty, after it was light enough for him and the brigade to have thoroughly examined the street. In the dining room Sule showed them several pieces of glass and fragments of half-burned cloth.

"It appears that a soda bottle stuffed with burning rags was lobbed at the cottage roof. I will be reporting it to the police," the captain said, accepting both water and a cup of tea from John, who'd arrived a few minutes prior and heard the story of the fire from Perveen.

"Apparently, a stranger came by yesterday asking Gita who stayed in the house," Perveen informed him. "And a wrought iron table was jammed against the door, prohibiting her escape."

"Most concerning!" Deepak Sule said, scribbling on a small pad he pulled from a pocket. "I'll make sure Dadar Police send a proper investigator to apprehend the scoundrel. Boys should not be playing with fire during the dry season."

After the fire chief left, Gita emerged from the parlor, where she'd been listening; she'd declared herself too upset to be present in the dining room. "Does he think boys were playing games? I don't!"

Jamshedji ran a hand through his hair. His curls were springing wild, and he was still in his sudreh and pajamas, which were now dusted with dark gray ash. "Gita, you have told us the man was most inquisitive about your name and also about the cottage. What about his physical description? How old was he?"

Gita spoke rapidly, as if she'd been saving up the details. "He spoke Marathi well, and he seemed in his late twenties, though it's hard to tell when someone has a mustache. He didn't wear any sort of turban or hat. He was friendly, but something about him seemed false."

"Well done, Gita," Perveen said, thinking that the lack of head covering meant it was impossible to guess his religion or regional background. She also wondered about whether whoever had set the fire had mistaken Gita, who'd never given her name, for Sunanda.

"Gita noticed quite a bit. She may remember even more, in the hours and days to come." Jamshedji's voice was encouraging. "Best to relax and let the thoughts come. Don't be afraid, dear; you are safe now."

"I want to stay with you all. I don't want to go to the police station." Gita looked anxiously from Jamshedji to Perveen. "Sunanda said the police are awful. They can lock you up and do other things, too."

Perveen thought of the beating Sunanda had received. But now was the time to reassure Gita, not elevate her anxiety. Softly, she said, "You are at no risk for arrest. In fact, you are the injured party, and your presence makes the charge against the man more serious. We will do our best to pressure the police to determine whether the aggressive stranger who spoke to you is connected to this arson attack."

"It seems so strange that anyone would want to hurt Gita!"

Camellia said. "I suppose we could think the man was punishing her for not speaking to him. But it's so unusual to have such a crime in our colony."

Perveen rose, smoothing her wrapper and coming away with soot on her hands. "I'm going to have my bath. It's a short while until the real day starts, and I am covered in dirt and ash."

"I'll ring Mustafa to say we're not coming into the office. I must be here to support Gita during the arson investigation." Jamshedji's voice was heavy.

"I'd still like to go into town today. I hope to speak with Sunanda," Perveen said.

"Yes, you should go. I'll stay with Gita." Camellia stroked Gita's hair, and the maid crumpled against her like a child.

31

THE OLD BOY

Washed and freshly dressed, Perveen felt determined to carry out her day. As Arman parked outside Gamdevi Station, she considered the hulking gray building with a different perspective. She'd hated for Sunanda to be trapped within it; yet now she saw it as offering some protection from an unknown foe.

It was a short wait until she was permitted back to the cell. Looking through the bars, she saw Sunanda lying on her back on a charpoy that had only a thin sheet covering it. On the ground was a second woman, gaunt and wearing rags, who appraised Perveen curiously.

"We must talk elsewhere," Perveen said through the bars to Sunanda, after she'd awakened with a start.

A guard grudgingly allowed Sunanda and Perveen to proceed to an unoccupied cell farther down in the block of barred rooms. Plenty of men were staying on the row, and they hooted and called obscenities to the two women as they passed by.

"How have you been feeling?" Perveen asked after they'd sat down together on a bench in the empty cell.

"My burn still hurts, but I think it's improving," Sunanda said, running her fingers through her hair made rough from sleep. "I go twice daily to the infirmary to get the cream. Dr. Penkar visited me yesterday evening. She convinced the jailers to bring a charpoy. But the prisoner who joined me wants it for herself."

Perveen grimaced, imagining that when Sunanda went back to her cell, she might have to fight for it. "I'll remind the guard about the charpoy being part of your medical treatment. Now, I am surprised that the police haven't called me about being present for any interviews. Have they spoken to you again? Have you suffered more blows or touching of any sort?" Perveen was determined to catalog the injuries her client had received.

"No." Sunanda looked at her expectantly. "Do you have any news about finding A. V. Tomar?"

"Not yet. However, something happened last night at our home. The garden cottage was set afire, and Gita came close to dying inside. Fortunately, we got her out through a window."

Sunanda drew in her breath. "How terrible! What is Gita's condition?"

"She's well enough to speak, but she has some injuries," Perveen said. "I want to talk to you about this." Perveen described the harassment and questions Gita had faced from the strange man twelve hours before the fire.

Sunanda was silent, and when she spoke, her voice sounded tentative. "Do you think that man set the fire to punish her for not speaking to him?"

"It's possible—but I was thinking that because Gita had told him that other people stayed in the garden house with her, he might have thought you would perish in the fire. Or he might have even mistakenly believed Gita was you. She wouldn't reveal her name when he asked for it."

Sunanda's eyes narrowed. "What did he look like? And what was his language?"

Perveen repeated Gita's description, and Sunanda hesitated before answering. "The description could fit many men. Just because he spoke Marathi doesn't mean he is a Maratha. It's the language of this area."

"You are thinking like a lawyer," Perveen said, coaxing a wan smile from her client. "Tell me—when you went to the Bhatias' on Friday, did you tell anyone there—or along the way—that you were living with us until the trial?"

"I told Oshadi. But why would she tell a bad man? She said to me she was praying for my trial to go in my favor."

Perveen agreed that Oshadi didn't seem the type to be so deceptive. And how would an elderly servant of little means have the power and funds to hire someone to commit arson with the intent to murder? "Dr. Penkar knew. I also told Uma Bhatia when I went to see her on Friday. My sister-in-law, Gulnaz, first heard about you when Gita told John that you'd vanished. Actually, Gulnaz was wishing for you to be Khushy's ayah—she had no anger toward you."

Sunanda nodded and said, "The man who talked to Gita must be the one who threw the fire-bottle into the cottage. Maybe he thought she would run out, and then he would get her. Men are like that—they go after maids if they think they are alone without protection."

Perveen didn't bring up the iron table jammed against the cottage door, because she thought Sunanda was hinting at something important. By now, she knew that she couldn't ask outright. She would have to do it piece by piece. "I'm trying to keep my facts in order about your case. It was a Saturday that you drank the tea. Where were you the Friday before? And what do you remember doing?"

"It was a busy day at Bhatia House." Her eyes looked past Perveen, as if she was imagining herself long ago. "I played with the children in the morning, and in the late afternoon Motabhai said the children were to come with him for a party at Juhu beach. It was some distance, so I would need to ride in the car."

"You said Motabhai?" Perveen said, remembering how Govind had said she'd used the term for "older brother" during a nightmare. Now she realized she'd overlooked that Sunanda might speak to an unrelated male who was older and deserving respect. "Does Motabhai work at Bhatia House?"

"Oh no!" she said quickly. "Parvesh Bhatia is the oldest son in the family."

Perveen was still for a moment, digesting the information. If Sunanda had called out for Parvesh in her nightmare, that meant he figured heavily in her thoughts.

"Did you mind having to travel with the children and Motabhai without Uma?"

Sunanda shook her head. "No. But at the party, a white memsahib was complaining that Uma hadn't come."

"Was she Begum Cora, the lady who gave money to you after Ishan's accident?"

"I remember very little about the tea party," Sunanda said. "When things are bad, I try not to think about it."

Perveen felt a rush of sympathy for her, but it was in Sunanda's interest for the back story to be understood. She was beginning to wonder if Sunanda's night terrors were connected with a sexual assault that had been committed by Parvesh.

"How was Motabhai's mood at this party?" Perveen had decided to use this term because it was likely how Sunanda thought of Parvesh Bhatia.

"I cannot tell you because I was off with the children. He told me that they could get their feet wet but not go in the water. But the other children at the party ran freely into the water. I was the only ayah there to watch all of them, so it was frightening." She closed her eyes for a moment, and when she looked again at Perveen, her eyes were luminous with fear. "The waves were huge. They could have been swept out and drowned."

Perveen could picture the scene. "Did you have to rescue anyone?"

"Nobody went too deep. We were getting quite wet, so I was glad when the house servant came to tell us the children's tea was served."

"Where, exactly?"

"On the veranda. One side was set up for the children, and the other side for the adults' party." Taking a deep breath, she said, "Do I have to say more?"

"Whatever you say stays between us." Perveen touched her hand lightly. "But telling might make it better. We won't know, unless you try."

Sunanda was silent for a while, and then spoke in a whisper. "When I was close to the veranda, a manservant said that the memsahib didn't like me being in the wet sari in front of everyone. The servant said he could watch the children while I went to dry my clothes. He pointed to a hut that was close to the water—the place where I'd gone earlier to dry the children's feet. I knew there were towels inside, so I agreed."

"Did the servant walk you there?"

"No. I ran through the sand so I wouldn't be away from the children too long and looked one last time to the villa before going inside. The man was watching over the children."

"What happened then?"

"I went inside and—" She shuddered and put her face in her hands.

Perveen softened her voice. "It's all right. You're not there anymore."

Sunanda's words were muffled. "I bolted the door. I thought I was safe. So wrong—"

"You did nothing wrong!" Perveen laid an arm across her shoulders, but Sunanda still would not look up.

"I dried myself." After a long pause, she whispered, "I was wrapping my sari when he came from the other side."

"Which side?" Perveen figured this would be easier to start with than the intruder's identity.

"The hut had two rooms—I didn't see it clearly because it wasn't very light. There must have been another door. But he came quietly."

Perveen could picture it so clearly that she felt Sunanda's terror spilling into her own mind.

"I called out I was sorry—I thought he was angry I was in

a place I shouldn't be. But he didn't speak—he just pushed me down. He smelled of drink, like what you gave me at your house. I turned my head and yelled, wishing someone would hear me." Sunanda's voice broke, and it took several seconds for her to gain enough strength to speak again. "He hit the back of my head. I thought he would kill me."

"What a terrible man." Perveen choked down the sob she felt, hearing the truth that Sunanda had finally shared. She knew that this might be the only time her client was willing to tell the story, so she would have to ask as much as she could. "Was it the male servant who told you to dry your sari?"

"The man was not a servant. He was rich. He wore a heavy ring on his finger when he pressed me down." Sunanda released the hands she'd plastered over her face and slowly came up to look at Perveen. "That's all I remember."

Perveen reached out to take Sunanda's clammy hands into her own. "You've done very well. What happened afterward?"

"I heard Motabhai's voice." Sunanda's voice was low, but calmer. "He came into that place, and he saved me, but I was so ashamed." Her voice broke into shuddering sobs.

"He surely came because he was worried about you!" Perveen said, her estimation of Parvesh rising. "Did the attacker run away?"

"I was hiding my face, so I didn't see much. Motabhai spoke to him in English. He said . . ." She paused, as if thinking carefully. "'Old boy.' I know those words because of the children's English class. Then he said, 'Challo.'"

"Challo" meant "let's go" or "I am going" and was employed in many Indian languages. The word was often used, including by Europeans living in India. Perveen inquired, "Did he speak any more?"

After a long pause, Sunanda said, "I don't remember any other words. I only heard the door opening, and then Motabhai told me the man had gone away."

"You say that Motabhai spoke to him in English. So could the man have been European?"

"I don't know." Sunanda looked helplessly at her.

"When the man pushed you down, did you see the color of his neck or his hands?"

"It was evening, so the hut was full of shadows." She shuddered again. "His hands were a light brown color, but it might have been because the place was so dark."

Perveen wondered if Parvesh had seen a European leave the gathering and walk down to the beach. Otherwise, how else would he know that Sunanda needed help? "Did you tell Motabhai you were going down to this beach hut?"

"No. But the children knew where I was going. Probably Ishan might have gone to his father. He runs about all the time, you know." Sunanda's words were coming more quickly.

Perveen was relieved that Sunanda had not broken down during the questioning and thought she might press a little further. "I know you weren't looking, but did you hear Parvesh threaten the man or perhaps fight with him?"

"No. He spoke in a way to him that was not angry—sort of like a joke. But it worked. The man who hurt me left the place. Motabhai said he would go outside the hut and stand watch so I could dress myself privately. He said that he would take me and the children home and that I shouldn't tell Uma-Bhabhu. She would become quite upset."

Parvesh seemed to have spoken as a man typically would, yet Perveen guessed that it had made Sunanda feel she was at fault. This made her all the more determined to identify the perpetrator. The facts should be known, even if only by Sunanda, Jamshedji, and herself. "Did you see anyone behaving strangely, or looking too much at you, when you left?"

"I felt like everyone was looking at me." Sunanda's voice broke. "My sari was still wet and now there was blood. On the way home, Motabhai stopped the car at a group of stalls on the beach road. He gave me money so I could buy a new sari while he gave the children kulfi to eat."

Perveen asked, "What happened to the sari that you wore to the beach party?"

"I threw it away behind the shop."

Perveen guessed the sari was long gone; spirited away by someone even poorer than her, who would wash it and give it to someone else to wear or cut it up to use for another purpose. "You said you drank the tea the very next morning. Does this mean you told Oshadi what happened?"

"I didn't want to say anything," Sunanda said tearfully. "But Oshadi noticed the new sari right away, even though it was almost the same color. She saw some bruises on my arms and neck and asked me who had hurt me. I said that I didn't know who. She said he was a scoundrel, and I should not think about it too much. That was when she said drinking some of her tea might make me feel better."

Perveen thought it seemed as if Oshadi had understood that Sunanda had been raped. "What did she tell you about the tea?"

"She said it was good for the health, but part of the treatment was that it caused a little bit of stomach pain. My monthly would come early, but that would help me. It happened that same day, just as she said."

"I'd like to speak to Mr. Bhatia privately about what happened. I believe he knows who the attacker was—"

"Please don't speak to him!" Sunanda implored. "Motabhai saved my life. He doesn't need more trouble."

"Your concern for Motabhai is admirable, but what happened to you was a crime. What is your feeling, now, about seeking justice? Shouldn't that man pay for hurting you?"

"No." Sunanda rose from the bench and stepped to the cell's corner, as if trying to get as far from Perveen as possible.

"But the man who attacked you should be in jail, not you!" Perveen heard her own voice rising in frustration.

"Already I have the charge of abortion. How could I find a job again, or return to stay with my brother, if people know that I'm dirty?"

Sunanda's whispered words were haunting—and all too realistic. Suddenly, Perveen hated the world they lived in—where men could violate women with impunity because they knew women were too ashamed to report them.

32

A SUSPICIOUS HUSBAND

"What is the address exactly?" Arman asked as they passed over the bridge to Bandra and along the coast.

"Varanpur Villa is in Juhu. The address on Cora's card says Beach Road," Perveen said. After what Sunanda had told her, she didn't want to delay any opportunity to learn more about the crime scene. Perveen had already been instructed not to pursue a case against the rapist, but she knew that identifying the rapist privately would probably lead her to the person who'd set up Sunanda with the false abortion charge.

"We will know the villa when we see it, maybe," Arman said. To their left was white sand and sparkling sea dotted with fishing boats. Along the sandy beach road, energetic boys hawked coconuts for drinking. She also saw the occasional shop selling goods ranging from foods to household items. When she passed a stand advertising kulfi set close to another store selling saris and shirts, she felt certain this was where Parvesh must have stopped to buy the replacement sari. All of that could be investigated later.

As they reached the limits of Juhu, Arman pointed out landmarks. "Mr. Tata was the first to build a beach villa in Juhu. Then others followed. Each house bigger than the next."

"How do you know so much about Juhu?"

"Your brother was contractor for a large villa a few years ago. At that time, there were very good sea views. Now the views are of houses." He waved at stucco villas, built tall with balconies on all sides. "I'm not sure I will be able to guess the nawab's residence. I will ask at that toddy shop ahead."

Arman parked, went out, and came back quickly. "He said the nawab's mansion is ahead. He said to look for a pink house and horses in the garden."

Perveen laughed. "Horses in the garden! Do you think he was exaggerating?"

"No reason for him to tease me when I bought one of his toddy bottles. Maybe he meant statues of horses."

The question was answered when, after the space of a few miles, they saw a fenced riding ring that contained three of the largest horses Perveen had ever seen, two of which were munching grass, while the other was sleeping. It always amazed Perveen that horses had the ability to lock their joints to remain standing while they dozed. Since the fire, her own body felt very tight; and rest seemed inconceivable.

After they'd passed the riding ring, they came to a tall gate set between two pillars. VARANPUR VILLA, 1921 was stamped on a brass plate along with a coat of arms showing a tiger and a horse. Under the shade of an umbrella stand, a young man in a turquoise-blue turban and suit was slumped in a chair.

Arman tapped the car horn, and the durwan jerked into wakefulness. Perveen's window was down, and she began her introduction, wishing her throat weren't so parched from heat. "Miss Mistry calling on the begum—"

"Go," he said, waving them along the long, narrow drive shaded by young palms on one side and a thick bank of bougainvillea on the other. Entering the grounds had been too easy, Perveen thought; it was remarkable that a nawab's security was so much less than that of Gulnaz's family.

The house was definitely pink: a three-story stucco villa built in a Renaissance style, with ornate floral wreaths carved of green stone placed above the windows, and long galleries with railings of the same green material which Perveen guessed was the Varun stone Cora had described. To Perveen's eye it looked like a rather pallid green, but perhaps that was because the sun was so blindingly bright.

Arman stopped the car before the wide front door. "Shall I step in with you?"

Perveen considered the fact that Sunanda had been attacked here. Although her instincts were that the assailant had been a guest, she couldn't be certain. "Very well. Let's go together to the front door."

To her surprise, nobody was waiting on either side of the door, which was ajar.

"This is a royal house? Where are the servants?" Arman muttered as Perveen opened the door fully.

"Hello? Is anyone here?" Perveen called out in English, hoping to attract Cora's attention. The house appeared so newly built that nobody had found the time to furnish it, although the wall near the door held a few pictures: a framed painting of a palace, and a professional photograph of Cora and the man who must have been the nawab, both dressed in formal palace attire. This was the first time Perveen had seen images of people on the walls of a Muslim home; perhaps the Nawab of Varanpur felt free of religious conventions when he was away from the watchful eyes of his state.

Ahead of her lay a long, glimmering hallway of black and white marble tiles. It was empty for just a moment. She heard a pattering sound, and from the distance, a small white dog ran straight toward her, barking and wagging its tail. Ruffling the dog's head, she guessed this pretty pet had been meant to receive the sausages Cora was carrying when they'd first met.

"I can't believe this tiny powderpuff is the chowkidar," she joked to Arman.

"Don't worry. We do have guards in the drive," said a sharp voice behind her.

Perveen turned to see that a stunningly handsome Indian dressed in riding clothes had come up behind them. About six feet tall, with broad shoulders and an athletic physique, the man had been gifted with a strong jaw, aquiline features, and broody eyes. If that weren't enough, he was as fair-skinned as a Baghdadi Jew—or Rudolph Valentino, she thought, remembering Cora's comment. Perveen could easily see why Cora had seen this man, who couldn't be more than thirty-five, as the answer to her prayers.

"Your Highness!" Perveen said in English, because that was the language he'd used with her. Belatedly, she ducked her head in a show of respect. "My name is Perveen Mistry. I'm a friend of the begum's. She invited me to call anytime, and here I am. I did not mean any criticism about the darling dog. She is very sweet."

"*He* is called Rover," the nawab said in a crisp boarding school accent. "I'll notify her maid about your arrival. You can wait for her on the veranda—through the doors straight ahead. Your driver should return to his car or go to the workers' courtyard."

Perveen assented. There was no reason for Arman to stay out in the heat in the car, when a courtyard would give him the building's shade.

"Oshadi!" the man bellowed.

Perveen felt a rush of surprise at hearing the name of the Bhatia family's head of female servants. From the far end of the hall, Oshadi began her lopsided gait, tapping the marble floor with her cane as she proceeded, stopping a good ten feet from the nawab, her eyes downcast.

Perveen was full of questions about how Oshadi had come to be working at Varanpur Villa, but she knew it was likely because of Uma, who had a pattern of helping her foreign friends with servants.

In Hindustani, the nawab instructed Oshadi to escort Arman and bring him a pitcher of water. After they left, Perveen hesitated. Why wasn't the nawab calling for someone to fetch Cora?

"Where is the begum?" Perveen inquired.

"She slept late today. So, upstairs. In our room." He looked at Perveen appraisingly. "Shall I bring you there?"

Perveen had no interest in going upstairs to a bedroom wing with a man who could have assaulted Sunanda. "I'm happy to look around outside until she's ready. She said the villa's beach is delightful."

"She loves it—she swims most days, unless she's riding," the nawab said. "In Varanpur, she'd hunt weekly if she could— but I haven't the time now that my stone exporting business is growing."

"I heard that you pledged a donation of stone for building the ladies' hospital," Perveen said, glancing along the hallway for more evidence of green. "Is that the stone I see in the ceiling moldings?"

"Yes, it is. And as for the hospital—just as well that it's cancelled." He smirked slightly as he spoke.

"Why?"

"Ladies have good intentions, but they cannot guarantee land or building materials. All of that is up to the husbands, and for us, business always comes first. There are other uses for Varanpur stone."

"I see," Perveen said, thinking that his casual attitude reminded her of Dwarkanath Bhatia's rescinded generosity. "I'll take my leave, then, and go to look at your famous beach view until the begum awakens."

"No need to go out the front door—down the hall and straight through those French doors will bring you to the seaside," he said, waving toward the faraway doors that Oshadi had opened. As he moved his left hand, she saw a heavy signet ring. One of Sunanda's few recollections of her attacker was that she'd felt his ring pressing into her.

Perveen walked cautiously down the hall, relieved that the nawab was going upstairs rather than following her. She hoped that he would tell Cora she was on the beach—but she didn't know if she could trust him to do that.

Outside, she stepped onto a long veranda paved in green Varanpur stone and furnished in cast-iron furniture painted in the bright white that had become fashionable. The veranda turned at the end, and she saw a shorter side to it, facing a small garden with a fountain. On this side, the white iron furniture was charmingly child-sized; a table and enough chairs for eight. The furniture seemed like an indication that the nawab enjoyed hosting his children from Varanpur. Cora was the approximate age of the ayahs working at Bhatia House, so she could easily have played with the young royals. Yet when Cora had been at Mistry House, she hadn't said anything about her stepchildren. She'd spoken of trying for a baby of her own.

Beyond the veranda was a pale sandy beach and then a small rectangular building, larger than the Mistrys' garden cottage, with simple walls made from reed mats and a bamboo ceiling. It reminded her of the shelters used for changing one's clothing that she'd seen dotting the sand at the seaside in England. At the time, she'd resisted Alice's entreaties to come in with her to don a bathing costume and wade into the Atlantic. She'd not liked the temperature of the air and imagined the water would be freezing.

Perveen slipped out of her sandals, stepped off the stone veranda, and moved along the sand. The white grains were very warm—but the nearby water beckoned. Perveen lifted the edge of her sari and hurried past the chairs to the place where the warm pliability of sand turned to damp coolness. At the water's edge, small, foamy waves lapped at her toes. Past them, the waves were strong, and she understood Sunanda's fear that the children could be swept out.

Perveen shifted to survey the beach hut. The short side closest to her had a door that was fixed with a simple peg on the outside. She approached it, moved the peg, and stepped inside.

It was dim, as Sunanda had reported, with the only light coming from the cracks at the top of the reed screens, and between the lengths of bamboo that made the roof. In monsoon, the hut would suffer a deluge, much like the shanties in Sunanda's neighborhood.

Perveen hadn't realized she was holding her breath. She let it out, feeling a heaviness that came from emotion and the closed space. Enclosed spaces made her nervous—and this one was especially fraught.

She could see somewhat in the gloom, and she walked around a pair of low benches to peer into a cupboard holding towels and an array of short clothing for women—bathing costumes, just like she'd seen Europeans wearing in magazine pictures. Unable to resist, she picked up a sleeveless dress with attached pants underneath the skirt. It looked as if it would end just below the knee—or higher, if Cora was wearing it.

There was a lightweight wooden wall on the far side of the room, and it opened to the hut's other side, where the cupboards held bathing costumes for men. A cowbell hung on a hook near the door, just as she'd noticed on the other side. Perhaps it was rung in the case of emergency.

A creaking sound alerted her that the door on the women's side of the little building had been opened.

Sunanda's trauma was not just in Perveen's mind anymore. Feeling sick with fear, she rushed through the door on the men's side and was out again, close to the water. She could go back to the house and see if Oshadi could take her to find Arman in the courtyard.

But in the next instant, the hut's other door opened and out stepped Cora, dressed in a knee-length silk wrapper, making it seem as if she'd just awoken. Shading her eyes with her hand, she regarded Perveen. "There you are! I was worried you might have gotten swept up in the waves!"

"I don't swim," Perveen said, feeling the rat-tat of her heart start to slow. "I wish I did know how, though. I was just looking around."

"In our cabana?" Cora crossed her arms, studying her with a skeptical air. "I'd have thought you'd take one of the beach chairs."

Perveen forced a laugh. "I've never seen such a little house for swimmers' use. Did you call it a cabana? I'm unfamiliar with the word."

"It might be Italian—or Spanish. I'm guessing. Never went to the kind of school where extra languages were taught." Cora sniffed and then looked toward the water. "We can set up sun parasols over the chairs to shield us while we have our drinks."

"That sounds very nice." Perveen would have preferred to speak to Cora away from the villa. She hadn't felt safe when she'd met the nawab. "Shall we go up to the veranda and tell Oshadi?"

"Just a sec." Cora went back into the cabana through the open door and came out with the cowbell. Swiftly, she loped a hundred feet or so toward the house and rang the bell vigorously. After a moment, a young man in blue began running down the lawn toward them.

Using her hands, Cora instructed him to drag the chairs close to where water lapped the sand and raise the umbrellas. The only words she spoke were about choices of drinks. To Perveen, she said, "I like my orange juice with a splash of champagne. How about you?"

"I'm a dreadful bore," Perveen apologized. "Because of this heat, I'm craving plain water."

"Any ice?" Cora asked.

"A luxury indeed!" Perveen said with a nod, repeating the same to the young man.

They settled in their chairs as the manservant went off. There was an awkward silence, so Perveen began. "Let me just say that I'm sorry about the last time we were together. I felt wretched after I spoke with you at my office."

"Have you changed your mind about representing me, then?"

Perveen hesitated, because she couldn't lie outright. "I would like to know more about the hospital committee from you. In the brief time I spoke with your husband, he mentioned that there wasn't enough support from the women's husbands. I want to know who is involved at this point." *And who might have attended the party where Sunanda was attacked.*

The begum bit her lip, smearing a bit of red onto the bottom of a front tooth. "You'll have to ask them yourself, because they won't answer my calls."

"Do you mean—the ladies on the committee?"

"Of course!" Cora's voice was impatient. "My title might be Princess, but the white ladies in this town have made it clear I'm from the wrong place."

"Australia is respected enough by Britain to have had dominion status since 1901!" Perveen didn't add that she thought the privilege had been given to Australia, rather than India, because of racism.

"I keep my mouth shut around them about my own family, just as I do about my dancing and singing career," Cora said glumly. "So it must be that they are thinking about Australia being founded as a penal colony. Australia is where men are supposed to go for horses—but not wives."

"Look, there's the bearer coming!" Perveen said. After the bearer had handed off their drinks, she told Cora, "I also felt like an outsider at the tea party. I heard Uma mention your title, so I thought you might be quite distant and perhaps even snobbish. But I saw your compassion during the emergency. You were so kind to Uma's ayah—Sunanda," she added, as if she'd forgotten that Cora already knew the name.

"Oh, yes." Cora sounded as if the praise had gratified her. "I gave her the money because I didn't think Uma's family was treating her well. The lowest of the low, she must be in their eyes. I hope she's doing well?"

The question held an expectation that Perveen could answer it. The only reason must be that Cora knew she was Sunanda's lawyer. "Well enough."

"It's a shame Uma didn't send her to me the way she sent an ayah to help Serena Prescott. Frankly, I could use her help as well as Oshadi's."

"That's very generous of you," Perveen said, thinking that maybe Cora still didn't know Sunanda had been arrested after all. But did Cora know Sunanda was the ayah who'd been with the Bhatias at the nawab's birthday cocktails? Did she have any idea she'd been harmed?

"You look so damn serious! What is it?" Cora's eyes were searching.

"I wanted to ask you more about the hospital donors, Madeline Stowe and Serena Prescott."

"Good lord." Cora sighed, and then took a luxurious sip of her drink. "The nawab introduced me to Madeline because he's close to her husband. Madeline was jolly good company until Serena arrived in town. Then they become bosum friends. The Stowes are planning to buy property near the Prescotts once some land comes available in the hills. Then I'll have even less of a chance to see Madeline."

Perveen saw the hurt in Cora's face and looked away, giving her the space to compose herself. Her eyes fell on Cora's toes flexing in the sand. They were such large feet—and with the toenails painted red, just like her fingernails.

"Did the Stowes attend your party in May?" As Cora's narrow, arched eyebrows rose in surprise, Perveen realized it might seem odd she knew about it. So she fibbed, "My sister-in-law talks to me about all the parties she hears about."

"Yes, they came. I invited many more ladies from the hospital committee, but only one other lady was there beside Madeline. And they didn't know each other well. It was more of a stag party."

"Another term I don't know." Perveen smiled, trying to make the younger woman feel more in charge.

Cora laughed heartily. "Stags are what you call male deer. A stag party is another way of saying a men's party. Manny's Bombay friends—horse-racing guys, and big wheels in business—tend to be rowdy. That night, I had a few too many myself."

"Weren't there children present?" Perveen prodded. Noticing that Cora was looking unhappy, she added, "I saw the dear little dining table and chairs on the veranda."

Cora smiled. "I chose that furniture. Yes, Uma and Paresh Bhatia's older kids came to the party. I specifically asked for them because several of Manny's offspring had come up on the train to visit. I couldn't watch them when I was hosting a gathering."

"And did the younger set have fun?" Perveen asked.

"I think so. They all speak Gujarati. It's a shame that Uma didn't want to come."

Perveen remembered Sunanda saying that Uma had only stayed back because of Mangala's jealousy, but she could not reveal her client's words. Instead, she imitated Cora's act of pushing her feet into the wet sand. She wanted to look relaxed.

"I noticed you've got Oshadi here. She might be able to oversee children at future parties."

"I think she's a bit too old and lame for that." Cora looked into her empty glass with a frown. "But I'm glad she's joined our staff."

Why? Perveen thought, but that would be too overbearing to ask. "When did she come?"

"She arrived by cart on Sunday." Cora raised her thinly arched brows. "Parvesh sacked Oshadi; that's why Uma felt bad and gave her the money for a ride out this way."

Perveen was shocked. "Why in heaven's name would the Bhatias throw out such a trusted family retainer?"

Cora glanced toward the house, and then back at Perveen. "Did you hear about Sir Dwarkanath's untimely death?"

Perveen was prepared. "The papers today said it was lead acetate poisoning. But what does that have to do with Oshadi being let go?"

"Men don't feed themselves, so such a poisoning must be blamed on the woman who did." Cora raised her eyes heavenward, then shut them against the bright sun.

"But Oshadi wasn't a cook." Perveen thought for a moment. "She did give the family tea."

"That's what she told me!" Cora said. "I think Parvesh thought it would be easier to get rid of Oshadi than for Uma to face rumors she didn't take proper care of her father-in-law."

This line of reasoning pointed to what had been made public knowledge: poisoning, but no police comment about whether it was intentional. Perveen asked, "Do you think Oshadi's speaking the truth?"

"I've no reason to doubt her." Cora tapped her fingers on the edge of the chair's arm. "It doesn't surprise me that Parvesh Bhatia would behave so despicably. I've suggested to my husband not to do business with him anymore."

"What kind of behavior do you mean?"

"He's a meddler," Cora muttered. "And everyone knows that the Bhatia Stone business has been suffering since Parvesh began taking on more responsibilities. And he ruined my party by leaving so early with his children. When somebody runs off, others follow."

"I suppose Parvesh's involvement with his wife's charity organization could be seen as a kind of meddling. I wonder if it really was Lord Bhatia who decided against donating the warehouses?"

Cora narrowed her eyes and said, "Uma doesn't strike me as a liar—although she can be evasive. She certainly didn't stand up for Oshadi when Parvesh sacked her."

"Most women don't feel they can disagree with their husbands outright," Perveen said, observing the surprise in Cora's eyes. "The important thing is that you've certainly given Oshadi a new life by employing her."

"Mmmm." Cora sniffed, and when Perveen looked at her, she said, "I love the seaside air. But today, I smell something rotten."

"Your nose is better than mine. Maybe a dead fish washed up somewhere?" Perveen sipped her water, wondering if Cora was obliquely expressing displeasure with her. In any case, Cora's drink was finished, and Perveen didn't fancy staying for another round. She'd make one last try. "By the way, do you have the guest list for that last party?"

"Maybe—but it doesn't matter. You'll come to another party with better people in attendance."

Perveen was glad that Cora hadn't reacted with suspicion. "You mentioned racehorse owners and businessmen coming to your party. Their names could be helpful for a new hospital fundraising list. The advantage is that these people are already in your hand—"

"No, they aren't!" Cora got up from her chair and plodded toward the sea. She waded a few feet, the water rising close to the hem of her wrapper.

Perveen followed, but only to ankle depth; watching and waiting.

"I try and try—but it's been so hard," Cora said. "Sometimes I think about going back, but what's there for me?"

Perveen felt a surge of sympathy. "What is so hard, my dear?"

"I don't know what the other women know," she said, running a hand through her hair. "I got dresses made not knowing the chic seamstress is Miss Marshall, rather than Mrs. Wilson. I didn't know I shouldn't get party invitations made at the printer in Santa Cruz; only Huddleston's in South Bombay is acceptable. Madeline said to me that engraving is the only acceptable style for people of our class. She's sweet to me, but I'm such a dunce."

"You are very young to be thrust into this position," Perveen comforted her. "And I don't believe snobbish people are ever satisfied. Not even with themselves."

Cora gave a last longing look at the sea before turning back to the villa. Shading her eyes against the sun, she said, "I spy Oshadi on the veranda. It might mean my husband wants to speak with me."

"The mark of good staff," Perveen feigned an overly upper-class, grand tone. "They are at hand when you need them, and invisible when you want privacy."

"Ha!" Cora snorted. "Can you believe I grew up without servants?"

Perveen absolutely could—and she was glad Cora felt free enough to be honest after her humiliating past encounters with her husband's set. "Shall we bring in the drinking glasses, to save Oshadi the trouble?"

"No, that boy who was here earlier will clean them up."

Cora walked a few steps ahead of Perveen, her bare feet plugging resolutely into the shifting sand. She had so much determination to her gait that Perveen felt certain that she might find a place in Bombay society after all. And if she couldn't, how might she find a meaningful way to live?

Once they'd reached the house, the same young man who'd brought them drinks appeared carrying two bowls of warm water.

"We shall sit down for our foot baths," Cora told Perveen, gesturing toward a pair of rattan chairs on the veranda. "Manny hates any grain of sand on the floors."

It was a peculiar, ticklish feeling to have one's feet hand-washed. After the boy had finished the ablutions and dried her feet with a soft cotton cloth, he laid out her cleaned pair of sandals.

"I'm checking on my husband," Cora said, stepping into a pair of high-heeled shoes that left her toes bare. "It's not likely I'll return, so—let's do goodbyes now."

Her words made Perveen think that she thought the nawab needed her; at least this would provide Perveen with some unexpected time with Oshadi. Gratefully, she said, "It's lovely to see you, Cora. Till the next time. Did you say you're going to the Lawyers' Ball?"

"I didn't say that, but I would like to go if you're there." A gleam came into Cora's eyes. "Probably I can convince my husband. Ta-ta, now!"

Perveen beckoned for Oshadi to come closer to the chairs from where she'd been standing at a distance, her body contorted slightly over her walking stick. Warmly, Perveen said, "We meet again. How are you finding this new place?"

Oshadi looked almost shyly at her. "It is strange. I don't know how to feel at home. I never saw such a modern house and people like them!"

"Please do sit down, Oshadi." Perveen motioned to the chair that Cora had vacated. "You will have a harder time later today if you don't take a moment's rest."

After some hesitation, Oshadi slipped into the lounge chair and carefully set her cane nearby. "How is Sunanda?"

Perveen considered how to answer; probably it was better not to worry the lady with details about the second incarceration. "Her burn is getting better. I know she would want me to say hello to you."

"She must miss Bhatia House like I do." Oshadi looked forlornly at the beautiful seaside view. "This is not the same. Uma-bhabhu said that I was part of the family. She knows I was the one who taught her what to do for her mother-in-law's care and how not to make Nana-seth angry."

"The nana-seth—you mean Sir Dwarkanath?"

She nodded. "Yes. It's what we called him because he was head of the house. That's Parvesh's title now. Though he hardly deserves it!"

Perveen imagined this was because Parvesh had sent her off. "Did you like Sir Dwarkanath much better? I mean, was he a good leader for the family?"

Oshadi's eyes flickered sideways, as if checking that they were alone. "He was fair to servants, although he was not always proper."

"What was improper?" Perveen asked, intrigued by Oshadi's chattiness. She was beginning to feel hope that Oshadi might know of the man's business enemies—anyone who might have wished to ruin his reputation by having a maid in his house accused of committing abortion. "Were his friends a bad sort?"

She shook her head. "No. I mean that he wasn't truly charitable—he never cared for the hospital. And he did things against Hinduism while pretending to be so religious."

"What did he do against religious rules?"

Oshadi raised her white eyebrows. "Very regularly, he drank alcohol. But it was such a secret that not even Motabhai knew. His father needed to maintain his image for other Hindus."

"And how do you know he drank?"

"I was household headwoman," she said. "I inspected the house every night before taking my rest—I had a small room there. The only staff member with a room," she added with pride. "Many nights I would pass through the house after all were asleep, and he would be inside the drawing room, fallen asleep from drinking. He would do this quite often when he had business troubles. I would find glasses with a trace of yellow or brown liquid stuck to the bottom. He took brandy. His son drank gin—and that was only with the British, to make them feel comfortable."

Perveen recalled that the one thing that had seemed imperfect about the elegant drawing room was a fingerprint on the glass of the liquor cabinet. Maybe it had been Sir Dwarkanath's. "Ah. Was the liquor meant as hospitality for European business visitors only?"

"Yes. But when I left on Sunday, Motabhai ordered all of the alcohol bottles removed."

Sunday was just a day before Perveen had accidentally met Inspector Prescott, who'd told her the cause of death was lead acetate poisoning. "Do you think the bottles were taken out because the police needed to check them?"

"Who knows? I was told to leave quickly. Sir Dwarkanath would not have wanted such a sight when mourners came to call."

Perveen felt eager to move on. She stood up, smoothing her sari. "Well, you are in a very different place now. I hope the begum and nawab are respectful and kind."

"Young madam wants to talk, but we always need someone in the middle to turn her questions into Marathi." Oshadi arose and pushed her chair into alignment with Perveen's empty one. As if satisfied with the appearance, she added, "The husband is unpleasant, but aren't most men? At least I can understand his Gujarati."

"I am happy to keep speaking Marathi with you." Perveen reached into her case and took out her card. "This has my home and office address, Marathi on one side and English on the back. I work at a place in Bruce Street called Mistry House. Everyone in Fort knows it."

Oshadi folded the card into her hand and reached for her cane. "What do I need with such a card?"

Perveen hesitated, wishing she could warn Oshadi that this was the place that Sunanda had been harmed, but being mindful of the professional obligation that had dominated her conversation with Cora. "I want you to have my address in case you'd ever like to speak."

On the way out of Juhu, Arman mentioned that when he'd been waiting in the courtyard, Oshadi had come and asked him a lot of questions about Sunanda's well-being. "I didn't say anything about her being back in jail. I never know what you wish me to keep private, so it's better to say nothing, isn't it?"

"Yes. You did well." Perveen suspected that Oshadi had asked out of sympathy, but still, the elderly woman shouldn't know details about the case. "On the way home, let's make a quick stop in Santa Cruz. I'm looking for a printing shop. And then I'd like to get a packet of sausages to take home to John."

"Portuguese sausage is very delicious," Arman said, his expression brightening.

Smiling at him in the rearview mirror, Perveen added, "And you will certainly get some for lunch."

33

AN IRON GRIP

When Perveen and Arman arrived home, it was already teatime. Her parents, Rustom, Khushy, and Hiba were gathered on the veranda, and Perveen noted that the chairs and tables had been shifted so they wouldn't have to stare at the bedraggled grounds leading to the garden house.

"Welcome back," Jamshedji said. "At least someone billed today!"

Perveen tried not to wince. "Did the police interview Gita?"

"Yes—and they are on the hunt for a man fitting the description." Jamshedji gestured to Rustom. "Watch your hand there. Khushy looks like she's drooping."

Adjusting the sleeping baby in his arms, Rustom said, "Finding the fellow will be difficult. How many men under thirty have mustaches? In fact, I may grow my own, now that Gulnaz isn't here to complain."

Khushy muttered slightly in her sleep, and Camellia smiled. "What a good father you are, Rustom. I think we can allow you a mustache if you like."

"I want to go inside and talk to Gita again. She's been anxious," Jamshedji said, rising to his feet.

"I'll go with you," Camellia said. "The heat is too much to bear."

After the parents went indoors, Perveen lowered the reed shade to block out sun from the veranda. Looking at Rustom, she said, "You look hot. How about a glass of water?"

"Please!" He chuckled. "I have been afraid to move."

"I'll get water for both of you," Hiba offered, rising from her crouch at the veranda's edge and going into the house.

Once they were alone, Perveen asked, "I wonder if you can help me with something. On Sunday morning, while you were in the drawing room inside Bhatia House, did you notice a cabinet holding liquor bottles?"

He shook his head. "No. If I had, I'd have been glad of a tipple. Especially with what was awaiting me at home."

"Fair enough." Perveen didn't want to brood on Gulnaz's departure. "My other question involves whether you might know some men I'm curious about."

Rustom peered at her suspiciously. "Why should I tell you?"

"Because it could help with a case. And it might possibly lead us to understanding who set the fire." Perveen had been pleased to acquire a duplicate copy of the nawab's guest list at the stationery shop in Santa Cruz. She hadn't identified herself, but just asked for it; something about her manner, or perhaps the way she'd mentioned Begum Cora, had led the man behind the counter to assist her without question.

Twenty couples, and a few bachelors, were on the list, none of them with immediately recognizable government connections. As Perveen read the guests' names to Rustom, he occasionally interrupted. Most of the names were known to him and a few were friendly acquaintances: Tigran Tata, a car dealer married to one of Perveen's batchmates from the Petit School, and Polad Shroff, who was a liquor distributor. The only whites on the list were a British South African named Austin Merrick, who was involved in horse racing, and Malcolm Stowe. Cora had complained that few of the invited ladies had attended—meaning that the invitation list didn't represent the full accounting of who was at Varanpur Villa the evening that Sunanda was raped. However, Perveen was becoming suspicious that Prescott's questions about the prosecution of elite men for rape were meant to help his friend.

Looking closely at Rustom, she said, "What can you tell me about Malcolm Stowe?"

"Our family's old business rival." Rustom shrugged. "I've spoken with him on many occasions when his company did the ironwork for some of our projects. The first time I saw him, I thought his appearance might indicate that perhaps his mother or grandmother was Indian. I don't believe he bothered with university, but he went to boarding school in Scindia, which set him up for close friendships with the Indian upper class—some of them royal."

Perveen remembered Sunanda's description of the color of her assailant's hands. "Did you ever ask if he was Anglo-Indian?"

"No—it's not important to me. He's a solid businessman—the company's in fine standing. As they say, he never leaves the card table without settling his debts—and when he lends money to anyone, he expects it to be repaid with interest."

"He sounds very upstanding, then?"

Rustom grimaced. "I wouldn't go that far. He once said to me that he took a long time to marry because a man's life should be fully enjoyed. He was known to play the field, as they say."

Perveen remembered Stowe looking away from Uma and her, as if to preserve their modesty, when they passed him waiting inside Bhatia House. "What do you hear about his behavior now?"

"Nothing dastardly," Rustom answered as Hiba returned to the veranda with two steel tumblers of cold water. "He found a British wife amongst the fishing fleet about ten years ago. He's got at least a couple of children. Tell you what, Perveen, if you want more, you should ask him. His office isn't far from mine in Elphinstone Circle."

"Thank you," Perveen said and then took up her glass for a long drink. Looking at Rustom cuddling Khushy, she felt as if her family was somehow growing. If not in size, in strength.

On Thursday morning, Perveen was still pondering how to discreetly investigate Malcolm Stowe. It was only after she'd gone
to the office and finished paperwork for two clients that she
broached the topic with Jamshedji. First, she told him about
Sunanda's revelation; and then about the list of people identified as invited to the party.

"I agree with you that knowing the identity of the fellow
who raped Sunanda could be most helpful for pre-trial conversations." Jamshedji put down his monocle and surveyed
her seriously from across the partners desk. "But identifying
the man can be hazardous. When you were at the beach villa,
you said that the nawab separated Arman from you almost
immediately. You had no protector. Anything could have happened."

Perveen fiddled with her fountain pen. "There were plenty of
servants, and his wife was home—"

"But what if she actually hadn't been?" Jamshedji cut her off.
"And I think he's as good a candidate as any for being a rapist.
Show me the whole list of names."

She took the paper out of her case and passed it across the
table, watching as he read it.

"I believe Tigran Tata, Polad Shroff, and Malcolm Stowe
will be at the Lawyers' Ball," Jamshedji said after a few minutes.
"And to answer your question of how I know, it is because I'm
on the ball's organizing committee. The party's two days away.
In the meantime, there's much to do. I looked at the Hariani
contract—which, by the way, was perfect. I made a small change
in phrasing, here and there, so he will know I've touched it."

"That's good," she said, heartened by her father's reassurance
of her acumen.

"I've booked two more barristers for you to interview, one
after the other, starting at two this afternoon." Raising a finger
at her, he added, "Mind that you're in to speak with them."

Perveen felt that her relationship with Jamshedji, which had become so fraught, was well on the way to recovery. She was grateful for her father's continuing attempts to help and his reminder about treading carefully made sense. Yet the identity of the complainant was the key to understanding her client's unusual arrest. She'd begun to dream of using the Indian Penal Code's Section 211, in which making false charges was a punishable crime. Another possibility was suing for damages using the civil action of malicious prosecution. But would Sunanda agree?

After Jamshedji went off to visit a judge at the High Court, Perveen told Mustafa that she was taking Jamshedji's edited contract to Mr. Hariani, and after that would stop downstairs at the office of Malcolm Stowe. She felt it important to mention the name, in case of adverse circumstance. In her mind, Mr. Stowe was a suspect.

Perveen had asked Arman to drive her, both for the security and because she felt it was crucial to appear fresh. On their way, she told him about the two offices she'd visit and said that she didn't expect to be inside for longer than forty minutes total. "Present yourself at Stowe Ironworks if I'm running late; I won't mind."

After Arman opened the car door for her, she stood for a moment regarding the first floor's bay window, which was probably the interior office for Stowe Ironworks. A whirring ceiling fan was visible, a good sign that Stowe might be in the room. But first things first; she left the revised contract in an envelope at Hariani's office, this time not asking to speak with the man. Then she went downstairs to Stowe Ironworks, walking through the door to see the same Anglo-Indian clerk who'd previously sent her off. This time, she smiled and laid her card on the desk.

"Good morning, once again. I'll introduce myself this time. My name is Miss Mistry, and I'm a solicitor with Mistry Law. I'd very much like to see Mr. Stowe."

The man looked from the card to her with disbelief. "Do you have an appointment—Miss Mistry?"

Of course, he knew she hadn't got one. Smiling at him, she said, "There was no time to call. It's all quite sudden. But important."

The young man ran his hand through a shock of black hair. Clearly, he was wondering if turning this surprise visitor away could cause trouble for Mr. Stowe. Maybe he thought it had something to do with Stowe's wife, whom Perveen had mentioned the first time. Rising, he said, "I'll tell him you are here. Will you please wait?"

Perveen straightened her sari's pallu as she looked herself over in the mirror over a settee—it was framed in wrought iron and was surely another example of the ironworks' production. She looked entirely presentable and would employ ladylike manners to reassure Stowe she wasn't a threat.

When the young man came back and told her that Mr. Stowe would see her, Perveen set her lips into the same pleasant smile she'd used to greet him.

He opened a heavy door—ironwork over teak—and stood back so she could proceed through.

Stowe's office was a replica in size and shape to Mr. Hariani's office above, although his furniture was different; more expensive, almost everything of Burma teak or mahogany. Looking at the slightly worn tapestry covering the wingback chairs, she guessed these pieces were from the past—just like the office door, which was of much heavier wood than was used in the twentieth century.

Even though she'd glanced at Mr. Stowe several times before, she hadn't really studied him closely before this moment. The man was slightly over six feet tall and had a stocky figure that spoke of heavy meals and drink, and he was well-dressed in a pale caramel-colored summer wool suit. He had been standing by the window and turned at the sound of the opened door.

"To what do I owe this unexpected pleasure, Mrs. Mistry?" Mr. Stowe smiled, exposing large square teeth that were more common to Indians than Europeans.

"I'm a solicitor who is involved in the women's hospital project—I came on quite late, at the invitation of Dr. Miriam Penkar. Also, my title is miss."

His dark eyes narrowed. "If you are a miss—that means you are not Rustom Mistry's wife?"

"I'm his sister. He's mentioned your business acumen." She tried to gaze at him as if he were an oracle.

"Is that so?" His full lips twisted into a grin. "I should buy him a drink. You know, our grandfathers used to drink whiskey together."

"Yes, I heard they were friends." She wasn't going to bring up the story about the poached ironworker. Stowe stepped toward her, holding out a hand. Now that he was close, she was overpowered by the smell of 4711, the *eau de toilette* from Germany.

Perveen allowed him to take her hand and he gripped it hard, shaking it up and down. She felt the hard edge of a ring. She withdrew her hand, trying to get a look at the ring, but he slid both hands into his pockets.

"And how might I assist you today?" he asked, retreating to the chair behind his desk.

Perveen sat down, noting the desk's contents: a bare blotter, a handsome pen-and-ink stand, and a stack of papers held down with an iron paperweight that resembled a small grenade, perhaps a relic from war production. Looking back at him, she resumed her mission of appearing like a charity committee member. "It's about the hospital. Dr. Penkar and other ladies are very much in favor of continuing with the hospital."

"I don't wish to disappoint you, but a few weeks ago Sir Dwarkanath told me personally that he had rethought the project. And now he has passed away. Very likely his warehouse and all the stone within will be sold to pay off the many debts he carried." Malcolm Stowe spoke in a businesslike tone, not showing the usual expressions of grief one would expect from a friend.

"Is that so? I feel that would be such a tragedy for the family, and also a loss for the city. To think that you and I were among the last to see him!" She took a handkerchief to her eyes, as if wiping away tears.

"And what do you mean by that? How do you know the last time I saw him?" He leaned back in his chair, studying her with suspicious eyes.

"I don't, actually. I was having tea with Uma Bhatia last Wednesday, and when I left you were in the hallway." She decided not to mention seeing him in Prescott's office.

"Oh, yes. I can't say I remember you—sorry, that's not a polite thing to say." He smiled wolfishly. "I would not miss noticing you the next time, Miss Mistry."

Perveen flinched, realizing that he was treating her boldly, possibly because she was young and unmarried. Now she wished she had approached his wife with questions rather than him. But she was stuck; she'd have to make the best of it. "I heard Begum Cora has taken an interest in leadership. What do you think?"

"Ha ha!" He laughed, spewing droplets of saliva into the air. "Now that would be ridiculous!"

Perveen struggled not to react to the spit that had just missed her. "Really? I think that Cora is the only one on the committee who is a woman of two worlds—West and East. And I believe her husband is quite generous."

"You're right about Manny—sorry, Mansoor. The Nawab of Varanpur and I have known each other since we were at Scindia School. In fact"—he turned his deeply tanned and sun-spotted hand forward, so she could better see the ring on his pinky finger, a flashing ruby oval inset into gold—"I still wear the blood brothers ring he gifted me with when we were twenty."

Perveen strained to see it without getting any closer; it looked exactly like the nawab's ring.

Noticing her attention, he said, "The ruby stone from Burma is carved with the letter *M*, for both of our first names. He is generous to a fault, even today. And I think that's why he married an Australian with few social graces and a bit of a reputation. I've said to him, don't let her make a spectacle of herself on the committee. It will only make things worse for you."

"I've heard she was a nightclub performer," Perveen said, widening her eyes with feigned shock while wondering what Malcolm thought was the nawab's existing disadvantage.

"Yes, she danced her way into his heart. I wouldn't be surprised if she tricked Manny into the marriage. And the poor bloke is finally getting the wool off his eyes. A showgirl can't transform into a begum."

Perveen twisted the handkerchief in her hands. "I know your friendship with the nawab went back to boyhood. I was wondering, is Mr. Parvesh Bhatia also a longtime friend of his?"

"Hardly! Parvesh is the orthodox type of Hindu who avoids socializing with Muslims," Stowe said. "But he didn't hesitate to use Manny when he needed money!"

"I did hear something . . ." She paused, remembering what Rustom and Cora had both said about the nawab lending money. "Never mind. We mustn't speak ill of the dead."

"What is it?" He looked keenly at her.

Perveen glanced toward the closed door, as if nervous the clerk would overhear. "Some people think Sir Dwarkanath gathered the donations to fatten his bank account temporarily."

"Absolutely true." Stowe picked up the round iron paperweight and dropped it from one hand to the other. "I've had to lend him money in the past. A number of contractors have done the same."

"But why would he go to contractors rather than a bank?"

"You are a nosy one, aren't you?" Stowe chuckled, amused

rather than angered. "He went to me because he knew that if I didn't help him, and the project was slowed or stopped, it would hurt me—after all, I'd spend thousands of pounds fabricating iron pieces to be used inside and out of the building."

"I certainly can understand that," Perveen said, watching him move the iron ball from one hand to the other. His words were calm, but perhaps the memory was making him feel restless or angry.

"The Wednesday that you saw me, I'd come to see if there was a problem brewing with our current project. The stone was late. But Sir Dwarkanath insisted that he'd got the funds and said not to worry."

The situation Cora had suspected—that Dwarkanath Bhatia was fattening his bank account in order to appear better-off to a bank loan officer—might not be so off the mark. Dwarkanath Bhatia could have deposited the ladies' checks on Friday morning and written his own check later that day to pay off the stone supplier. When the building was finished, the customer would pay him, and he would reimburse the women's hospital fund.

"So the Bhatias' situation is very different from their public image," Perveen said.

"It wasn't always so," Stowe said, walking toward his bay window to look down on the street. "Sir Dwarkanath began as a middleman between stone quarry owners and contractors. When he was flush with money, he bought his own quarry west of the city. He did well selling this stone for many government buildings coming up. But the quarry was eventually depleted, and he found buying stone from suppliers more expensive than before. And there's another problem with stone, but I'm sure I don't have to explain to a clever lady like you."

Perveen remained in her seat, thinking frantically of what he expected her to know. All that came was the memory of Sunanda's brother and the other men she'd seen in Kalbadevi laboring with heavy carts. "The weight?"

He chuckled. "No, my dear. The biggest challenge arises when the stone reaches the city to be cut into bricks. There are sections of stone in a quarry that are more brown than gray, or more green than yellow. Therefore, the stone has sometimes been manually colored after being cut into bricks. Sometimes the colored bricks have been placed in the wrong parts of the building—the facade, for instance—and the color could wash away within a single monsoon. That has happened with more than a few buildings recently."

"I see." Perveen was pleased at how forthcoming he'd been—especially since she was a woman making an impromptu visit. She wondered if he had an alternate motivation. "How widely known is all of this?"

"Your brother knows," he said, his gaze turning toward Mistry Construction's building across the circle. "Some property owners have complained and wanted replacement or other restitution. Sir Dwarkanath didn't own the quarries, so he could blame the people there."

"Were all of these quarries in Bombay Presidency?" Perveen asked.

"No. Some are in princely states."

Previously, Perveen had thought the British would be the likely beneficiaries of the new maps Colin was drawing. Now she saw that redrawn boundaries between British and princely India might allow Bhatia Stone to buy another untapped area rich with stone for themselves. It might be the true reason that Sir Dwarkanath wanted a bank loan.

Abruptly, Stowe left the window and returned to his desk. He didn't sit down, just leaned his hands on its edge, so he faced her in a more aggressive posture than before. "Why are you really here?"

She felt warmth in her cheeks. "Trying to move the hospital forward—and feeling grateful for what you've explained about the Bhatia family's difficult position."

"Yet you are grilling me on the stone business. Tell me, did your brother send you?"

"No!" She was shocked by the cold look in his eyes. "Mistry Construction is your ally, not a competitor. I don't know much about stone—I thought you were interested in teaching me."

Sensing her time was finished, Perveen rose from her chair, feeling shaky. At least he hadn't figured out her deepest intention: evaluating him as a suspect in the attack on Sunanda.

"Your brother will have a chance at development at the same time as the others," said Stowe, moving around the desk to stand imposingly over her. "You tell him that—and not to send another hen into the fox's den."

Perveen thought Stowe's metaphor was ridiculous, but of course, the company's heritage was welding fanciful animals into ironwork. She didn't answer and was close to the door when she realized she'd left her legal case near the desk. She walked back to fetch it, but when she bent slightly to pick it up, she was shocked to feel the iron grip of Stowe's hand squeezing one of her buttocks.

Feeling a mix of nausea and terror, she wheeled about, thrusting the case hard against his belly. He swore and she stumbled away, her mind reeling. Sunanda hadn't been able to fight off a man—how could she?

"Are you all right, Miss Mistry?" he asked unctuously as she rushed for the door. She scrabbled for the doorknob, realizing with horror it was locked.

In the next instant, Stowe was opening it with a key from his waistcoat yet taking pains to make sure he was close enough behind her that she experienced the full length of his hot, heavy body pressed against hers.

"Do watch yourself!" he said with a chuckle as she almost tumbled into the waiting room.

The clerk who'd let her in earlier half-rose from his chair at the counter, looking with confusion at the two of them.

Perveen righted her posture and turned back to face Stowe. She realized that from the way she'd half-fallen, it might appear to the clerk that Stowe had thrown her out. She had to behave normally, or there was a risk a rumor would start—and, of course, the one whose reputation would be injured would be her.

Perveen spoke in the pleasantest voice she could muster. "Thank you, Mr. Stowe. And please give my best wishes to Mrs. Stowe. I can hardly wait to see her."

Stowe's eyes narrowed, as if he understood the threat within her words.

Moments later, Perveen was out of the office and hastening out to the street. She felt relieved that Jamshedji would be out and she wouldn't have to immediately mention where she'd been. If her father learned she'd been alone in an office with a man they both knew could have raped Sunanda, he would be furious. And because Stowe had been bold enough to touch her buttocks, he had made it seem extremely likely that he was inclined toward assaulting females.

"What is wrong, Perveen-bai?" Arman asked with concern when she ran out to the car.

"Nothing at all." Taking a deep breath, she said, "I had a difficult interview. I finished it."

"And the delivery of the contract to Mr. Hariani?"

"I did that first. Now let's go home."

As Arman put the Daimler in gear, Perveen looked up at the window. As she'd feared, Stowe was looking directly at the car. The distance was too great to make out his facial expression, but she imagined that he thought he'd got the best of her.

34
THE DOCTOR'S DEPUTY

*P*erveen spent the first half hour after she returned to Mistry House with a cup of tea, debating how much she could tell Jamshedji about Stowe. If he heard all the details, he might restrict her entirely from further investigations of the guest list. And although she'd hinted to Malcolm Stowe she'd be talking to his wife, what purpose would that serve? If the two of them had attended the nawab's party, she might indeed know of his guilt—but according to law she would never be forced to testify against her husband.

Perveen finished her tea and closed her eyes. She'd heard the door opening below and knew that one of the barristers coming for an interview must have arrived.

The first lawyer, Sushil Rao, regretted being unable to assist due to a close relationship with the Bhatias. The barrister who came next, Atul Narayan, also listened carefully, but concluded he wasn't well enough versed in issues of feminine health to speak about the case in court. Jamshedji was present for both interviews and tried to persuade them otherwise, but neither would agree.

Perveen and her father went home shortly thereafter; the car was silent with gloom. Jamshedji called the police department and learned nobody had been found meeting the vague description of the arsonist. Khushy was in a sulky mood, turning away from Perveen in favor of Hiba.

Friday looked as if it would also be a difficult day. Instead of working on Sunanda's case, Perveen decided to plow through some paperwork for a client whose English-language bookshop was looted during last November's Prince of Wales riots. But she could only read through the papers for a half hour before feeling faint. She remembered what Stowe had said in unctuous tones: *Are you all right, Miss Mistry?*

How could she, the hen who'd escaped a fox's den, ever feel all right? Even worse was knowing her family home had been targeted by someone who hadn't been caught and could strike again.

She jumped up at the sound of Mustafa's footsteps in the hall. He came in without his usual tray with tea. Instead, he handed her a paper. "Dr. Penkar telephoned at nine-thirty."

Perveen was annoyed to have missed the call. "I was here! Why didn't you call me?"

He looked stricken. "As I was about to get you, she rang off. An urgent medical emergency, she said."

"I hope that everything's all right." Perveen rang Dr. Penkar's office and was surprised when the warm answering voice was that of Miriam's mother, Bathsheba.

"Good morning, Mrs. Penkar. Perveen Mistry here. I thought I was ringing the clinic. I apologize."

"Oh, Perveen! Don't worry. It's the same line. I book many of the appointments," Mrs. Penkar reassured her. "What is Miriam calling you about?"

Perveen suspected Mrs. Penkar was thinking about her daughter's legal situation. "I don't know. I'm only returning the call."

"Well, she is with her patients now. Why don't you come here this evening, if you can arrive before sundown? Because it's Friday, we will serve you a Shabbat meal. There will be much more food than teatime snacks."

"Mrs. Penkar, I would enjoy that another Friday. Can you carry the message I called back to the nurse downstairs? I hope that Miriam can ring me back."

"Very well—I shall do that."

"Thank you."

Half an hour later, Perveen had finished a cup of tea and made some headway in research for the bookshop's damage case. She looked up, glad for a break, when Mustafa appeared in the door.

"Dr. Penkar is calling again."

Perveen launched herself out of her chair and hastened downstairs. She didn't bother with hellos. "What's happened?"

"It's about Ishan Bhatia." The doctor sounded breathless. "Uma rang to say that he's ill and asked for me to see him. I want to ask you to go."

Perveen was perplexed. "But I haven't any medical training. Don't the Bhatias have their own pediatrician?"

"No. They use a general practitioner who treats the whole family, but he's still away on holiday. Remember, he was unable to see Sir Dwarkanath."

Her mention of the deceased man made Perveen even more anxious. "Couldn't you suggest someone to them?"

"I already suggested that Uma take Ishan to Cama Hospital and let the diagnosis be made there—however, the house is full of relatives who've arrived for a mourning ceremony, and she said Parvesh doesn't want to cause any type of upset. He thinks the child ate too much and the situation will pass."

Perveen thought Parvesh's attitude here was consistent with what Oshadi and Sunanda had told her. He was a good man, but he cared about appearances. "Are you thinking that Ishan might have encountered the same poison as his grandfather?"

"It crossed my mind." Miriam's voice was grave. "I would see him, as Uma requested, except I must attend to a birth today. You are one of the ladies I know in possession of an automobile. Can't you please drop in to look at him? You could offer to carry Uma and him to hospital. Don't let Mangala dissuade you."

The mention of Uma's competitive sister-in-law made Perveen stiffen. She hadn't thought of Mangala as being the agent of poisoning. But she couldn't rule this out, especially if Ishan had the same symptoms as his grandfather. "I suppose that I could."

"Now, do you have a pen?" Miriam described an exhaustive array of symptoms of many likely conditions, from appendicitis to dysentery and poisoning, that Perveen duly noted in her book. She also ordered Perveen to look for items in Ishan's room or that he used for dining that might contain something poisonous; this should be carried in a bag to the hospital for analysis. "When you reach Cama Hospital, remember to explain about Sir Dwarkanath's lead acetate poisoning. That fact will surely put a fire under their pathologists' feet."

After Perveen hung up the telephone set, she ran upstairs to tell Jamshedji the urgent reason she needed the car. As expected, he told her she was in no position to play doctor.

"First off, I'm not going to attempt any guess at a diagnosis," Perveen responded, mindful of the stern look on her father's face. "I am only going to make it possible for Ishan to get to the hospital. And I certainly won't take him against his mother's wish."

"Given what happened to Sir Dwarkanath, they should allow it," Jamshedji opined. "And be sure that either one of the parents accompany you or give medical power of attorney. Take a boiler-plate contract with you." Pressing his fingers against his temples, he asked, "And when can I expect your return?"

"Late afternoon?"

"I require the car here before four. Arman is taking me to Harroways in Kemps Corner for the final fitting, which is at four-fifteen sharp. And you were coming with me, remember?"

Her father had said something earlier about his tailor appointment, and she'd forgotten about how he'd wanted a new suit for the Lawyers' Ball. "Must I? Surely the tailor knows more about the fitting of waistcoats than I do."

"Come if you can." He gave her a sulky look. "It's important that we both look respectable at the Lawyers' Ball. It's tomorrow, remember?"

"I wouldn't dream of missing it!" Perveen kissed his cheek, gathered the medical notes into her briefcase, and dashed out.

The road to Ghatkopar had become very familiar. Perveen no longer paid attention to the sights along the way, but upon reaching Bhatia House, she saw a marked difference. Not only the driveway but the grounds were filled with parked carriages, as well as horses and drivers. And more children were outside. A group of young boys played together in the garden, kicking a ball between them. The girls sat on the side, watching and calling out to them. When one girl ran to join, Chandini, the ayah she remembered from before, rushed to pull her back.

After Arman parked the car, Perveen walked behind a family that was heading inside. The father was speaking to another man about the distance they'd come: a long train journey from Gujarat. Several men had shaved heads, signifying they were family members who had participated in the cremation. Some mourners wore white, and others pastel colors; no gold borders or designs were in evidence.

The spacious rooms of Bhatia House were crowded with people, many sitting cross-legged on the floor, or on cushions. The only area that was devoid of people was the front hallway: a space about the size of a long mat that held a clay water urn and a lit brass lamp. Perveen heard a woman telling children that this was the spot where Sir Dwarkanath had been placed before he was taken for cremation.

Perveen meant to go upstairs to look for Ishan in his bedroom, but she paused to glance into the drawing room, which was filled with mourners. At the center was Parvesh Bhatia, who looked weary, with a drawn face and shadows under his eyes. She imagined he was losing sleep because of his father's death, his new work burdens, his ailing son—and perhaps something more. Cora had said that Parvesh was a meddler; what if he actually knew that his father was a secret drinker and had decided things would be easier if he were gone?

Perveen gazed at the cabinet that had once held alcohol bottles. Just as her brother had told her, all the bottles were gone. Either Parvesh or Uma could have discarded them; especially if one of them knew a bottle had been contaminated with poison.

"How kind of you to pay condolence. Your brother also came a few days ago." A wide-shouldered lady was studying Perveen, who jerked her eyes away from the cabinet. It took Perveen a few seconds to recognize Mangala Bhatia. Today she was dressed all in white, and the modesty of the color made her look less fearsome than on their previous encounters.

"Yes, Mangala-behen. Our family has many ties to yours and we are so very sorry for the loss of your father-in-law."

"I'll introduce you to our cousins who've come from Gujarat. Tomorrow is Asthi Visarjan, the scattering of ashes in the ocean. They will tell you about our religious custom." Mangala took her elbow in a firm grip.

"I'm sorry, but I have a duty here." Perveen shook her elbow free. "Dr. Penkar asked me to check on Ishan."

"Uma's already upstairs. And you are not a nurse." Mangala gave her a combative look.

Perveen stepped closer to her, a slight act of intimidation remembered from her encounter with Malcolm Stowe. As she'd expected, Mangala took a faltering half step backward. Perveen lowered her voice. "As I said, Dr. Penkar has deputized me into service. I also have a car waiting in case Ishan requires transport into town."

Other women were looking at them, and Mangala's face pinkened. Very likely, she did not want them hearing how sick Ishan might be. In a low voice, she said, "You don't know where his room is. I'll show you."

Mangala led Perveen up the stairs and past the row of rooms

in the bedroom wing. She opened a door to reveal a nursery with low shelves full of books and toys. The charpoys were stacked in a corner, unused, and mattresses covered the floor. So Ishan was sleeping amidst others, even though he wasn't well.

"We must sleep on the floor during our time of mourning," Mangala said, as if noticing Perveen's frown.

A woman with unkempt hair in white was crouched over a small body on a mattress in the far corner. Hearing them, the lady turned to reveal a puffy and exhausted face.

"Uma-behen," Perveen said, shocked at the change in her appearance. "Did Dr. Penkar tell you I was coming in her stead?"

"Don't worry, I am managing everything quite well," Mangala interrupted, giving Perveen a scornful look. "I told her the truth; he's sick. Looking at him won't help anything."

"Dr. Penkar said she'd try to see if you could help." Uma offered a wan smile. "Our doctor's away, and I'm very worried about Ishan."

"I am so sorry that Ishan's suffering," Perveen said, moving closer to take a look down at the child.

Uma didn't answer, but her eyes filled with tears.

"It's too much trouble for you to endure this, isn't it?" Mangala put a commanding hand on Uma's arm. "Now she's seen Ishan, she can go."

Perveen remembered the dark thought she'd had earlier: if Ishan passed away, Mangala's sons would eventually inherit the business. And Mangala probably didn't know how troubled the finances were; that the inheritance was not necessarily a prize.

Uma shrugged away from her sister-in-law's touch. "It's all right. Mangala, you may leave us."

Mangala gave Perveen a venomous look, but she stalked out, closing the door tightly behind her.

"Come take a look at him," Uma said, resuming her position kneeling by the child.

Perveen knelt down. Ishan's knees were drawn up against his

chest. His eyes were shut tight, but they fluttered open, as if he sensed someone new was nearby.

"Ishan-beta!" Uma spoke coaxingly, using the endearment for child. "This nice aunty is Dr. Penkar's helper. You don't remember, but she was right there when you were hurt at the tea."

Ishan murmured something unintelligible, and Uma told Perveen, "He's got a terrible stomachache. It started yesterday, but today he is confused."

"I should note that," Perveen said, reaching into her legal briefcase to take out the checklist she'd created from Dr. Penkar's instructions. "Dr. Penkar wanted me to ask whether he is thirsty."

Uma rubbed her hand across her damp brow. "No. He hasn't asked for anything, and you'll see there is a glass of water right beside him. Now that I think about it, though, he's not asked to use the toilet since yesterday afternoon. But he isn't strong and wanting to play—he said his legs feel too heavy."

"Any vomiting?" Perveen asked, checking on another symptom the doctor had mentioned.

"Fortunately, no. He is just very tired. You see, we are talking about him, and he cannot answer for himself." Uma stroked Ishan's head.

Perveen knelt so she was at eye level with the child. "Beta, look here. Can you say the different feelings happening inside your body?"

Slowly, he opened his eyes. "My stomach hurts. My eyes are tired."

Perveen watched Ishan close his eyes and turn away. Remembering another of the doctor's wishes, Perveen asked him to open his mouth.

Ishan did so, and Perveen noted something strange—a blue tinge on his gums. It was a warning sign, Miriam had said—but Perveen saw only the hint of a line. "Uma, can you see that his gums are slightly blue?"

Uma peered into her son's mouth. "I've never looked so closely, I'm afraid. Does it hurt, beta? The area on top of the teeth?"

"No!" Ishan's eyes fluttered open, but they didn't focus on her.

Perveen rattled off the warning signs that she knew from her conversation with Dr. Penkar. "Confusion, lack of thirst, and the color of his gums might indicate lead poisoning. He should be examined by a doctor straightaway—and at a place like a hospital, which has a laboratory. We must also gather up things in his room that might contain lead or anything else that isn't safe for consumption."

"So it's the same as happened to my father-in-law." Uma's voice broke, as if she realized her son might be close to death. She buried her face against his and started to sob.

"Ishan is young and strong. I've seen him run. He is a fighter!" Perveen could not get a response from Uma, so she moved on to sort through the scattered toys on the floor. Most of them were wood, some were metal. The metal ones she put together in a pile. As she crawled along the floor, she noticed a small paan box under Ishan's bed. If the mattress had been covering the slats, she wouldn't have seen it.

She reached under the bed and lifted the little box meant for keeping betel nut rolls.

"That's my treasure box!" Ishan murmured, suddenly coming into alertness.

"I'm sure he found the box empty. I wouldn't give the children paan. It stains the teeth and makes them too excitable." Uma's voice was defensive.

Opening the box, Perveen found a number of small divided spaces, all of which were filled. The space she looked at first held what looked like a stale rolled paan. As she picked it up, she didn't see the typical black-red mixture inside, but something white. Carefully, she unrolled the leaf and pulled out a tightly rolled ten-rupee note.

"Whose money is this?" Uma looked in shock at her son, who was still appearing unfocused. "There is money in your treasure box."

"Baa, I am only keeping it safe for her," Ishan whimpered.

"Is it Sunanda's money?" Perveen asked.

"Yes, it's hers—nobody should have it!" Ishan moaned. "Do you know my Sunanda?"

"Oh, yes! She is my very good friend."

"When did Sunanda give you all this money?" Uma interrupted in a terse voice.

He didn't answer, and Perveen said, "Perhaps it was shortly after the tea party."

Perveen continued inspecting the box's contents. She identified a red cashew pod, a soda-bottle stopper, a dusty red rubber ball, and a flat shiny piece of brass that looked like a lady's compact.

"Did Sunanda also give you this?" Perveen asked, opening the round brass compact, which had traces of pinkish powder inside.

"No. I found it in the garden." Ishan took it in his hands, looking at his face in the little mirror.

"When did you find it?" Uma asked.

"Yesterday. The others came after me and wanted it, but I was first. You know: finder keeper, loser weeper." He looked at his mother, who shook her head, not understanding the English phrase.

"Whose compact could this be?" Perveen asked Uma.

Uma raised her hands heavenward. "I don't know. The color is wrong for every woman in the house."

Perveen's memory snapped back to the tea party. There had been three European ladies and one Australian present. "It might have been dropped by accident by someone at the party; and cosmetics can sometimes be poisonous. It's worth taking this along with us to the hospital. Don't you think so, Ishan?"

"You won't take it from me?"

"No. You will be in charge of bringing it," Perveen said, striving to sound cheerful. "The doctors will like to admire what's in this treasure box."

"But not the money—someone in the hospital could steal it!" Uma looked at Perveen with concern. "And I'm very sorry that Sunanda was sent off when she needed to get what was rightfully hers."

"I could keep it for her in the safe at Mistry House, if you'll allow it," Perveen suggested. "Later, I can give it to Sunanda."

"Where is my Sunanda?" Ishan's voice rose. "Tell me!"

Perveen hesitated. She didn't want to say anything that would make him more upset. "She's in the city. I know she would like to see you again, but before that, we must fix your stomachache."

Uma looked helplessly at Perveen. "As lady of the house, I'm supposed to stay here and receive condolences. I told Miriam I couldn't leave."

"I can go," said Mangala as she stepped into the room. "I'm Ishan's favorite aunt!"

Perveen had been on the verge of offering Uma the chance to sign over power of attorney to her, but she didn't want to do it in front of Mangala, who might persuade Uma not to. So she said, "What a kind offer, Mangala-behen! However, Ishan is a child, and the doctors will insist on the presence of one of his parents, who are considered his legal guardians."

"Parvesh cannot go, so I suppose that I must." Uma sounded resigned. "And did you have your own car, Perveen?"

"Yes, and my driver is waiting to go. Nobody from your household needs to be troubled." Perveen turned to Mangala, who looked ready to keep protesting. "Mangala-ben, you have been hosting everyone so capably. Nobody could do it better than you."

Mangala smiled as if savoring the praise. "That is true. Don't worry about the guests."

Mangala went downstairs with a quick step, and Perveen latched the paan box and put it inside her legal case.

She wished she felt free to tell Uma her suspicions about Mangala, to warn her that Ishan might continue to be in danger. However, to say something like that could result in quite a bit of trouble if it turned out the poisoner was someone else. Instead, she said, "It's settled, then. Let's go."

Uma kissed Ishan and spoke to him softly. "Beta, we will be taking a ride in a nice car; the air will flow by your face and cool you. We shall bring your treasure box and another toy that you will choose."

"My bear," Ishan said, pointing to a stuffed animal on the far side of the floor.

Perveen retrieved the bear, and then Uma lifted Ishan into her arms.

Arman was standing in front of the Daimler, arguing with a driver who was attempting to park his horse-drawn taxi in front of it.

"No parking there! We must leave right away for the hospital," Perveen said to the man.

"Wait!"

Perveen turned and saw Parvesh Bhatia racing out of the house toward them. He called, "Let me see him!"

When he was close enough to look down at his sickly child, his expression grew serious. "He doesn't look well at all. He's worse than Mangala was saying to me."

"She didn't want him to be treated." Uma pressed her lips together, as if she was beginning to quietly awaken to the dark thoughts Perveen had felt unable to voice. "Miss Mistry is kindly taking us to Cama Hospital."

Perveen half-expected a challenge from Parvesh, but he only reached out to take Ishan into his arms. "Listen to what Baa, Miss Mistry, and the doctors say you must do. And you must get better. Please."

"You're going to frighten him!" protested Uma, who had slid into the car and was holding out her arms to take her child back.

Parvesh handed over Ishan, kissing his head one last time before closing the car door.

Perveen had waited outside the Daimler, and as she watched Parvesh, she could see how downcast his face was. His father had died a few days earlier; surely he was worrying he might also lose his son. She motioned for him to step away from the car so they could speak privately.

"We are bringing some toys, in case there's a chance they are made of lead or contain anything similar to what poisoned Sir Dwarkanath." Perveen kept her eyes on the man's anxious face. "We also discovered a cosmetic compact, and some money that Ishan was protecting for Sunanda. It was the ten rupees the begum had given."

He smiled ruefully. "He would do that. She was his favorite."

Taking note of his reaction, Perveen asked her next question quickly. "Did you know that Sunanda was jailed once again after visiting here last Friday?"

Parvesh dropped his head and muttered that he did not. "What has she done?"

"Without thinking clearly, she violated her bail restriction. She wasn't supposed to come to this place, but she believed she needed that money Ishan had. My father and I are serving her free of charge, but a barrister needs to be paid."

"Let's not speak of such things." He cast a glance over his shoulder.

Perveen was determined to get some acknowledgment from him. "Just tell me—is it true that you went to a party in late May in Juhu with your children and Sunanda?"

Parvesh looked toward Uma and Ishan sitting in the car, and then back to Perveen. Rapidly, he whispered, "She mustn't be blamed. I wish you the best in defending her."

"Fair enough," Perveen said. "But did any man show improper behavior at the party?"

"I don't have the strength to remember much." His voice shook with anxiety. "Please allow me to mourn my father. It is considerate of you to bring my son to the hospital." Parvesh turned and walked back to the house, so fast it looked as if he were afraid Perveen would follow.

He was protecting the attacker's identity. Why? Perveen stood, looking after him, feeling a mix of confusion and despair. If Parvesh was brave enough to intervene on Sunanda's behalf, why wouldn't he want a lawyer to go after the rapist?

"What were you saying to Parvesh? He looked quite distressed," Uma asked as Perveen got into the Daimler's front seat.

Perveen saw no way to bring up any of it, although if Uma knew something, it would be beneficial. Did she? Turning her head to look directly at her, she said, "I was asking about when he and the children went to the party in Juhu for the nawab."

"Yes, it was a birthday party," Uma's brow furrowed. "Princess Cora was upset I didn't go. That's why I gave her so much attention at my tea party the following week. But why would you ask about it?"

Uma's reaction made it clear that she had no idea of the assault. And as Sunanda's lawyer, Perveen didn't have the right to disclose the violation that her client wanted to keep quiet.

"Not in front of Ishan," Perveen said, shifting her position so that she faced forward.

"To Cama Hospital, then?" Arman asked, glancing sideways at her.

She answered, "As quickly as you can."

35

THE OPENED COMPACT

ama Hospital, founded in 1886, was the brainchild of Pestonjee Hormusjee Cama, a wealthy Parsi with great social concerns. He wanted the city to have a hospital that would specialize in the needs of women and children and set a goal for a predominantly female hospital staff when he made the grant donation of one hundred thousand rupees to establish the building. But Mr. Cama passed away seven years after its founding, and only a few European women doctors had ever been hired. The social reality was that the hospital's management preferred to hire men.

Remembering how Miriam's application to the hospital had been refused, Perveen was anxious about the attitude and abilities of Dr. Anand Mehta, the young pediatrician who came to see Ishan Bhatia after they'd waited for an hour in a small cubby of a room. She watched closely as he held his fingers to Ishan's wrist and kept his eyes on his pocket watch.

"This number is fine, and he has no fever." The doctor smiled at Uma, who'd been introduced as the patient's mother. "No need to worry."

"I don't want to be a bother." Uma spoke timidly. "But his stomach hurts. And he's not urinating."

Perveen spoke loudly. "We've brought this very ill child here on the advice of Dr. Miriam Penkar."

"An obstetrician who works in town," Dr. Mehta said, glancing at Perveen with irritation. "And who are you, madam?"

"Perveen Mistry, solicitor at law." She looked steadily at him. "There was a poisoning in the family's house recently. Ishan has some of the same symptoms as his grandfather, who died from lead acetate poisoning. Maybe you heard about the case? It was in the newspapers."

"Do you speak of Sir Dwarkanath?" The tenor of the doctor's voice lowered with respect.

Uma glanced at Perveen, as if understanding that they needed to assert the family's status. "Yes. My Ishan is his grandson."

Dr. Mehta's voice warmed slightly as he spoke to Ishan. Reaching into his bag for a battery torch, he said, "Little boy, open your mouth, please. I want to look inside."

"I don't like him!" Ishan moaned, burying his head in his mother's bosom.

"Please, Ishan-beta. Open nice and wide. The doctor has a magic light!" Perveen entreated. When Ishan finally parted his lips, Dr. Mehta shone the torch inside. Softly, he asked, "Does your throat feel sore, Ishan?"

Ishan snapped his mouth shut and said it didn't.

"His throat is not red, which is a good sign," Dr. Mehta said to Uma in a reassuring tone.

"Doctor, when you were looking, did you note the blue line on his gums?" Perveen asked.

"No. I saw nothing of the sort."

"Do you mind looking again?" Perveen gave him an ingratiating smile.

"Ishan, please. Open your mouth again. When you are done, I have some sweets." Uma opened the pouch she carried and held a laddu aloft.

Ishan did as he was told, and the doctor looked for a long time. At last, he took away the light and looked at both women. "The gums are looking a bit unusual. I have decided to check his blood and urine for evidence of toxins."

"I am grateful that you are being thorough." Perveen

spoke as if she hadn't had to point it out herself. "Lord Bhatia's symptoms began on a Thursday and he expired within forty-eight hours."

The doctor turned back to Ishan. "Little boy, were you chewing on toys?"

"No!" Ishan pouted. "I don't eat toys. I'm not stupid."

Perveen pulled out the compact she'd found in the nursery. "Please check this when you are doing tests. I've heard that cosmetics sometimes contain lead. We have brought other things as well—"

"That's mine," Ishan wailed. "Give me!"

"We can't. You have your teddy bear!" Uma said brightly.

Because Ishan looked unconvinced, Perveen said, "Your bear will be frightened if you don't comfort him. He doesn't know this place."

Ishan's crying stilled and he gripped his bear tightly, while Uma gave Perveen a grateful glance. In an undertone, she whispered, "It's hard to believe you don't have children."

Perveen didn't answer but felt herself glowing inside.

Taking the compact in his hand, the doctor clicked it open. His brow creased as he looked at the grains of pinkish-white powder. "We will certainly test this."

After placing the compact on a tray, the doctor washed his hands and continued the examination, palpating Ishan's abdomen until he moaned. After examining the boy's limbs, Dr. Mehta said, "I'm recommending that a nurse draw his blood and take samples of other bodily fluids. It is likely he will stay here overnight, perhaps longer."

As the doctor bustled out, Uma whispered to Perveen in English, "If he stays overnight—that means he must be very ill. I cannot bear to lose him."

Perveen gripped her hand. "This is what we wanted—for thorough testing to occur. It cannot be any other way."

"I did not treat you well before. I'm sorry." Tears shone at the edge of Uma's eyes. "Your coming today may have saved Ishan's life."

Perveen shook her head. "What I did for him was an ordinary act of help. I wasn't brave—not like Sunanda. And she is still suffering."

"You're right. And I turned her away—"

"It was a difficult time." Perveen softened her voice. "The true way to make things right is to support her from now on. And to talk to your husband about speaking with me again. He might know something that could help Sunanda's legal situation."

"Baa! Where's Sunanda?" Ishan moaned, and as if that had taken too much energy, he closed his eyes.

When Perveen returned with the car to Mistry House, Jamshedji was eating lunch downstairs. "All back in good time. What was the outcome?"

"We are awaiting results." Sitting down at the table across from him, she explained about Ishan being admitted and the various items that would be examined for possible lead acetate poisoning.

"So—he could also die?" Jamshedji's eyes bored into hers. "To think that I didn't want you to go!"

"I don't know. I'm sure they'll be there at least one night. I gave Uma our number at the office as well as at home," Perveen said. "If she doesn't ring me by five o'clock, I'll walk to the hospital to check how Ishan is."

"Very well. We're off to the tailor's in a few minutes. You're going to check my trouser length, remember."

"Pappa, please trust the tailor to recommend the best length. I don't feel comfortable being far from the phone—do you mind if I stay here?"

He assented, and Perveen was glad to be ready for the telephone call that came just after her father had gone out and the clock struck four.

"Mrs. Uma Bhatia is calling," Mustafa said. "She said to come quickly because it's a hospital telephone."

Perveen hurried downstairs and picked up the receiver. "How's Ishan?"

"The nurse said the doctor has results and will be with me soon. Can you return to be with me when he's here? I'm afraid I won't ask the right questions."

Perveen put away her worries and told Uma she'd be there as fast as her feet would allow.

The late-afternoon sun had created an inferno, so Perveen changed her plan and hired a horse-drawn taxi to take her the remaining blocks. The driver agreed to wait with the promise she'd pay him for the extra time.

Ishan had been admitted to a ward with eleven other beds filled with children, most of whom had family members nearby amusing them with toys or feeding them from tiffin cases of home-cooked food. Ishan's teddy bear was tucked snugly next to him, but he appeared to be fast asleep.

Uma waved to her from his bedside. When Perveen joined her, she whispered, "He cried so much during the blood-drawing that he fell asleep. But then I thought, is it dangerous for him to sleep so long? He might not ever wake."

Perveen held her hand tight, wishing she could reassure her that everything would be fine. That was probably what the family had thought when they'd taken Sir Dwarkanath to Sir J. J. Hospital.

They waited quietly together until Dr. Mehta arrived, looking more harried than before. Nodding at Perveen, he said, "Miss Mistry, you were correct in pointing to the blue gums. That was a sign of a particular type of lead poisoning."

"What kind?" Uma cried anxiously, as Perveen absorbed the news, feeling relieved that she'd lobbied hard for the laboratory testing.

"It's subacute lead poisoning. It is less serious because a smaller dose is in the body. Acute lead poisoning occurs when someone ingests a large dose in a short time. That was probably the case for Sir Dwarkanath. What is interesting is that the trace of powder left in the compact was highly concentrated, so much that even a spoonful could cause a fatality."

"Does this mean that the lead acetate present was more than might be found in a cosmetic formulation?" Perveen asked.

"Correct. It seems that pure lead acetate was added to the container. However, that does not mean poisoning was intended, because nobody knew the boy would find the container." Dr. Mehta gave the sleeping child a reproving glance. "Now, shall we speak of treatment?"

"Please," Perveen said, and Uma nodded vigorously.

"Our hospital pharmacy has a novel medication from Britain that binds the lead to it and then passes through the body, thus preventing lasting damage. I would recommend this for a quick return to full health."

"Doctors tried to use a kind of medicine at Sir J. J. Hospital for Sir Dwarkanath," Uma said. "I'm not sure what it was, but it didn't work."

"Your father-in-law's organs were probably already in failure," Dr. Mehta said. "The other choice for treatment is the old-fashioned remedy of milk."

"Oshadi would recommend the milk," Uma said. "I don't know what to do!"

"We are offering you the chance for a medicine that not every child receives," Dr. Mehta said sternly. "The chelating medication is costly, and our supply is limited."

"What more can you tell us about the medicine, and where it's been used?" Perveen asked.

Dr. Mehta explained the medicine had originally been used to treat poison gas victims in war, and when that was proven effective, it was used by British doctors treating workers made ill from glazing pottery with lead finishes. He assured them that Ishan would receive a small amount of a chelating formula that was appropriate for his body weight.

"What should I do?" Uma asked Perveen at the end of the recital.

Perveen imagined herself in the same situation with Khushy. "I also like home remedies, but in this situation, I would trust in modern medicine. If the amount given to Ishan is small, the risk is probably also low. But you are his guardian. You should do what you think is right."

Slowly, Uma nodded. "I wanted the best medicine and surgical care for Bombay's women. I should give my son a similar chance."

After the medical order was written, Perveen said goodbye and went out to her waiting taxi. She felt relieved that Mangala hadn't been part of the decision-making and resolved that at the first private opportunity, she would explain her concerns to Uma.

Perhaps Mangala had been the one who tampered with the compact. But as she'd said to Dr. Mehta, they had to consider whether the lead acetate from the compact had poisoned Lord Bhatia. Oshadi believed that she was the only household member who knew about the man's drinking. But others might have guessed, either from the smell of his breath or the changing level of bottles within the liquor cabinet.

Her thoughts returned to Ishan. How remarkable that he'd kept Sunanda's money for her and that he continued to express so much love. It was news that might give her client something to cling onto, although there was certainly no guarantee she'd be able to work at Bhatia House again.

"Bhaiyya?" Perveen addressed the driver. "I won't go to Bruce Street straight away. Do you know the way to Gamdevi Police Station?"

At the jail, the duty officer clerk told her that she needed to wait. This was nothing unusual, except the reason was that Sunanda was being allowed a brief outdoor exposure with other women. Time in the jail's small courtyard was probably considered a privilege; but in such blistering heat, Perveen wondered whether it could be enjoyable at all. In fact, the misery of the weather might have been the reason that the prisoners were being allowed exercise now, rather than earlier in the day.

Shortly after six a guard said Sunanda had returned. Perveen followed him, noting the shafts of bright light from small windows spilling into the dark, humid passageway. Sunanda's cell, though, was as gloomy as before, and her cellmate was gone.

Sunanda was sitting on the edge of her charpoy, looking tense. At the sight of Perveen, she stood. "You are here again! This is soon."

"Please, make yourself comfortable. How are you today?"

"Not so well. I'm scared." Sunanda's voice cracked.

"About the trial?" Perveen was, too.

Sunanda shook her head. "I don't feel well staying here. Since last time we talked, I keep seeing what happened to me. It's like very bad dreams all the time."

"I am so sorry. You were brave to tell me. But today, I only want to talk about the Bhatias." Seeing her face tighten, she said, "About Ishan."

"Ishan!" Her eyes sparkled. "What about him?"

"I went there today and received your ten rupees from Ishan. He loves you so much—he misses you. He explained about the money he was protecting for you. I had to argue very hard to get it from him—but now I have it for you."

"Ah. That is very good."

"I'm not going to use it for legal fees—but I'll keep it in my office safe so you have something when you get out. Another thing: he was poisoned from lead, just like his grandfather. But the doctors at Cama Hospital say it's a very mild case, and he will recover quickly because he's getting a special medicine."

Perveen had aimed to sound reassuring, but Sunanda's expression had turned to panic. "But who poisoned him? Who would kill an innocent child?"

"All that is known is that the poison was found by him in a cosmetic compact in the garden. Do you know what that is?" When Sunanda shook her head, Perveen described the round metal tin with a mirror inside. "Have you ever seen such an object?"

"No! I only remember him finding the bottle cap. The other items he kept as treasures he found himself." Sunanda shifted position, and Perveen caught a dreadful stench. "Because I knew about the treasure box, I asked Ishan to hide the begum's money that Oshadi gave me inside an old paan."

"You thought this was better than keeping the money at your home?"

"Amla would have taken it," Sunanda said in a flat voice. "And I couldn't leave it in the ayahs' cupboard because the other ayahs were speaking jealously about how I'd got the money. I thought either of them might steal it."

"Remind me, how many ayahs work at Bhatia House?"

"When I was still working there, we were three. Padma and Chandini and me. But Padma left the day after the tea party."

"Do you mean she quit, or was she let go?" Perveen wondered if the Bhatias thought she'd been derelict in her duty. Or had something worse happened to the girl?

"One of Uma-bhabhu's foreign friends badly needed a maid, so Uma-bhabhu offered to send Padma. Padma speaks the most English of any of us."

Perveen was surprised that Uma would give up an ayah—although she couldn't have known she was also about to lose Sunanda. "Did you ever tell the other ayahs about drinking the tea?"

Shaking her head, she said, "I didn't tell anyone I was drinking it, but afterward Padma was near me when the cramps began, and then the heavy bleeding. So I think she could have guessed. Uma-bhabhu drank it often."

Perveen felt her mind turning with new ideas. "Uma's European friend, Serena Prescott, hired Padma. Did you see her at the tea party?"

"Yes. Prescott-memsahib was at the tea party. The day after I was burned, she came to the house in a fine car and took Padma away to become her ayah. I remember Chandini being cross because now it would be quite difficult to care for all the children. But Uma-bhabhu said Padma had to go away because she had promised the lady about it. And Uma-bhabhu said that I should work, if I felt well enough."

"If you were on duty for the Bhatias continuously after your burn, they worked you too hard!" Perveen exclaimed.

"But I would rather have work than jail!" Sunanda said bleakly. "Tell me again, when is my trial?"

"July seventh. That is about three weeks from now." Perveen spoke calmly, trying not to worry about whether the infection would become so bad that her client wouldn't survive.

"Such a long time." Sunanda sounded desolate. "But I am sure Ishan will be well by that time. Just tell Uma-bhabhu to add sugar, so Ishan will not spit out any medicine. And tell him from me what a good boy he is, and that I am happy you are holding my money now."

How well Sunanda understood Ishan. Perveen wished that the ayah could have the choice to work for the Bhatias again, although she was worried about the working conditions. Perveen had seen Uma appearing regretful about how she'd treated Sunanda, but was it just temporary emotion?

36

A CONTINUING DANGER

When Perveen returned in the hired taxi to Bruce Street, it was almost six-thirty.

Arman was parked in the Daimler outside Mistry House. He got out and stood frowning as he watched Perveen pay the taxi driver. "And now Mistry-sahib gives you license to ride in taxis?"

"Don't worry. I'll explain it to him myself." Perveen realized that Arman might be worried he could be displaced; that not only she, but other family members, would turn to taxis for transportation.

Inside Mistry House, Mustafa said that her father had been anxious about her whereabouts. Perveen headed upstairs, readying herself to apologize. Jamshedji looked up when she came in. In a strained voice, he asked, "And how's the patient?"

Perveen explained the doctor's prognosis and apologized for keeping her father late at the office on a Friday afternoon.

"No matter. I spent extra time at the tailor, which allowed the coat sleeves to be adjusted to my taste." Smiling at her, he said, "I have just a few more names to look through on the party list for tomorrow's ball. Surely I will spot the name of someone we can approach about Sunanda's case. It was too annoying with those barristers refusing us yesterday."

"I would almost think word's gone out among the barrister community that this is a losing case," Perveen said.

"Who knows? Let me spend another half hour on it. Is there anything you can find to do?"

Taking advantage of the extra time, Perveen decided to go

downstairs and ring Bhatia House. Fortunately, it wasn't Mangala who answered, but a female cousin who agreed to fetch Parvesh. He came swiftly, and she explained about the lead poisoning. Hearing Parvesh's gasp, she reassured him that the doctors felt certain the chelating medicine was sure to clear the lead.

"The important thing now is to find out whether this poison that Ishan accidentally consumed was the same substance that killed your father." Perveen deliberately used the word "killed" because she hoped to inflame Parvesh to the point that he might say something useful. When he didn't, she said, "Dr. Mehta at Cama Hospital has assured me the compact containing the lead will be taken to the laboratory at Sir J. J. Hospital. Do you recall what else the police took from your home for testing?"

"Nothing was taken. They asked me if there was any food left over, but we do not eat kept food. Anything unfinished is gladly taken by our servants. The cooks prepare fresh food for every meal."

"The parlor cabinet no longer holds any of the bottles of liquor. Did the police take it for examination?"

"No. And why should they have taken it? My father didn't drink. The alcohol was only there for offering to Europeans." Parvesh's tone held a slight echo of his father's contemptuous style.

"So, why is the alcohol gone?"

"Because it's inappropriate to display at a time of mourning!" he shot back. "I told a bearer to put the bottles away on the shelves where Oshadi used to keep medicine. All those dusty old teas were already disposed of."

And so was Oshadi. Perveen thought of telling him how lost Oshadi seemed at her new job, but she restrained herself. "I understand my questions are strange. I'm asking about all of this because locating the source of poison is very important. It was found in the compact, but it might also be somewhere else, like the bottles. Perhaps your father did drink, now and again.

May I ask how often you take alcohol, and whether you have a preferred drink?"

"I don't mind your asking. I know that your people—the Parsis—are drinkers." His voice held a note of accusation.

"Even among us ladies," Perveen said, trying to put him at ease. "For us, champagne and brandy and sherry are considered proper. And, on occasion, mixed gin drinks."

"The British take a gin and tonic as a remedy for malaria. That's why we kept an ample store of both gin and tonic in the cabinet. It's usually what I take. But I don't need your questioning; this is not a courtroom! Ishan is going to be well, and I am grateful to you for taking him—"

"Mr. Bhatia, my goal is not to put you on the witness stand. However, it may happen. And think about what all of this means: if it turns out that any of the bottles are contaminated, it might seem that your father or even you were targeted for death."

"By whom? Who would wish ill of us?"

"You have business relationships." She paused, hoping he would bring up Stowe or the nawab. When he didn't, she said, "There are also complications inside every extended family; I can't guess how deep rivalries might run. But the first thing is for you to tell the police what happened to Ishan, and that there's reason to believe poison is still present somewhere, and thus is a risk to all."

"Are you saying"—Parvesh's voice dropped—"that all my guests might get poisoned while eating and drinking at Bhatia House?"

"If the poison is still on the property, yes. What are the cooks serving as mourning foods?"

Quickly, he answered, "Simply prepared vegetables—but we are also giving rice and rotlis at the meals. And tomorrow we travel to the river for Asthi Visarjan."

"Before you leave, I suggest you ring the police. They can take the bottles while everyone's away. Just tell your head servant."

"Oshadi," he muttered. "Too bad she's gone. I'll have to tell our cook."

Perveen said, "Mr. Bhatia, would you also ask the police to test these substances?"

"No!" he said, his voice rising in anger. "I shouldn't call the police while the relatives are still here. We are in mourning."

Perveen thought that she was beginning to know Parvesh Bhatia. Very likely, his hesitation to stand up for others—and himself—was because his father had been the one who'd always done that, and who had criticized him for not living up to expectations.

"I think that your family, and the workers of Bhatia Stone, understand that you are now the nana-seth. They will come to respect you the way they did your father."

"Why are you saying this?" he asked wildly. "I really cannot speak with you any longer."

"Wouldn't you rather know that your household supplies are safe? Not just for you, but for your family and your guests."

"Sorry, they are calling for me."

She heard a click, and then the phone went dead.

For any number of reasons, Parvesh couldn't hear another word. She could only hope the ideas she'd raised would haunt him.

37

THE LAWYERS' BALL

"Look, Khushy. Aunty's pretty tonight!"

Hiba was crooning to Khushy, but Perveen knew the words were meant for her own ears. Both Hiba and Gita had commented on Perveen's unusually quiet manner all of Saturday. Her tension since the telephone conversation with Parvesh was obvious. How frustrating it was to know that he had knowledge that could help the case, yet it was being withheld. Maintaining a proper social image seemed to be his priority.

And tonight, her own appearance mattered. She was headed off to the Lawyers' Ball and needed to look just right; not so glamorous that others would doubt her ability, but she could not fade into the woodwork.

Jamshedji had told Perveen that her shoulder-length hair would look improper when wearing a sari at a grand occasion, so she'd asked Gita to buy hair for her at Crawford Market. Gita, whose favorite job responsibility was hair and dress, had brightened at this challenge and made a series of tiny, tight braids that she pinned into hanging loops around Perveen's head. The process had taken forty minutes, and the result reminded her of Medusa, the mythical Greek woman with snake-like locks. Gita had listened raptly as Perveen told her about Medusa, and at the end, offered to change the style to prevent bad luck.

"Don't be silly. I adore this," Perveen assured her. It was a dramatic look that was as heavily ornamental as the long gold earrings with inset pearls that dangled almost to her shoulders.

Camellia and Gita together helped Perveen decide on a

lustrous dark purple crepe silk sari with gara embroidery. Running her hands over the dark green vines, blue-green parrots, and deep pink roses, she thought about those who'd spent hours embroidering it in Hong Kong; just as she'd thought about the women who'd grown hair and had it cut as a commodity.

Perveen also wondered if the unworn sari her mother had pulled out of her almirah had actually been intended for Gulnaz, who loved the flower she was named after. Regardless, the sari made her feel like someone much more glamorous—a woman without a care in the world.

"I approve!" Jamshedji said when she went downstairs at five-thirty. He wore the new black dinner suit with tails. "Formal but not frivolous. That is what's called for tonight."

"And your dinner suit is absolutely dashing," she said, walking around to inspect the long-tailed coat. "Are those spats new?"

"Yes, indeed." He lifted his shiny black shoe, showing the smooth white leather adornment. "My feet will flash fire when I dance with my daughter."

"I'd rather not go out on the floor. I feel like enough of a spectacle these days."

"You had two years of dancing classes—you and Gulnaz both!" In a less cheerful tone, he added, "Rustom visited the Bankers' house this afternoon. Once again, Tajbanu declared Gulnaz to be asleep. I told him he should have stayed to wait, but he's wary of pushing too hard."

"At least Rustom is rising very nicely to the challenge of fatherhood. He said he's going to spend all his time with Khushy this evening and will lay her down in the cot himself." Perveen wished her father could understand that their status quo wasn't so bad.

Jamshedji fiddled with a cuff link. "There's a danger in encouraging Rustom to become so entwined with Khushy."

"That's old-fashioned thinking!" Perveen went to him and

finished closing the cuff link on his right sleeve. "What are you and I, if not entwined?"

"Thank you." Jamshedji stretched out his wrists, looking at the perfectly matched result with approval. "We must also be aware that if Gulnaz files for marital separation, the likelihood is that she will be granted custody of Khushy. For Rustom, losing his daughter could break him."

And it could break me, too. Perveen swallowed the lump that threatened. "But it's worse not to love, isn't it? Please, Pappa, we must have good thoughts."

Jamshedji acknowledged her advice with a bittersweet smile. "You speak truth. And now it's high time for us to get off to the Lawyers' Ball."

When they arrived at the entrance to the Ripon Club, there was already a queue. Perveen saw Nariman, the Mistrys' favorite waiter, checking the arrivals against the official guest list printed in script on a series of ivory papers. While they stood in line, Perveen surveyed the backs of the people ahead of them: many Parsi lawyers and accountants who belonged to the club, as well as other people invited to the fundraiser. Still, there were dashes of cream everywhere: British officers in the Indian Civil Service, especially judges and magistrates. Once checked in, these men stepped to the front of the line for the club's small elevator, as if nobody else mattered.

"Mr. Mistry and Miss Mistry's boutonniere and corsage are marigold," Nariman instructed the junior waiter assisting him when they reached the head of the check-in line.

Jamshedji tied the corsage on Perveen's wrist. As she pinned her father's flower into his lapel, her irritation at the delay getting into the party rose. She muttered, "I would rather wear roses than marigolds, especially with what we paid for our tickets."

"It's an identification plan!" interrupted Vivek Sharma, who'd been standing nearby. "All solicitors wear gold."

"Hello, Vivek. How were these colors decided?" Jamshedji smiled at the barrister, as if Jamshedji had forgotten that Sharma had declined to take Sunanda's case.

"The law school committee members. Your lot wears gold because it's closest to the color of bullion. We barristers get red roses for drawing blood in court. Prosecutors are the prover-bial white knights—they take the white plumeria, and judges and magistrates have a spray of green leaves as representation of justice."

"And how about the guests who aren't in these categories? The businessmen, civil servants, and so on?" said Jamshedji.

"You'll see them upstairs. Proud purple, the color of roy-alty." Vivek raised his eyebrows in a slightly sarcastic gesture, reminding Perveen of his affiliation with the freedom move-ment.

"Pappa, let's not wait for the elevator. It's overly hot, and I smell something rancid." Perveen was annoyed that Vivek was alluding to being a progressive when he had been the first to shy away from helping Sunanda.

As they climbed the spiral staircase, Jamshedji said, "You shouldn't have made that comment. Many others could think it was meant for them."

"Oh, I'm sure everyone saw me shooting daggers at Mr. Sharma," Perveen fumed. "Let them wonder what's wrong with him!"

Dryly, Jamshedi said, "Creating gossip is not going to find us the barrister we need."

Upon reaching the third floor, Perveen saw the results of the previous day's labors. Every column was wrapped in ribbons, and fairy lights twinkled close to the ceiling. The vast floor, usu-ally filled with widely spaced tables, was completely clear, with waiters weaving their way among attendees with trays of food and drink.

A band in the corner was playing a waltz, and half a dozen

couples danced smoothly. Several of the ladies had undraped their heads and tossed their saris' long ends over their shoulders, looking free and modern.

"Very different from last year," Jamshedji said, accepting two glasses of champagne from a waiter for himself and Perveen.

"Cheers, Pappa." Perveen sipped, relishing the bubbles on her tongue. "Yes, it's nice with this band. The songs are new."

"And among the dancers, I see your dear friend."

Perveen followed his gaze and saw, a few inches above most of the men, Alice's golden hair. Perveen knew instantly Colin was her partner; although he was facing away from them, she recognized his wavy dark hair and the unevenness of his movement. Jamshedji had met Colin only briefly and didn't appear to notice him, which made Perveen feel relaxed enough to watch the two of them a bit longer.

Her attention shifted when a magistrate named Oswald Packham approached her father. Jamshedji introduced her as his daughter, the city's first female solicitor. Packham merely nodded and launched into a conversation about the replacement of the Bombay High Court's chief justice. Who did Jamshedji think was in the running? As the conversation about seniority versus performance became intense, Perveen took her leave. She'd seen that Alice had departed the dance floor.

"And here you are," Perveen said, kissing her friend on the cheek. "How stylish you are."

"Mummy surprised me with this dress." Alice looked down at her navy silk frock trimmed with black fringe that hit the knee. "I felt awfully exposed when I first tried it, but I'm getting used to it."

"It suits you. And the length must be very good for dancing."

Alice's purple bougainvillea corsage flopped on her wrist as she adjusted the silver headband circling her sweating forehead. "Well, we all know that I've got no grace, and Colin is hardly better. He saw the buffet whilst we were dancing and now has thrown himself into sampling everything. Tell me, is there somewhere a bit cooler where we can talk?"

"Yes, let's go to the gallery." Perveen led her through one of the club's many doors.

Leaning against the railing outside, Alice said, "When Colin and I were dancing, three different men cut in on us. It was absolutely annoying—until the last one boasted that he works in the prosecutor's office. His name is Mr. William Randall."

"How fortuitous you met a prosecutor!" Perveen raised her glass in a toasting gesture.

"He's a clerk," Alice said, winking at her. "So much more candid than a prosecutor would be. Mr. Randall said Rippington isn't here tonight because he is a junior and can't yet afford to make big donations. The only reason Randall came was someone gave him a spare ticket." Alice leaned against a column, taking a deep swig of her glass of champagne. "Randall didn't say anything about Rippington being corrupt, although he did say that he was inexperienced. He's lost a few cases based on confusion about evidence. We fell into a conversation about whether enough crime was being successfully prosecuted. Apparently, part of the trouble is the prosecutors have been requested to push forward more cases than they have time to manage well. And Randall said the Bombay Police are behind it."

"Interesting."

"I asked why Mr. Randall thought the police would be acting in such bad form, and he said the pressure comes from a consultant from the Imperial Police who started with the police department." Alice sighed heavily. "And who might that fellow be?"

"That doesn't surprise me, but it's certainly troubling." Perveen took another sip of champagne, thinking about how it seemed increasingly possible that Prescott was the man who'd set up the complaint that led to Sunanda's arrest.

"I did what you asked, and the night is still young," Alice was saying. "Anything else?"

"Let's go to the far end of the gallery, where it's quieter." Perveen wanted to be sure nobody would overhear the rest of their conversation.

Finishing her drink, Perveen gave Alice the names of the men who'd attended the nawab's party, and who were also at the Lawyers' Ball: Stowe, Tata, Shroff, and the nawab.

"Polad Shroff donated all the alcohol for tonight. There's a sign saying so at the bar." Alice twirled her empty glass in her hand. "I could ask around until someone can identify him for me, and then I can offer him my sincere thanks."

"Be very careful not to walk into an area where any of these fellows might be able to strike," Perveen said. "Certainly, the presence of a few dozen people didn't dissuade Sunanda's attacker."

The two of them decided there was no need to interview Malcolm Stowe, given Perveen's earlier meeting, and that Perveen would interview Tigran Tata because of her family connection.

"I'll dance with the nawab, if I can persuade him to ask me," Alice said with a grin.

"That could be tricky with Cora. She's wildly enamored of him and might take offense," Perveen mused.

"I suppose so. When Colin and I were dancing, I spotted him with one of those tiny young blonde girls—the type my mother wishes I'd be," Alice said ruefully. "She did look enchanted by him. Is that the lucky princess?"

"No—Cora's a redhead." Perveen looked through the long shutters that had been unfolded in order to provide entry from the club's main room to the outdoors. Several foreign women were dancing with men or chatting in small groups, but none of them was Cora.

"Miss Mistry! Alice! There you are!" An Englishwoman's voice carried over to them, and Perveen realized she must have been gaping too openly.

Coming from the far end of the open-air gallery, three women walked together, two of them British and one Indian.

Serena Prescott, looking fashionable in a lightweight lavender silk frock, was leading Miriam Penkar. Miriam wore a white silk brocade sari with silver and gold paisley embroidery. She had a few gold bangles and a simple chain around her neck. Right behind them was Madeline Stowe, wearing a dark blue dress—a bit matronly, but clearly expensive. The dress seemed to fit with what her husband had said about her not wishing to be in the limelight.

"Good evening, everyone!" Alice said enthusiastically.

"Dr. Penkar, it's a happy surprise to meet you here." Perveen decided to greet the doctor directly, because her expression seemed a bit anxious.

"I didn't know I was coming until this morning. Mrs. Prescott invited me." From the way Miriam glanced at her companion, Perveen sensed the doctor felt like an interloper in the room dominated by men who either held government power or big bank accounts.

"I think many potential donors for the women's hospital are here and should meet Dr. Penkar." Serena put an arm around the woman's shoulders, and Miriam flinched. "We will convince them to give."

Now Perveen wondered if Malcolm's idea that Serena Prescott should take the hospital project was bearing fruit. But why hadn't he suggested his own wife? She glanced at Madeline Stowe, who looked straight back at her without smiling. Curious about where the power now lay, Perveen asked, "Are either of you taking the helm of hospital leadership?"

"Oh, no. My husband keeps me far too busy," Madeline said with a smile that didn't reach her eyes.

Perveen wondered if Madeline said this because she didn't like the idea of hours away from her husband—or because she wanted to keep careful oversight. She wished she could find a way to ask Madeline about any unusual circumstances at the nawab's party, but the lady was unlikely to incriminate her spouse, if he'd been Sunanda's attacker.

"Neither will I!" Serena sounded jovial. "Uma sent me a note saying she intends to continue with the hospital project after mourning is complete. Apparently, her father-in-law's dying wish was for it to be reinstated."

"I hadn't heard until Mrs. Prescott told me today. Such good news!" Miriam grabbed each of her companions' hands and squeezed them, a girlish gesture that seemed to affirm that she felt the hospital gang was back together.

Uma hadn't said anything earlier to Perveen, no doubt because of her anxiety about Ishan's health. Or—as Gulnaz had presciently observed—the dying wish of Lord Bhatia might be a convenient invention. Still, Uma's wish might never turn to reality. "Mrs. Prescott, did Uma say that Mr. Parvesh Bhatia also supports this plan?"

"Obviously," Serena said, loosening her hand from Miriam's. "After mourning is over, Parvesh will locate the deed for the warehouses in his father's papers. But we truly need you, Perveen, to assist with formalizing the hospital trust and accepting the deed. Things weren't properly done before."

Perveen thought that Serena did seem to be taking a leading role, despite what she'd said about Uma. And she thought again about the compact, which could have belonged to Serena. What if she'd given it, filled up with poison, for Uma to accomplish the unthinkable?

"We are going to completely reorganize the committee!" Serena's warm words broke into Perveen's troubled thoughts. "Some ladies won't be coming back, and we want new blood. How about you, Alice?"

"Normally, I don't follow my mother around," Alice said

with an eye roll. "This is a very important cause, though. If Perveen's in, so am I."

Perveen smiled, but she didn't answer. She wanted to help with the project, but if Lord Bhatia's death was ruled as murder, the women would have more complications than anyone could imagine.

Alice announced she needed more champagne, so the five women walked back into the ballroom, which was considerably more crowded and louder. Once drinks were in hand, Miriam, Serena, and Madeline noticed an important man they wished to introduce to Dr. Penkar.

After the three women had sailed off, Alice lowered her head to speak softly into Perveen's ear. "What do you think of Parvesh's change of plan?"

"Even if his father didn't say what they believe he said, Parvesh Bhatia is now the family head and can do as he likes," Perveen said. "But why would he give away valuable real estate when the company has financial trouble? Or is he leveraging the tea party's donations, as Cora and the nawab thought Lord Bhatia intended to do?"

"I do wonder if Uma is fully aware. Not only about the company's finances, but how Serena is pushing herself forward." Alice looked intently at Perveen.

"I wish Uma were here tonight, but I suppose mourning makes that impossible! Never mind; I've just spied Tigran Tata, Bombay's king of cars. My work begins." Perveen gestured toward a lean gentleman whirling a Parsi woman in a European dress around the dance floor. "He's with his wife. Shireen was a few years ahead of me at school."

"Gather up Colin and dance alongside them," Alice suggested. "Where has he gone, anyway?"

"Never mind about Colin." Perveen tried not to look as if she'd secretly been keeping her eye out for him. "I'll wait for the Tatas near the dance floor."

"You do that." Smirking, she added, "I believe Colin would be awfully glad to meet you on the upper floor, whenever you have time."

How devilish Alice was! Perveen's face flushed pink as she walked off toward the dance floor. As the song finished, Tigran and Shireen caught sight of her smiling at them.

"Do have a drink with us, Perveen. I've been telling your father he could trade that Daimler for a Benz. You use the car just as much as he does. What do you think, maybe a new brand such as Maybach?" jested Tigran, a handsome man in his late twenties who was not as tall as Colin, but solidly built.

"That's a car for maharajas and nawabs, not ordinary lawyers. Oh, no more champagne for me! Juice please," Perveen said, and accepted the glass of orange juice that Tigran handed her from a passing waiter. Tigran had a heavy ring on his right hand—a big sapphire surrounded by diamonds.

"You are more than lawyers—you are luminaries," Shireen said, taking a generous sip of champagne. "Perveen, you should not be hiding your hair in modern company. I see the bottom of what looks like a very interesting hairstyle."

"Very simple braids—whilst your hair is a work of art," Perveen said, gesturing to Shireen's upswept pompadour, which was not only uncovered, but studded with pearl-embedded pins. "By the way, have you seen the Varanpur royals?"

"The nawab came alone. Perhaps it's because of what happened last month."

Shireen pursed her painted red lips.

"What do you mean?" Perveen remembered that Shireen had always been a chatterbox at school.

Shireen glanced around, as if trying to speak confidentially. "There were a lot of children, and I think it must have flustered the begum, who's barely more than a child herself. She drank like a fish and muddled the dinner. From appetizers to pudding, it was a very unorganized night. And their servants are always quitting, so the ones working didn't know left from right."

Perveen was disappointed that Shireen had nothing but mockery of a naïve young woman to offer up as information. Looking toward Tigran, she said, "What do you think?"

"I felt bad for them," Tigran said. "Guests started leaving after the first course. Even the nawab disappeared."

"How long?" Perveen asked, thinking about the short walk from the mansion's veranda to the cabana.

"Oh, I've no idea. I was drinking a bit myself. That's the only thing worth doing when a party's falling apart," Tigran said with a chuckle.

"I stayed with Cora because I didn't want her to be the only lady left—and in her intoxicated condition." Shireen spoke piously, in the true manner of someone pretending not to gossip. "It's such a shame the British can't receive her socially. That's another reason the nawab might not have included her in his plans tonight."

"Although he could hardly introduce that young gal on his arm," Tigran joked. "Look at her!"

Perveen followed Tigran's pointing finger to the dance floor's center, where the nawab, dressed in a black dinner suit, was dancing very slowly with a fresh-faced European girl in a short silver dress.

"How old do you think his little blonde companion is?" Shireen asked with a giggle.

"She shouldn't be any younger than eighteen. You know the club rules as well as I." Perveen felt a rush of sadness as she thought about Cora, who at nineteen, believed she was the center of her husband's universe.

"Royals break the rules because they think themselves above all authority. I will have to pray that the nawab's young companion wakes up in her own bed and not the Taj Mahal Palace

Hotel. We heard that he keeps a permanent suite there for his trysts." Shireen smiled archly at her.

Perveen watched the nawab smoothly spin his companion around the floor, smiling charmingly down at her. He was a big man and had even more rings on his hand today. All the better to press into a woman and hold her down. He wore a dinner suit, like the others, and his oiled hair waved away elegantly from his forehead. He could have been a European gentleman, had it not been for the color of his skin.

The band changed from a waltz to a popular song, "Let the Rest of the World Go By."

Shireen clapped her hands together. "Brennan and Ball's best song. Perveen dear, will you excuse us? It's my favorite."

"Go ahead."

"Very well. Cheers!" Tigran steered Shireen onto the dance floor.

Perveen watched the harmoniously dancing couple, thinking about how they'd split up at the nawab's party, when Shireen was keeping Cora company. Where had Tigran gone during this time? She also couldn't disregard Tigran's physical size, and his heavy ring. Yet he'd said the nawab had gone off alone for some time during the evening. This could be significant.

38

THE GAMES ROOM

So much was spinning in her head—ideas about men, about the Bhatias. She shouldn't have had two glasses of champagne without food. She needed air. Taking a deep breath, she walked out to the hallway and up the flight of stairs to the club's fourth floor. Alice had hinted that Colin might be waiting for her, but he was nowhere in sight.

She stepped into the games room, which took up most of the floor's space. The lights were on, revealing a room empty of people but packed with excess furniture removed from downstairs. The billiard and card tables had been shoved up against the wall to make room for dining tables and chairs. She was about to leave when she heard the sound of footsteps coming up the stairs. For the sake of caution, she crouched down between the two nearest tables.

"Perveen?"

Recognizing the warm sound of Colin's voice, she popped back up. Smiling with relief, she said, "Were you following me, all of this time?"

"Thirty steps behind." He smiled at her, and she thought how dashing he looked in his black tailcoat, white shirt, and tie. His collar wasn't entirely buttoned up and his bow tie was slightly askew, proof that he'd had trouble putting together the elements of evening dress. Her pulse raced as he approached the sea of stacked-up tables where she'd moored herself. Taking her right hand in his, he whispered, "Alice told me you'd gone up this way."

"And she told me you'd be waiting. What a conniver she is!" Perveen said with a chuckle.

"Let me look at you," Colin said, and she turned to show the draping of her sari and her fantastical hairstyle. "I can't fathom seeing you looking this beautiful in such an odd place. All these tables and chairs! I could use a few of them in my flat, don't you think?"

"I won't join you in any thieving," Perveen said, intending to teasingly pinch his cheek, yet finding her touch turn to a caress. "Normally, this floor is used for game playing—mostly cards and billiards. The dining furniture was temporarily carried up to make space for dancing below. But I agree—it's a strange place for our chat. There's a rooftop terrace just this way."

Perveen led Colin by the hand through the jumble of furniture and past one closed door to another leading out to the club's flat rooftop terrace, where they could look down at the sight of Elphinstone Circle, softly lit with gas lamps. Her beloved city— no, their shared city. He had come here for her.

Colin stood beside her, looking down at the city. "We could small talk some more, but I've got something to tell you. I was weighing whether I could manage it."

Perveen felt her stomach drop. Usually, a pronouncement like this meant a change. "Please tell me."

He was still staring down at the lights in the street as he spoke. "I was angry when you suggested there might be an agenda behind redrawing those maps. It was my first paying job here. I thought, what can I ever do that meets your approval?"

Perveen thought about how, just a few months earlier, he'd quit the civil service, an employer that would have paid him comfortably the rest of his life. She had never credited him for the act. "Oh, Colin—"

He held up a hand, and she halted her intended protest.

"It was good that you warned me. Prescott and Stowe showed clear hostility after I delivered the revised maps. And I wondered why they had hired me rather than going to an official source for help." He turned his head, and she saw the disillusionment in his eyes. "They must have asked because Prescott knows I'm tight on funds. I'd do what they wanted, they thought. Yet I couldn't give them that."

Perveen tried to understand his words. "Are you saying that you found something specific about the borders between British and princely India that was difficult?"

"Quite," he said crisply. "And although I gave them the maps I'd made, I had the original tracings. I made new maps from these and sent them to an officer friend of mine in the Kolhapur Agency."

Perveen had the sense he was on the verge of a big revelation, but she had pushed him too far before. She would be more patient this time. "Varanpur is one of the states overseen by the Kolhapur Agency, isn't it?"

"Indeed. And when he looked at my map, and the three maps that came before, he concluded that I hadn't made a mistake. Varanpur is currently being shown as two thousand square miles smaller than the original definition of its boundaries in 1850."

"So the nawab should be credited with more land than he is currently using?" Perveen was secretly annoyed that such a dislikeable man might benefit from Colin's careful research.

"That's just it. And the agent I queried seemed to have evidence that over the last few decades, the government sold off some areas for development that weren't really theirs—the nawab's land. For instance, there's a hydroelectric dam in question."

"Goodness!" Perveen said, realizing the financial implications. "What did the agent say about that?"

Colin took a deep breath. "He said that the news will be shocking to the government. Quite unwelcome, but it must be known."

"It means the nawab could accuse the government of

encroaching on his land," Perveen said slowly. "And what happened to the areas in question? Were they all developed?"

"Not all of it's been sold. There are vast swaths of undeveloped hectares that the government is interested in selling to buyers who are keen to build plantations, hotels, and even retirement bungalows."

Prescott, Perveen thought to herself. He was close to fifty, which meant he'd already fulfilled the minimum twenty-five years expected in the civil service. This was where he wanted to go, and the Stowes would have their place nearby.

"What are you thinking, Perveen?"

She took her time before answering. She had so many thoughts—which could she share without endangering Sunanda's case? "Ever since Britain took hold, it's been rare for a nawab or maharaja to be granted more land. What's more typical is for a royal to lose land."

"On what grounds?" Colin asked.

"Typically, it's because the royal has done something the British can label as illegal. They can't put him in prison, but they can seize part of his land." Perveen paused, thinking back to legal cases she'd studied. "When did you meet with both men to tell them about your findings?"

After a short pause, Colin said, "It was the first Friday in June."

"June second," Perveen said, recalling that by the following Tuesday, the complaint about Sunanda had been forwarded to the prosecutor. And that two days later, the police had arrested Sunanda. Prescott hadn't attended the nawab's birthday cocktails, so he hadn't witnessed Sunanda crying and disheveled after the attack; but it was likely that someone had gossiped about it to him. And this brought two new thoughts to her.

First was that Stowe could not have been Sunanda's rapist, because Prescott wouldn't wish for his friend's name to be exposed in such a light. She had disregarded Tigran Tata as a suspected attacker, but now she needed to seriously think about the nawab. It was possible that Prescott had heard something about the attack on Sunanda involving him; and if there was a court case, in which Sunanda reported the man's name in exchange for leniency, there would be grounds for the government to take land from him.

At Sunanda's expense.

"You've gone dead quiet." Colin interrupted her thoughts. "What is it?"

Perveen felt an overwhelming urge to tell Colin exactly what she was putting together—but nothing could be said until she was sure—and after Sunanda's case was settled. So, she improvised. "Do you hear the orchestra playing downstairs? It's familiar, but I can't think of the title."

"'I Ain't Got Nobody.' Roger Graham wrote the lyrics. I used to play it at Oxford when I was with the student orchestra."

"That's right; you once told me that you played piano." Perveen tilted her head, concentrating on the moody song drifting up from the third floor. "It's a lovely song, but I can't say that I could define the word 'ain't.' American slang, isn't it?"

"That's right. In the song's context, it could mean 'have not,'" Colin said, putting his arm around her. "The song is about feeling alone. Now that I've told you about the map—I don't feel that anymore."

"Oh, Colin." Perveen turned to face him. As she tilted her face upward, he stepped closer to her and slipped two fingers into one of her looped braids.

"I've been wanting to do this all evening," he said, stroking the fine braid. Perveen thought of telling him the braid wasn't made from her real hair, but it would spoil the moment.

Colin finally bent his head to kiss her. *This is a dangerous kiss,* she thought as it began. She realized this might be the only time a Parsi had ever kissed a British person inside the Ripon Club. The touch and melding of their bodies felt like a silent challenge to the city itself.

Colin's hands gripped her shoulder and waist as she opened further to the kiss. As she was beginning to lose herself, she heard what sounded like heavy furniture grating on a floor. Wordlessly, they parted and looked toward the half-open door into the games room.

"It's probably Alice," Colin murmured. "The mischief maker."

Perveen shook her head. Alice had contrived for their upstairs meeting—why would she interrupt it? On the other hand, Malcolm Stowe and Nigel Prescott had a grudge against Colin and might have followed him.

Perveen's pulse raced, as she imagined what power Prescott would hold over her if he caught her in a compromised position. Even if someone else was creeping around, that person could repeat whatever they wished about Jamshedji Mistry's outrageous daughter and an amoral Englishman.

The two of them had to separate and somehow get downstairs, but what was possible when they were on a rooftop in the middle of the city? It seemed the only escape was to go through the games room, but then they'd meet up with the intruder.

"Maybe we should wait it out?" Colin whispered.

"Too risky." She shook her head, wishing she could press herself flat into the wall.

The wall!

As they'd made their way out to the terrace, they'd come close to the room's back wall, and she recalled noticing a door. Now she remembered how waiters sometimes appeared on the floor carrying trays of drinks and snacks for people playing card games—and for the spectators. The door surely led to a staircase down to the third-floor kitchen.

"I know a way down. Stay quiet," she instructed him in a whisper.

Perveen felt along the back wall for a door and hit several chairs before she found the doorknob. Blessedly, nothing was stacked in front. She opened the door, hating its loud creak, and looked down. Light streamed up from the third floor, as well as the clatter of dishes and the shouts of the club's head chef.

Looking back at Colin, she led him down the stairs, unable to use the railing because one hand was occupied with lifting the edge of her voluminous sari, and the other hand was in Colin's. The escape took less than a minute; as Perveen stepped through the lower door into the kitchen, a waiter shouted in surprise and a pot lid dropped to the floor.

"Sorry!" Colin raised his hands upward, as if he were facing a savage bully.

Perveen gave him a pitying look and then turned her attention on the crowd of cooks and waiters. In Gujarati, she said, "I discovered that the foreign gentleman is feeling poorly. I led him down this staircase because he was embarrassed to be seen by his company manager. Please forgive our intrusion, but he needs to sit down and perhaps have a glass of fruit juice."

"Don't worry, Miss Mistry!" Nariman stepped forward, motioning for an underling to get off the stool on which he'd been sitting. "We'll give him orange juice. I know that a lady doctor is on the premises. You find her."

"Good idea." Perveen gestured for Colin to sit down on a stool, and he did so, looking morosely at her.

"Mr. Sandringham, you must take a rest." Perveen looked at him sternly. "Once you feel recovered, please come out to the ballroom. In the meantime, I'll ask someone to call you a taxi."

Colin's face was flushed with annoyance, and Perveen hid her smile as she walked confidently out of the kitchen and into the ballroom.

She was sure Colin would make his way out in a few minutes. In the meantime, she would locate her father. She'd stay by him, just in case the person who'd been snooping around upstairs arrived downstairs and tried to harass her. Fortunately, the room had been so dark that nobody could have seen Colin.

Perveen drew a quick breath. It occurred to her that when she'd gone up to the fourth floor, the electric ceiling lights were on. But when she and Colin had come back inside, the room had been completely dark.

Someone had switched off the lights. Chances were a club employee had seen the lights on for no reason and shut them off. It could be as straightforward as that. It could also mean that someone had come up specifically looking for her . . . or for Colin.

Perveen moved along the edge of the room, looking for people she recognized. She saw that Alice was conversing with the Nawab of Varanpur, whose hand was resting on his blonde companion's back—as if they were quite cozy already. Tigran and Shireen Tata were dancing, and as they passed, she caught sight of the Stowes dancing together with comfortable familiarity. The sight of the married couple beaming at each other made her think it unlikely that Malcolm had been upstairs. It struck her that Madeline was enamored with her despicable husband, just as Cora was with her own cheating prince.

Perveen glanced away and spotted her father in conversation with someone: a silver-haired man with his back to her. A European, she guessed from the hair and pinkness of his neck.

"Here she is," Jamshedji said, as Perveen joined them. "You've been busy everywhere."

"So many people to meet and greet!" Perveen said cheerfully, her smile wavering as she recognized Jamshedji's companion as Nigel Prescott.

"Hello, Miss Mistry. I'm glad you took up my invitation to come to the ball!" His voice was jovial, and he included her father in his wide smile.

Jamshedji's eyebrows drew together in disapproval at the word "invitation."

Desperately, Perveen tried to reframe Prescott's words to reflect the truth. "Good evening to you, Mr. Prescott. As I was saying to you at police headquarters, my father and I attend this function every year. And how nice for you to have a chance to visit the Ripon Club."

"The food and music are positively spiffing! I can't complain about anything except for the heat, but what else is new?" Prescott ran his hand through his silvering hair, and she saw sweat shining on his brow.

"It should rain in a few days' time. Then we will all be lamenting how difficult life is." Jamshedji smiled pleasantly, appearing to have survived his initial dismay at Perveen's familiarity with the police official. "Mr. Prescott, before my daughter joined us, you were describing your history in India. Were you always attached to the Imperial Police?"

"No. I joined relatively late—a transfer from the ICS."

"Were you with the police when you were in Rajputana?" Perveen asked, remembering the sword in his office.

"In those days, I was a young political agent connected with the Western Rajputana States Residency. The Imperial Police keep themselves to Delhi," he said, self-consciously touching the elaborate brass pin on his uniform.

"Except for the ones who work as consultants to the Bombay Police," she said, watching his eyes narrow.

"Inspector Prescott, you must be an expert in Rajput culture!" Jamshedji chortled, and Perveen wondered if he was also thinking about the police complaint carrying a Rajput name.

"I made some very good friends. I can't claim to much more than that."

Now that Perveen had gathered some important threads, she was ready to sew. "I've been wondering about the name Tomar. Is it a Rajput name?"

Prescott paused, taking time to rub the stubble on his chin. "What is this about? ICS officers study one Indic language, and mine is Urdu. Might you ask another person about the name?"

"Of course she can." Jamshedji gave her a reproving look.

"Right in this room, probably. There are as many names in India as there are immigrants."

Perveen wasn't ready to let go of the topic. "Given the friendships you made there, and your love of wide spaces, would you ever try to return to Rajputana?"

"It's almost time for retirement," he said, shaking his head. "And now that my wife is involved with the women's sailing team, I don't know how we could leave Bombay. However, the cost of living is quite high."

"I wonder where you might buy land, then?" Perveen asked, as if it were an idle question.

Jamshedji gave her a warning look, and then turned a smile toward Prescott. "Inspector Prescott, would you like to meet Mr. Kanga, the new advocate-general for Bombay Presidency?"

"I'd like that—but I did promise a dance to my wife." He affected a rueful smile. "Since coming here, she says I have become an administrative bore, and I'm determined to prove otherwise. Have a good evening, both of you."

"And to you as well," Jamshedji said as he steered Perveen deeper into the crowd.

Perveen murmured to her father, "What do you think of him?"

"I'll tell you once we are dancing."

She'd thought he'd wanted to speak with Mr. Kanga, but apparently not. Out of the corner of her eye, she saw that Colin and Alice had taken chairs close to the long line of windows. Alice's shoulders were heaving with laughter, and she imagined Colin might have told her about escaping through the kitchen.

The band was playing a waltz. Perveen's left hand folded into her father's right, and they box stepped, with more distance between them than most of the couples. This was befitting for a father and daughter, and Perveen was glad the song was slow enough that the two of them could move gracefully and even talk.

"Prescott said you're in the running to work for him. A women's safety bureau!" Jamshedji looked accusingly at her.

"I didn't go to him!" Perveen protested in a low voice. "He pulled me into his office when I was in the police station. I had to sit and listen to his nonsense. Of course, I said no."

"And why would someone who believes in women's rights throw away such a chance?"

"Because we are law partners! I also know that his offer is false. He's trying to stop me from pursuing the truth about why Sunanda was arrested."

Jamshedji's grip lightened as they turned to dance in the next direction. "And where is the gentleman, anyway? For all he said about needing to dance with his wife, I don't see him."

"I'm sure he was only making an excuse to get away from us."

"And besides spinning new theories—what have you done this evening? Any barrister contacts?"

Perveen's face warmed as she thought of the kiss with Colin. "Not quite. I've circulated, doing some background checks on the guest list at the nawab's party."

"We agreed you wouldn't pursue that angle." Jamshedji's frown reminded Perveen that he'd admonished her against pursuing any rape investigation.

"I'll explain later," she said, imagining that he might be impressed with the conclusion she'd drawn about Prescott's framing job. "But I think I've got an idea about a possible civil suit resulting in damages paid to Sunanda."

Her father answered swiftly, "Waste of time."

"Why?" Perveen wasn't certain of Sunanda's rapist's identity, but she was well on the way to it.

Her father paused, as if taking care with his words. "Any civil suit would be a costly effort, with a small likelihood of winning."

"But you don't yet know what I've found out!"

"Stop finding things out. Your job here tonight is to interview barristers."

Feeling upset, Perveen missed a step and fell against her father. She pulled away from him, knowing the hard truth in what he was saying. A trial was looming, and she couldn't possibly begin to defend Sunanda without a man to speak for her. And it made her furious that she had to bow to the rules of a legal system created in Britain, by British men.

"Never mind, Perveen." He was soothing her in the same tone he'd used when she'd been ten and lost the badminton championship to Gulnaz.

"I do mind!" Her voice was shaking. "I can't dance along, knowing I will always be seen rather than heard."

"And what are you talking about?" Jamshedji looked at her with concerned eyes.

"I need to sit out for a spell." Perveen glanced at the massive clock on a pedestal near the entrance. It was just ten o'clock. She stalked off, feeling that her emotions paired with the heat of the room were unbearable. She thought of going to Alice and Colin, but what good would that do? Colin didn't know anything about the case. She couldn't tell him.

She walked out of the ballroom and onto the landing where the elevator and grand staircase down offered her a quiet invitation. Getting out to the street could be refreshing. She would smell smoke and spices, not perfume and gin.

The vestibule was empty, but as she approached the elevator, she saw the cables flexing and rising. She felt slightly dizzy from emotion and champagne. Why not wait to take the elevator rather than manage her sari down three flights?

As the barred metal compartment settled loudly onto the third floor, she suddenly lost her breath. Shoving aside the heavy brass door, Malcolm Stowe stepped out of the elevator, followed by Nigel Prescott.

Giving Perveen an oily smile, Stowe bent his head so close that she could smell his breath, a mix of whiskey and his own foul scent. "Miss Mistry, are you playing the wallflower?"

"Not at all. I'm thinking of getting some air," she said, giving him a look that she hoped told him that she'd never forgive his behavior at the office. "I imagine that's what you two were doing as well?"

"No smoking in this club," Prescott said, raising his eyebrows as if this was the ultimate ridiculosity. "I just learned from Malcolm that Parsis forbid smoking."

"For most of us, that's correct," Perveen answered, realizing that she'd been stepping back so much from the men that she was practically against the wall. "Some elites take exception."

"And what's the reason for the taboo?" Prescott crossed his arms as he regarded her with a cool smile.

Perveen realized that she'd shaken Prescott's sense of security, and he was trying to push her back into place. "Fire is holy. We treasure precious smoke from ceremonial fires. We avoid the foul smoke from burning waste and other things, like tobacco. Maybe that's why we are so healthy."

"But you Parsis do drink alcohol!" Stowe said with a hearty laugh. "I've never seen as many Indian ladies drinking as tonight."

If Perveen had still been holding a drink, she would have adored flinging it at his smug face. "There is no law against enjoyment of life in our faith. Or moderate consumption of alcohol, meat, cheese, and eggs." She shifted one foot forward, trying to force the two of them to allow her space to leave. "I'll take my leave now, if you don't mind."

"Just a moment, please." Although Prescott was smiling, she could tell he was angry. "You said something earlier that I've been thinking more about. The name Tomar."

Perveen stepped into the elevator, but Prescott held his hand on the folding metal door, stopping her departure. Looking straight into his cold eyes, she said, "Yes, I have been interested in that name for quite some time. It was on a police complaint. The odd thing is that neither the prosecutor's office nor the police have any record of Mr. Tomar ever meeting personally with someone to deliver his account. For all I know, he's in Rajputana—or in someone's imagination."

Stowe's voice cut in. "You never should have—"

"Let me talk!" Prescott harshly interrupted. Grimacing at Perveen, he said, "Miss Mistry, don't worry so much for your client. If she speaks truthfully about the history of her situation, the prosecutor might even withdraw the charge."

His words were proving her theory right. But it was frightening to come close to such an unscrupulous operator; and she also noted that Malcolm seemed nowhere near as calm about it. Stowe's face was flushed, and he was looking venomously at Prescott.

"Tell the maid she must explain to the judge about who caused all the trouble for her," Prescott purred. "She was wronged. It's as I was saying to you: women must be defended."

Perveen's dizzy feeling was worsening. Wondering how she could evade Stowe and Prescott, Perveen stepped out of the elevator and glanced toward the entrance to the ballroom, which was blocked by a weighty British judge talking with a pair of young British lawyers. Perhaps instead the long louvered doors that led to the gallery? As she glanced at the closest door, she caught a blur of motion behind it.

Is it a camera lens? Perveen kept her eye on what looked like a flat, dark spot. No. The party photographer would not shoot photos from behind a louvered door. Whoever was lurking meant no good.

"Someone's there," she said in a low voice, subtly gesturing toward the shutters, as she edged back toward the open elevator.

"Where? What nonsense are you speaking—"

The rest of Malcolm Stowe's rejoinder was lost amid a deafening blast.

39

LINKED MOTIVES

$\mathcal{P}$erveen watched in horror as Stowe pitched forward amid a splatter of blood. Prescott reached out his arms to catch him but ultimately crumpled to the floor under the weight of his burly friend. There was a second shot. From her crouch in the back of the elevator, Perveen didn't see whether it hit flesh, because she'd already rolled across the floor, trying desperately to place herself out of range.

Screeches, shouts, and epithets in English, Gujarati, and Marathi filled the void that was left after the second blast. A rush of people from the ballroom filled the vestibule.

"Someone's been shot!" a woman gasped. "Oh dear, oh dear!"

It wasn't until the words were said that Perveen understood that the menacing flat circle had been the barrel of a gun.

Nigel Prescott clumsily rose to his feet. His black dinner suit was covered in rivulets of red. Wearily, he gasped, "Imperial Police here. Secure the premises. Everyone should get back inside the ballroom!"

Did the gunshot come through the louvered shutter doors? As if belatedly realizing he could escape the unseen shooter, Prescott stumbled after her.

"Are you hurt, sir?" Judge Packham said, taking hold of Prescott's shoulder.

"I don't know!" Prescott bellowed, tears at the edge of his eyes. As a team of waiters rushed to the vestibule's edge, two barristers shouted at them to drag Stowe's prone body to safety.

Servants were expected to risk their lives; here as well as at Bhatia House.

"I saw the end of a gun between the louvers," Perveen told Jamshedji, who had arrived at her side. A few feet behind him, Colin and Alice stood together, looking anxiously at her. "I'm quite all right!" Perveen said, hating the way that her voice shook.

"Gunfire came from outside that door!" Prescott said, pointing toward the landing. "No civilians are to enter the landing. I need someone who's in charge of the building. Now!" As the club's manager stood at the ballroom's entrance, wringing his hands, Prescott added, "Everyone stay in the ballroom. Please. I need a chair."

"Go on, sir, do your police work!" someone called from the crowd.

Another man yelled, "Are you trying to make us all sitting ducks?"

Miriam Penkar had pushed her way through the gaping crowd. In a commanding tone, she stated, "I'm a physician. Was anyone hurt?"

"Mr. Stowe," Perveen told her. "Mr. Prescott's just shaken."

Glancing at Perveen, Miriam muttered, "The only time in memory I've gone somewhere without my medical bag, and just look!"

"Yes!" Perveen heard herself laugh, despite the awfulness. "I don't have my legal briefcase, either."

"There's blood splatter on you," Miriam said, eyeing her sari. "Is that all of it?"

"I'm not hurt." Perveen looked down to see red droplets coating her arms and the upper half of her sari. Now she wondered who the gunfire had been meant for: Stowe, Prescott, or even her?

Miriam Penkar turned her attention to Stowe, who'd been laid out on a tablecloth set on the ballroom floor. Examining him gently, she said, "The good news is that it only looks like a shoulder wound. Mr. Stowe, can you hear my voice?"

"Are you sure it's not worse?" Stowe groaned. "I want a British doctor. Prescott, why in blazes are you here? Catch the crook!"

Perveen thought it was likely that Prescott wasn't pursuing a suspect because he was part of the Imperial Police, a university-educated administrator who'd not had the same training as regular Bombay Police officers. It was also unlikely he'd carried a weapon anywhere in his slim-fitting suit. Serena Prescott was motioning for her husband to come to sit on a chair near her next to the bar area. Madeline Stowe had pushed her way through the crowd and knelt next to Miriam. Her eyes were streaming with tears as she regarded her husband.

"Malcolm, I love you," she whispered. "I may have said some things, but I never wished this to happen—"

"Mrs. Stowe, if you want to help, please bring me some clean kitchen towels and a bowl of water," Miriam interrupted. "And make sure someone's rung for an ambulance. I see no point in removing the bullet here when there are skilled surgeons at the European Hospital."

"The Parsi Ambulance Company is already alerted," Nariman said breathlessly as he handed a stack of towels to Madeline.

The club's president, Xerxes Bhesania, stepped forward.

"Please, everyone! Back to the party!" he called out in a rolling voice. "We have already barricaded the doors to the gallery. There is no danger of intrusion, and the bar is still open!"

Perveen was reminded of the accident at Uma's party and the impossibility of continuing to socialize. Yet most of the crowd did wander back toward the dance floor. After all, the building was supposedly secured, and the bar was still serving champagne. She imagined people thought the assailant had gotten away. Perveen realized she was the only person who had seen the gun. She should explain what she'd seen to the Bombay Police when they arrived, though she imagined Prescott would try to take control.

But the next face she saw was Colin's. He stood just behind her father, and she could not refrain from giving him a wan smile. Jamshedji turned and looked thoughtfully at Colin. "Sir, you seem familiar. Where have we met?"

"My name is Colin Sandringham—"

"Oh, yes. You helped us greatly last November. When the Prince of Wales was here." Jamshedji smiled warmly at him. "Quite an evening, isn't it?"

"Yes," Colin said, looking stunned by Jamshedji's reaction. "I was wondering where Inspector Prescott has gone. I wished to tell him that I learned the club has a second stairway running through the kitchen. It goes up to the roof—I don't know if it also goes down to the street."

"Frankly, I also don't know. It seems a question for the staff, who seem to be doing a bit more than our good inspector." Taking Colin by the arm, Jamshedji led him to the club manager.

From the twenty-foot distance, Colin sent Perveen a look that seemed to implore her to join them.

Instead, she sent back a message with her eyes.

I love you. These were words she'd never said aloud to him, but that she hoped he could understand.

Madeline Prescott had returned from the errand to bring towels and resumed her spot near Malcolm's face. She'd stopped sobbing, and she spoke in a quick voice that was full of outrage. "I just saw your so-called friend resting on one of those long wooden lounge chairs. What a bastard—he did nothing to save you, let alone apprehend the shooter!"

Whatever Malcolm muttered back to her was unintelligible, but Perveen had the thought that Madeline Prescott would be worth seeking out for further conversation.

"Perveen!"

Perveen saw her father was motioning for her to join him, although Colin was no longer there.

"Go on, Perveen," Miriam said, glancing at her. "I'm fine here. I see some waiters are bringing the water I asked for."

Perveen made her way to her father, who at last took her into his arms. He held her tight, and she realized from the wetness on her forehead that he was weeping. Speaking into her hair, he said, "I almost lost you. But God has given me a second chance, and I must become a better man."

"You are a great man, Pappa. Don't fault yourself because I got close to a bullet!" Perveen said, feeling uncomfortable to see her father's vulnerability.

"I was seeing myself only as your father. But you are my partner. That means—I must listen more and talk less. Tell me what happened in the landing. All of it."

It was a roundabout apology, but she would certainly remind him of his words in the office, the next time she felt overstepped. "I only remember that I suddenly could see something between the shutter's louvres. It was so strange—I couldn't understand what it was right away. And I really didn't know that it was a gun aimed for Mr. Stowe or Prescott. I wonder, was it an anti-British attack, or something connected with our case?"

"There are reasons to think the shot was meant for you." Jamshedji dabbed with his handkerchief at a blood spot on her sari. "We are the ones who suffered a fire at our home—it must have been a warning. You are defending a woman who was violated by a very powerful man, and that man is showing his power."

"Perhaps," Perveen said. Stowe and Prescott had been working together—had the powerful man struck against them? In the next instant, she wondered where the nawab had gone.

"Pappa, have you seen the Nawab of Varanpur anywhere?"

"I haven't. But I want to tell you that I feel more than ever Sunanda must be represented. If no barrister will work with us, I'll put on my wig."

As Perveen hugged her father tight, she heard Alice's voice.

"There you two are!"

"Hello, Alice," Perveen said, accepting her friend's embrace.

"I come bearing news," she said, looking at the two of them.

"I hope it involves the arrival of some actual police?" Jamshedji said.

"Yes, there's a spot in the back of the club where I could hear the bells of their arriving vehicles. Two horse-drawn carts and an automobile," Alice added. "By the way, it seems that Nigel Prescott has single-handedly ruined the reputation of the Imperial Police. It's been more than half an hour since the shooting, and he's made no attempt at a search. The criminal most likely has escaped."

"An officer alone is a man alone," Jamshedji opined. "We think of police as being brave, but they are only human."

"I was walking around, and I didn't see the Nawab of Varanpur anymore. Or his companion," Alice added sarcastically.

"Miss Hobson-Jones, who are you referring to, exactly?" Jamshedji inquired, his eyes alight with curiosity.

"The nawab was inseparable from a young blonde who I heard just sailed out to visit Bombay a few months ago. Husband-hunting, probably . . ."

Perveen stopped listening to Alice's gossip about the mystery woman. The police had arrived and were fanning out through the club. A constable directed everyone to the rear lounge area. She followed directions but felt her mind turning back to her conversation the previous week at Mistry House, when Cora had visited and talked about her husband's various abilities, which included the hunting of game. What if the young lady with him tonight had been his smoke screen? Mansoor of Varanpur could have seen her off in a taxi and slipped back into the club. Perhaps he had done so because Malcolm Stowe had become disaffected with Prescott's plan and had warned his boyhood friend.

Yes, Perveen thought. It was all quite likely. But the police would be set on finding the shooter by themselves. They'd regard anything that she suggested with the same respect Magistrate O'Brien had shown her.

Too much was on her mind; she needed to steady herself. She stepped away from Alice and put a hand on the wall. It was warm. Everything was too hot.

"Perveen doesn't look well," Alice said, putting an arm around her as she looked at Jamshedji. "Do you think one of the people sitting would give up a chair?"

"Oh no!" Perveen protested. "I think I need to go to the ladies' lounge."

"I'll walk you there," Alice said, putting a hand on her arm.

"Make sure she comes out with you," Jamshedji said, watching with a worried expression as Alice escorted Perveen toward the back of the ballroom, where one set of French doors had been left open for access to the lavatories. As they entered the space just before the lavatory, she could see the outdoor gallery was now filled with police, who were particularly concentrated on the larea where Perveen had seen the gun's barrel.

"I'll go inside by myself, Alice. It's quite small," Perveen said when they reached their destination.

"Of course," Alice said. "I'll wait for you right here, just as I promised your pappa."

Another woman was already in the small room, washing her hands at one of the sinks. Perveen took her spot at the vacant sink and turned on the taps. Her first goal was to get some water on her face, neck, and arms. She was covered in sweat, from both the heat and fear. As the cold water revived her, she lifted her face and looked at herself in the mirror, no longer elegant, with several of her coiled braids hanging loose. Glancing sideways, she saw the woman at the other sink was Begum Cora, wearing a black silk evening gown trimmed with a gold fringe collar.

"Well!" Cora said, her voice scratchy as she caught sight of Perveen. "You look divine tonight!"

The nawab was gone, and Cora was here. It was an awkward situation. Perveen didn't know what to say, so she said, "How good to finally see you. I remembered you saying you'd come, so I've been looking."

"I arrived later than my husband—my hairdresser was late," she said, touching her red curls. Her eyes were large and luminous, framed with thick black mascara. "I haven't seen the nawab anywhere. Do you think he went home?"

"I don't know." Perveen thought about the nawab's dance partner; should she tell Cora? "I don't know."

"Did he leave with a pretty girl?" Cora asked, her tone almost cheerful.

"I don't know. I saw him dancing with someone I didn't know." Perveen let out her breath. She'd been honest and allowed Cora the truth. She felt Cora staring at her even harder, which felt uncomfortable, so she lowered her eyes.

That's when she noticed the frothy soap all over Cora's hands was tinged black, and there were black smudges in the sink. Gunpowder?

She must have stared at Cora's hands a beat too long, because Cora was suddenly chattering at her. "Oh dear, I see you've got blood on your sari! Let me help you wash that off."

Cora reached for Perveen's sari's pallu and pulled the end under the running tap in the sink. Trying to gently release her sari from Cora's grasp, Perveen met resistance. Affecting gratitude, she said, "Thank you, dear. I don't think we can do much more for my poor sari tonight. My maid will take care of it."

Holding fast to Perveen's sari, Cora shook her head. "You mustn't go. A wet sari is too revealing."

The words were reminiscent of what the nawab's servant had told Sunanda the day of Cora's beach party. Begum Cora didn't want a young maidservant in wet garb to be seen in areas near her guests. Her husband might have overheard her and been inspired to take advantage.

"Do you know what the trouble is with this country?" Cora's voice was tight.

Perveen thought frantically. "There are too many troubles to count! My father sometimes says that's why law will always be a reliable occupation. We can try to right the wrongs done to people."

"But you don't want to represent me." Cora studied her coldly. "It's because you knew."

"Knew?" Perveen heard her voice crack, and she wondered if the gun was close by, or hidden somewhere else in the club. Perhaps upstairs.

"Yes, you know all of it. Just because people like to talk to you! You are received socially—and I am not."

"But not by everyone—"

"Who told you, Parvesh Bhatia or Malcolm Stowe?" Her eyes drilled into Perveen.

Perveen had trouble answering. "About what?"

"About what happened to Sunanda. And why did everyone care? That girl was just a maid. A nothing." She narrowed her eyes as she scrutinized Perveen, as if willing her to disagree.

"To you she meant nothing," Perveen said, unable to forget Sunanda's weeping in prison—the memories that were coming back and sickening her. "But what your husband did was violent and wrong. It also dishonored you."

"Parvesh Bhatia is the one without honor!" Cora said darkly. "He borrowed, and what did Manny get in return?"

Now Perveen understood that debt was the reason Parvesh had felt unable to speak the nawab's name, even though he'd been horrified by the assault on Sunanda. Yet Cora believed Parvesh *had* told her, or maybe others. Had she shot Stowe because he was at the party, and she thought he knew?

Perveen was trying hard not to aggravate her, but to align with her instead. This was the best way for a lawyer to gain information from a hostile witness. "You must love your husband very much."

"Yes. And I will have good news for him when he finally drags himself home." With a giggle, Cora said, "I'll tell him that we've got two thousand more acres of land."

"I think you overheard my conversation." This gave Perveen hope, because surely it would paint Colin and Perveen as helpers rather than enemies.

"Yes, who was it you were snuggling with?" Cora put on a mock-scolding tone. "I didn't know you had a secret beau."

Perveen flushed, unwilling to answer this particular question.

"Look at you, living in fear!" Cora said mockingly. "When you were brave enough to help me with the dogs."

Perveen recalled how frightened Cora had been that day at Bhatia House. And that gave her another thought. After the dogs had been chased off, Cora had collected the fallen items, shooing off Perveen when she'd tried to help. Cora had behaved that way because she had been carrying an item she didn't want to be noticed. The compact was something she'd already owned; the lead acetate—a substance meant to kill her unborn child, or even her, by one of the other begums—was most likely found by her in the Varanpur Palace.

Thoughts flashed like cars of a train hurtling at top speed. Cora had feared that Parvesh Bhatia would tell about her husband. It might be that the poison was meant for him, yet Sir Dwarkanath had consumed it.

"What's worrying you, my dear?" Cora asked, her eyes pinpoints of concern.

"It's just that—just that I want to go outside. The air is quite close, isn't it?"

"Bombay is hot everywhere," Cora said. "And why shouldn't you suffer a while longer? You are such a schemer, posing as a friend when it's always been about destroying me. You think I'm a stupid git, don't you?"

"On the contrary—you have one of the sharpest minds I know." As Perveen flattered her, the fear rose. If only Alice had come inside the lavatory with her!

"And I'm a sharp shot." Cora bit her lip, and when she spoke, her front teeth bore red smudges. "I meant to finish Stowe off. If you hadn't been there to raise a ruckus, he wouldn't have survived."

"Cora, I don't think you're well." Perveen was striving to sound comforting, rather than judgmental. "We should talk to Miriam Penkar about this. You know her and trust her. Let's go out of this wretched little room—"

"Not yet." Cora had never let go of Perveen's sari, and now she twisted the end so hard that Perveen was jerked forward against her will. "I don't want you talking to any doctors about me. If only you'd been the one to burn."

Perveen's fear was tinged with confusion. "Do you mean— the fire at my garden cottage?"

"I thought you were with her."

"What?" Perveen paused, thinking. "Do you mean, you thought I was staying in the garden house with Gita?"

"With Sunanda," she said. "And don't try to pretend she wasn't there. My driver spoke with her."

"The stranger?" Perveen said, remembering the inquisitive man who'd frightened Gita. "But she wasn't with us anymore. She's in jail."

"Jail? What a wretched place. I thought she was with you?" Cora wrinkled up her nose, and Perveen could see straight into her nostrils, which had a faint covering of white. If it wasn't face powder, could it be a drug? Cocaine might be the agent behind her rambling, wild conversation.

Perveen took a deep breath, striving to appear focused on Cora's face. If only she could edge closer to the door, she'd be able to seize the knob. "Sunanda's been at Gamdevi Station since last Saturday."

"I wish I'd known!" Cora still had hold of the sari's pallu, and when she yanked, Perveen was brought closer. Still, Cora's bold focus gave her an opportunity to slowly reach behind her toward the knob without being noticed. She almost had it.

"There's no reason for us to leave," Cora said with an eerie smile. "Why are you being so silly?"

There was a knocking at the door. Perveen shouted, "Help!"

Cora's outsized eyes bored into hers and she pulled sharply on Perveen's sari so it circled her neck. Instinctively, Perveen backed away, but the noose tightened. Dizziness rose, and her hand slipped from the doorknob.

How long could she last without breath, she wondered, just as she heard a dull banging behind her.

How can Cora be strangling and shooting at the same time? she wondered, but in the next moment, the door pushed into her back.

"Good God!" Alice Hobson-Jones shouted at the same time Perveen heard a crisp slap. Suddenly, the grip on her pallu was gone.

In a moment, Alice was between her and Cora. Fiercely, she said, "I heard everything you said through the door!"

"Oh, you shouldn't be speaking to me! Don't you know, I'm not received?" Cora retorted, her eyes darting wildly from Alice to Perveen.

"I'll do bloody well what I please!" Alice slapped Cora again before hauling Perveen out of the room to the club's hallway.

Two constables crowded past them into the small lavatory, and Alice called after them: "That woman was trying to strangle Perveen! And look at the traces of gunpowder on her!"

How quickly Alice had put things together. It was a relief because Perveen's throat was raw. She would have plenty of words to say, but not for a while.

As the constables emerged with the handcuffed princess, she sobbed, "Not a word without my lawyer!"

Now Perveen was doubly glad she'd never had the woman sign a retainer.

Alice knelt beside Perveen. "I had a feeling something was taking too long. But the door was locked—"

"It was—just my hand!" Perveen answered between coughs.

Alice lowered her head to speak into her ear. "The police found a rifle on the third floor and a crumpled servant's uniform. They went upstairs because of what Colin told them about the back staircase."

"Does it seem that she did the shooting alone?" Perveen still had her suspicions about the nawab.

"I think it's most likely." Alice chuckled, adding, "Apparently, the police already located the nawab and his girlfriend in flagrante delicto at the Taj!"

40

THE ARRIVAL OF RAIN

"I trust you to go alone, but I'd very much like to be there." Jamshedji spoke quietly as he faced Perveen from across the partners desk. Three days had passed since the headline RIP-PING MURDER ACTS AT THE RIPON had run in the Monday edition of the *Times of India*. In that time, Princess Cora of Varanpur, nee Arbison, had been formally charged with cul-pable homicide in the death of Lord Dwarkanath Bhatia, and the attempted murder of Malcolm Stowe.

"I prefer to be together," Perveen said honestly. Her working relationship with Jamshedji had become easier in the last few days. They had cast a wide net while conducting personal interviews, finally deciding that the sworn statements they'd gathered from Colin, Sunanda, Padma, Madeline Stowe, and a certain Ripon Club waiter were the most crucial. "After all, you were the one who made the appointment with the advocate-general's secretary. Now, are you sure all the sworn statements and their copies are packed in your legal case?" Perveen asked.

"Quite sure." Her father smiled, as if remembering all the times he'd asked her the same.

The advocate-general's office was on the grounds of the Bombay High Court, just steps from where trials were decided. Strolling distance from Mistry House. Arman wouldn't be needed until later on—after they knew what had happened.

"We might need umbrellas," Jamshedji said, looking

suspiciously at the sky as Mustafa opened the door for them to leave Mistry House.

"The cloud looks twenty miles away," Mustafa said. "Likely no rain until midday."

For the last few days, both men had predicted the monsoon's onset and been wrong about it. Today, the only thing that needed to go right was the conversation with Mr. Kanga—*Judge Kanga*, Perveen reminded herself. Retired judges were called by their titles for the rest of their lives.

Armed soldiers stood with hands on their bayonets as the Mistrys walked onto the High Court grounds. Jamshedji murmured to her that it seemed the government was still worried that Indians entering might try to assassinate British employees— even though, in 1919, an act had been passed aimed to reduce Indians' access to firearms. Aware of the continued scrutiny, Perveen motioned for him to lower his voice.

The advocate-general's office was housed in a *G*-shaped building of rubblestone that opened in 1874, four years before the massive High Court was completed. As they walked along the ground floor's corridors, Jamshedji mentioned that the Bombay Bar Council and various offices for senior Bombay Presidency administrators were on the upper floors. It seemed too quick a walk past the prosecutor's office to the door with a plaque marking the office of the advocate-general.

When Perveen and Jamshedji entered, an Anglo-Indian clerk asked their names and business. Then the clerk said, in a voice devoid of expression, "Your arrival is anticipated by Judge Kanga. I will bring you to him."

Bring you to him. Perveen realized how different this meeting would be than being in court. And how should this impact how she spoke to the man? Because he still technically had the title of judge, he might not allow her to open her mouth.

Their escort opened a door at the very end of the hall that

bore the name Jamshetjee B. Kanga, advocate-general of Bombay Presidency.

Advocate-General Kanga sat behind a wide mahogany desk that was neatly piled with books and papers. He was a long-faced, sober-looking man, and he rose from his seat when he saw them. Another inversion of the usual process in a court room. "Do come in, Mr. Mistry and Miss Mistry." Jamshetjee Kanga's eyes fell on the lone chair facing his desk, as if he'd just realized that his chamber was not prepared for the two of them.

"Terribly sorry, Your Honor. I'll bring another chair," the clerk said, hastily exiting, although it was a peon who returned carrying a heavy rosewood armchair.

Perveen seated herself in the first chair, while her father took the second. She tried not to obviously stare at Judge Kanga, the very first Indian appointed to Bombay Presidency's highest legal position. His demeanor aligned with that of a learned and strict man; yet behind his gold-rimmed spectacles, his eyes looked kind.

Perveen imagined that he was also making his own inspection of them. All parties were Zoroastrian, so he'd probably be wary of behaving in a manner that could be considered favoritism. But would that mean that they'd lose?

A bearer stepped into the room carrying a silver tray laden with chinaware stamped with Bombay Presidency's coat of arms, the two leopards supporting a shield topped by a prancing lion. The first cup went to Perveen, but she didn't take a sip until the others had been served.

The judge spoke in a neutral voice. "I understand you wish to speak about what you perceive as some irregularities in the department of the Bombay City Prosecutor."

"Thank you, Your Honor," Perveen said, hearing a squeak in her voice. "We've come to respectfully request your consideration of whether a person or persons within the police and prosecutor's office worked to perpetrate fraudulent grounds of arrest."

Judge Kanga's voice was cool. "That is quite serious. Was the matter brought earlier to the chief prosecutor?"

Perveen stiffened as she thought about how they had not addressed the chief prosecutor. Jamshedji had agreed with her that it was possible that the chief prosecutor was in Prescott's hand. But now she saw that the advocate-general might refuse to listen any further.

"No, we did not!" Jamshedji cut in, as if observing her hesitation. "After all, the chief prosecutor's name was on a warrant that we can prove never had legal standing. I'll leave it to my partner to give the full details."

"You may proceed, Miss Mistry," Judge Kanga said, looking at her with slightly narrowed eyes.

Perveen found her voice. Slowly, she described the circumstances of Sunanda's arrest—and the witness named Arvind Vikas Tomar who had no address, and was unknown by everyone connected to the case, including the police—everyone save for Nigel Prescott, the consultant to the Bombay Police.

Kanga's face had been expressionless as she told the tale; she wished she could rush forward, but she and her father had rehearsed the best way to tell the story.

Now it was Jamshedji's turn. Softly, he said, "Our defendant client, Miss Chavda, does not know of Mr. Tomar, and neither do her family or neighbors in Ghatkopar. The Bhatia family household's members and servants also don't know anyone with that name. Nor do the workers at Bhatia Stone. Interestingly, Tomar is not a Marathi or a Gujarati name. It's common to Rajputana, a place that Mr. Prescott considers his home away from home."

Kanga's eyes flickered behind his gold-rimmed spectacles. "Indians emigrate and work in different areas. It's not inconceivable that Mr. Tomar lives outside Rajputana."

"I agree, sir," Perveen said. "That is why I submitted a request for information on Mr. Tomar, so I can depose him before the pending trial. However, the department sent no response to us. We also have learned that Mr. Tomar never had a personal appointment with anyone in the police when making the complaint. Supposedly, he mailed a letter with the information—a letter containing no return address."

"Are you stating that the prosecutor used a typed letter—rather than any witness interviews—and used that as a basis for an arrest?" Behind the thick spectacles, Kanga's eyes had widened into an expression of incredulity.

"Your Honor, we really can't be sure," Perveen said, feeling a rush of insecurity as her words came out. "You see, Mr. Nigel Prescott, a consultant from the Imperial Police, was the person who approached the prosecutor's office with Tomar's letter. And although I have asked for and been denied the chance to see the original signed letter, I was finally granted a copy yesterday. Having examined it, I believe it's possible that the letter was composed by someone other than Mr. Tomar. The language is typical of a highly educated person in England."

"Maybe he studied in England—like you and your father did," said Judge Kanga. There was a hint of frost in his voice, and Perveen remembered hearing that the advocate-general had started off as a solicitor educated at Government Law School in Bombay.

"Please consider these exhibits," said Jamshedji, who brought forth several papers. The first was the letter signed "A. V. Tomar," which was written in upper-class language, and used words like "nanny" in place of "ayah," and terms such as "whilst" and "carried on." There was also no translator's stamp—meaning the change of language could not be attributed to another person's taste.

Kanga's face was expressionless as he read it. Then he slid the other papers in front of him and adjusted his spectacles. One paper was handwritten in Marathi, the other was typed in English, with a translator's certification stamp. Perveen said,

"The Marathi paper is a sworn statement from Padma, a maid-servant in the household of Inspector Nigel Prescott. We had the translation made and certified yesterday."

Kanga read it slowly and then looked up. "Quite convoluted. Was this statement taken in person?"

Perveen felt a rush of anxiety and was glad to hear Jamshedji answer in a steady voice. "Yes, Your Honor. Padma spoke with us in our office two days ago. The gist of Padma's sworn statement is that both Mr. and Mrs. Prescott questioned her in great detail about Sunanda, pressing for details about the date that Miss Chavda sipped an herbal tea. Padma also reported over-hearing Mr. Prescott tell Mrs. Prescott that the nawab could be jailed or lose property if Sunanda said his name in court. Padma reports that Mr. Prescott spoke with excitement and enthusiasm about it."

Kanga did not comment, so Perveen pulled another paper from her legal case. "We have brought another sworn statement from Mr. Nariman Engineer, a waiter at the Ripon Club. He witnessed Malcolm Stowe and Nigel Prescott smoking outside the club, arguing about a letter. He heard Malcolm Stowe say to Nigel Prescott, 'Hard luck. You shouldn't have bothered.'"

"Cryptic," Kanga said, examining the document. "How can it mean anything for certain?"

"We would like very much to see the letter. We believe that Stowe was talking about the letter we showed you earlier that was supposedly from Tomar. Mr. Stowe might be implying that he wished Prescott hadn't sent that letter to the prosecutor's office."

"But Mr. Engineer's statement does not mention anything about an alleged rape, or the name of Sunanda."

"That is because two co-conspirators were chatting, and they had no need to regurgitate facts already known. The important thing, in my mind, is to examine all of these witness statements in connection to each other." Perveen could not keep emotion out of her voice. "Mr. Prescott anticipated that if threatened with prosecution for abortion, Sunanda would speak aloud the name of the nawab in exchange for having a lighter sentence—after all, this is what Detective Vaughan promised when he interviewed her in prison."

"You are suggesting that Prescott made a highly contrived plan," Judge Kanga said. "Highly devious."

Jamshedji cleared his throat. "Your Honor, what we have learned is that Mr. Prescott had an interest in buying land to use for business and personal life after his retirement. He had asked Mr. Stowe to help him understand the actual boundaries of land between British India and royals. Prescott suggested that Mr. Stowe approach a naïve young vice president at the Royal Asiatic Society named Colin Sandringham. Miss Mistry has taken Mr. Sandringham's statement."

Perveen watched the advocate-general's eyes move slowly down the typed interview, which included the details of payment, confidentiality, and Prescott's anger with Colin's revised map showing more land in the nawab's territory.

"Complicated," the advocate-general said after a pause. "It's a possible theory—but still lacking in substantiation."

"This brings us to the recent conversation I had with Madeline Stowe," Perveen said, pulling out a paper. "Mrs. Stowe wrote in a statement that she had mentioned to Mrs. Prescott that she'd been at a party at the nawab's house where she had seen the nawab pulling together his clothing shortly before Parvesh Bhatia took a weeping maidservant and his children home. She suspected that the nawab had either assaulted the maid or the children. In any case, she was disturbed enough to tell another lady." Perveen watched Kanga's eyes run over the paper, and she hoped she hadn't gone too far. If the case did go forward, she'd just provided a very good reason for the prosecution to argue that Sunanda had committed abortion.

As if sensing Perveen's anxiety, Jamshedji gave her a reassuring nod. When it was clear Kanga had finished reading,

Jamshedji said, "Your Honor, I was quite struck by the fact that Mrs. Stowe also mentions that Serena Prescott brought up to her the notion of buying a hillside estate in the next year or two. As you'll read in the statement, Mrs. Prescott told Mrs. Stowe that some undeveloped mountain land would come into the hands of Bombay Presidency. According to Mrs. Stowe, Mr. Prescott requested a transfer to Bombay because he wanted to build relationships with government officials within Bombay Presidency."

Mr. Kanga was maintaining a poker face, but Perveen could see his feet below the desk. He was twisting one foot back and forth, as if aggrieved. What did this mean?

Jamshedji picked up the thread. Leaning forward, he modulated his voice to a low, suspenseful tone. "Malcolm Stowe attended a party where we believe the nawab may have assaulted our client. We believe that he mentioned this attack to Prescott, without any expectation that Prescott would use the information gathered in a calculated scheme to dishonor the nawab. That's what we believe caused Stowe and Prescott's argument overheard by the waiter outside the Ripon Club."

Perveen listened with appreciation to Jamshedji's careful language, which did not violate attorney-client privilege. Three days earlier, she'd already explained to Sunanda that Cora had spoken words implicating her husband in the attack. Sunanda had given her agreement to their mentioning the attack to the advocate-general.

"Judge Kanga, it does not seem ethical that an innocent woman be prosecuted for a non-cognizable crime. The case appears to have been brought about as a means to make real estate purchases. And of course, if there is a trial, it will ruin Sunanda's life," Perveen said, daring herself to look straight into the advocate-general's stern face. "If an unmarried woman is exposed for having had intercourse, she is likely to lose the chance to work in a respectable occupation, or to remain accepted by her parents and family. She would likely never find a groom willing to take her in marriage. And she is only twenty years old."

"Putting Sunanda Chavda on trial sets a dangerous precedent for the office of the Bombay prosecutor," Jamshedji chimed in. "The accounts we've gathered point to the prosecutor going forward with a case that had far too many irregularities. And when has a woman ever been charged for abortion before quickening has occurred? Surely the prosecutor knew this case did not fit standards for justice within Bombay Presidency."

Kanga sat in silence. Then he slowly stacked together the papers, making them neat as the others on his desk.

It seemed that he was putting away their arguments. Perveen's dread grew as she saw he was about to speak.

"I will have discussions about the ethics of the particular prosecution with the chief prosecutor—as is the usual process," he said heavily. "In the meantime, I'm using the authority vested in me by Bombay Presidency to write an order for the release without bail expense for Sunanda Chavda. Did you say she's at Gamdevi Station?"

"Yes, she is!" Perveen said, feeling tears threaten as she sensed Sunanda's nightmare was almost over.

"As I'm sure you've realized already, there are solid grounds for investigation. Section 219 prohibits any civil servant from corruptly or maliciously involving himself in any stage of a judicial proceeding. It's a serious crime punishable with a heavy fine and a term of up to seven years." Judge Kanga rose, a signal that the meeting was finished.

"Thank you," Perveen said. "Thank you so much."

"I am also grateful, Judge Kanga," Jamshedji said, practically hopping up. "By the way, we were both wondering if you've heard anything about the fate of Princess Cora?"

"The suspected shooter," he said, nodding. "Generally, foreigners accused of crimes are extradited to their home. She will face legal consequences there. As you know from your experience with the courts, very few Europeans serve time in Indian jails."

"No—it's our people who fill them," Perveen said, thinking about Gandhi, three months incarcerated and perhaps with years to go. But she had a feeling with the new advocate-general, it would be harder to argue that free speech, and peaceful gathering, was the same as sedition.

A sharp knock at the door interrupted her thoughts.

"Come in, we are just finished," Kanga said, his tone considerably more relaxed than before.

"Sorry, Your Honor. Mr. Prescott insisted on seeing you!" announced the clerk.

"It'll be only a moment." Nigel Prescott, dapper in his police uniform, set a foot in the door. Catching sight of Perveen and Jamshedji, his smile faded.

Kanga's long face seemed to stretch another few inches. "Mr. Prescott, the procedure for our office is to request an appointment with my secretary."

"I come on police business—to apprise you of necessary information. The real facts," Prescott added, looking dourly at Perveen.

Prescott's choice of words made Perveen's stomach roil. If he delivered false statements in his typically smooth manner, the advocate-general might be deceived and change course on his corruption investigation.

"I'll be calling you in later," Kanga said coldly. "Good day, Mr. Prescott."

Perveen looked quickly at her father. She'd never heard an Indian speak to a British person with such a tone. And Prescott seemed just as taken aback, because two red spots appeared below his cheekbones. He appeared poised to say something, but in the end, pressed his lips together and left the room.

Perveen looked at her father, who motioned for her to collect the papers that the advocate-general had reviewed. But as she touched the stack, Kanga put his hand on them.

"As you know, it's contingent on the office of the prosecutor to dismiss a pending case," Kanga said. "As I begin my discussions with the head prosecutor, I would like to share these sworn statements you brought. May I?"

"Certainly. We brought with us certified copies," Jamshedji said, opening his legal case.

Yes, Perveen thought. *We will protect the evidence. No matter what.* Taking a deep breath, Perveen said, "Your Honor, I am most grateful."

"No need to keep thanking me." Giving her a warm smile, he said, "Remember, I saw what happened at the Lawyers' Ball last Saturday evening. You delivered the shooter to the police. And you probably saved a number of people from being shot—including Mr. Prescott himself."

Two hours later, the advocate-general's directive to release Sunanda Chavda on bail had reached the desk at Gamdevi Station, where Perveen was waiting.

"It's so bright outside!" Sunanda said, shading her eyes as they emerged.

"Yes, but I notice clouds rolling in." Perveen chuckled inwardly as she heard herself sounding like her father. "The first time you and I left Gamdevi Station, we feasted at a restaurant around the corner. Shall we do that now?"

Sunanda shook her head. "I'm too happy to be hungry. There is no room for food inside."

"Then come home. Everyone is excited to welcome you." While Perveen had been waiting for Sunanda to be released, Jamshedji had gone home to tell Camellia and Gita the news.

"Your family is so kind to take me again. I only hope that I can wash before they see me," Sunanda said, running fingers through her matted hair.

"Of course! And we must tend to your burns," Perveen said.

"And when I'm healed, should I go to Gujarat?" Sunanda

rattled on. "I don't know whether my family will let me return."

"We can be your family," Perveen said. "As for the rest, we can talk in the car."

Arman opened the back door to the car with a flourish. "Welcome back, Sunanda, and congratulations. And, of course, congratulations to you, Perveen-bai, for a successful outcome."

Perveen thanked him. Having a case dismissed wasn't as satisfying as winning at trial would have been. Winning an abortion trial could have exposed the hypocrisy of the laws that controlled women. It could have set a precedent.

To have had that trial, though, all Perveen's arguments would have been spoken aloud by a male barrister. And what would it have felt like to see him parroting the words that she would have suggested? She doubted that a man could speak about a woman's menses without showing some discomfort. Ultimately, her client had been spared the shame of such a trial and had her freedom restored.

As the car rolled into motion, Sunanda spoke again. "You told me there's a new baby nurse living at your house. Does your sister-in-law like her better than the other one?"

Perveen explained, briefly, that Gulnaz was still staying with her parents, adding, "Khushy will be fine staying with us. Hiba is in no rush to go."

Clearing her throat, Sunanda ventured, "What do you hear about Uma-bhabhu and Motabhai? I was worried that they thought I did something to hurt Sir Dwarkanath."

"They know it's not true," Perveen said, squeezing her hand. "Parvesh finally told the police to come and check the liquor bottles and they found a brandy bottle was tainted by lead acetate. The begum told me that she'd done it."

Sunanda gasped aloud. "The redhead memsahib who wears a sari? Why would she do such a terrible thing?"

"It's too long a story for this car ride." Perveen was also eager to tell Sunanda that she'd heard from Alice that the nawab was no longer received in Bombay society and had even put Varanpur Villa up for sale. He might never go to jail, but his reputation was ruined.

To fill the time, Perveen turned the conversation to the situation of Oshadi, who had received a surprise visit from Parvesh and Uma, who'd driven together to Juhu to apologize for firing her. They'd asked her back with a raised salary, and Oshadi had happily agreed.

"When I visited Bhatia House, I noticed Oshadi was helping Mangala and her children pack up to go to Lonavala," Perveen said. "Mangala boasted about getting her children into the best schools in the hills. She will stay nearby, with her husband in their own family bungalow."

"Probably everyone will be happier about that!" Sunanda said, after Perveen had described the visit. "But tell me more about Ishan, please. And also—Motabhai."

From the way Sunanda had mentioned Parvesh, Perveen guessed that he would always hold a special place in her heart; the place of a protective older brother.

"Ishan was well enough to play in the garden, and I'm sure he'll miss his cousins. He wanted to make sure I'd given you the money he'd been keeping—and I will, my dear, if you come to the office with me tomorrow. Bhatia Stone's future is less certain. Parvesh-bhai wishes to donate the warehouse space for the hospital, and he may depart the stone business forever."

"But what else could he do? How would they live?" Sunanda's face was tight with concern.

"Parvesh-bhai told me that he and Uma are thinking about selling some of their vast property in Ghatkopar to be developed for housing. And now, I've got a question for you! Given all that's happened, would you ever consider returning to Bhatia House for work?"

Sunanda sighed happily. "It's all I want! Oshadi is like a mother to me."

Perveen squeezed her hand, feeling pleased. Uma dearly wanted Sunanda to return, with a raise similar to Oshadi's. But Perveen would let Uma tell Sunanda that herself.

They'd entered Dadar and were slowly traversing the colony, passing the street where the Bankers lived. She knew her parents would task her with continuing to visit Gulnaz. But today she thought, *Why go to Gulnaz right away? Let it rain first. Everything changes with the rain.*

"Thank you for bringing me back to your house. I was wrong to leave," Sunanda said as the car stopped in front of the duplex. "This is a good place."

"Arre!" Perveen felt a drop on her arm. "Did you just feel that?"

The first drops of the summer monsoon were spread several seconds apart. They landed hard, like small stones, and Perveen held up her arms, watching the smile on Sunanda's face widen.

The two young women, linked by coincidence, danced and twirled in the rain, playing as if they were ten years younger, and not separated by society's rules.

After a few minutes, Perveen caught sight of Camellia standing in the open door, holding Khushy's small, chubby hands out to feel the first touch of rain. Then, Jamshedji emerged, hurrying toward Perveen and Sunanda with a large black umbrella.

"I told you it would rain!" he called out to Perveen. "But did you listen?"

Laughing, Perveen put an arm around Sunanda, and as the skies broke open, they ran in.

GLOSSARY

Aadab: polite phrase and gesture of greeting among Muslims

Anna: small unit of money equal to four paise or one-sixteenth of one rupee

Arre: exclamation meaning "hey there"

Ayah: maidservant tending to a woman or child

Baa: direct address for one's mother

Bai: suffix meaning "honorable sister" that's added to her name

Badmash: bad guy

Baksheesh: tip, charitable gift or bribe

Bapuji: direct address for father-in-law

Begum: respectful term of address for a Muslim lady of royal, aristocratic or high-born status that's added to her name

Behen: suffix meaning older sister or "good lady" used by Hindus, especially Gujaratis

Bhabhi: sister-in-law

Bhabhu: eldest sister in law in a Gujarati Hindu household

Bombay Presidency: a large administrative subdivision of British India that had Bombay as its headquarters

Challo: let's go

Charpoy: rope bed

Dai: midwife

Durwan: watchman for the home or a public place

Fetah: tall, stiff hat worn by Parsi men

Garbhapaat: death of a fetus from miscarriage or abortion

Gujarat: British-ruled region of Western India

Gujju: slang term for an ethnic Gujarati

Gymkhana: sports arena club

Hai Ram: Hindu exclamation meaning "Oh God" that can be used in religious and secular life

-ji: suffix used to add respect among Hindus

Kolhapur Agency: the British colonial government's grouping of twenty-six princely states in Western India that later became known as the Deccan States Agency

Kurta: collarless tunic

Kusti: Zoroastrian sacred cord worn around waist

Lathi: stick used for fighting

Maharaja: Hindu ruler of a Princely State

Maratha: name describing the people of Western India's descended from warrior clans

Marathi: language spoken in Maratha-dominated areas, including Bombay

Mathabana: thin white cloth tightly wrapped to cover a Parsi woman's hair

Memsahib: term of address for a superior-class woman

Meri Mai: exclamation of distress meaning "My Mother"

Nawab: Muslim ruler of a Princely State

Oh Khodai: exclamation of shock or excitement meaning "My God"

Pallu: the hanging end of a sari

Pandit: Hindu priest

Parsi: Indian-born member of the Zoroastrian faith

Poona: important business and military town in Bombay Presidency

Purdah: custom of women living in a separate area of the home and rarely going outside in order to avoid the male gaze

Rupee: unit of currency equal to sixteen annas

Sahib: term of respect for upper-class man, European or Indian

Sanskrit: ancient language that is the base of many languages in South Asia

Sudreh: light white undershirt worn by Zoroastrian men

Thali: a personal platter used to serve a meal

Thalipeeth: savory pancake

Vakeel: advocate who can be a person's public pleader, lawyer or agent

Varanpur: fictional princely state in Western India

ACKNOWLEDGMENTS

J was inspired by the late Padma Laxmi Mehta Parikh, who was a founder of the Laxminarayan Maternity Home and Hospital in Kolkata. Very special thanks to her daughter and my stepmother, Manju Parikh, who generously read this manuscript.

Sifra Lentin, the Mumbai-based author and historical researcher, was a fount of knowledge about Bombay's Jewish history and Dr. Jerusha Jhirad, Bombay's first Jewish Indian woman physician. I'm grateful for location suggestions from Simin Patel, the historian and owner of Bombaywalla Historical Works; and for backstage architectural details from Xerxes V. Dastur, Chairman of the Ripon Club. Jehangir Patel, publisher of Parsiana magazine, and Farrokh Jijina, a Parsiana senior editor and Khaki Lab volunteer, and Farida Guzdar were all extremely helpful on matters of Parsi traditions.

Many thanks to Mitra Sharafi, the Evjue-Bascom professor of law at the University of Wisconsin Law School. In addition to kindly reading my manuscript, her article "Abortion in South Asia 1860–1947; a Medico-Legal History" in the March 2021 issue of Modern Asian Studies provided the base of knowledge I needed to set up Perveen's big case. I also learned many details about the court process from two Mumbai-based lawyers, Parinaz Madan and Mehernaaz Wadia, and Baltimore attorney Erica Schultz.

I'm grateful for the review of Gujarati culture from Manushi Dave and Radhika Subberwal and Mamta Shah. Also, I loved the special view of Ghatkopar from Sonal Parekh, Gopika

Parekh Mehta, and Vandana Palan. For Australian history and slang, I owe it all to the author Fiona Stager!

Publishing a book takes a team, and I couldn't have done it without the patience and support of my dear agent, Vicky Bijur, and my fabulous friends at Soho Press: Juliet Grames, Bronwen Hruska, Rachel Kowal, Rudy Martinez, Paul Oliver, Steven Tran, Taz Urnov, Yezanira Venecia, and Alexa Wejko.

Finally, I lift up the names of my husband, Anthony, and our son, Neel, as well as Pia, the daughter who left this earth too early, but who will never leave my heart.